DO ANYTHING BUT BREATHE, BLACKSTAFF, AND SHE DIES.

A hook-nosed vulture of a man held his knife at Vajra's throat, his other arm holding her up and pinning her back to his grimy hauberk. Another slovenly rat-faced man, his beard growing only in clumps around many scars, held Vajra's legs and aimed his rusty short sword at her midsection.

Throw the staff down, Blackstaff, and you both might live a while longer. Kessik, grab those books.

The Blackstaff dropped the books from the crook of his right arm to hold his staff with both hands.

You had better not harm her . . .

FORGOTTEN REALMS

ED GREENWOOD
PRESENTS
WATERDEEP

FORGOTTEN REALMS

ED GREENWOOD
PRESENTS
WATERDEEP

BLACKSTAFF TOWER

STEVEN E. SCHEND

Wizards OF THE COAST

Ed Greenwood Presents Waterdeep

BLACKSTAFF TOWER

©2008 Wizards of the Coast, Inc.

Published by Wizards of the Coast, Inc. FORGOTTEN REALMS, WIZARDS OF THE COAST, and their respective logos are trademarks of Wizards of the Coast, Inc., in the U.S.A. and other countries.

All Wizards of the Coast characters, character names, and the distinctive likenesses thereof are property of Wizards of the Coast, Inc.

Printed in the U.S.A.

Cover art by Android Jones
First Printing: September 2008

9 8 7 6 5 4 3 2 1

ISBN: 978-0-7869-4913-7
620- 21813740-001-EN

U.S., CANADA,
ASIA, PACIFIC, & LATIN AMERICA
Wizards of the Coast, Inc.
P.O. Box 707
Renton, WA 98057-0707
+1-800-324-6496

EUROPEAN HEADQUARTERS
Hasbro UK Ltd
Caswell Way
Newport, Gwent NP9 0YH
GREAT BRITAIN
Save this address for your records.

Visit our web site at www.wizards.com

DEDICATION

To my grandparents, Mildred and Edward Hayward, for instilling in me a love of history over many summers in New England.

ACKNOWLEDGMENTS

No book is ever conceived of or produced in isolation. In a book about heroes rising to the fore, I must acknowledge those heroes who helped bring it forward.

First and foremost, I humbly thank my wife for her patience and love; crafting novels is never simple, but this one got easier with your support along the way.

Ed Greenwood, as always, you're a far better friend and mentor than you'd ever acknowledge or possibly realize. My thanks, always.

Susan Morris, my editor, has my thanks and many huzzahs for making this better.

Jeff Grubb, thanks for letting me bring your Osco Salibuck back from the dead.

Thanks also go to friends who became heroes with me in DUNGEONS & DRAGONS® many years ago: David Gehring, Alan Holverson, Bob Andrea, and Dave Beaulieu. This book of emerging heroes is for you guys.

Last but hardly least, I need to thank Gary Gygax and Dave Arneson for opening up new worlds to all of us through their game DUNGEONS & DRAGONS. It's a debt we can never truly repay, save by crafting new stories and sharing that sense of adventure.

INTRODUCTION

Back in 1966, fascinated by the fantasy tales crammed into my father's study, I started creating the FORGOTTEN REALMS® as the backdrop for my own stories, looking over the shoulder of the swindling old merchant Mirt the Moneylender as he wandered the Sword Coast a mere boot-stride ahead of local authorities and furious rivals.

Well over thirty years passed, and a game known as DUNGEONS & DRAGONS® got invented and soared to wild popularity. The Realms became part of it and literally hundreds of novels, short stories, game products, and articles appeared, all detailing facets of the Realms—building a long, detailed, and complex history for this entirely imaginary place. What I dubbed "Realmslore" started to pile up deeply in some places (such as Waterdeep) and around some characters, such as powerful wizards, who've always held an attraction, and the Chosen of Mystra, servants of the foremost deity of magic, who have an allure all their own.

You may have heard of one of them: Elminster, the sly old meddling rogue. Or perhaps the Seven Sisters, who in the Realms aren't oil companies, priestesses, or princesses (though they sometimes behave like all three), but silver-haired women who share a mother: Mystra herself.

Then there was Khelben "Blackstaff" Arunsun. *The* Blackstaff. The gruff, grim, self-righteous, straight-arrow counterpart to Elminster. A man (?) of as many mysteries as Elminster, but of a very different style. I created him to be "there but aloof from the citizenry on the streets" in Waterdeep, married to Laeral of the Seven Sisters, the two of them providing enough magical firepower to keep the dreaded Mad Mage, Halaster, down in Undermountain, and to prevent all the wizards attracted to Waterdeep's riches or hired by its various ambitious and unscrupulous nobles, wannabe nobles, and guildmasters from blasting the city to ruin every second night as they got into spell-duels with each other, or experimented with a newer, mightier Swarm of Suns spell.

Enter Steven Schend. One of several long-suffering "traffic cops" of the Realms, the staffers who have to rein in not just me, but everyone else with a fun, wild, and crazy idea they want to try out in the Realms, and coordinate the whole ongoing circus. Steven's way of handling the job was to understand why conflicts happen through history—the imaginary history of the Realms. He adopted Halaster (and Undermountain), Khelben (and Waterdeep), the coastal kingdoms of Amn, Tethyr, and Calimshan, and the fallen elf realm of Cormanthyr, and *really* steeped them all in history.

Which is why he was the ideal writer to pen the novel *Blackstaff*, and why he is really the only person who could tell the tale you hold in your hands, *Blackstaff Tower*.

Oh, you're in for a treat. Not a trudge through dusty history, but a tense clash of intrigue in Waterdeep a century after the events of *Blackstaff*, A story built on the secrets of the past that charges boldly into the future.

I couldn't wait to read it, the first time through—and when I was done, I couldn't wait to read it again.

Ed Greenwood
March 2008

PROLOGUE

*The North has sinfully warm days late in the year, which some call
elf summers, that merely bulwark the wary for the inevitable chills of
winter to come.*

Malek Aldhanek, *My Travels,*
the Year of the Gem Dragons (812 DR)

20 MARPENOTH, YEAR OF THE AGELESS ONE (1479 DR)

"Are you sure you need to do this right now, Samark?" The young
woman's short black hair rippled in the light breeze, never
obscuring her bright indigo eyes. "I know it's important, but it's
too nice a day. Why spoil our picnic by rifling through that tomb?
Stay here, where it's warm and bright."

Vajra Safahr stretched languidly on the blanket. She luxuriated
in the sun and playfully clamped her toes on the edge of Samark's
robes. "Aren't there *better* things we could do with such a marvelous day?" She let one dusky shoulder slip free from her gray
tunic as she leaned toward Samark and winked.

The old man, Samark "the Blackstaff" Dhanzscul, smiled. The
smile contorted three parallel scars running from his right cheek-
bone down to his jaw. "Tempting, lass," he said. "Deliciously so.
Hold those thoughts. My task here won't keep me long. Especially
with such a motivation putting wings to my aged feet."

Samark turned to face a hillock covered in vines. The flat-sided
boulder he approached showed a few graven letters through thick
crawling ivies. Samark placed his left hand flat atop the near-hidden

KH, and the crystal atop the twisted metal staff in his right hand flashed a bright green. He uttered a few syllables and stepped through the stone as if it were air.

The small tomb smelled dank and close. The green light from Samark's staff lit up the tiny space. Dust and cobwebs covered every surface and cloaked the wizard as he stepped inside. Magic crackled in the air, reacting to his presence, but it subsided after he whispered, *"Suortanakh."*

The old man walked down three steps and knelt at the bier dominating the tomb's floor. Complex marks tiled its sides, all glowing a dim blue beneath a spider-spun shroud. The gray carving of a tall man with a full beard rested atop the stone sarcophagus, his hands holding a glass globe atop his chest. After a brief prayer, the old man sent a pulse of magic into the globe held by the effigy. The energy cleared the webs off the glass globe, and it shimmered with emerald-toned magic.

Samark rested his left hand on the glass and said, *"Aegisbiir n'varan colroth aegismiir!"*

His ring and the globe both flashed. The omnipresent illusions of dust and webs dissolved, as did the illusory walls of the tomb. The tomb revealed itself to be the entry chamber atop a long stair that led down into a chamber far more vast than the hillock outside. At the top of the stairs, bright silver bars prevented entry. Samark willed his staff's crystal to glow brighter. The brilliance made the staff's carved metal claw appear to hold a small emerald sun.

Samark leaned heavily on the staff as he walked up to the silver metal bars where the back wall once stood. He placed his left hand flat on a featureless metal plate where a lock might normally appear, and the crystal on his staff pulsed. The bars and the plate grated into the ceiling and floor. Samark shuffled down the stairs. During his descent, he glanced toward the chamber on his left, a gallery of sorts at the foot of the stairs. Twenty-five items rested atop short white marble columns, each amid a bright spotlight. A realistic centaur reared atop the nearest column, carved from a single gourd-sized ruby. Beside it, an undulating ribbon of gold and platinum turned and twisted end over end on its velvet pillow. Beside that, a crown carved from thick bone and set with sapphires seemed to hug shadows to itself, despite the bright light overhead. The rest of that chamber held more than a dozen rods and staves standing on end with no visible supports, as well as eight swords of various makes, all unsupported. Samark walked past the chamber, turning his glance toward the opposite chamber.

Inside this room, a septet of bookshelves all loomed a man's height above his own. As he crossed the threshold of the room, he spoke to the empty air. *"Diolaa siolakhiir. Melkar of Mirabar's Journal. Alsidda's Tome. Te'elarn'vaeniir. Love at Llast."* In response, four books pulled themselves off their separate shelves, floated across the open air, and landed gently in his hand. Tucking the books under his left arm, he turned and walked out to the foot of the stairs and turned toward the far end of the room.

Samark moved slowly down a long hall lined with portraits. As he walked, torches flared to life two paces ahead of him, lighting the paintings and the names embossed in brass on their frames—Rarkin, Strathea, Larnarm, Rhinnara, Phesta, Kitten, Brian, Sammereza, Durnan, Mirt, Ruarn, Pellak, Shilarn, and at least a dozen more. He chuckled as he walked, and muttered, "How many knew the regard with which the Blackstaff held them, I wonder? So few Lords gained Khelben's respect, let alone that of the other Blackstaffs . . ."

At the tunnel's end, Samark entered a tall triangular chamber, two statues flanking him on either side. He bowed his head in reverence, scanning the names of each statue and whispered to each, "Greetings, honored Open Lords. Lord Caladorn Cassalanter. Lord Piergeiron Paladinson. Lord Lhestyn Arunsun. Lord Baeron Silmaeril." Samark stopped, turned to the point of the room, and raised his eyes. "Honored greetings, Open Lord Ahghairon."

This statue gleamed brightest and tallest, its height dwarfing the other four in this chamber. Samark marveled at the workmanship.

He sought but never found a chisel mark anywhere on the robes, staff, or even the intricately tangled beard of the bald wizard before him. His eyes darted to the gold ring encircling Ahghairon's left index finger and the sapphires-among-silver amulet resting on his chest—the only things not carved from the marble cliffs of Mount Khimbarr.

Samark set down the books and released his staff, which floated beside him. The wizard wove a complex series of gestures and a longer series of arcane words as he walked sunward around the statue three times. On the completion of his third circuit, he proclaimed, *"Aonaochel. Enakhel adomanth, adoquessir, adofaer. Lakrhel eislarhen aonaoch."* The metal ring and amulet both shimmered and reappeared on Samark's person, albeit scaled down to fit his human form.

Samark smiled, knelt at the foot of the statue, and said, "Thank you, Great Protector. I do thy bidding and that of our predecessors in all your names."

>———W———<

Vajra Safahr sighed as she watched her mentor dissolve into the tomb. She wondered how that old man made her heart beat so fast, and her mother's words returned to her. "Never question love—it makes its own rules each time anew." Waterdeep, Crown of the North, was a tolerant city, but a few still saw their partnership as odd, both due to their ages and because Vajra was a dusky-skinned Tethyrian, not a native Waterdhavian. Even so, none questioned that Vajra Safahr was the Blackstaff's Heir in duty and love.

Vajra rolled onto her back and stared up at the clear sky. After three years in the Sword Coast North, she knew that they had precious few days left before Auril drew a perpetual gray blanket across the skies for the winter months. Vajra could have gone inside with Samark, but she preferred the sun and leaf-scented wind to the dank.

As she lay there, movement seized her attention. A stone arced across her line of sight and fell directly in front of her at the edge of her blanket. She sat up and peered closer it.

The rock spewed a cloud of greenish gas. Vajra scurried back and started a spell to repel the vapors when she felt a sudden pinch. She reached for it and felt a dart in the back of her neck. She turned to see a dark-clad figure rise from the overgrown tomb, his hooded face revealing only a wicked grin as he tucked a blowgun back in his belt.

"She's unable to speak, lads. We should be safe."

The man laughed, and through the roaring in her ears Vajra dimly heard others approach around her. She focused her attention on the laughing man, and willed magic out her eyes. Three bolts of amber energy felled the man in mid-laugh.

Thank the gods Samark taught me how to cast at least one spell without movement or sound, she thought.

Vajra tried to rise but found her legs would not support her. She fell backward as her eyes began to cloud over. She stared straight upward and raged at her body's betrayal. Her foes closed around her, blades drawn. None had seen the business end of a bath house or a razor in some tendays.

"Is she out?" The skinniest of them asked, his pinched face, scars, and patchy beard reminding Vajra of a rat.

"No, she's staring at us. If looks could kill, eh?" The taller man's face bore a beak of a nose, making him the vulture of the lot.

"What do you mean, Rivvol? She's smiling." A pudgy, inquisitive face peered down at her. Realization dawned on the black-haired ferret of a man and he reared back.

Fools should have learned the first time, she thought.

Vajra's contempt for her opponents eked into her smile and spell as she willed more missiles at the three foes. Each of the men staggered back, clutching their faces in pain. One wiped tears from his eyes and kicked Vajra hard in her side.

Another voice from behind the trio said, "You were warned not to underestimate even the apprentice, fools. Now, prepare her and yourselves for the Blackstaff's return."

Vajra wished she could move to see who that voice belonged to. The man's kick turned her away from them, and she stared at the boulder marker of Khelben the Elder's tomb. She tried to move or speak, but failed at both. One of the men picked her up, keeping her eyes directed up and away from himself and his compatriots.

Samark the Blackstaff walked out of the tomb and through its covering vegetation as effortlessly as he'd entered it. "I have them, Vajra. Now, where—"

"Do anything but breathe, Blackstaff, and she dies!"

A hook-nosed vulture of a man held his knife at Vajra's throat, his other arm holding her up and pinning her back to his grimy hauberk. Another slovenly rat-faced man, his beard growing only in clumps around many scars, held Vajra's legs and aimed his rusty short sword at her midsection.

A third man sidled alongside Samark, a crossbow at his shoulder. Pressing the point of his quarrel to the side of Samark's throat, he said, "Throw the staff down, old man, and you both might live a while longer. Kessik, grab those books."

The old wizard dropped the books from the crook of his right arm to hold his staff with both hands. "You had better not harm her . . ."

"Shut it, you. And drop the staff!" The vulture's blade pressed closer to Vajra's neck, drawing a bead of fresh blood atop older gore still encrusted on the knife.

"Listen to Rivvol, Blackstaff. He gets twitchy around wizards, and he's likely to kill even one as pretty as that Tethyrian." The speaker moved over next to his comrades, his crossbow always at his shoulder. Kessik let go of Vajra's legs and scurried over to the pile of tomes next to Samark.

"Fine." Samark threw the staff at the ground among the four of them. As he let go of the staff, he clapped his hands, and his form shimmered with cerulean magic. The staff hit the turf right at Vajra's feet and flashed a verdant pulse in all directions. The top of the staff tipped forward onto Rivvol's arm, and he screamed as emerald lightning crackled from the staff into him. He screamed and collapsed, but his dagger fell as well. Vajra collapsed in front of him, her body unharmed by the staff, but her neck gushing blood from Rivvol's knife.

The crossbow's scrape and twang drew little of Samark's attention, but he saw the bolt glance off his protective shield. His face wrinkled in concentration, Samark launched a purple pulse at Vajra, pointing with his other hand to aim a second bolt at the crossbowman. The energy swept through Vajra and looped around to strike the crossbowman. The woman's wounds healed quickly, but the crossbowman's throat opened just as hers had been, and he fell to his knees, his breath and lifeblood bubbling out of the wound.

"Ammol!" Kessik stood open-mouthed. Both his allies had fallen in mere seconds. "What'd that green stuff do to me?" Kessik asked, his eyes filled with terror as he crawled away from Samark, the tomes forgotten.

"Absolutely nothing, boy." Samark said. "It merely undid some spells to reveal your master to me. Now flee, before I become less patient or he decides you're expendable too."

Kessik paused a moment, then turned and fled as fast as he could. Samark barely watched him, his attention focused on the tall, hooded man who had shimmered into visibility when the green energy washed over him. Wearing nondescript olive robes, the man stood with his scimitar drawn, its edge shimmering with red light. The mage's most outstanding features, aside from a very thick, singular eyebrow, were the ornate rings flashing on every digit of both hands. The man's razor-thin salt-and-pepper mustache and goatee framed his sneer.

Samark touched the scars on his own cheek and said, "I wish I could be surprised, Khondar. Your betrayal was inevitable—though, I confess, sooner than I expected."

Khondar "Ten-Rings" Naomal said, "Blackstaff, this reckoning has been coming a long time. I'm glad you know it was me who ended your life and that of your strumpet."

"And how do you plan to do that?" Samark stepped closer to Vajra and his fallen staff. "Far better than you have tried, you know."

Khondar Naomal's response was an angry slash of his scimitar while he uttered an incantation. The blade resonated with magic and a slash of midnight shredded the air between the two wizards. The dark energy shattered the blue shield Samark had around himself, much to the Blackstaff's surprise.

"You've gotten better toys, Ten-Rings," Samark said, "but you've always relied too much on them."

Samark braced himself and summoned energy around his hands and arms as Khondar rushed forward. Ten-Rings chopped downward with his glowing scimitar, and Samark clapped his hands, trapping the blade in mid-chop. Both men stood eye-to-eye, their hatred as powerful as the magic that trapped them together.

"You should have stayed in Sundabar, Khondar. You'd have been the big wizard there, rather than fighting your betters over imagined slights every tenday."

Samark couldn't move or cast without disrupting his active spell and releasing the blade. Luckily, Ten-Rings also could not move without losing his weapon.

Three amber pulses slammed into Khondar's side, and he howled in anger. Taking a quick look to the side, the Blackstaff saw the still-paralyzed Vajra had collapsed facing their battle. Her eyes glowed with arcane power and anger.

Samark chuckled, "Vajra can harm you even when paralyzed, Ten-Rings. Having an ally helps, but having some one who loves you . . . well, that makes all the difference."

Khondar's grin disarmed Samark. "Very true, Blackstaff. I couldn't agree more." The ten-ringed man let go of his scimitar and backed away. "Don't you, Father?"

Samark saw his foe's gaze wander past his own left shoulder toward the tomb. Samark said, "Father? Then you're—"

"My son, and your doom, fool," Khondar's voice rang out behind Samark.

An energy ring blinked into existence around Samark and clenched shut around his midsection, teeth biting into him as it contracted. Samark's last word was a pleading "Vajr—"

Then the spell rent him in two.

Khondar moved quickly behind Vajra and clubbed her on the back of the head with his scimitar's pommel. As he did so, his form blurred and shimmered. Rings faded from his hands, as did his mustache. His hair darkened, and his robes became a black tunic and breeches. The younger man, who shared the singular eyebrow of his father, looked up and said, "She's out at last."

"Thank you, Centiv," Khondar said to his son, as he floated off the ivy-covered tomb toward him. "Your illusions, as always, are excellent. I'm glad Samark's trick only removed your invisibility. It kept him focused on you. Now, stay back. There's going to be power in play here that should keep her from being a bother."

As if on cue, the two halves of the Blackstaff's body sizzled with energy, darkening the gory remnants even further. A tempest of dark lightning crackled out of Samark's remains and arced in two directions—into his staff and into Vajra, who arched her back and legs as if screaming before she fell into spasms. In one breath, the energy cascade ended, and the meadow lay still again. The only sounds were Vajra's uneven breaths and the triumphant howl of Khondar's laughter.

"Rejoice, Centiv! She's the last obstacle we have to conquer, and her secrets will lead to our joining the Lords and ruling the city!"

Vajra lay unconscious, but Khondar approached her warily. He nudged her with the toe of his boot. He gestured and her garments rewove themselves, binding her arms and hands. He looked up briefly and scowled at his son's rapt leer at Vajra. "Centiv, I don't need your help right now. Go chase down Kessik and make sure he cannot talk about this to anyone."

Centiv nodded and cast a spell before he leaped across the landscape in the same direction Kessik fled.

Khondar turned to the remains of Samark. His eyes shone as he reached for the blood-spattered amulet on Samark's chest. He patted down the pockets and body. As he wrenched a gory gold ring off Samark's finger, he muttered, "The power of the Blackstaff lies nearly within reach. Soon, the tower will be mine . . . and I'll gain the secret of long years so far denied humans. I shall become the Blackstaff, and Waterdeep shall know its savior! The rightful rule of wizards is at hand for the Crown of the North again!"

CHAPTER 1

The Watch is for our people's safety, not solely his Lordship's security or whims, and should be used thusly.

Open Lord Piergeiron Paladinson to a Masked Lord,
Lords' Court Transcripts,
21 Uktar, Year of the Helm (1362 DR)

8 NIGHTAL, YEAR OF THE AGELESS ONE (1479 DR)

The tavern was hardly his first choice of venues, but it had grown on him after Faxhal first dragged him here last month. Renaer Neverember liked that the usual hateful, conceited social climbers and all-but-nobles that constantly badgered him for his attentions and his friendship rarely came here. This tavern at the edge of Sea and Castle Wards was well-kept and honest, and its patrons were a wide array of Waterdhavians, not just one group or social stratum. Renaer appreciated that, as he did its dark brew and its night black loaves. Atop all that, another small part of it made Renaer agree to meet his friends here repeatedly. Tucked back in the eastern corner away from the doors was a small sheltered nook with shelves on the back wall. Mostly empty, the shelves held a random assortment of broadsheets at all times, though often a few days out of date. Renaer managed to read a few of the more recent issues of *The Vigilant Citizen* and *The Blue Unicorn* before his first friend arrived.

Lord Torlyn Wands tossed a heavy oilskin-wrapped bundle on the table in front of Renaer. "The weather's getting that winter sting to it," he growled as he tugged off his soaked half-cloak. The clasp on his cloak snagged his light gray linen shirt, pulling it out of his belt and exposing his slender yet exceedingly hairy chest.

A few patrons whistled at the young noble, while a passing serving maid ran her fingers across his chest, making him blush. When she looked up and locked eyes with him, she blushed even brighter and stammered, "My apologies, Milord Wands," and rushed away.

Torlyn turned his attention back to Renaer as he tucked his shirt back into his breeches. "Damned shirt! My sister keeps replacing my functional clothes with these 'things that are in style,' and they drive me mad!" He slumped into the seat opposite Renaer and put his boots up on another chair. "Look at these soaked boots! All the trouble to dye the calfskin blue, but they didn't bother to waterproof the blasted things!"

"Ah, the costs of noble fashions and the maintenance of social airs." Renaer smiled, tipping his flagon toward Lord Wands in mock salute. "You have my sympathies, milord. Bad form, really, to not treat the leather well, I agree. I can suggest a few cobblers who can fix those up for you or make you better ones right away."

Torlyn laughed, his irritation at fashion forgotten. "Speaking of better leatherworking, I'm amazed you didn't dive on that parcel the moment it left my hands. I wanted to show you my latest acquisition, since few appreciate a good book more than you." Lord Wands's broad grin was not concealed in the least by his long mahogany locks or full beard. He whispered thanks to the still-blushing tavern maid who brought him a large tankard of the tavern's dark ale, and then Renaer's attention shifted from his companion to the parcel. Two sharp tugs undid the leather lacings and he opened the oilskin wraps around a large book.

Renaer ran his fingers over the ornate leatherworked cover and the bindings, his eyebrows rising in appreciation. He gingerly opened the volume to its initial page and let out a low whistle.

"The Compleat Dragonhunter?" Renaer asked, looking up at Torlyn without letting go of the page or the book.

His companion laughed. "Had it for two days now, along with *Gold Amid Dragonfire*. They were hidden among a lot of dross I picked up when I absorbed the last remnants of the Estelmer and Melshimber collections last month."

Renaer chuckled. "You and your dragon books, Torlyn. Are you rebuilding your family's library or gathering a hoard?" Renaer flipped through a few pages, nodded at the good workmanship and calligraphy, and rewrapped the book to protect it.

"Very funny, Ren." Torlyn smiled, swallowed some ale, and asked, "You're one to talk, he who snaps up every book on Waterdeep's past that's been written. Say, did you find *Folk of Renown* yet?"

"No. Well . . . yes and no," Renaer replied. "I found a copy on the market up in Longsaddle last month, but I bought something else."

Torlyn shifted his blue boots off the chair, then stood. From the way Torlyn tugged at the bootcuffs and then shifted how he sat, Renaer could tell Torlyn's clothes and boots were too new and uncomfortable. He noticed Renaer's attention, shrugged, and cleared his throat before sitting down again and asking, "Why? For Oghma's sake, you've wanted that book forever, Ren."

"I know, I know," he answered, amused to see his audience taking the bait. "Instead, I discovered the final pieces for my Savengriff collection."

"You found a complete copy of *A Palace Life?*" The young lord slammed his tankard down in disbelief. The dark-stained table shined with the newest sluice of spilled ale, though neither man cared, save to move the wrapped book to a drier, safer spot.

Renaer leaned back. "I bought all three volumes with an identically bound copy of *Piergeiron as I Remember Him* thrown in for good measure!"

"Nice. 'Tis no wonder you're the new sage of local obscure lore."

"Sage?" Renaer asked. "I'm a mere dabbler and an inveterate reader, 'tis all."

"Still, I'm impressed. The only known library with every mundane work of Aleena Paladinstar and her wizardly husband Savengriff." Torlyn Wands looked down in dismay, then raised his eyes with a smile. "At least my collection still has the only full set of nonmagical books by the Seven Sisters—or at least it will when you return my copy of *Lifelong with Regrets* to me."

"Soon, Torlyn, soon. It's a fascinating read, and I'm grateful for the loan. Laeral's handwriting and her inscription to your great-great-grandfather add a whole new understanding to her." Renaer drank and waved a servant over to their table. "Another round, please, Arlanna." He flipped a taol toward the tavernmaid, and turned back to Torlyn. "When are Faxhal and Vharem due to join us?"

"Patience, Renaer, patience," Torlyn said. "I hear Vharem spent most of his day chaperoning the youngest Phullbrinter sisters in their shopping for the Gralleth feast."

"Ah, what that man does for his coins," Renaer said. "He'll need stronger drink than this, then."

The door to the tavern opened, and two of his oldest friends entered. Renaer stood and waved them over to the table. Faxhal smirked a perfect mimicry of Renaer's own grin back at him. Faxhal resembled Renaer in many ways—broad-shouldered and brawny, clean-shaven, shoulder-length brown hair, square-jawed with chiseled features—but his claim that he was the better-looking of the two urged Renaer to remind him he was shorter and had thus concentrated Renaer's charisma. Vharem wore an expensively tailored night blue cloak in contrast with his unkempt blond beard and scuffed brown boots.

"The Watch is hunting for you again, Renaer. We had to shake a patrol on our way here." Vharem rolled his eyes along with Renaer as he related the news. The tall blond man signaled Arlanna to bring two more tankards as he shrugged his dark cloak open and sat down next to Torlyn. The two men traded nods as greetings.

"What have I allegedly done this time to displease his Open

Lordship, my father?" Renaer sighed, rising to let Faxhal get past him to a seat.

The shorter of the two men shook his head, then rushed forward and vaulted over the table, using one hand to catapult himself onto the bench in the corner of the tavern. Renaer grinned and muttered, "Show-off," as he sat down again.

Faxhal said, "Not a thing, so far as we know. It's just a few new shieldlars and their patrols trying to impress their new captain and tonight's valabrar—and unfortunately, tonight's overseer for the Watch in Castle and Sea Wards is Kahlem Ralnarth."

Torlyn choked on his drink and coughed. "How did *that* inbred noble idiot get promoted? What have I missed the past two tendays?"

"Only a marvelous chase across Field and Sea Wards not three nights ago," Vharem said with a snicker. "A dash across the Northbeach is not something I want to repeat before spring."

"Yeah," Faxhal said. "You'd think he'd be grateful we led them right to those smugglers at the Lancecove. Capturing a septet of forgers and smugglers was shine on his sword, to be sure. His promotion from aumarr should have made him more grateful."

Renaer looked up, dropping his sly grin quickly, as he said, "I think he's worried his superiors will regret that promotion if they find out he only caught *them* due to chasing and trying to arrest *us* for assaulting a city official and defiling a holy place."

Torlyn gasped, and Renaer and Faxhal chortled. Vharem draped an arm across Lord Wands's shoulder and whispered, "Kahlem staggered into us after leaving his favorite festhall—er, 'newest shrine to the Red Knight'—and took offense that we happened to be using the midden abutting its wall after a night at Raphen's tavern on Imar Street."

Torlyn's eyes widened, and he said, "Don't tell me . . ."

Vharem nodded. "He pushed Renaer and me to one side, and *this one*"—he jerked his thumb toward Faxhal—"turns and asks,

'What beems to see the broplem, occifer?' as he finished relieving himself on the man's boots!"

"Kahlem's not a bad Watchman," Renaer said, "but his water-headed ideas on how to investigate crimes—"

Faxhal interrupted, "—led the fool to believe we're smugglers too!" He punched Renaer's shoulder and laughed. "Now get ready. I've got time for one drink before we give them the run-around." Faxhal grabbed and downed Renaer's drink in one gulp, and then belched loudly. He pulled two hooded mantles out of his bag and tossed one to Renaer. "Let's give them the old seeing-double bit, yes? I've needed a good run all day."

Renaer marveled at his friend's desire to intervene for him and said, "You know, I could actually let them take me in for a change. Clear the air and settle things with Kahlem?"

To their credit, the four men kept straight faces for nearly two full breaths before snickering. Renaer and Faxhal pulled the stylish dark blue hooded mantles over their heads and atop their black cloaks.

Vharem said, "We'll meet you at the Grinning Lion by the next bell, then?"

Lord Torlyn Wands groaned and asked, "Gods, why does it have to be that place?"

Faxhal asked, "What's the matter with it? Argput always has a table for us. Besides"—his voice dropped to a whisper—"the food's better there than here."

Torlyn groaned, "It's become a watering hole of late for the Thongolirs, and I'd as soon avoid their ilk until the solstice balls where I've no excuses to avoid them."

Vharem said, "Sacrifices must be made, milord, in the name of friendship. Besides, you'd have no problem if the Lady Nhaeran would give Lord Terras an answer on his suit."

"Which, as you're all aware, is an unequivocal *no*, and you know my sister cannot tell him that until after we clear up the debts that Hurnal set up with the money-grubbing old bastard." Torlyn sighed. "My cousin's even opened up our old hunting lodge for rent by hunting parties a tenday at a time. Our family's private hunting lands have become just another asset for him to exploit."

"I'd be happy to help, milord Wands, truly," Renaer said, his face losing its smile as he locked eyes with his friend. Faxhal, for his part, adjusted Renaer's hood so the two of them looked nigh identical.

"Appreciated, but impossible, sirrah." Torlyn shook his head, avoiding Renaer's eyes. He cleared his throat, then chuckled nervously and said, "Be off with ye, nigh-noble rogues. Your sport awaits and the night is young! Vharem and I can't wait to hear about the latest ways you two've found to avoid Watch pursuit."

Renaer and Faxhal looked at each other, sketched salutes at their friends, and bolted for the door. Before they even reached it, Renaer heard Vharem shout, "Ten taols says the Watch comes up empty again tonight! Do I have any takers?"

Renaer looked back once to see Toryln raise his tankard in salute before he was lost behind the quickly massing crowd around their table, all gambling men eagerly betting on successful escape or pursuits.

>===W===<

Renaer and Faxhal found Darselune Street relatively empty. The slate-roofed wood-and-stone buildings across the way had been cleaned by the past night's sleet and ice thawing that day and rinsing soot off the buildings. Ice and frost returned with sunset, and moonlight twinkled on slate and slats alike. The two men passed a carriage tied up in front of the Slaked Sylph, and Faxhal shrugged toward it, his eyebrows rising in question.

Renaer shook his head. "Why actually do something illegal to add merit to their pursuit of me in Lords' Court?"

They jogged across Gulzindar Street, their boots scraping the frost-rimed cobbles on the road. They saw a Watch patrol heading west toward the Field of Triumph, their backs to them.

Faxhal belched loudly, and then bellowed, "Have you no manners, Renaer?" The man grinned and then sprinted south toward the Spires of the Morning, leaving Renaer a few steps behind.

The watchmen spun on their heels and the armar shouted, "There he is! Renaer Neverember, hold! We have a—! After them!"

The broader avenues like Julthoon Street, Calamastyr Lane, and Swords Street glowed brightly in the moonlight due to the diligence of the Dungsweepers' Guild and a lighter shade of cobblestones used on the major roadways all across Waterdeep. As the two men dashed across a carriage's path, they heard their pursuers curses at their path being blocked by that same vehicle soon after.

Renaer kept quiet as the opulent and well-tended buildings of Sea Ward receded. Faxhal was already past the temple to Amaunator, its pink marble courtyard walls glistening with frost and icicles. Looming ahead were the more utilitarian domiciles and row buildings of Castle Ward, though there were exceptions to the common buildings, like the gargoyle-infested Charistor looming three stories tall over the intersection with Swords Street, or the squat white stone of Jhurlan's Jewels with its quaint Old Cormyrean wall merlons atop its roof at Tchozal's Race.

"We'd better split up," Renaer said to Faxhal.

"Last one to Argupt's buys for the night," Faxhal replied, whispering so as not to lead their pursuers to their final destination. "I'll head east up the Walk—you lead some south!"

Both men turned south down Swords Street at full speed, laughing as their pursuers howled their plans aloud. "Head over to the Street of Silks and head them off at Keltarn!"

The two friends pointed ahead and firmed up their plan. Faxhal shouldered an uneven stack of crates stacked alongside the mouth of Elvarren's Lane as he passed. The moldering boxes teetered and fell behind him into the paths of the Watch and a few passersby.

The two saluted each other, and Faxhal whirled off to the east, turning left and racing up Zelphar's Walk. Renaer expected him to run up to Armin's Cut and swing back up to Tchozal's Race to lead a few of the Watch in circles.

Renaer slowed his pace slightly, nearly allowing two young members of the Watch to come within ten paces of him. Reaching into his pocket, he readied his weapons as his ominous target loomed out of the darkness.

Blackstaff Tower seemed to make the night around it darker. No torches lit its windows, nor did any brighten the dark steel and stone of the curtain wall around its courtyard. Renaer raced past the gate, admiring the metalworked roses and staves that entwined the metal bars. Looking over his right shoulder to make sure they were within range, Renaer tossed a handful of stones at the gates to Blackstaff Tower and immediately doubled his speed, leaving his chasers behind. Suddenly, the night lit up, a sea green glow emanating from the metal gates into the surrounding street. The woman and man slowed, appearing to run but moving only at a snail's pace. Renaer smiled but shook his fascination away and kept running. "I wasn't sure that was going to work. First time I've ever used Blackstaff Tower's spell defenses against anyone."

Renaer dashed left, heading east up Tharleon Street. The Flagon Dragon Inn's three stories dominated that corner, the stone dragons at the base of the walls all gouting fire. He waved at the two dragon-helmed guards at the door as he ran past, and both returned the wave. He'd have to drag Torlyn back here again soon—he liked this place, even if it did cater more to those of less-than-noble class. Renaer jogged into the Silkanth's Cut, ducking behind Rarknal's Whitesmiths and running up the outer stairs leading to the rooftop garden on the adjoining building.

Renaer never slowed his pace and continued to run up to and past the roof's edge, launching himself toward the clothesline that angled over the eastern arc of the cut. He grabbed it and used his momentum to swing himself further up and onto the parapet of a row house. Keeping up his pace, he ran across that roof as well, leaping over the low wall that marked where that building abutted the next. As he ran east across that roof, he headed toward the stone arches that arced over Hoy's Skip below. Since the Spellplague, many of the row buildings had arches to support the buildings.

Renaer deftly ran over the arch as if it were a dry street instead of the ice-rimed bridge it was. He continued south, vaulting over or climbing above the abutment walls among the buildings lining the Street of Silks. When he stopped, dropping into the shadows next to an overlarge chimney, he could look across the street and beyond to see into the well-lit windows of the Smiling Siren festhall.

Renaer waited. The young Lord Neverember heard the Watch stumble past him on the street below, their armar chewing out the new recruits and barking orders. Looking down, Renaer knew he'd run many a scamper with this armar, the bald patch on his head exposing a familiar birthmark.

The balding armar's voice traveled in the crisp winter air. "No, he's not a Shar-worshipper to draw shadows around him! You're just incompetent! Now look down to Keltarn and see if he's heading east. He likes to take Cymbril's Walk, not the Prowl, because the taverns along there like him. We'll head up to Bazaar and investigate parts east. If we don't find him by the Street of Bells, we regroup at the Singing Sword and . . ." The words grew muffled as they moved out of Renaer's hearing range.

Renaer smiled, then something tapped him on the shoulder and he felt his stomach lurch. He turned and found himself facing the tabard of a barrel-chested Watch valabrar standing less than an arm's reach from him, a watchman's rod in hand. In Selûne's pale light, Renaer stood, and said, "At least it was you and not Ralnarth. Well, Officer Varbrent? Am I a prisoner?"

The grizzled older man rubbed his salt-and-peppered beard with the end of the rod, smiling slightly at Renaer. "Nah, but you're getting almost predictable, lad. You've come here twice before. You don't scout too well ahead of yourself or you'd have noticed me waiting here for you. Slow night?"

"Slow enough. I didn't find any other things to lead them toward."

"Like those smugglers the other night? Ralnarth caught a good reward there, he did."

"And we both know he doesn't deserve the promotion, Morrath. He's a bully with coin and a noble name behind him, that's all!"

"Aye, lad, but he's connected in the right places, so he moves up the ladder. Besides, for his faults, he serves a purpose."

Renaer smirked at the Watch captain. "Someone for you to laugh about back at barracks?"

Morrath snorted and said, "No. He's vain, so his uncle's money gets him and his Watchmen better equipment, but ultimately that's only good for the city. Don't worry—we both know why he's got his recruits chasin' you. That'll die down in another day or so, assuming you and your friends stay out of his nose. Kahlem won't bring things to the notice of your father. Not while I'm about."

"Thanks, Morrath," Renaer said, clapping the watchman on the shoulder.

"Boy, your rat-scampers are handy for training the young 'uns or punishing those who've o'erstepped their places. I just wish you or your friends would join the Watch to train them directly. You'd be a farsight better officer than Ralnarth."

Renaer winked and said, "You can't afford me, Morrath."

"Well," Morrath said, "can't blame a man for trying. Just keep yourself from trouble, boy."

Renaer and Morrath both clambered down a stone rose trellis from their rooftop perch. Renaer dropped the last few feet, landing in a crouch onto Swords Street again.

"Do you want to share a carriage?" Renaer asked, but when he turned in Morrath's direction, the man had disappeared. "Well met, Morrath. Have to learn that one some time."

Renaer stepped out of the shadows at the mouth of Scarlet's Well and flagged down a carriage. The single horse and its young driver both started from his sudden appearance. He didn't blame them, for the area was known to be haunted, albeit by a harmless woman's spirit still weeping bloody tears for her lost love. The boy got over his fear quickly when he saw the quartet of taols Renaer held up. The boy reached eagerly, but Renaer closed his hand around all but one of the square coins. "The rest are yours if you get me quietly to the Grinning Lion in less than two songs."

The boy nodded enthusiastically as Renaer slipped inside the carriage. Renaer found no comfort inside, as the matted cushions provided little relief from the hard bench or lurching ride.

Renaer enjoyed the chases with the Watch, but he bristled when the law enforcers—including his father the Open Lord—flaunted power over him and others. Dagult and Kahlem Ralnarth's abuses of authority showed the people that the Watch did not work always for the greater good of the city—just the whims of officers or the Lords. Worst of all, he didn't know what his father wanted, other than obedience and for Renaer to only act within the limited confines of Dagult's imagination. Renaer heard his father's words often enough—"You're a dupe, a wastrel, and you're throwing money away at every church across the city! I won't have my son waste his life!"

Renaer whispered, almost in prayer, "I want more for my father and for Waterdeep. This used to be a city where dreams came true and gods walked the cobbles. Now, the grime of commerce and greed covers everything, including the once-shining helms of the Lords. The Crown of the North still rules all commerce and politics, but it can't remotely claim to be the City of Splendors. This city needs heroes to bring back its life and luster. But gods know if I have it in me to be one."

Many hours later, Renaer crept quietly up the stairs to his rooms, a task not terribly difficult given the stone steps and carpets. He expected to be alone, but lights still blazed beneath the door to his father's study.

"The man is the Open Lord," Renaer muttered. "Why in the gods' names doesn't he use his offices at the palace?"

Despite his aggravation at the delay in sleep, Renaer smiled. He discovered years ago that he learned more when folk didn't know there were others within earshot. He slipped silently into his room, closed the door, and stripped for bed. Folding his clothes neatly on a side dresser, he shivered from the cold despite the small fire in the fireplace near his bed. Renaer burrowed beneath the furs and quilts, all the while keeping an ear cocked to the voices carried through the chimney shared with the next room's fireplace.

"We've not learned nearly enough, Dagult." Renaer didn't know this thin reedy voice, nor did he like what the man had to say. "She is as stubborn as her master was."

"We know the Blackstaffs have always had access to unknown magic," another unrecognized voice said. "I got her talking about the masked Lords of the past, but she would not say how they controlled them."

The thin-voiced one said, "The secret of long years, of course, is the most profitable of secrets we could glean from her. I always suspected they bargained with elves or dwarves for those secrets."

"Three tendays! That's what you told me! And it's been seven!" Dagult slammed his hand down on a table. Renaer knew his father's temper well, and Dagult's roar meant he was frustrated but not yet angry. That's when he'd get very quiet. "You claimed I would have the Overlord's Helm to help me uncover my fellow Lords' secrets. *That* is what you claimed would make this gambit worth it! Well?"

The second voice joined in again. "We can't get her to focus. She's been mad ever since—"

"Focus?" Dagult snapped. "What do you think you have Granek for?"

The thin-voiced man coughed and said, "Yes, well, his methods are—"

"Only slightly more successful than your magic, apparently," Dagult said. "Now, when are you going to deliver what you promised? You've already received far more reward than what you've delivered in return, but I'm still prepared to bring you into the fold, should you gain results before the solstice."

Just who was Dagult conspiring with here? Renaer wondered. He *never* put more on the table unless he could hang someone with the other end of the deal. And to deal with wizards . . .

"We shall celebrate together before another tenday passes, milord Neverember," the reedy voice replied. "The three of us shall free the city from the Blackstaff's interference for the first time in two centuries—or at least ensure the Blackstaff is aligned in full with the Open Lord's policies."

Renaer heard the door open, and the men wandered out of his earshot. He saw three shadows pass his doorway, and one returned back to Dagult's office. Renaer heard the thud and hiss of another log being tossed on Dagult's fire grate. The bluster and volume had dropped away, and the cold quiet tone chilled Renaer despite the fire and the furs. "Just make damned sure that this never soils my hearth, wizards, or you'll find out I've more power than even your wizards' guild can muster."

Dawn nearly reached his windows before Renaer fell into a fitful sleep.

CHAPTER 2

It's a trip neither pretty nor pleasant, but delve the sewers if you truly want to learn what goes on in Waterdeep.

> Orlar Sarluk, *Down the Drain:*
> *A Life in the Guild of Cellarers and Plumbers,*
> the Year of the Worm (1356 DR)

Laraelra Harsard knew she needed help and needed it quickly. She looked over the assembled crowds milling around Heroes' Garden. Over the past few decades, each ward seemed to adopt its own unofficial gathering places for swords for hire, where Caravan Court, the White Bull, and Virgin's Square once sufficed for mercenary hiring. The snow-covered hillocks of the garden were already soiled from foot traffic, even though it was barely past sunup. Laraelra wove her way around the statues of heroes of Waterdeep's past. Scanning the crowds, she noticed someone had knocked the right foot off of Lhestyn's statue. Above a skinny man in black leathers, the outstretched stone arms of Lords Oth Ranerl, Tanar Hunabar, and Cyrin Kormallis held only broken blades or sword pommels. Laraelra moved deeper into the Heroes' Garden, searching for strong-backed hirelings but only finding jokesters had stolen the head of Rarkul Ulmaster for the fifth time that year.

If more people respected what it takes to work stone, Laraelra thought, they'd not be so quick to ruin it.

Laraelra had dressed for the weather and the task ahead of her. Her heavy woolen cloak covered her oiled leather tunic, pants, and her sealskin boots—necessities for mucking about the sewers. The black color of her clothes made her seem even paler in the morning cold. Despite her thick garments, Laraelra hugged herself to stay warm. As she rounded the back-to-back statues of Mirt the Merciless and Durnan the Wanderer, she patted their knees and thought, *Milords, help me find men of your mettle before it's too late.* Then she spotted the largest group of sellswords in the Garden—or more properly, they spotted her.

"Right here, Milady Harsard!" A stylish young bravo rushed ahead of the pack, his spotless purple cloak flaring behind him. He swept off his large feathered hat and bowed before her.

Behind him thundered a muscled tree stump of a young braggart, his first beard coming in thin patches and barely covering his pimples. "Ignore that fool. I'm your man, Laraelra!" To prove his point, he kicked the bowing man over on his way to intercept Laraelra.

"Hardly," she replied, striding past with a twitch of one arched eyebrow. Laraelra pulled her cloak closer to ward off the breeze and the light snow on it. Scanning the crowd, she looked for men at least her height, then winnowed down candidates by how strong or capable they seemed.

Finally, she approached one man leaning against the statue of some centaur hero. The contented young man was more interested in his roll of sausage and onion than in catching her eye. Blond hair avalanched across his shoulders and brow. Until she got close to him, Laraelra did not see the few days' growth of pale blond beard on his face. When she stopped in front of him, the man was in mid-bite, though he smiled close-mouthed at her around the steaming food.

"You'll do," Laraelra said, "assuming you can focus on a task as much as your meal."

She smiled as the man hurriedly chewed, swallowed, and then choked and coughed in surprise. He stood two hands taller than

Laraelra, his shoulders twice hers, and his arms were as large as her legs. Strapped to his back was a greataxe, much-abused but serviceable, like the dagger pommels she saw in his boots. Despite the cold, his cloak was open, exposing well-worn leather armor over a broad chest.

She pressed three silver pieces into his hand and said, "You'll get that much every bell you have to accompany me today, if that's acceptable to you."

The man nodded and coughed a few more times while he tucked the coins into his boot.

Laraelra motioned for him to follow, then turned her back and headed for the copse of trees at the southern end of the Heroes' Garden. "You'll want to finish that before we enter the sewers, I wager."

She half-expected him to stop walking once she mentioned the sewers, but the young man gamely followed her without hesitation.

Laraelra extracted a ring of keys from her belt pouch as she approached the stone hut that covered a sewer shaft among the trees. After she unlocked the access shaft and cracked the door, she turned to her companion. "In case you didn't know, I am Laraelra Harsard. And you are . . . ?"

A broad, beaming smile spread over the man's massive jaw. "Meloon Wardragon, at your service, mistress. What'll need doing this morning?"

Laraelra grabbed a torch off the wall inside the access hut, and lit it as she talked. "I am investigating a problem for the Cellarers and Plumbers' Guild down in the sewers. I simply need you in case anything or anyone tries anything untoward." She raised her eyebrows as she looked Meloon up and down. "You'll be a snug fit in some of the tunnels, so you might want to unbelt that axe of yours ahead of time. Never hurts to be prepared, after all."

Meloon nodded and pulled his axe free while Laraelra descended the rung ladder in the floor shaft.

"Just curious, mistress, but why choose me when all those other swords wanted your attention?" Meloon asked. He wrinkled his nose a bit at the overwhelming smell wafting up the shaft, but sighed and took a few deep breaths to acclimate himself to the odor.

The shaft and tunnel beneath Laraelra added a hollow echo to her words. "Most of those bravos up there dressed to impress and would balk at a morning spent in the sewers. Those who weren't dandies were trying to impress me and get in good with my father. I'd rather have someone who's more attentive to the job at hand. Besides, your boots were already covered with dung, so you're obviously someone who worries more about the work than appearance." Laraelra stepped off the rung ladder to the side of the tunnel before she looked up to see Meloon clambering down. "At least it's warmer down here than it is out on the streets. Wetter, but warmer."

Meloon said, "My father used to say, 'Never trust a man what's not got a little stuff on his boots. If a man's worried about where he's stepping, he's not working hard enough.' Glad to see that wisdom's alive in Waterdeep."

Meloon stepped onto the side ledge that lined the central sluice, and his left boot slipped in slime and slid sideways into the muck. Meloon sighed, looked up at Laraelra, and shrugged, a sheepish grin on his face. Laraelra wrinkled her nose as she smiled at him, then she turned and moved a bit up the path to allow him to shake the offal from his boot.

The pair stood at an intersection of three tunnels, all equally foul in appearance and stench. Walled all around in stone, the passages were twice as far across as Meloon's broad arm span, though the tunnel behind them leading southeast was smaller than the others. Laraelra spotted light flickering at an oval tunnel entrance outside of their torchlight long before she heard the voice.

"If ye and yer new lad're done exchangin' pleasantries, we've need of a strong back, lass!" A gravely voice echoed up the tunnel.

Laraelra darted forward with her torch. "Harug, is Dorn still all right?" she called out.

"No, he's far from that, lass," Harug replied. "He's trapped under rubble in a puddle of rising filth."

Laraelra and Meloon moved to the left side of the passage, as the ledge continued only on that side. They turned into the lit entrance of the smaller tunnel, the close confines of which concentrated the stench. The light of their torch merged with that of two others, and they could see the situation.

Part of the side wall had collapsed inward, though the ceiling arch overhead remained intact due to support pillars on both sides of the collapse. Sewage flowed out of the gap in the wall, cascading atop the pile of loosened stones and dirt. A makeshift shield of rocks kept most of it from splashing onto the two dwarves. The mobile one worked to move rocks while the other laid still, his legs trapped beneath the fall.

"About time ye made it back, lass," Harug snapped. "It's getting deeper around me nephew there, and I can't stop the flow long enough to redirect it."

The old dwarf seemed exhausted, his shoulders sagging, but he kept moving, barely facing them before he returned to repairing the crude screen that kept the worst of the sewage off his fallen companion. He kept darting glances up at the dark recess that had opened in the wall above him.

Laraelra's eyebrows arched in surprise and anger, and she felt a flare of heat flush across her face. "Why aren't Parkleth and Narlam here helping you clear rubble?"

Harug turned and shot her a knowing look.

"Those tluiners just left you here?" she said. "Oh, when I get my hands on those parharding wastes of air!"

"How 'bout me first, Elra?" The trapped dwarf opened his eyes briefly and chuckled. "The cowardly bigots can wait."

Her temper cooled, and she dashed toward her old friends. "To be sure, Dorn."

Laraelra knelt by her friend, brushing some mud away from his eyes. She hoped her face didn't betray how concerned she was about the gash on his forehead or the muck rising around him. To hide her worry, she talked over her shoulder at the other men. "Meloon Wardragon, meet Harug Shieldsunder, the most cantankerous dwarf in the city and one of our guild's best tunnel workers. The muddier one here is Dorn Strongcroft, his vastly more pleasant nephew. How can we help?"

"Move yer skinny self out of our way and get the lad to brace his back against that pile," Harug said. "If he can lift that main pair o' rocks for a trice, we should be able to pull Dorn free without the whole thing crushing all of us. Can ye do that, lad?"

"Aye," Meloon said, as he leaned his axe against the wall and ledge. He stepped over and straddled the fallen dwarf, making sure his footing was secure. He squatted and reached behind his back to grab the two largest rocks. He nodded at Laraelra and Harug, who grabbed the groaning Dorn by the arms. The three of them nodded in unison, and on the third nod, Meloon grimaced and lifted, using his legs and arms to pull the weight of the pile off of the dwarf. Rocks and sluice water, now free of the temporary dam, engulfed the tall man, and he gasped at both the stench and the cold water as it soaked him from head to foot.

Laraelra and Harug yanked Dorn free of the rubble, the wet muck making a sucking noise as he slid free. The dwarf himself only made a perfunctory grunt, then his head lolled back as he passed out. Laraelra and Harug pulled Dorn more than three body lengths away from the collapse and up onto the ledge before they stopped.

Sighing in relief, Laraelra called back, "Meloon, you can let go now," and heard him groan as he lowered his burden. The rocks and dirt rumbled slightly as they settled into the space where Dorn once lay. More rocks tumbled from the broken wall, widening the dark gap.

Laraelra focused on Dorn, whose crushed, mud-encrusted legs were twisted unnaturally. She shuddered, remembering the far-lesser pain of a twisted ankle, and she thanked Tymora that

Dorn had fallen unconscious from the pain. She needed to keep his wounds clean and determine if any bones broke through his skin. She closed her eyes, focused on the image of a sunbeam becoming a rainbow, and summoned her power. She opened her eyes and spread her fingers in a fan over his legs. The mud shimmered and separated, the water flowing away and the dirt and offal falling off of Dorn's legs in chunks. After a breath or two, she relaxed, not seeing any blood staining his now-dry clothes.

Within the piles around Dorn's legs, Harug spotted the glint of one gold and one silver ring, and he snatched those up. "Delvarin's daubles," he grunted at the sorceress, pocketing the jewelry.

She replied, "You're better off using that digger's treasure to pay a cleric to heal him, Harug, or he'll never walk again. Now why did you send a runner to the guildhouse claiming you needed protection down here instead of a pump crew and an engineer?"

"Fixits always come later, lass. I figured you'd have to bring somebody big enough to help do that more quickly." Harug thumbed toward Meloon, who was busy coughing and wiping the worst of the muck off of his face, arms, and torso. "Oh, and to deal with those, too."

Harug picked up a rock and threw it past Meloon's shoulder to strike a lettuce green mottled lizard in the snout as it appeared atop the pile of rubble. The mastiff-sized lizard's response was a hiss and snap of its jaws, and Meloon punched it in the nose, forcing it back into the darkness. Meloon peered into the wall cavity and said, "There's a lot of noise and movement back here, folks. I think it's a lot more of these things."

Laraelra stood, squaring her shoulders and facing the old dwarf. "Harug," she said, "strap Dorn to a board and get him to safety. We'll take care of those things. When you've heard it's clear, I want you down here to rebuild that wall. Father may favor Rodalun for the engineering jobs, but I don't trust that drunken sot to do it right. Besides, I don't want any others—especially my father— knowing about this breach in the tunnels."

"Finally," Harug chuckled, "I'm glad ye respect dwarves, even if some other Cellarers don't. Thanks, Elra lass." Harug clapped a thick calloused hand over hers and looked in her eyes. Softly, he said, "We owes ye both, lass, that we does."

Laraelra felt the solemnity of the dwarf's promise, and she knew her longtime friend Harug now pledged his life to hers.

Harug's eyes snapped toward Meloon. "Watch them sewyrms, lad. Them lizards're stubborn, but their bite's only half as bad as their tail lash."

Meloon smiled and said, "Thanks!" He stepped over to retrieve his axe, keeping himself between the lizard and Laraelra. In that moment, two sewyrms hopped atop the rubble pile and a third splashed into the sewer stream behind the rocks. Laraelra had to reassess her initial impression of Meloon. She watched his eyes and ears catch everything moving around him and plan his attack accordingly. Sweeping the greataxe as he spun back around, Meloon beheaded one lizard as it leaped at him. The second lashed its scaled tail over its body like a scorpion, slapping the warrior's arm and drawing blood. Meloon grunted and lopped off the lizard's tail on the return swing of his axe. That creature screeched in pain and leaped back into the darkness, out of reach.

Laraelra watched Meloon's axe slide in his grasp from all the water and filth covering him. She stepped closer and cast her spell again. Water and offal slid off of Meloon, his clothes, and axe.

He shook his head and said, "Who did that? I'm grateful, but . . ."

While many still feared magic since the Spellplague, Laraelra reveled in her small and growing sorceries. Even with her paltry few spells, she knew how to winnow down the opposition from lizards at least. Behind Meloon's massive back, Laraelra said, "If you'd move to one side, I'll do more than help dry you off. I can make this battle a lot simpler."

"A skinny little thing like you? A sword's weight could knock you over." Meloon chuckled.

"Don't forget who's *paying* you," she said, and she tried to push by him, but Meloon swept her back with his left arm.

"Unless you've a fireball or two in your sleeves, you'd best leave the fight to me. *That's* what you're paying me for." Meloon swung his axe up and cleanly decapitated another lizard.

The lizards hissed loudly. Three more leaped atop the pile as the survivor jumped down into the sewer stream alongside. The tunnel filled with splashing and hissing sounds loud enough to drown out the near-constant dripping.

"Meloon!" Laraelra said. "We can't pick them off one by one. Pick me up!"

"Hardly time for that, though I'll be happy to oblige later, milady." Meloon smirked as he shoved the greataxe into the rubble pile, reducing it in height but also dislodging and knocking all three sewyrms back behind it.

"Hold me up so I can see into the cavity, fool!" She punched Meloon in the side in frustration. "I'll disable most of them with a spell, instead of us getting overwhelmed by them. Then we can *both* take care of the stragglers, yes?"

"Oh. Why didn't you say so?" Meloon swung his axe one more time to ward off the sewyrms clambering up the pile, then reached around with his left arm, grabbed her around the waist, and held her high up on his torso. "That high enough, milady Harsard?"

"Fine." She muttered a few arcane syllables, breathing deep and thinking of a dragon's head, and a radiant cone of color flashed from her outstretched hands. The brief illumination showed her a deep cavity that used to be a cellar or tunnel, its entirety choked with the green sewyrms. All of them hissed in pain, though most fell unconscious, stunned by the clashing spray of color.

She leaned back against Meloon's shoulder and chest and said, "The few that are still moving are blind and more easily dispatched now. Promise to never underestimate me again and you can call me Elra."

"Done, Elra," the blond man said as he set her down at the edge of the cavity. "You didn't mention you were a wizard."

"I'm not," she said. "I don't tell many people about my hidden talents, given how most feel about magic since the Spellplague. And I'm a sorcerer, not a wizard."

"Doesn't matter to me—for friends or a fight," Meloon said. "We're still striding. That's what matters."

Laraelra smiled, but that vanished when a scream echoed toward them. Before Laraelra could give him an order, Meloon shouldered his way through the loose rubble pile, widening the opening. The two of them clambered up and over into the cavity, haunted by the sounds of their breathing, the hiss of a few sewyrms, and the echoing screams. Laraelra grabbed one of the torches and brought it to light their way.

Meloon's first steps sank ankle-deep into mud. What lizards they found were soon beheaded and shoved out of the way.

"What is this?" Meloon whispered. "Where are we?"

Laraelra said, "There are a lot of hidden cellars, tunnels, and old foundations beneath the northern wards, some of which have been mapped, others not so much. Many places here are decades older than the city around them. As long as they never interfered with the sewers, the Lords and the Cellarers and Plumbers' Guild turned a blind eye to them all. The money that buys these places also buys secrets."

"I can't tell where the screams are coming from," he said, his knuckles white around his axe haft.

"Just up ahead and to the right," Laraelra replied, pointing ahead to an obvious intersection of tunnels. "After a few trips down here, you learn to ignore the echoes and focus on the sources of sounds. Now let's go quietly."

Meloon swept a protective arm to keep her back as he moved ahead. Laraelra bumped into him when he stopped. They stood on the edge of a drop well beyond their torchlight, blackness yawning before them. The pavement fell away here, the walls looking slightly melted, rippling from brickwork to smooth flow-stone. Laraelra could see a tunnel entrance outlined indirectly by flickering torchlight far below her and to her right. A woman's ragged gasps and whimpers of pain grew to another anguished scream. The screams echoed up from the depths, along with the murmur of a man's voice.

"Wizards!" The man's spit of disgust and phlegm resounded through the darkness. "You all think you're better than us, but they can't get secrets out of you with magic, so they call on Granek. Wizardry or no, without fingers, you'll be naught but a hard-coin girl after we're done, if you don't yield your secrets."

Laraelra and Meloon paused high above, sharing a look of horror and revulsion as they listened.

"Tell Granek what he wants to know, and we'll stop. For now. Resist, and we'll do worse to your hip than we're doing to your knee."

The woman's ragged sobs and panicked breathing were audible even where Meloon and Laraelra stood far above them. Laraelra hugged herself, her eyes tearing up at hearing the utter hatred in the man's rough voice. She knew people could be cruel, but she'd never heard it so plain. Fear, anger, and her breakfast all warred in the pit of her stomach and she gulped to hold it down.

Meloon paced and smashed the butt of his axe against the wall, loosening stone fragments to clatter down into the black-ness. In the firelight, Laraelra could see the anger in his clenched jaw and knew his imaginary target was the torturer down below in the gloom.

"Well?" the man asked, but there was only a long pause. A hollow laugh, a moist crunch, and a deafening scream followed.

Laraelra and Meloon both jumped in shock. Meloon's face shifted to stern resolve. "Can't we help her?"

She nodded, and whispered, "Let's see if there's a way down."

Laraelra grabbed a stone from the floor, cupped it in her left hand, and whispered at it. In a whirl of sparkles, the stone glowed with a steady blue light. She tossed the stone down into the abyss, and it dropped more than five people's heights before it rattled to a stop. The pale azure light revealed a shattered and nebulous system of tunnels, many of which had melted or collapsed together on at least two levels. Her stone's light merged with the outer edges of their torchlight, showing them at least a drop of at least thirty feet.

"No way we can get down there without ropes and hooks." Meloon groaned.

"No," Laraelra said, "but that doesn't mean we can't guess who's doing this."

Laraelra handed her torch to Meloon and pulled a scroll tube out of her belt pouch. She opened the tube and pulled out the parchments within it, flipping through them until she found what she sought. She explained, "My father keeps detailed maps of every sewer connection and tunnel he knows of down here, and he notes who owns the properties above them as well. I've made copies for whenever I need to come down here."

She squinted at the map and motioned for Meloon to bring the light closer.

"If I'm reading this right, we're beneath Kulzar's Alley and Rook's Alley," she muttered, deep in thought. "There's a block of three conjoined buildings up there."

"So who do we go fight?" Meloon asked.

Laraelra stared at the map, then folded it back up sharply. "No one. We can't do anything."

"Who owns this block?" Meloon asked. "We can't let them get away with this!"

"We have to," Laraelra said. "The block is owned by the Neverembers."

"The Open Lord?"

"I doubt it. Lord Dagult wouldn't do this. Even if he would, he's got far more secure locations in Castle Waterdeep or beneath the palace." Laraelra thought aloud, "We could go to the Watch, but who will they believe? The Open Lord or the daughter of a paranoid guildmaster and her hired sellsword?"

"I don't care," Meloon said. "I need to help that woman. Nobody deserves that—servant, coin-girl, or peasant. And if we have to go the palace and confront the Open Lord, well . . ."

"No," Laraelra said. "Lord Dagult's too busy with the city. His son Renaer manages all his properties, allegedly. Let's go pay a visit to and get some answers from Lord Neverember the Younger. Unless you'd like to stay down here a while longer?"

"No," Meloon said coldly. "My axe and I want words with Renaer Neverember."

CHAPTER 3

Whether a lord knows in his castle what hap or no, his sovereignty
makes demands of him for it nonetheless, and any who wouldst gainsay
that deserves neither loyalty nor obeisance.

Myrintar Hasantar, *Things a Knight Should Know,*
Year of the Mace (1307 DR)

9 NIGHTAL, YEAR OF THE AGELESS ONE (1479 DR)

"Milord?"

"Yes, Madrak?"

"Apologies at interrupting your breakfast, but you have unexpected callers."

Renaer looked up from his trencher of fried eggs and potatoes and stared at the white-haired halfling whose face barely cleared the table top. Renaer swallowed and said, "Anyone who knows me would not call on me before midmorn. Who is it?"

Madrak cleared his throat and said, "The Lady Laraelra Harsard, daughter of Guildmaster Malaerigo Harsard of the Cellarers and Plumbers' Guild, and one Meloon Wardragon, sellsword." Madrak's tone left Renaer little question as to his opinion of them.

"I've met Laraelra before at the Wands manse, but never more than to say hello," Renaer thought aloud, "but why she would need a sellsword to come here?"

The halfling harrumphed and said, "They claim to have questions for you about your properties on Kulzar's Alley. They appear to have come directly from the sewers to your door. I took the liberty of receiving them around back at the stables."

Renaer smiled. "Thank you for that."

"No thanks needed, young lord. After all, you'd not be the one to clean up the foyer after such, would you?" Madrak said, and then asked, "Shall I tell them to call another time?"

"No," Renaer said, and he got up from the table. "Odd that the guildmaster's daughter herself brings me news of some problem with the cellars or somesuch. It's the sort of thing normally channeled through low-level guild members and servants." Renaer pulled his napkin out of his shirt front and wiped his mouth, then looked down at the butler at his side. "Could you have Bramal bring me the deeds and keys to those properties? I don't know who's renting them at present, if anyone. That way, we'll be able to deal with any problems directly."

"Very good," Madrak replied. "I took the liberty of asking my son to do just that before I came in here. He'll join you around the stables. Now, don't let these strangers take advantage of you. I've heard tell that the cellarers can back the sewers up into one's vaults simply to shake coins loose from an unsuspecting young lord such as yourself."

Renaer chuckled and patted Madrak on his shoulder. "I appreciate the warning, old hin, but I didn't just fall off a dung-sweeper's cart. Let's see what they have to say before we accuse them of trying to separate me from my gold, hmm?"

Madrak snorted and said, "Lad, you just learned to walk a short tenday ago in my eyes. I'm looking out for you as I promised your good mother when she placed your swaddled self in my arms. You've a good ear for sniffing out falsehoods, but your head for business isn't nearly as keen as your love of books."

"And *that* is why Bramal conducts the bulk of the family business as my proxy." Renaer knew that Madrak's son and his children were vastly more capable than he would ever be at keeping track of his holdings, collecting rents, and the like. "I trust you and them, Madrak, but today at least I wish to have a hand in my business."

"Does our hearts good to hear that," Madrak said. "It's high time—"

"The Brandarth holdings were seen to by me, not my father?" Renaer said, and the old halfling flushed.

"I'd never say that, young master," Madrak replied, and he and Renaer said in unison, "for it's not my place nor my concern."

Renaer knelt at his butler's side and rested both hands on his shoulders. "Madrak, you and your family have been at my side since I was born. I know that Dagult would have put you out, save for my insistence and the conditions of Mother's will. Never fear. Your family will always have a place in my house—and not just because of the hin-sized servants' passages. You never have to mince words with me, old halfling. I trust your judgment more than my own."

A wry smile appeared on the halfling's lips. "Then you'd best stop leaving guests awaiting your pleasure, milord Renaer. Time to start living up to all your potential and being more than a shut-in scholar or a rake-by-night racing with the Watch." Madrak shooed the young man off. He waved a dismissive hand at the cloak rack by the doors leading into the stables. "Oh, and wear that heavy cloak, milord. Auril's blessed us with a biting cold this morn."

Renaer grabbed the cloak off its peg and swung it around his shoulders as he shoved open the door. The smell of hay and horse manure wafted around him as he closed the door behind him. He waved to Pelar, the groom, who was brushing down Ash, Renaer's favorite stallion. While all the servants answered to Madrak, not all were halflings related to him. By necessity, the grooms were humans capable of handling the larger animals.

Renaer spotted two strangers standing a few paces to his left by the servants' entrance off of Senarl's Cut. He turned and walked briskly toward the scrawny woman and broad-shouldered man. She stared out at the stream of carts and people heading toward Tespergates at the southern end of Senarl's Cut. She hugged herself, but Renaer couldn't tell if it was from the cold or nervous habit. The young man seemed more interested in admiring Neverember House's carriages and horses.

"Milady Harsard? Master Wardragon?" Renaer asked when they turned to face his approach. "What seems to be the problem today?"

Laraelra spun on her heels and pointed an accusatory finger in Renaer's face. Her face switched from angry to surprised, as if she had shocked herself. "Who's living in Roarke House right now?"

Behind the three of them, the rasp of a sword being pulled from its scabbard preceded Pelar running forward to defend his young master with a shout of "Back away, woman!"

Renaer noticed the blond man with Laraelra—noticed especially his hand reaching for the axe on his back.

Renaer held up both hands and shook his head. "Calm yourself, Pelar. This lady has a lot on her mind. No threats here, right?" Renaer shot a smile at Meloon, whose grip relaxed on his axe hilt.

Laraelra sighed and stepped back. "My apologies, milord. It's been a tense morning." She hugged herself again and stared away. Pelar stopped, sheathed his blade, and slowly returned to Ash's stall.

Renaer exhaled and began again. "I'd invite you in for a warm cup, but the state of your clothes presents a problem for my staff." He smiled at Laraelra's answering blush and continued, "Now why do you ask about Roarke House? I've got someone fetching me the deeds and details on that property as we speak. Is there a problem with the sewers beneath it?"

"Not as much as—" Meloon started, but he stopped when Laraelra elbowed him in the stomach.

"I just need to know who's living in that building, Lord Neverember," she said. She grabbed some errant black hairs that waved in front of her pale face and pulled them back inside her hood.

"Lord Neverember is my father," Renaer said. "Call me Renaer, but don't expect me to part with my business if the Cellarers and Plumbers' Guild won't tell me why they need to know it."

"This isn't guild business. It's—"

"Someone's torturing someone in the cellars beneath your property, man!" Meloon blurted.

Renaer's jaw dropped.

Pelar stepped forward again, fists up, and said, "Take that back, and apologize to the saer."

Even though Meloon was nearly a foot taller than the stable hand, he stepped back, surprised by the anger in the man's eyes.

Renaer rested a hand on the older man's shoulder and said, "Thank you again, Pelar, but I don't need to be saved from everyone with a cross word for me. Besides, I want to hear what's got these two all wound up and angry with me this morning."

Pelar's eyes never left Meloon's, but he lowered his fists and muttered, "They should show more respect to you, saer, that's all." He dropped his hands, nodded to Renaer, and then returned to brushing the horses.

The door behind them opened and a halfling with his long, dark hair tied at the nape of his neck entered the stables. He juggled a few scrolls, and keys jangled at his belt. He cleared his throat, and said, "Milord, a word. In private." Despite being less than half the size of Meloon, this halfling cowed both him and Laraelra with a stern look when they tried to follow Renaer. Once Renaer was close, he knelt in front of the halfling to block their line of sight to his face.

"What is it, Bramal?" Renaer said. "Do you have the papers on Roarke House?"

The halfling whispered, "No, milord. That's what I came to tell you. They're missing, along with two sets of keys. I didn't sell or lease out the property. The last dealings I had with that house was in renting it this past summer to some guests of Lady Nhaeran

Wands. As far as any of us know, Roarke House should be vacant. There're only four people with complete access to those records and keys. You and I are two of them, and the others are our fathers."

"Very well, Bramal, thank you. Don't worry about it, but do give me the other set of the keys to the place." Renaer stood as Bramal put the ring of keys into his hand. "Was there anything suspicious about the deeds on the adjoining properties?" Renaer asked this loudly for his guests to overhear, and Bramal took the hint.

"No milord," he replied. "The Gildenfires remains, as it has for thirteen years, in need of repair and a tenant to do so. We replaced the roof year before last to keep the building intact, but your father insisted we not waste money fixing up anything a tenant might do for us. The warehouse between that festhall and Roarke House has those long-term leases with Houses Ammakyl and Gralleth. At last autumn's inspection, half the warehouse was filled with older furniture and other decorations from the last three times Lady Ammakyl decided her mansion was not quite up to the leading edge of Waterdhavian fashions. The other half, the Gralleths have filled with materials from former noble villas when they absorbed the estates and interests of the Bladesemmers and the Markarls."

"Well, Laraelra? Meloon? Feel up to walking to Roarke House?" Renaer said. "We can inspect the property, and you can tell me more about whatever is 'not guild business.' "

Laraelra had rarely been in this neighborhood, even though it bordered on the Heroes' Garden where she met Meloon earlier. The buildings she noticed lining Skulls Street were better-kept row houses with stone foundations and wooden upper floors, none of which loomed less than three stories high. Once they turned into Rook Alley, the building quality and size plummeted, most of the structures of one or two stories and in ill repair. The roof slates became rough wooden shingles with moss-encrusted gaps, the foundations simple brick rising to knee height and continuing with dark stained wood. While the outer buildings surrounding Rook Alley celebrated the richness of Sea Ward, those hidden within reflected the ill fortunes visited on the city in times past and present.

Following Renaer's lead, Laraelra and Meloon came to a stop on the stoop of an imposing three-story building. The well-kept stone front was freshly scrubbed and cleaned, unlike most other buildings to the south and east. This was one of two stone buildings in the general vicinity, the other being the Halaerim Club directly across Kulzar's Alley. Roarke House's columned frontage seemed ostentatious, compared to the slightly rundown nature of the buildings attached to it. This neighborhood had fallen on bad times in the past decades, and now Roarke House was among a well-tended few. The cleaner buildings here and there along Skulls Street did suggest gentrification might be returning to this part of Sea Ward, but it would be some time in coming.

Laraelra sniffed and said, "Very clean for a vacant place, Renaer. Hiding a rich friend from the Watch?"

Renaer glared at her. "Would I have brought the daughter of one of the loudest mouths in the city with me, if I were?"

Meloon rested hands on both their shoulders. "Hey, I'm sure there's a simple explanation for all this. Can't we be friends here?"

"No," came the simultaneous reply from both.

Renaer put the key in the lock of an ornately carved duskwood door, its surface a relief of stars and crescent moons. The door knocker, lock, and door pull were all silver crescents, as was the decorative end of Renaer's key. The lock clicked, and the door swung easily in silence. Renaer's eyebrows rose in surprise, which Laraelra followed with one arched eyebrow.

Renaer shrugged and said, "Last time I opened this door, the hinges shrieked. Someone's oiled them. Shall we?"

"You're not worried about us fouling your floors here, milord?" she asked.

"Drop the tone, Laraelra," Renaer said. "The walk here cleaned your boots."

The trio stepped into an echoing entry hall, its stone floors and high ceiling dominated by a sweeping grand staircase that hugged the walls of the room as it led upstairs. Overhead loomed a three-stories-high atrium, a glass skylight shining light down to the ground floor. Tiles covered that floor in a continuing pattern of stars, moons, and random pairs of eyes. Two doors bracketed an open archway opposite the front door and beneath the stairs. Additional doors flanked the front wall of the house. All doors were closed, and aside from their footsteps, no sound could be heard.

Meloon let out a low whistle then said, "Why the eyes and moons and stars everywhere?"

Laraelra said, "Roarke House was built by Volam Roarke, an exceedingly devout worshiper of Selûne, right?" She smiled with Renaer's answering nod, and continued. "He financed the restoration of the House of the Moon after the Spellplague collapsed it."

Renaer nodded and said, "The Roarkes had even reached the nobility about seventy-five years ago, but their family fortunes dried up over the years since. By the time they lost their noble status and other riches forty years ago, my grandfather bought their holdings in the city. Last I'd heard, the Roarke clan owned only two inns along the High Road between Leilon and Neverwinter. This place has had about half a dozen long-term tenants over the years. It's only been the past four years that it's been a summer rental. Most of the folk who rented it out never even knew about the sub-cellars."

Renaer walked to the door on the left. "This door leads to the cellars. Now, tell me more about what you saw—no, heard down below. It seems like we'll need to update the maps for the sub-cellars. Wonder if the Rook's Hold was part of what you saw down there?"

"The Rook?" Meloon asked.

"A thief of some repute more than a century ago," Renaer explained. "His hideout was in the subterranean crypts after which Skulls Street outside was named. It sounds like the tunnels and crypts may have collapsed and merged a while back. I never knew they extended beneath this house. They've always been blocked off, or so I was told."

Laraelra chuckled. "Renaer, the amount of things beneath the streets that the city chooses to ignore or not know about would stagger your imagination."

The three of them entered a small stairwell that spiraled down into darkness. Renaer grabbed a torch out of a wall sconce and lit it.

"And I thought I heard you complaining at the last Wands feast that you wanted nothing to do with your father's guild," Renaer said. He took the lead on the stairs, the smoke from his torch rising and stinging Laraelra's eyes. "Why were you poking around beneath the streets this morning?"

Laraelra cleared her throat and lowered her voice. "Someone has to stand up to the bigots in the guild. The dwarves deserve equal pay and equal treatment, and some of my father's foremen will hardly bother with that. Parkleth, one of the worst of them, would have left a friend of mine to drown this morning as a lesson for the dwarves to stay out of sewer work. We only uncovered your house's secrets by accident."

"My—" Renaer stopped dead and glared up at Laraelra. "That's it. We're done here. That's the last insult you get at my expense, when I've been naught but accommodating."

Laraelra's face felt hot as she realized what she'd said, and she slumped her shoulders. "I'm sorry. Truly, Renaer, before the gods, I apologize. I'm tired, angry, and I spend too much time around my father, who's all too eager to blame everything on nobles or the ruling class."

Renaer resumed their descent to the cellars, and Laraelra knew she had to watch her tongue around the young Lord Neverember. His clipped tone told her he was still angry as Renaer said, "I'm neither of those things, really."

"Yes you are, whether you admit it to yourself or not," Laraelra said. "Even without noble title, you're one of the richest land-holders in this city. When you add your father's holdings to yours, only House Nandar and a handful of others own more properties. Even if you don't acknowledge or use it, that gives you power over a lot of people, Renaer. Now, can we finish what we started here?"

"Not even my father would put up with an accusation of being party to torture," Renaer said. "The only reason I'll continue is to prove this has nothing to do with me and mine." Renaer continued down into the main cellars.

Meloon put his hand on Laraelra's shoulder and whispered, "Maybe it's not my place to say, milady, but I don't think he knows what's going on any more than we do."

"Then we're all in for an education, aren't we?" she whispered in return as both of them joined Renaer in the vast cellar. To the right of the stairwell lay cords of firewood carefully stacked from floor nearly to ceiling. Open and empty earthenware jars rested on shelves to the left, while hooks dangling from the ceiling were empty of the usual smoked meats that might hang there. Across the room was an archway leading farther into the cellar. The trio moved into the next room, where stacked furniture and chests completely filled the right-hand side of the chamber. The long left-hand wall was covered with wine racks, though only a few bottles remained on the shelves.

"Now," Renaer said, "if someone were living here right now, those shelves back there and the wine cellar would be far better stocked, wouldn't they?"

Laraelra waved her hands and said, "Fine. We believe you. Now will you show us where these secret sub-cellars are so we can prove that we weren't lying?"

Renaer approached the wine racks and counted the rows. He reached out, grasped one section of the racks, and pulled. The rack slid out easily and then turned on a hidden hinge to expose a section of the wall behind it. He stepped forward, chuckled lightly, and pressed a small stone on the wall.

Nothing happened.

"Well?" Laraelra asked.

"This should have opened!" Renaer said. "The door leading to another stairwell should be right there!"

Meloon motioned for Renaer to move. He rushed forward and slammed his shoulder into the wall. "Ow! If there's a door there, it's well-braced or locked."

"Or held by a spell," Laraelra said.

In the house above them, shouts filled the air.

"Someone's in here!"

"They've gone down into the cellars! Come with me!"

Renaer shoved the wine rack back into place, and then held Meloon from drawing his axe. He whispered at Laraelra, "Time later to talk on all this. Do you know any spells to help here?"

"Only if you're spoiling for a fight, and they'll only stop someone temporarily," she said. "Nothing that will get us out of here without notice."

"No need," Renaer said, as the three of them rushed back into the front cellar chamber. "I'll explain."

"I hope so, young lord, for you have much to answer for." The white-haired man leaned on a duskwood staff, its presence as much as the speaker's own notoriety identifying him as Samark "Blackstaff" Dhanzscul. The premier mage of Waterdeep, the Blackstaff glowered at them while the crystal atop his staff pulsed a bright purple.

"Indeed they do, friend," said the other man descending the stairs. Bald with a tightly trimmed gray mustache, the man exiting the stairs walked with confidence and strength belying his scarecrow frame. His fingers steepled in front of his face and his prominent eyebrows, the ornate rings on every digit of his hands reminded her of his full name—Khondar "Ten-Rings" Naomal, the Guildmaster of the Watchful Order of Magists and Protectors.

Khondar asked, "Shall I call the Watch or the Cere-Clothiers, Ossurists, and Grave-Diggers' Guild? Your choice, children."

CHAPTER 4

I watched a wolf cub challenge his pack leader this morning. The guile and experience of the old wolf won out again, despite the younger's strength and speed. Would that youth did not always rely on bluster and newfound strength . . .

Laeral of the Nine, *Thoughts on Life and Wizardry,*
Year of the Snow Winds (1335 DR)

9 NIGHTAL, YEAR OF THE AGELESS ONE (1479 DR)

Khondar surveyed the intruders carefully. He recognized the one at the forefront. Khondar maintained his neutral face, but bristled inwardly at the surprise intrusion. "Renaer Neverember, would you care to explain your presence here? Have you taken to hiding from the Watch here now?"

Renaer spread his arms wide and bowed to both him and the Blackstaff. "I apologize for our intrusion, Guildsenior Naomal. My clients asked to see Roarke House, but there seems to be some confusion as to its current status for tenants."

"I am its current tenant, as of the tenday last. I have a copy of the signed deed upstairs."

Renaer arched an eyebrow at that and said, "I handle all Brandarth and Neverember holdings within the city. And yet, you and I have never spoken aside from pleasantries at parties more than five months ago. Apparently someone on my staff failed to tell me about this transaction."

"Apparently." Khondar disliked this boy more with every breath, since he remained calm and unreadable. Khondar tamped his temper down by focusing on Renaer's companions. The woman he had seen before, but he could not place her face or gaunt form. What made him seethe was the lack of respect for him in her scowl. Beside her, the young blond bear-of-a-man twitched with nervous energy, ready to fight anyone, but he seemed held in check with her hand. Khondar tired of the pretense and asked, "Do you need to see the deed to believe me, lad?"

The Blackstaff interrupted, "My time is short. Surely explanations can wait another time?" He stamped his trademark staff upon the stone floor, its silver-shod end ringing dully. "I'm sure these young people have other matters to which they can attend."

The larger man stepped forward. "No we don't! We need to know—"

The woman stopped him by slipping into his path.

"—if there's anything we can do to make your new home more comfortable?" said Renaer. He turned on his heels, showing Khondar his back as he swept his arms at the walls. "Would you like, perhaps, a few bottles of a lovely Farlindell Red from Tethyr's Purple Hills for these racks? As an apology for our interruption?"

"The only apology we shall need, young Neverember," Khondar said, "is the keys by which you entered this house, followed by your swift exit."

"We have a few questions yet, milord," Renaer said. "My friends Ararna and Pellarm were hoping to purchase this or another house in the same general area. They want assurances that there are no problems with either neighbors or the infrastructure. They don't believe me, as I'm trying to sell them property, but perhaps you could offer a more objective opinion."

Renaer's companions flinched when he said their names aloud, and Khondar knew that Renaer had given them false identities.

"You try my patience, all of you." Khondar sighed. "Such questions will wait for another time, if at all. If you insist on remaining trespassers, the Watch shall be summoned."

"Fine!" said Pellarm. "Maybe they can find out who you're torturing and where you've hidden her!"

Khondar froze, though the Blackstaff's outrage was apparent as he howled at the warrior. "Boy, you delay two archmages in important work with foul accusations! Where is evidence to back your claim?"

"Only what we heard from the street." Pellarm shrugged. "We heard horrific screaming as we walked by—and I for one don't ignore pleas for help."

Khondar smiled mirthlessly as he watched the boy spin his poor lies. He seemed ignorant of just how close to the lion's maw he put his head. "You're obviously new to the city, Pellarm. I'll not waste our time relaying all the sordid ghosts that haunt this and other nearby neighborhoods. That is why we're all in my all-too-empty cellar with neither woman nor tortures at hand." Khondar stepped off the stairs and into the cellar, motioning back toward the stairs. "Now, while I'll happily receive new neighbors at a later date, the Blackstaff's time today is more precious even than mine. Please, *remove yourselves.*"

"Again, my apologies, milord," Renaer said, and he backed up toward the stairs, taking each of his friends by their elbows. "When would be a good time to call again?"

"Enough!" the Blackstaff shouted, his patience at an end. He swept his staff in an arc and his other hand wove a pattern in the air. A haze of colors shimmered into existence on the stairs next to the three young people. Renaer and Pellarm both stared fixedly at it, fascinated at its shifting color weave.

The alleged Ararna shook her head and glared at the Blackstaff. "The Watch shall hear of this!"

"Hardly," Khondar said as he finished his gestures and snapped his fingers to get the woman's attention. They locked eyes and his dominating enchantment burrowed into her mind. *You cannot communicate anything you've seen here. Follow your friends and do not come back to this house.* Khondar enjoyed this spell's usefulness in dominating people for days or whole tendays and wiping their memories of its use later. Before he let the spell lapse entirely, he'd find out what she really knew and why they were here, but now was not the time.

As the Blackstaff willed his own iridescent illusion up the stairs, the two young men followed it without hesitation. While the woman had initially struggled against the magic, she followed them as ordered.

After a few moments, the Blackstaff returned to the cellars and said, "I'm sorry if I acted out of turn. Too many questions."

"It got them out of here, and that's all that matters to me right now," Khondar replied. "If the woman hadn't resisted your spell, I'd not have had to waste one on her. Still, should we need to, I can influence her and keep watch on her activities over the next tenday or more."

"Well, not one person blinked as the pattern led them out onto the alley and headed toward Trollkill Street," the Blackstaff said. "I've put an arcane lock on the front door so we won't be disturbed easily now. I'll set up other defenses later."

"They should have been in place already," Khondar said, turning away from his son. "Let's get to work, then."

Samark flinched, looked back upstairs, and then asked, "Shouldn't we ensure they don't talk to anyone? Or at least find out what they know for certain?"

"They may actually prove useful. She cannot say anything due to my spell's enchantment. As for Renaer, his well-known habits for avoiding responsibility and his reluctance to implicate his father should keep him quiet as well. The sellsword . . . well, who's going to believe a sellsword over the Blackstaff and the Watchful Order?"

The Blackstaff's eyes shifted to gray as he spoke, "True, but they could cause problems—like they did here. There's no way they could have heard her, Father." His form wavered, then solidified into Centiv's younger leather-clad form. The pale, balding face melted into one far younger with a full head and beard of chestnut-colored hair.

"Well, they heard *something*, Centiv, and it led them here," Khondar said. "Just open the door, while I figure out what to do next."

Centiv approached the wall and opened the rack-door as Renaer had earlier. His ring flashed bright blue, and when he pushed the rock in the wall, a door recessed into the wall, exposing a well-lit spiral stair leading down.

"I have enough friends and influence to turn the public's trust against them before they can interfere," Khondar said as they descended. "They've played into our hands perfectly. After all, many saw them come here, while we enter and exit invisibly. Should anything get exposed, they're the ones caught on the hook. Dagult will most likely protect his son from the worst of it, which makes the brunt of it fall on that skinny girl and her barbarian friend. Either way, it forces all parties to cover for us, should anything leak out."

"I know I've seen that scrawny woman before, but I can't place her," Centiv said. "She's not a member of our guild, though perhaps she should be, given her resistance to my spell."

"What she should be is grateful I chose to waste that domination spell on her instead of blasting her and her meddlesome friends to ashes." Khondar punched his fist into his other palm. "Now we lose another day before I can get answers!"

Centiv said, "Then that's another day in which we find more folk to rally to our cause—freeing knowledge for the guild from the grasping hands of private mages like the Blackstaff."

"Yes, yes, of course," Ten-Rings said, as they reached the bottom of the stairwell. The chamber they entered was merely another nondescript cellar by all appearances. The elder nodded to his son, who used the staff he carried to tap three stones in succession at one corner of the ceiling. In response, a secret door slid open, the walls and floor unfolding into yet another secret stair. Screams pierced the air.

"That's the only part I hate." Centiv shuddered. "I know we're doing all this for the city's good, but do we really need to torture her to get the answers we need?"

"Unfortunately, we do, lad." Khondar sighed. "Samark and all the Blackstaffs keep secrets they should share with the guilds, the Lords, and others. It's how they maintain their mystique, their stranglehold on power—they keep their secrets, even when it harms the City around them.

"We do this only because this woman, like too many, would rather maintain the way things have always been done." Ten-Rings sneered. "She wants our fair city to stay under the control of the money-grubbing merchant classes and foreign interests. Wizard rulers would never allow Sembian shades to infiltrate the palace. We'll restore things to right, son. We will. We'll clean up this city. All we need are the keys to the tower and its magic. The sooner that outlander bitch gives them up, the sooner her pain will end."

Ten-Rings exited the stair into a tiny chamber only as wide as a staff's length. Set into the wall facing them was a small niche holding a handful of tomes and beneath it a number of vials in a wooden box. He snatched up a vial as he stormed through the open doorway to the left of the stair. A pair of doors lined the hallway on both sides, and all the noise came from the nearest room on Khondar's right.

The woman lay strapped to a rough wooden table, bound spread-eagled with each hand and foot bound to a corner of the table. Her clothes were whole, though rent to expose her limbs and her midriff. Blood dripped or dried on nearly every exposed bit of skin. A large metal clamp encircled her right knee, bending it unnaturally to one side. Obscene black bruising and bleeding around a clamp at her left hip showed that her interrogator had also shattered that bone in his ministrations. Numerous cuts along her arms, legs, and stomach had long since scabbed over. Her face held half-healed bruises days old, and her lower lip was a mass of scabs. She lay senseless, breathing heavily but irregularly, and her eyes were closed. Her short dark hair lay matted to her head with sweat and grime. Blood—both dried and otherwise—coated the table beneath her.

The man standing over her shoved a dirty rag into the pulsing wound on her left forearm as he withdrew a nail, sighing as he did so.

"Has she told you anything, Granek?" Khondar asked, and the man whirled around. Granek was short, stripped to the waist, and covered with hair, dirt, and blood. His graying hair hung loose and long, its receding hairline making it look like his hair slipped to the back of his head. The eye patch over his right eye failed to cover the two scars that crossed his forehead, temple, and upper cheek. He dropped the nail and hammer onto a side table and wiped the blood from his hands onto a rough leather apron and breeches he wore. Granek shook his head and went to a water bucket, raising the dipper to his lips.

"The lass has spirit, aye," Granek said after wiping his mouth with his forearm. "As we'd planned, she had two days to heal before we went at her again this morning. All she's given me are screams and a few insults directed at me mam. Oh, and a few for you as well, Khondar."

"Address him as Guildmaster, dog!" Centiv snapped "Show some respect!"

Granek glared at the younger man and said, "You need me, and I still need to be paid. Gold gets you my respect, as I've done more for you than you've for me. Besides, we're all out on the plank together here. Show some manners yourself, lad."

Centiv's fingers crackled with energy and he began mouthing a spell, but Ten-Rings rested a hand over his fingers and said, "Enough. You should not be so easily baited." He then turned his attention to Granek, and said, "And you should not presume to be more important than you are, hireling, or you shall find out how adept I am at doing magically what you do mechanically. Now, give her this, so we might talk." He handed the vial through the bars to Granek, who snatched it away with anger.

Granek stalked to the woman's side, muttering, "Waste of a good potion, ask me." He opened her mouth, but stopped as Ten-Rings cleared his throat.

"Maybe you should remove the clamps to allow her to heal?" said Ten-Rings. "We already know how well she screams, and don't need to hear it for this discussion."

Granek frowned and tucked the vial into a pouch. He removed the clamp from her left hip, and she groaned. Even Centiv shuddered as Granek removed the knee clamp and her leg moved like its bones were no more than gravel in a bag. Granek retrieved the vial and poured its contents into her mouth, manipulating her throat to force her to swallow. He then pulled the rag out of her forearm, which made blood flow freely again.

Within moments, the blood stopped flowing and the woman's old and new bruises faded beneath her dark skin. She shed the scab on her lip as that wound healed, and her hip and knee returned to their normal positions. Her indigo-colored eyes darted open and she snapped her head up to stare at Granek, then beyond the bars at Centiv and Ten-Rings.

"Does that feel better, Vajra?" said Granek.

"I'd thank you for healing me, but I know you don't do it for my sake. We've danced this dance before, Khondar," Vajra said. "I won't give you the knowledge you seek."

Ten-Rings sighed and said, "To think you came to this city to join my guild—"

"*Your* guild?" she laughed. "Does the Watchful Order know they're your personal servants?"

"Better that than lackeys of the Blackstaff," he said.

Centiv added, "Or whores of the same."

"Centiv"—Vajra shook her head—"so much power stunted by sycophantic adulation. Thirty years here and still no life without Father?"

Centiv's knuckles cracked as he clenched his fists.

"You wizards are all the same—all talk, no action," Granek said. He leaned onto Vajra's recently healed knee, and she inhaled sharply and grimaced. Granek cackled. "Just 'cause you're healed don't mean you're healthy. So tell us what we want to know. Tell us how to enter Blackstaff Tower safely."

She opened cobalt blue eyes and stared past Granek at Khondar. "Ye only need courage and a Blackstaff. Dare ye pick one up?"

"Tell me what the books are for," Ten-Rings said, "and we'll stop the pain. Grant us entry into the tower, and we'll end this once and for all."

Vajra laughed a deep laugh, and then opened wine purple eyes to stare at Centiv. "Why did your father bring you here from Sundabar, Centiv? Did he need a scribe? Or were you just his only child to swallow every lie?"

"Keep this up and you'll part with your life, Vajra Safahr," Ten-Rings whispered. "We saw the Blackstaff's death give you an influx of power. Who's to say that power won't transfer to one of us upon your death?"

"We've been threatened by worse than fools like you who conjure enemies whenever he's denied any desire," Vajra said, glaring at him with sea green eyes. "The enemies you've always seen—from Sundabar to Athkatla to Waterdeep—were all your own fear or your own incompetence. Now, you tell yourselves you do this for Waterdeep. You delude yourselves. You do it for yourselves alone. The power you seek you neither deserve nor understand. Your teachers weep in the afterlife for your failures."

Granek growled and struck Vajra hard in the stomach, knocking the wind out of her. As she fought to breathe, he said to Ten-Rings, "I'll get more answers out of her and tell you later. You'd best go, as all you three do is trade insults."

Khondar shook his head and punched his palm in anger. Centiv stalked out of the dungeon, through the entry chamber, and through the other door past the stairwell leading up. When

Ten-Rings caught up to him at the end of the long hallway, the two of them stared at the Duskstaff, which hovered a foot off the floor in the center of the circular chamber

"It took a lot of magic to bring this here," Centiv said, "but with some illusions and Cral's ring, I can make it seem like I'm carrying it. We *could* take it to the tower and see if that truly does get us in. Beyond that, I'm sure the two of us can handle whatever the tower throws at us. It's obvious *she* doesn't deserve the powers hidden away in there."

"I've no doubt, Son," Khondar said, "but patience. She has secrets yet to be slipped, and I'd rather not face that tower without knowing we'll easily exit again. I'll not walk into a trap laid by Samark or one of his predecessors. We've wasted too much time. Go wander a bit and be sure to be seen as Samark. I have a guild meeting to attend. Do make sure the house and these cellars are properly warded this time."

CHAPTER 5

Were this humble scribe to note all those who fell before and behind to place such heroes upon their path, this account wouldst be lengthier still for all the blood and bone upon it.

Khel Largarn, *Heroes Legendary and Others Still,*
Year of the Quill (1397 DR)

9 NIGHTAL, YEAR OF THE AGELESS ONE (1479 DR)

Selûne and her Tears gleamed in the clear night sky, the lunar satellites illuminating the steam that rose from the mouths of those arguing in the cold night. The figures worked their way cautiously off Heroes' Walk and around to the south along Gunarla's Dash. Their boots scraped the frost-rimed cobblestones. Although they were among the few out on foot in this neighborhood, they did their best to remain in the shadows, hugging the rough wooden walls of the buildings. The moonlight glistened off the tile roofs up ahead, but Renaer couldn't spot anyone standing watch over the alleys. He waved his friends along, but their bickering continued.

"I'm just saying if you're a sorceress, why not conjure a few lights and save us the lamp oil and the smoke?" Vharem whispered.

"Magic is more precious than lamp oil, fool," Laraelra snapped. "Besides, it *also* attracts drifting glow-globes, so it would make it harder to hide. Now would you get out of my way?"

"Why do you need to be right next to Renaer?" Faxhal asked. "Sweet on him already? Fast work, Neverember."

Both Renaer and Laraelra hissed, "Shut up!" Faxhal merely grinned in response.

"Hey," Meloon said in an excited whisper, pointing to his right. "I've been in that tavern. Had my pocket picked, but recovered my loss in the fight after. Anybody else try The Mysticslake?"

"Will you all be quiet?" Renaer said. "We don't want to draw more attention than we already have."

"There's no one else out here, Ren," Vharem said.

"I want to keep it that way," he replied. "Besides, don't you always say that's when you should be more nervous? When you can't see who's watching?"

"What're you so worried about?" Faxhal asked.

Renaer threw his hands up. "We're about to break into a powerful wizard's house—even *if* his ownership of it is suspect—and you're asking me what I'm worried about?"

Renaer paused at the alley intersection. The rest halted behind him, and Faxhal bumped into Laraelra. A lamppost illuminated the north side of Roarke House, the south sides of another of his warehouses, and the slate-tiled Kendall's Gallery. From this angle, the group could see the lights ablaze in the windows of the Halaerim Club across Kulzar's Alley. The windows of Roarke House were all dark. Renaer tugged his hood low and rushed past to the door of the building on his left. Renaer shrugged and then rotated his shoulders a few times, releasing some tension along with a long exhale. He rummaged in his belt pouches for the key he needed.

"I get it," Faxhal whispered. "He's worried because of you. He doesn't know if he can count on you."

"He can count on us," Meloon snapped at Faxhal. "You're the ones late to the party, as I see things. Laraelra and Renaer spent most of the day reading up on the old passages 'neath these buildings. You and he just showed up looking for a free meal and drinking."

"Like we always do," Vharem said. "We weren't expecting a home invasion on Gunarla's Dash. Not that lack of planning makes it any less fun."

"Please, let's keep talking until the Watch finally hears us," Laraelra grumbled.

Renaer grunted as he turned the key in the long-unused and rusted lock, and he pushed the scraping door inward. He turned and nodded at Vharem and Meloon, who both lit their lanterns and brought them up as the five of them shuffled inside. Renaer barely spoke louder once inside. "Welcome to Gildenfires, friends. Watch where you step."

The long-abandoned festhall still had some furniture and décor intact, but all could see why the place had been abandoned since the reign of the previous Open Lord. Scorch marks marred the paintings and half-burned gold draperies along the walls. Massive holes yawned in numerous places in the ceiling and floor.

"What happened here?" Meloon asked.

"A battle among some wizardly patrons," Vharem said. "No one could get any charges upheld, though. These men had so many people scared or bought. Rumor has it they were high-ranked members of the Watchful Order. Because the festhall operators couldn't claim restitution, they went broke and this building's been empty for twelve years. Dagult chose not to fix the place and just had it boarded up."

"Too bad, really." Faxhal sighed. "This place had some great attractions in its day."

"How would you know?" Laraelra asked. "You would have only been twelve or thirteen when it closed."

Faxhal winked at her in response, and Renaer chuckled as he saw Laraelra blush.

"Let's keep moving," Renaer said. He led the five of them past the piles of rubble and around the holes in the floor toward the kitchen. Other than their footsteps on the creaking floorboards, the squeals of rats fleeing were the only sounds.

"So remind me again why we're not out having a fine evening entertaining our new companions?" Vharem asked.

"*I'm* having fun," Meloon said.

"How many times do we have to tell you?" Laraelra said. "Meloon and I heard someone being tortured somewhere beneath this area. We just couldn't get to her."

"So why don't we use the way you two came before?" Faxhal asked.

"We couldn't reach it before," said Laraelra. "The guild should already be at work repairing that breach. Besides, I don't want word to reach my father that I'm—"

"Fraternizing with the high and mighty oppressors of us all?" Renaer smirked, his tone rising to a rough voice with a nasal high pitch.

Laraelra's jaw dropped and she said, "By the gods, that's a pitch-perfect impression of him! I didn't think you'd met him that often."

"Once was enough, I'm afraid," Renaer said. "Your father's rants disrupted a rather pleasant party I attended at the Jhoniron Club last summer down in Castle Ward. As for the impression, my apologies. I don't always realize when I'm mimicking someone's accent."

"You should hear him do Watch Aumarr Krothyn Slakepike!" Vharem said. "His impression's so good, he can get the Watch to abandon their posts by shouting orders in his voice."

"True enough, but now there's enough of us to get caught," Faxhal replied. "It's easier to rat-scamper or avoid being seen with only two or three. This mob's too easily caught, especially the big guy there. I doubt he can move his monstrous feet fast enough to run."

"Don't mind him, Meloon," Vharem said, as he drove an elbow into Faxhal's stomach. "He's just jealous he's the least handsome and shortest one here. He's always been one to pick fights with the biggest guy in the room."

Faxhal spat loudly, landing a gobbet right in front of Vharem's boot. "So how do you know something is amiss? Other than those two *strangers* heard screaming. Bells of Belshaba, I hear screaming in half the taverns every night!"

"Not like this, little man," Meloon muttered, his voice low and serious.

"If you'd heard it, you'd know someone was being tortured," Laraelra said. "Last time I checked, torture was still a severe offense in the city."

Renaer said, "We also saw the Blackstaff and Ten-Rings working together. Willingly. What does that tell you?"

"They're up to something magical?" Faxhal asked.

"Probably," Renaer replied, "but let's look a little beyond the obvious. They acted like old allies, when in fact—"

"Those two can't stand one another!" Vharem said.

"And so?" Renaer spun his questioning eyes toward Faxhal.

Faxhal shrugged. "I don't know. You know full well I'm going to ignore local politics unless it involves pretty women. I make it a point to ignore wizards always, even when it *does* involve pretty women."

Renaer rolled his eyes and said, "One of them wasn't who he seemed to be. Perhaps both of them weren't who they claimed, and they're trying to point blame at targets that no one dares accuse. In any case, the Watch won't believe our word against the supposed Blackstaff, so if anyone is going to do anything to stop them or at least save that woman, it's going to have to be us."

During their conversation, the five of them had inched their way across the creaking and dangerously sagging wooden floor to the cellar door. The floor was stone in the back third of the building where it met the walls and doors. The kitchen yawned off to the right, an icy draft coming down the chimney and stirring the cobwebs at the long-cold fireplace. The party chose the door opposite, leading to the cellars.

Renaer opened the door with some difficulty, its boards having warped over time. He stepped into the stairwell that led down to a small landing before turning into the main part of the cellar. He descended to the landing but stopped and turned to stare up at the rest of them on the stairs.

"Everybody needs to move past me on the stairs. Vharem, bring that lantern closer. Elra, help me look for that trigger." Renaer knelt down on the slab and began scraping at the edge of the upper stairs as the others walked past him.

Faxhal nudged Meloon. "Elra? Have they been getting chummy all afternoon? They've got pet names for each other."

Meloon smiled. "She asks her friends to call her that. Why? You jealous? I'll give you a pet name if you—"

"Will you two *please* be quiet?" Laraelra said as she knelt next to Renaer. "When we find the door to these tunnels, we don't want you two yammering away and giving our foes warning."

"I don't think there's much chance of that," Renaer said. "There are at least three sets of tunnels and chambers we'll pass through to get beneath Roarke House."

"So what're they there for?" Vharem asked. "Your forebears smugglers or something, Ren?"

"Or something. The tunnels were either built by or expanded upon by three or four different ancestors." He pulled off his gloves for a better sense of touch along the wall and step. "One of them was among the earliest guildmasters of the Cellarers' Guild, which explains how they all managed to bypass any mention on official or unofficial maps."

Faxhal, irritated and impatient, asked, *"Why* are they here?"

"Imagine my surprise to find that my great-great-grand-uncle was none other than Kulzar Brandarth."

"The old pirate?" Vharem asked.

Renaer nodded. "Kulzar had been disowned by the family and wasn't allowed to use his family name, but they granted him a house that used to be here. He buried his final treasures somewhere around here, but no one's ever found them in the two centuries since. Of course, the family reclaimed the deeds after his passing, just in case."

Renaer beamed as he and Laraelra both found bricks in the walls alongside the third stepface that each tipped inward.

Faxhal gasped. "We're going after pirates' treasure?"

"Unlikely," Renaer said. "The tunnels were built during the Guildwars for the resistance against the guildmasters' rule of the city. I suspect someone's found part of the tunnels and is using them for a foul purpose."

"Kulzar's treasure might explain the involvement of those wizards," Laraelra said, "but I think the woman they were torturing might be able to tell us what they wanted. If she's still alive."

She and Renaer reached into the hidden trigger points and pressed the stone buttons set into the side of the third step. The upper stairs began sliding silently and swiftly downward, stranding them on the landing but reforming as a new stairwell leading deeper than the Gildenfires' cellar.

"So far as we know, no one's used these tunnels since before any of us were born." Renaer unfurled a parchment from his sleeve, showing a map. "Some of the tunnels shifted or melted together during the Spellplague. They may not be as they're marked. In any case, I'll want to keep the maps of these tunnels current. Vharem, you've got the rope, if we meet any drops?"

Vharem nodded, shrugging his cloak aside to reveal the rope looped around his torso.

Renaer led the way down the stairs, but slowed his pace as the steps grew taller and more difficult to descend. He noticed the tunnel shrank as they descended, and soon all but Laraelra had to shuffle sideways, as the corridor wasn't wide enough for their shoulders. The third landing, which turned them to the right one more time, was partially melted, and the direction the tunnel turned was all a smooth stone ramp.

Vharem unfurled the rope, handing one end to Meloon and the other to Faxhal. Renaer cleared his throat and raised an eyebrow in question. Vharem usually deferred to Renaer's decisions, but he looked him right in the eye and bypassed him, giving Faxhal the rope.

Faxhal clapped Renaer on the shoulder and said, "He wants me going first in case there's trouble, Renaer. No offense, but I'm a little better in a fight than you are. If we meet someone who wants to talk, you're our fellow."

Renaer rolled his eyes but motioned them to continue.

"Why don't I go, then?" Meloon asked.

"Because I need *you* to help me anchor the rope while the others go down ahead of us." Vharem clapped Meloon on the shoulders and braced his feet against the corridor's walls. He'd wrapped the rope around his waist once and fed it through his gloved hands. Once Vharem was braced, Faxhal saluted them, eased his way past his friend, and picked up the rope and Vharem's lantern.

"You can hardly hold onto the lantern and the rope, little man," Laraelra said. "Allow me." She whispered a few words, causing her fingernails to glow a light blue, and slid that blue light onto the pommel of Faxhal's dagger. He smiled, handed Laraelra the lantern, and kissed her hand as she took the lantern from him. He then slipped down the twisting slide, feeding out rope as he went. After a minute or so, his blue light was out of sight.

The rope suddenly wrenched through their hands. It pulled Vharem off his feet, but Meloon braced his feet and stopped them from sliding more.

"Yow!" Faxhal's feet slipped out from under him after the sharp turn in the tunnel, and he slid a ways before he slowed his fall with his feet against the walls. He yelled, "Sorry!" back up the tunnel before he looked below and found himself above a vertical opening in the ceiling of a chamber. He said, "Another drop coming!" up the shaft to warn Vharem, then jumped free, smiling as he slid quickly down more than twice his own height to land on the floor.

The blue light Laraelra placed on him barely reached the ceiling, and Faxhal noticed the opening he'd come through was the highest point in the ceiling—the arc of the ceiling and odd shape of the room made him think of an egg. Stalactites of stretched out and warped brick and mortar hung from the ceiling in places. Faxhal knelt and looked along the floor, easily seeing its uneven slope toward the center.

"Definitely egg-shaped," he muttered. *But why such an odd shape?*

The only other features in the room he could see were copious amounts of webbing and spiders.

Faxhal tugged on the rope and yelled up, "Nothing down here but spiders! All clear. Send Ren down!"

He untied himself and fastened the line to a small clump of stone beneath the opening. *It'll take Ren a little while, so I'll look around a bit*, he thought.

Faxhal paced around, finding the room's walls and clearing away the veils of dusty webbing with his sword.

Renaer arrived with a, "Fair day down here, then, friend? Good to have a little light again, that's for sure." He tugged on the rope to signal he was down. "What's the situation?"

"Not much here," Faxhal said, "and the room's warped floor to ceiling like an egg, though I don't think it was built like this. I was just walking the perimeter and clearing away webs to find any doors."

"Well, it'll give us something to do while the others descend."

Faxhal and Renaer stayed together, using their swords to sweep away webs and a few rotting tapestries here and there. Under nearly a solid mound of webbing, they discovered a long-dry cistern, its edges merged with the slope of the wall.

"So what befalls below, gentles?" Laraelra's voice drew their attention up toward her. She descended, a lit lantern floating along-side her while she slid down. Faxhal found himself dashing over to help her down, his hands at her very skinny waist before he even thought about it.

"What exactly are you doing, Faxhal?" Laraelra flinched from his touch and swung slightly to the side on the rope to drop to the ground. She looked irritated and suspicious—reactions with which Faxhal was very familiar.

What wasn't common to him was the nervous feeling of disappointment in his gut. He looked at her arched eyebrows and muttered, "I meant no—nothing. Just, nothing." He stomped toward an unexamined corner.

The three of them diligently and carefully pulled back more and more dust and webs to find the room had once stored old food crates and wine barrels, all since emptied by rats. Faxhal sighed in relief when his probes with his sword finally revealed a door.

Faxhal pressed his ear to the door and listened, but he heard very little.

"Is it safe to drop the rope?" Meloon said. "Are we going to need to climb back up?"

"Unless you found somewhere to anchor it, we'll have to trust in luck that these other corridors can lead us out of here again," Renaer said.

"Could be worse," Meloon said. He tied the rope around himself as Vharem shrugged it off, then braced his feet, and said, "You first, Vharem. I'll jump after you're down."

"You sure? It's a long fall," he said. Meloon answered with a nod. "Very well, friend."

Vharem held the rope on both sides of the loop around his trunk. He slowly played out the rope, sliding down into the chamber, and let himself fall the final few feet to land near what seemed to be a long-dry cistern, its back corner rearing up like a stone wave. He moved forward and waved up to Meloon, who let the rope drop to the floor. As soon as Vharem had gathered the rope, Meloon jumped, landing hard but rolling forward to save his legs from injury. "Whew! There's a jump! You sure we're not in Undermountain, Renaer?" Renaer smiled and offered him an arm to help him up.

"I've scouted a little ways ahead," Faxhal said. "Once beyond these first rooms, there's lots of ways to choose from. Most have no noise behind them, but I didn't open any of them yet. Renaer probably knows what they are, so let's go and let him show us his great brains." He winked at Renaer as the five of them moved through another door and into a very tall but slim door-lined corridor. Renaer took out a small chapbook and flipped pages, nodding as he read and counted out sixteen various doors, eight on each side of the corridor.

The high ceiling echoed their steps back to them. Renaer tried his keys on each of the doors. While some opened into long-empty storehouse chambers, a few opened to reveal melted walls and contortions merging with sewer lines. Laraela shook her head, and muttered, "Either there's older sewer lines we don't know about, or there are breaks in the system we haven't found."

More than half the doors would not budge though, their locks either rusted or the doors jammed by the shifts in the corridor. Faxhal nodded toward one and Meloon and said, "Care to help me knock?" The two men shouldered the door in, and it splintered, falling off its hinge. All they revealed was another warped room with sewage bubbling up in a back corner. After the second of such discoveries, Faxhal gave up helping and just waited on Renaer to open a door with his keys.

The group reached the end of the corridor, which was covered by a carved stone demonic face taller than any of them, its mouth snarling to reveal large fangs the length of Faxhal's forearm. Far above, they could see a light coming through at the ceiling, a vent helping the airflow among the subterranean chambers.

Renaer walked forward, consulted his notes, and reached out to push the demon's head horns closer together on its forehead. An audible *click* followed, and the demon's face moved slightly. Faxhal could feel a draft rushing out the gap, but when he put his hand on the stone to open it, Renaer cleared his throat and shook his head. Faxhal and Vharem exchanged looks and both of them rolled their eyes. Faxhal whispered, "Ren, either let us help or show us what your precious books tell you."

Renaer moved past the others to the nearest door on the right side of the corridor. He reached up, pushed hard on the doorframe, and the stone lintel there slid upward and clicked. Renaer then opened that door and walked through it. "One of the builders had a dwarf's help in some of the stonework. Good distractions and good traps. If we'd used the corridor behind that demon's head, there's at least four pit traps beneath weighted tip-floors. This is the safe way."

"Fine," Faxhal said, "but let us go first."

Renaer opened the door, and Faxhal and Vharem entered the room. After a small tunnel about three paces long, Faxhal entered a small round chamber filled with gold light from an enchanted ceiling. Inside the room was a pair of writing desks and a set of tall shelves heavy with parchments and bound books. The desks held old, desiccated parchments and the ink in the wells had long since dried. Faxhal probed ahead with light toe touches and his fingers ran along the walls, feeling slowly for any triggers or traps. He was especially careful by the only flat wall—opposite the entrance—in the chamber, as it was covered by a bas-relief carving of two trolls battling three Watchmen in antiquated garb. Once Faxhal knew the floor was clear, he examined the carvings carefully and identified one trigger to lock a hidden door from this side and a second to open the door. He left those alone for now and continued checking the chamber.

After one circuit of the room, he nodded at Vharem, who waved the others in. The room became crowded with all five inside, and Faxhal hissed everyone quiet when he heard a voice cry out, "Samurk! Samurk . . ."

"I hear someone crying," Faxhal whispered. "A woman. She keeps muttering a name or something."

A loud snore buzzed through the room, causing everyone to look at each other in surprise.

"We're well beneath both the warehouse and Roarke House," Renaer said. "This is a listening post built earlier for the resistance to spy on guild loyalists to whom they'd rent out the chambers beyond. Everything said, every noise made, in the two lower

71

chambers can be heard here, where scribes used to sit and copy down everything said for use as evidence or blackmail."

Faxhal interrupted, wanting some of the attention, "And there's a secret door in that wall carving there, right?"

Renaer stared at him a moment, then grinned and nodded. "Yes, and it opens to a tunnel that leads back beneath Roarke House and ends in another secret door."

"Why would anyone use those chambers if they knew they could be spied upon?" Meloon asked.

"They didn't know anyone could hear any of that until we gave that away this morning," Renaer said. "According to our records, all of these secret tunnels and chambers were unknown by old Volam himself when he built Roarke House over the existing cellar and foundation. Others found those chambers, linked them to the house, and converted them for their personal use, but they've been unused since Grandfather bought the building decades back. At least, as far as I know." He nodded toward Laraelra and Meloon and added, "You two probably heard things coming from this chamber filtered through some of those links with the sewers."

"Why didn't anyone else find out about the tunnels?" Meloon asked.

"If you don't know to look for something," Faxhal said, "you'll never be bothered to find it. That's why I always keep looking— and getting accused of poking around where I shouldn't."

"Faxhal's right," Renaer said, taking care to keep his voice down, "at least the first part. We can spot the triggers that are almost invisible on the other side."

Faxhal pointed out the lock triggers—the stonework swords wielded by the Watchmen in the battle scene. Renaer checked his journal and began moving the stone swords. Faxhal shook his head when Ren moved the second Watchman's sword. "You just locked the door shut again, chief. Just the two outer swords pushed outward should trigger this door."

Renaer nodded, scribbling corrections in his notes, and he turned toward the group, who stood around a scraped arc on the floor—the door's obvious path on this side. He said, "Everyone, get ready. They may have defenses ready in their cellars, even if they aren't expecting any company from this direction."

Renaer shifted the final trigger, and the door slid in toward them. They looked into a pitch black corridor, lit by the gold light spilling through the now-open door.

"Good." Faxhal chuckled then he drew his long sword out and brandished it in the air a little before he nodded at Renaer. He hoped Laraelra was impressed, and he added, "Been itching for a fight all day."

A sudden twang, and Faxhal snapped backward, a crossbow quarrel lodged in his throat.

"Careful what you wish for, boy," came the hoarse chuckle from the dark.

The thief felt both the impact at his throat and the crack at the back of his head when he slammed back on the stone floor. *I expected that to hurt more,* Faxhal thought. His breath caught in his throat and he found it hard to breathe or move. He lost his grip on his sword and heard it rattle on the stone floor. *Oh stlaern, I never got the chance to tell her how pretty her eyes were . . . or save her from this . . .*

The last thing Faxhal heard beyond his own heartbeat was a plaintive gasp from Laraelra's throat as she looked down at him. *No love poem, but I'll take it,* he thought.

The noise, the smells, the sensations all faded. Faxhal felt lighter and lighter with each heartbeat. Until the heartbeat ended.

CHAPTER 6

Even on the slowest night, the dark is never quiet in Waterdeep.
Borthild "Steelbard,"
One Season's Nights and Days Waterdhavian,
circa the Year of the Prince (1357 DR)

9 NIGHTAL, YEAR OF THE AGELESS ONE (1479 DR)

Laraelra gasped as Faxhal almost flipped backward. Her signal of true danger was the spray of blood arcing past her own shoulder. She looked down at Faxhal's fallen body in disbelief, the mixture of annoyance and amusement he triggered in her already shifting to horror.

"Down!" Meloon ripped his axe out of its harness, swinging it up into his hands.

Vharem grabbed Faxhal by the collar and pulled him out of the way. By the time Vharem had his friend behind the door near Renaer, Faxhal had stopped moving and his eyes were open and blank. Renaer pulled out a potion vial from his pouch and looked at Vharem, pleading. Vharem shook his head and reached down to close their friend's eyes. Laraelra couldn't hear everything he said, but she did catch ". . . farewell, little fox."

Laraelra shouted out a spell, and blue light rippled out of her, clearing the darkness from the corridor. They faced two men in Watch garb, one kneeling and holding a spent crossbow while next to him an older man with an eye patch waited with a sword and shield. Behind them both stood Samark "Blackstaff" Dhanzscul, the gem atop his staff flaring red.

Samark waved his hand and red bolts flew from his fingers. Two slammed into Meloon's broad chest, and he grunted but held his ground. Three more arced at Laraelra but skittered around her, feeling like lightning-charged rain on her skin, before they launched themselves back at the Blackstaff.

Laraelra focused, despite the distraction of the Blackstaff's spell, and cast another spell of her own. She pulled up an amber energy that crackled among her fingers until she pointed at Samark and said, *"Drialrokh!"*

That bolt hit its target unerringly—his throat. Laraelra smiled as she watched color drain from the already-pale face of the Blackstaff when he realized he could not speak. The wizard turned and ran, to the surprise and anger of his two guards. The eye-patched one stepped forward, yelling, "Get that crossbow restrung or draw your blade, boy! They'll not be much bother for us, e'en without hisself."

"Meloon?" Laraelra shouted as she stepped back and to the side of the opening.

Meloon jumped into the corridor, swinging his axe wide with both hands, forcing the corridor's two guardians to shuffle back a bit from the door. "Hope I'm bothersome enough, one-eye."

The older man grumbled and spat in Meloon's path, but he and his companion backed up farther from the swinging axe.

Laraelra looked down at Faxhal, caught both Vharem and Renaer's eyes, and whispered, "Avenge him."

Renaer's reached into his wide sleeves and pulled a dagger from each one.

Vharem drew a short sword out of his belt and whispered to Renaer, "Didn't think we'd need these, but thanks for the loan."

The sorceress looked up and saw the younger guard raising his spanned crossbow. She concentrated, waved her hand, and the crossbow quarrel flipped out of the stock just as he pulled the trigger.

Renaer dived and rolled in a somersault, staying low but moving forward. Vharem stepped into the corridor's opening after Renaer, holding a dart in one hand and a short sword in the other. Renaer stopped in a crouch before the guard, adding the momentum of his roll to his two thrown daggers. One missed, sailing past the guard's shoulder, but the second one hit him in his hand, forcing him to drop the crossbow. The guard kicked out at Renaer with little effect. Vharem let his dart fly and hit the young guard in the thigh. He stayed back behind Renaer and Meloon, who parried the older man's blade with his axe.

"You've had good teachers if you're not taking the first swing at me, boy," the gravel-voiced man said to Meloon. "Too bad you gave up your only advantage." The older man stabbed his long sword forward and Meloon brought his axe up, making the blade scrape along his mail shirt instead of piercing it. Meloon countered by swinging the double-bladed axe back down toward the man's side. The older man brought around a shield, and the loud clash of weapon and shield filled the corridor.

Laraelra stood back at the corridor's opening, harnessing her anger at letting the Blackstaff escape as she thrust quicksilver-colored missiles at the two guards. She willed one upon each of them, and the young guard fell over with a choked cry.

"You little traitors'll pay for that," the man grunted, as he stabbed again at the dodging Meloon. "You have no idea what you've stumbled into."

The man backed up the corridor, his features masked in hatred. Meloon pressed forward, and Laraelra could not see his face.

"Granek Ruskelver, I remember you," Renaer said. "You were drummed out of the Watch last year for accepting bribes and conduct unbecoming a Watchman."

Granek flinched, looked down briefly at Renaer, and his singular eye shot him a look of revulsion. "You got no idea how this city really is, rich boy. You'll find out what happens when you trip over the plans of the mighty. I did my job well for Ten-Rings, and no young sellsword's gonna drop me!" Granek swung hard and fast at

Meloon, who brought his arm up. The sword scored a long, wound along his left forearm, crossing two thick white scars from some previous battles. When Meloon shoved his axe up to force the blade away, the sword's point stabbed into the mortar in the wall.

Granek's eyes widened as he tugged to free his weapon, and Meloon brought the axe down hard on Granek's overextended right leg. Granek screamed as he fell to the ground, clutching the stump of his leg and groaning. After a few moments, he passed out.

Meloon whispered, "I'm still striding. How about you?"

Renaer stood, noting he and Meloon had both been sprayed with Granek's blood from his leg wound, and blood already covered the floor. Vharem shoved his way past both of them, muttering, "Want to get that wizard before he can cast on anyone again."

Laraelra yelled, "Vharem, no! Don't be a fool!" *I don't think Renaer could handle another death tonight,* she thought. *I don't think I could either.*

Meloon reached out for him and grabbed a handful of his shirt, pulling Vharem short. "Don't let Faxhal's death make you run to your own."

Vharem shot Meloon a look mixed with anger and grief, then shrugged off Meloon's grip, only to find Renaer blocking his path.

"Don't lose your head," Renaer said, his eyes welling with tears. "We will get that wizard, but I don't want to lose another friend tonight. We're here to save someone, not lose everyone."

"Caution is good," Laraelra said, "but we do have to hurry. That spell I hit the Blackstaff with won't last long. I can try it again, but he may have some defenses up against it now. Our best bet is to find and save that woman. We'll avenge Faxhal another night."

"I'll take point. I'm a bit tougher than the rest of you," Meloon said. He kneeled by the fallen young Watchman and ripped off his sleeve, then wrapped his bloodied forearm in one scrap of cloth and wiped off his axe blade with the rest.

Laraelra moved closer and helped him wrap his makeshift

bandage around his forearm. She whispered, "Thank you, Meloon. If he'd run on ahead . . ."

"I know," he muttered. "Seen it happen before."

"Don't think that you won't get paid," Laraelra said, "just because we're becoming friends. You'll be compensated as agreed this morning." She put the finishing touches on the bandage and pulled it tight, then smiled at the blond bear of a man.

He returned her smile and said, "Friendships are better currency anyway." From his crouch, he grabbed the empty crossbow off the floor and stood. "Well, what's the plan, Renaer?"

"All we know about the end of this corridor," Renaer said, "is on my maps and notes—and the fact that we've a very angry archmage, or someone powerful enough to impersonate him. I want to get to the bottom of this, but I don't want to die."

"We are *not* leaving without killing him!" Vharem choked. "Don't let Faxhal's death mean *nothing!*"

"He meant as much to me as to you," Renaer said, "but I'm not willing to risk our lives. We can go back and I can hire many more sellswords—"

"And he'll have us arrested for trying to attack the Blackstaff," Laraelra said, "the Watchful Order, or some other trumped-up charge. *And* he'll have this area so well protected we'll never get in again *or* find out who they were torturing or why. We *have* to do this now, Renaer, risks and all. Let's find the woman we came to save—*that* is what Faxhal died for."

The four looked at each other, nodded, and Renaer said, "Very well. Our secret corridor—which they discovered somehow—exits behind a privy. We should turn left and into a corridor lined with doors."

Vharem lined up behind Meloon, leaving Renaer and Laraelra to cover their backs. As the others moved forward, Laraelra felt something touch her foot. She looked down to see a very weak and trembling Granek, whose lone eye locked on hers. "Help . . .," he pleaded.

Renaer stepped over and said, "Even before tonight, Granek, before your lackey killed my friend, you deserved this death. Alone, in the dark, no one to mourn you."

Renaer kicked the man's grasp loose from Laraelra's boot and moved away, taking the lantern with him.

Shadows falling on his form, Granek pleaded with Laraelra, "Lass, mercy."

Laraelra hugged herself, staring at Renaer's back, but she understood his cold anger, remembering her own when she heard his words earlier. She looked Granek in the eye and said, "Nay, before the gods, torturers deserve no mercy. Ask it of Kelemvor when you see him." She snapped her cloak tight around her as she turned to follow Renaer.

>===W===<

They moved quickly and found Meloon and Vharem stopped by the opened secret door, the privy seat still attached to it and turned to one side.

"What's the problem?" Renaer asked.

"No pit," Meloon said, his brow furrowed. He dropped the crossbow and kicked it across the floor, only to watch it disappear through apparently solid stone and clatter loudly as it fell down a shaft. "Hmph. Neat trick, that."

"How did you know that was there?" Laraelra asked.

Meloon grinned. "Saw the seat and knew someone had to have dug one. You dig those enough times, you remember how much work is hidden beneath a lot of dung." He knelt, grabbed a loose rock and scratched an **X** at the near side of the pit. He reached back and said, "Lend a hand, please." He grabbed Vharem's forearm to keep from falling into the hidden shaft and then leaned forward, closing his eyes and tapping ahead with the rock in his hand. When he touched solid rock again instead of illusion, he scratched an **X** there as well, and said, "Haul me back, Vharem, and then everybody, jump past the second mark!"

He got to his feet, took his axe in both hands, and jumped across easily. The rest of the group followed suit. As Renaer landed, a woman's harsh screams rang out around the corner.

The quartet ran around the corner into a slim corridor, two doors lining each side of it. The screams seemed to come from the one on the far right. Meloon started forward, but Vharem bolted ahead of all of them. He ran to the door, reached for the handle, and his hand passed through the illusion. He stumbled forward, off-balance, and Vharem's world went red as fire exploded all around him. The blast knocked him off his feet and threw him back down the corridor. His sword, dislodged from his left hand, bounced across the hall and hit the opposite door. This too exploded in a blast of flame and heat, but Vharem was already down and the explosion passed over him. With the explosion came another shriek from beyond the door.

"Vharem!" Renaer yelled, and he rushed to the fallen man.

His leathers and hair all smoking, Vharem tried to talk but just coughed. Much of his long brown hair fell away in singed clumps, and his face and hands were blistered, but he fought to stand again.

Renaer dragged him back against the wall and away from the doorways, saying "Rest here, friend. Catch your breath."

Vharem winced as he flexed his fingers and watched thick, blackened flakes of his skin crack off his hand.

Renaer pulled out a small vial from his belt. "Drink, V." He poured the contents of the vial over his friend's cracked and soot-stained lips, and the cracks instantly healed. The worst blistering on Vharem's face and hands subsided and returned to his normal skin tone. Even his hair began to regrow.

"Wow," Vharem said, looking at Renaer and then the vial. "Who knew healing draughts tasted like clover honey, mint, and zzar all in one?"

"Don't get used to them," Renaer said. "They're more expensive than your usual bar tab for a tenday."

"Didn't you need that for whoever was down here?" Vharem asked as Renaer helped him to his feet. "Help her get back on her feet?"

"I've one left," Renaer said. "Besides, you needed it more. I don't want to lose another friend tonight." Renaer opened his mouth to say more, and then simply hugged Vharem and asked, "Elra? Meloon? Find anything?"

"Look at the marks on the floor," Meloon said. "It's weird that the blasts stay in the doorway and never slip inside the door. They're also not wooden doors, see?" Meloon shrugged toward the farthest doorway Vharem had approached, and the wooden door was now a prison door of metal bars and naught else.

Laraelra's concentration showed her the world she loved—the world of magic. She looked at Renaer, her eyes filled with a sea of stars, then she looked intently at the corridor, the doors, and the floor. "I'm seeing magic all around here. The remnants of the spells Vharem triggered match the auras on those two other doors." She pointed at the doors they had all run past, one on each side of the passageway. "I'm also seeing some lingering but powerful magic. I think it's an illusion of some kind. It's dotting around here, as if it's—"

"Footprints?" Renaer asked.

"Exactly," she replied, snapping her fingers. "You're right, Renaer. Whoever's posing as the Blackstaff only wears his shape. If nothing else, I think he's gone, as the trail heads up the passage and turns."

"Help me!" A voice cried through the first left-hand door.

Laraelra snapped her head in the door's direction, her concentration shattered. She held up her hand and waved everyone away from the door, then tossed some pebbles at the door. The illusory door exploded with flaming fury, but no one stood in its path. Renaer and Vharem found it was a locked wooden door, just like it seemed. The pair kicked it twice before the lock broke and the door swung inward, scraping against the stone floor.

Inside the room, a young woman lay spread-eagled and strapped to a table, blades and other torture implements on the tables around her. Her long red hair matted on the table or to her head with sweat and blood. The gown she wore was reduced to tattered rags, and her feet were visibly injured within iron boots with ankle screws. She saw her three saviors at the door and whimpered, "Please! Get me out of here before he comes back!"

Vharem and Renaer rushed forward, pulling at the blood-soaked leather straps and unscrewing the iron boots. Laraelra wove a minor magic to repair the woman's tattered gown. The woman gasped, "Don't know what they wanted, but they kept hitting me! And my feet! Oh blessed Ilmater, my feet!" She wailed as Laraelra and Vharem removed the boots, but her black-and-blue flesh hardly resembled feet at all, given how many bones were shattered in them.

Vharem asked, "What's your name?"

"Charrar," she replied. "I'm a dancer at the Ten Bells on Brondar's Way."

"What did they want with you?" Laraelra asked.

"I don't know!" Charrar said, but whimpered slightly when Vharem picked her up off the table. "They just kept hurting me, and the Blackstaff just stood there smiling!"

Laraelra started to ask, *When did they bring you here?* but stopped herself. Something didn't smell right here, though the stench of blood was real enough.

Renaer reached into his belt pouch and said, "I've got something that may help."

"Hang on, Renaer," Laraelra said, resting her hand on his forearm and another over the cork-stoppered ceramic tube he held. "Wait, in case someone has lethal injuries, hmm?" She looked around the room and asked, "Where's Meloon?"

A loud, piercing scream came from out in the hall, and Meloon stuck his head in the room to say, "Elra, come look over here. I hear the screaming, but there's nothing here. It's really irritating . . . and repetitive."

Laraelra walked to the doorway, but as she passed Renaer, she arched her eyebrows at him, her back to Charrar. His eyes widened, but he nodded.

Laraelra exited that room and breathed deeply, then coughed. I don't know what's worse, she thought, the smell of blood in there or of singed Vharem out here.

She crossed the corridor where Meloon stood, angry. "I ran down that way while you checked the room. That bastard sealed off the corridor leading out of here with stone. I couldn't find a door, even though I saw scratches where a door scraped the floor for years."

"That's probably an illusion of a solid wall," Laraelra said, "if not a conjured wall itself."

"Did I mention how much I hate illusions?"

"So which room again?" Laraelra asked. As if on cue, the scream pierced the air again. Obviously coming from the room on the far right. "You're right. *Really* irritating." She shared a smirk with Meloon as they approached the room, and Laraelra concentrated, summoning her ability to see magic. The prison-bar door stood partially open from Vharem's disturbing it, and Laraelra looked at the threshold. "There's an illusion set right inside the door." She tapped her toe lightly on the blue-gray puddle of magic, and the screams ended abruptly. Her eyes widened, and she peered intently at the far corner of the room. "This room is clean. No other magic in play that I can see."

"Are you sure?" Meloon asked. He tried to push past her and look in the room himself. He had to stoop, since the doorway was low, and bumped into Laraelra as she turned to leave, knocking her off balance.

She tumbled into the room and said, "Watch it, you—" and fell flat on her back, banging her hip and an elbow. However, before the pain ended her spell, she saw a large gray-silver field of magic above the door. "Meloon—there!"

"What?" Meloon reached down to help her up, and a blood

drop plopped onto his outstretched arm. He turned and looked up, just inside the doorway, but he saw nothing. Another blood drop appeared out of thin air and fell onto his shoulder.

"Something's hidden there," Laraelra said, then pointed. "Look at those iron rings in the walls. See if there's a hammock up there. I think it's been made invisible, and it's hiding something inside it."

Meloon poked upward with his left hand. He felt rough cloth and something heavier above that. He pushed harder and heard a low moan. Meloon started feeling around the edges of the invisible cloth, as the woman inside moaned in a foreign language.

"You know what she's saying?" he asked. He found an edge to the invisible cloth. He pulled it open, finding a bloodied and dirtied dark-skinned woman with very short black hair and multiple wounds all over her body. Her eyes were open and staring, but instead of regular pupils, her eyes were dark orbs filled with crackles of red energy. "Whoa."

"Renaer?" Laraelra yelled out into the corridor. "We've got another one here! And she needs help more than Charrar! Hurry!"

Laraelra wanted a closer look at the woman, but if she was right about this, they were in a far worse game than they knew.

Meloon stretched the invisible fabric of the hammock out of the way and rolled the wounded woman down into his arms. As she moved, a chorus of voices—men's and women's both—screamed in pain.

"Selûne preserve her, she definitely needs this more," Renaer said, as he arrived to see the dagger protruding from the woman's stomach. "Hold her, Meloon."

Renaer held her head up, poured the potion into her mouth, and pulled the dagger free. Her body spasmed in reaction to the pain, but the belly wound closed up, as did the lesser wounds on her face and body. She began breathing easier, and her eyes flickered open briefly, but they remained storm-clouded orbs of black. Renaer looked up at Meloon, who just shrugged, but Laraelra pressed in behind them.

"Don't you recognize her?" she asked.

Renaer nodded, but the others shook their heads.

"That's Vajra Safahr—the Blackstaff's lover!" Laraelra said. She didn't want to say more until she knew for certain, but she had the nagging suspicion that Ten-Rings and his associate were trying to steal the power of the Blackstaff—and she wondered how long the illusion-wearer had posed as Samark. Her thoughts were interrupted by Vharem carrying Charrar out into the hall toward them.

"He tortured her too?" Charrar said. "I heard others being tortured down here, but not her." She clung to Vharem, who minded not one bit, and then said, "Get me out of here before he comes back again!"

"Good idea," Renaer said, and he took Vajra into his arms. "Meloon, Elra, see if there's any other way out. Charrar, I'm sorry, but I've no more healing potions. We'll have to carry both of you out of here."

Charrar nodded, but then tearfully put her head down on Vharem's shoulder and sobbed. Vharem held her closer just enough to ease his short sword back into its scabbard.

"What are you doing?" Renaer snapped. "You might need that!"

"And how are we going to fight if we're each carrying someone?" Vharem said. "If we go back the way we came, we can at least block off some passages and hole up until we can all move better. We know what's back there already."

"Yeah," Renaer said, his eyes dropping, "but it's the things we don't expect that kill us."

"The alleged Blackstaff sealed the corridor with some spells or illusions," Laraelra said. "We'll have to go back the way we came."

"What about Faxhal?" Vharem asked, his eyes pleading with Renaer.

"Later," Renaer said, his face cold and impassive. "We'll come back to bury him and mourn later. For now, let's move."

>=====w=====<

"How do you know where we are, Elra?" Meloon's whisper echoed in the sewer pipes.

"Can't tell you guild secrets," Laraelra replied, as she spotted the keystone in the archway over the intersection. This led into one of the secondary sewer lines beneath the city, and that rune told her they were heading north again. She was trying to get them back to the surface shaft at Heroes' Garden she and Meloon had used that morning. "Hear those picks? That means there're cellarers at work." She motioned for him to turn left, and they saw another light other than the lantern that she held.

Two figures looked up, startled, when the lantern's light came into their tunnel. Laraelra smiled as the familiar gruff voice of Harug called out, "Who delves? Cry out or face blades!"

"Less noise, old daern," Laraelra said. "It's Elra and friends."

When they met up, she moved ahead of Meloon to clasp forearms with both dwarves, thankful to see more friendly faces. It was obvious to Laraelra the dwarves had spent the past day clearing the channel and reshoring the wall.

She looked closely at their work. "Nice secret door you seem to be installing here, Harug." When he scowled at that, she whispered, "It'll be our secret, old daern. Father needs not know."

Harug gripped her forearm and muttered to her in his native Dwarvish, *"Lass, be careful. Best not take this shaft up to the garden. There be folk waiting for ye up there. They don't talk like no Watch I ever seen. Fools forget voices carry down this way as well. Take the next one west up to Shank Alley. That'll leave them like orcs waiting for a gopher that's left its hole."*

Laraelra nodded, then turned as Dorn clapped hands with Meloon. "Dorn Strongcroft pays his debts with friendship!" He spit into his hand and held it out for Meloon to shake, which he did. The young dwarf's eyes widened as he saw the man's weapon. "When that axe needs some work, you come see me cousin in Fields Ward. Ask for the Strongcroft smithy and mention my name. They'll steer ye arights."

"Ow!" Charrar's voice echoed loudly in the subterranean tunnel. She continued her complaints as Vharem approached with her in his arms. "Vharem, aren't we getting out of the sewers soon? I don't like it here!"

Laraelra wasn't sure Charrar could make more noise if she tried, and she watched the woman, wondering what didn't settle in her mind about her. She put her finger to her mouth and signaled for silence. Then she motioned for them to follow, and they inched past Harug and Dorn.

Laraelra let Meloon lead and, as she half-expected, Charrar pointed at the access ladder leading up and yelled, "Hey! There's a—"

Laraelra clapped a hand over her mouth and glared. She whispered, "Someone's lying in wait for us up there, so we're going *this* way. Now *keep quiet*."

Charrar's eyes narrowed, and she slowly nodded.

When they did finally begin clambering up another surface shaft a while later, Laraelra went first and shoved the sewer shaft cover aside as quietly as she could. Next, Charrar clung to Vharem's neck as he climbed, whimpering as she bumped against each iron rung of the ladder. Meloon climbed up and lowered down a rope. Renaer, the last to leave the sewers, waited while the others reeled the unconscious Vajra up with a makeshift harness on the rope. Laraelra pretended to watch Vharem and Meloon stretching their arms and shoulders out, but she remained watchful of the sulking Charrar, who perched on some crates behind them.

Charrar shifted her position and shoved a barrel to make her perch wider. Two empty crates clattered down into the alley. She flinched away and bumped her left foot into another barrel. She let out a scream and clutched her leg, whimpering.

"Shut it, woman!" Vharem snapped. "You'll draw every cut-purse and Watchman in earshot!"

Dawn was just breaking across the sky, and Laraela could see where she was. Between the smell of fish guts and one particularly gruesome demon's head painted on the back of the tallest building in the center of the alley, she figured out their location. "We're in Shank Alley. That sign faces out on Morningstar Way for the Demondraught tavern."

"If you say so," Meloon said. He turned toward Renaer. "Hey, you're probably tired, and I'm not. I'll carry Vajra for a while." He had hauled her up by rope and held her in the crook of one arm as he coiled the rope up with his other hand. His axe lay on the cobbles beside them.

Renaer shook his head. "No, but thanks. I'll carry her, in case we have to run. I can keep up with you even while carrying her. I'd rather you were ready for anyth—"

"Drop all weapons and surrender!" The shout came from the alley's mouth to the west of them.

"Like that?" Laraelra asked.

CHAPTER 7

A man's home, like a man's wife, holds many secrets from those who
don't respect her or know how to hold her in the proper regard.

Rhale the Wise, *Maxims*,
the Year of the Halls Unhaunted (1407 DR)

10 NIGHTAL, YEAR OF THE AGELESS ONE (1479 DR)

Meloon, help me!" Renaer ran forward, and slammed his shoulder
into the tall pile of crates near the alley entrance. Renaer and
Meloon shoved the crates over just in time, seeing the surprised
looks on the Watchmen's faces as the boxes of seaweed and shellfish
toppled upon them.

"Surrender!" Charrar shouted. "Renaer Neverember and
company, you're in the custody of the Watch!"

Vharem whipped around, reaching for his short sword,
only to find its point at his throat. Charrar stood, despite the
apparent wounds on her feet, and she had stolen his weapon.
"Charrar, what—"

"Don't embarrass yourself further, Vharem. I'm neither your
woman nor your grateful rescued victim. Seems a shame, though,
what the Blackstaff'll do to you—such a waste of a good body." As
Renaer and Meloon approached, she moved the sword point closer
to Vharem's throat. Meloon groaned as he noted she stood on the
head of his axe, pinning it to the ground. Charrar called to her
compatriots, who struggled from beneath all the crates. "Hurry!
We need to get them off the streets!"

Two flashes of quicksilver slammed into Charrar's eyes and sword hand. She crumpled to the cobblestones.

Laraelra stood in the shadows, the same silver color fading from her eyes. "I *thought* something wasn't right about her."

"Run!" Renaer pointed up and to the right. "Go north on Morningstar Way!" His hands, however, waved to the south. Renaer scooped up Vajra and Meloon picked up his axe, while Laraelra grabbed the stunned Vharem by the shirt and dragged him into motion. He stumbled forward, holding his throat, and finally snapped out of it and broke into a run with her. The four of them slipped around the northern side of the Demondraught and ran south along Morningstar Way.

Renaer stopped where Aureenar Street crossed Morningstar near the gray-stoned Stormstar Ride, and he noted that most every building was dark, the street-level shops closed and the homes above asleep beneath their brown-tiled roofs. He whispered, "Vharem, Ravencourt!"

Vharem slowed and hooked arms with Laraelra to help her keep pace with him. Meloon turned, brandishing his axe, but Renaer shook his head. He inhaled a deep breath and let out a piercing whistle. Shouts behind them and sudden movement in the shadows from the debris- and cat-filled Shank Alley told Renaer they'd taken his bait. He launched himself and Vajra forward again, with Meloon running alongside again.

"Why'd you do that?" Meloon asked. "We could have gotten away!"

"I've no doubt we will get away, Meloon." Renaer said. "We lead them on a path of my choosing. I truly doubt they are the Watch—just sellswords wearing the colors. If they're working with that fake Blackstaff, they're up to no good."

"And what does this Ravencourt have to do with anything?" Meloon asked as he followed Renaer's direction further up Aureenar's Arc directly toward one of the Field Ward's watch towers.

"Revenge," Renaer said. He took a look behind to see three

figures in pursuit with a fourth trailing behind. He heard the farthest one yell, "They hurt Charrar! Get them!"

Renaer cut a sharp right turn around a whitewashed stone-walled
baker's shop, hooking his way into an inner courtyard. While the
surrounding buildings were all one- and two-story taverns and shops,
the four larger buildings within the courtyard each stood three stories
high. Atop the gables on each of them loomed stone ravens. They
didn't have time to admire the architecture as they caught up with
Vharem and Laraelra, who had stopped, undecided which direction
to go. Renaer barreled past them with a sharp "Follow me!" as he ran
for the lone shadowtop tree at the far end.

"There's no way out there, Renaer!" Vharem said, though he
followed once he heard their approaching pursuers.

Laraelra shouted out a spell, and a cone of bright colors filled
the air just as the quartet of pursuers came around the corner. All
of them yelled and stopped in their tracks, one of them falling
senseless to the street. Laraelra broke into a run after her friends
and called, "Who's after us—the Open Lord or the Blackstaff?"

"You'll find out, lass," the lead man growled as he shook his
vision clear and raced after her.

Renaer ran to the far side of the tree, where he stopped.
Meloon, Vharem, and Laraelra caught up quickly, surprised to
see that Renaer had stopped again. "Are we letting them catch
up again?" Meloon asked.

"No. You and Vharem should try and clear the alley between
the third and fourth buildings there." Renaer pointed at the western
buildings a moment. "Elra, a little light here will help."

Vharem and Meloon attacked the debris-laden midden,
trying to create an exit. Laraelra sidled next to Renaer as the
three remaining pursuers arrived. The three men drew swords
out of their scabbards.

"See, friends?" Renaer called. "The Watch *never* draws steel
on unarmed foes, only rods or staves. They're our foes' hirelings,
be sure."

Laraelra's spell took effect, filling the air with blue light.

The lead pursuer responded, "Only thing folks'll believe is what we tell—Huh?"

The thug fell silent as the outline of the black-barked tree appeared atop the trio. A low moan seemed to issue out of the tree trunk along with a rustle and crackling of nigh-dead leaves and branches. The first man ran forward, intent on Renaer, when black shadows lashed out of the tree to wrap around his sword arm and body. He yelled, and his friends stepped back—too slowly. Leaf-enshrouded black vines lashed out at them too. All three screamed and howled when the vines crushed where they gripped, but their voices grew still as three final vines descended from the tree and looped around their necks as nooses. Branches cracked and groaned as they stretched under the feet of the three, raising them high above the street. With a loud crack, the branches all broke away, leaving the three men to freefall until the nooses ended their falls with the snapping of three necks.

Laraelra watched, morbidly fascinated, as the tree's shadow seemed to shift and not resemble the tree's silhouette but a judge's gavel. She looked at Renaer, who had a grim look on his face. "Did you *know* that was going to happen?" she asked.

"Yes, I expected something like that, but not nearly as dramatic," Renaer replied. "Guess old Magister Nharrelk gets angry if he doesn't claim any guilty souls in a century."

"You led us under that thing, *knowing it could attack us?*"

Renaer turned with Vajra in his arms, locking eyes with Laraelra as he turned. "We were always safe from the Hanging Tree of Ravencourt."

"Why are you so certain?"

"You haven't avoided punishment for any capital crimes in the city, have you?" Renaer said. "Those are the only ones who get judged by the Magistree."

Vharem had watched what had happened even while working to free a passage, and his eyes were goblet-wide and staring at Renaer.

"How many times have we led a rat-scamper through here and that never happened? And why now?"

"Seven times, friend, all of them successful escapes," Renaer said. "As for them, they were guilty of hanging offenses. Consider it some justice against those who killed Faxhal."

Renaer saw the slight path and kicked-over fence that allowed them to pass up and over a refuse heap. He nodded his approval and began climbing out of Ravencourt while still talking to the group.

"We must go back to Neverember Hall before too many folks question why I'm carrying someone. There's not many people about yet, but that'll change swiftly. Meloon, sling Elra and Vharem over your shoulders. That way, we're simply carrying our drunk friends home from their cups."

Laraelra rolled her eyes and said, "I don't think so. I can stumble home, thanks."

Meloon lashed his axe to his belt and then reached for her. "C'mon, Elra, it'll keep anyone from being suspicious."

She smirked. "Vharem's looking awful, there, Meloon. Why don't you take one arm and I'll take the other? We can walk *him* home, since we're both taller than he is."

Vharem laughed as he threw his arms over the shoulders of Meloon and Laraelra. "It's not as if this isn't closer to a typical end to a night with me and Ren!" As they walked away, Vharem muttered, "Gods speed you to rest, Faxhal, and may the guilty swim in razor-strewn dung for their afterlives."

The late morning sun shone brightly through the windows at the far side of the room, though the windows facing Mendever Street remained cloaked behind heavy curtains. In the shadows on the bed, a man loomed over Vajra's prone body, his hands glowing green and white. His voice was low and his prayers were barely audible over Renaer's own as he knelt to pray in the sunlight.

"Valkur, speed his path, fill his sails, and calm his seas. Amaunator, light his way and warm his face. Tymora, grant him the luck to be at his reward before his misdeeds are counted in full. Kelemvor, judge him worthy to pass the veils. Gods above, grant my friend the happiness he found so rarely on Toril out among the stars."

Renaer's eyes welled up, but no tears escaped until he turned his head toward the light touch on his shoulder.

Renaer looked up into the peaceful eyes of Wavetamer Garyn Raventree, whose own prayers had ended moments before. "A good prayer, if a bit random."

"How is she?" Renaer asked.

Garyn shrugged and said, "I've healed her, so she's physically as strong as she can be. But mentally . . . I don't know. She's under the influence of some magic I've never seen. Given that she's linked to the Blackstaff, that's not surprising."

"So why won't she wake up?"

"I asked for clarity on her condition, and all I know is her soul now carries twenty or more lifetimes."

"What does that mean?"

"On that, Valkur puts me on still seas, friend."

"Well, thank you for everything, Garyn. I'll be by within a tenday and we'll talk about my debts to you."

"Consider this but payment for our own debts, for the young Lord Neverember has been a staunch friend of Valkur and his faithful."

Renaer stood up, walked over to his desk, and withdrew a small purse, which he handed to Garyn. "In that case, let me pay for some prayers to be sung in Faxhal's name."

"Of course. His ship will sail the stars on the waves of our prayers, friend. While he wasn't the best sailor, he was a good comrade to many of our faithful."

The priest bowed and exited the room just as Madrak came in bearing a pair of copper kettles, their contents piping hot. He poured both kettles into a basin by the window, the steam rising in the sunbeams.

"It would seem that only the lady Safahr has slept well since your adventures began yestermorn, milord. Can we not urge you and your friends to sleep? To eat? At least I can insist you not waste the hot water for your morning ablutions."

Madrak had been starting his normal day just as Renaer and his friends returned to Neverember House. Since then, he'd sent runners to Valkur's temple on Sul Street and another down to the palace to hear of any news or gossip and to notify the Watch or the Lords that the Blackstaff was not who he seemed.

"Later, Madrak," Renaer said. "I want to know what the reaction is to our news before I collapse either into bed or a trencher. Who did you send down to the palace to tell about the Blackstaff—about the duplicity?"

"Varkel. I gave him the Saddelyn pony to make sure he got there as quickly as possible."

"Good. He'll remember every single word spoken to him and around him. Are the others well?"

"Master Vharem is sullenly distraught, but has remarkably stayed away from the liquor cabinet. Mistress Laraelra has been quietly meditating in one corner, while only Master Meloon shows any sense in eating and catching some sleep. Of course, he has placed his filthy boots up on the tables and ruined the tablecloth, but . . ."

Renaer had wandered away from Madrak to approach the bed. Vajra looked vastly better, now that she had a clean robe and had all the grime and blood washed out of her hair and face. Renaer just wished she would wake up and give them some answers to help get them out of this mess.

"The fact that you have the Blackstaff's Heir in your care— however her condition—speaks well for your story, Renaer," Madrak said. "No matter how thickly the lies fly, truth is like a sunlit breeze that scatters them."

"Where did you say the others were?" Renaer asked.

"The dining room, master," he replied. "I'll check with the staff to see what other word is on the streets and meet you there. After you've refreshed yourself and dressed."

The two of them pulled the curtains around the bed closed, allowing Vajra even more warmth and silence to help her sleep. Madrak approached a tall cabinet and pulled on a decorative design between the two drawers, producing a small set of steps on which he stood to open the tall wardrobe doors. The butler began pulling out new clothes, while Renaer stripped off his old clothes and threw them to one side. Renaer splashed the hot water on himself, scrubbing himself clean and thoroughly dousing his head and face multiple times before he put the basin on the floor and soaked and cleaned his feet in it. By the time he was done, Madrak had assembled a new set of black leather pants, green muslin shirt, a black ermine-lined vest, and a new wolf-furred cloak. Madrak withdrew to let his master finish dressing.

As the latch clicked shut on the door, Renaer finished rubbing himself dry with the towel, only to realize he was being watched. Vajra's face stuck out from between the curtains, a mischievous smile on her lips. While Renaer was hardly embarrassed, he was surprised, especially as he watched the woman's eyes shift between normal looking eyes to dark orbs to a pair of mismatched eyes, all as she rambled incoherently. Her facial expressions also constantly shifted, as if she were at war within herself.

"Tasty, just like a good strong lad he carried us all the way wish I could things he needs know protect me is he the Heir can he help something's wrong with the we need help fight Ten-Rings problem is son recover the Dusk owe him pain oh let me play . . ."

With that final reach and one of the most lascivious looks Renaer had ever received, Vajra fell unconscious again, her head and left arm resting on and over the end of the bed. Renaer pulled on his pants quickly and then got Vajra resettled in bed. Even when he lay beside her to pull up the furs and coverlet, she did not respond at all to his presence.

After he finished dressing, Renaer came down to the dining room. As he entered, Vharem turned toward the sound of the door. Laraelra's eyes also opened and locked on his. Meloon's light snore continued as the tall man's chin rested on his chest, his feet on the table, and his chair precariously tipped beneath him.

Madrak entered the dining room, cleared his throat, and said, "Varkel has returned, master. He—"

A blur pushed the door further open and rushed past Madrak. He ran right up to Renaer, his face red with exertion and wind-burn, his hair slightly frosted from the cold. "Master Renaer!" he shouted, and the noise woke up Meloon, whose sudden start tipped over his chair, and the young blond man fell flat on his back on the floor.

Varkel hardly noticed the crash or Vharem's snickering about it. He started talking very fast. "Master Renaer, they're saying such awful things. I could hardly stand there and listen to them spew such lies about you—what with how well you've been to us all these years. Now mind you, were I not to know that these kind folk were associated with your lordship, I might be inclined to believe—"

"Varkel, slow down," Renaer said. "Take a breath and simply tell me what's news on the streets. What happened when you told them about the Blackstaff?"

"I weren't never getting the chance to, master," Varkel said. "The crowds were so thick, and when they gave the pronouncements, I figured I should highstep it back here right soon!"

"What did they say?" Meloon asked.

The sandy-haired halfling took a deep breath and began speaking very quickly. "Rashemel Steeldrover, the Watchlord of the North Towers, she gave the pronouncements from the steps of the palace, which seemed odd, considering—"

"Varkel! Focus!" Madrak and Renaer said simultaneously.

"There are warrants out for the arrests or information leading to the arrest of Renaer Neverember and any present associates, including Ararna, Pellarm, Vharem Kuthcutter, and Faxhal Xoram, for having allegedly conspired against the Lords' Rule, having knowingly undermined and interfered with the guild business of the Watchful Order of Magists and Protectors, having trespassed upon private property and caused extensive damage thereupon, having caused grave harm to be visited upon the Watch and other persons, and other sundry charges to be visited upon those so warranted at the time of their arrest and summoning for trial."

Laraelra surprised herself when her response was a light chuckle of disbelief. "But . . . that's . . ."

"Fully fabricated and false, I know, but actionable as far as the city's citizens are concerned," Renaer said. "Still, it's another sign that we're in slightly over our heads until we get some help equal to the quality of that stacked against us."

"We better get going, then," Vharem said. "I've a few ideas, Ren—know a few places we can go."

He shook his head. "Thanks, but I've got the perfect place in mind. I meant to take you, Faxhal, and Torlyn earlier, but things got busy."

"They're right, master!" Varkel cried. "You have to flee! Shrunkshanks and I ran as fast as we could, but we've not the speed nor the longest of legs to stay ahead of a battalion of Watchmen."

A loud pounding reverberated from downstairs, a mailed fist against the solid oak door.

Varkel hopped up onto the seat by the bay window, looked out, and said, "There's about a dozen Watchmen outside, and they've brought a battering ram to get through the doors."

"It doesn't look like they're going to use it," said Meloon. "They're talking to someone at the door."

"Nolan has gone down to stall them," Madrak said, "and while he is capable of confusing them awhile, he cannot stop them, should they lose patience."

"Right," Renaer said. "If they're in the front entry hall, we can't go back the way we came." The young Lord Neverember moved to the window to confirm Meloon's observation, talking over his shoulder to the halfling. "Madrak? The garden path?"

"I understand," Madrak said. "I'll fetch what you need." He shuffled out of the room just as a loud boom signaled the end of the Watch's patience.

Renaer sighed. "They've thrown Nolan into the street and started using the battering ram. Here's what we have to do. Meloon, look under those window seats there and there"— Renaer pointed to the bay windows across the room—"and grab as many furs as you can. We'll meet you upstairs once you have them." He put his finger to his lips and then pointed at Vharem. "Can you dash to the kitchens and have Ellial put together some quick provisions for the five of us? Meet us up in the garden. Elra, with me, please."

Renaer motioned for Laraelra to join him and they half-ran out of the room. They turned down the hallway and entered the library. Laraelra breathed in the smell. She loved the scent of tanned leather and vellum and that slight hint of mildew and dust common among old books. Bookshelves lined the north wall from floor to ceiling, but there were large gaps among the books in them. Two tables at the room's center held large piles of books, some opened and some stacked haphazardly. Renaer moved to the large fireplace on the eastern wall. He grasped the corner cornice and slid it upward into the mantle. The nearest bookshelf clicked, and its lower half swung open, revealing a hidden area behind it.

"We'll need these. I don't have time to check which ones, so we'll take them all." Renaer pulled the bookcase open further and he and Laraelra knelt down. Set into the stone wall was a recessed shelf on which were five books bound in black leather with ornate silver clasps. Renaer pulled them out and loaded them into her arms.

"Whose books are these, and why do we need them now?" Laraelra asked. The books thrummed beneath her touch—she could feel there was magic within them. The drumbeat of the battering ram echoed through the mansion.

Renaer shouldered the shelf back into place and headed for the door. "I'll explain later. Right now, we've got to get out of here."

"Let me guess—there's a hidden slide in the walls that'll whisk us to the alley out back?"

"Even better, but we need to hurry."

Loud retorts joined the battering ram's blows as the door started to crack. Renaer heard someone yelling down in the entry hall, "The door's cracking! Get the bar up here now!"

The two of them ran from the library and up the stairs to the third floor. They met Meloon, his arms piled high with various bear, wolf, and ermine pelts.

Laraelra asked, "Renaer, why aren't you carrying something? The rest of us—"

"Fine," Renaer snapped as he opened the door to his room. "I'll let *you* carry Vajra, then, and I'll take Varad's books."

He crossed the darkened chamber to his desk, pulled open the right-hand drawer, and pocketed a large ring of keys. He then moved over to the bed. Vajra lay beneath a heavy fur cloak, which Renaer kept on her as he picked her up gingerly. She groaned and threw an arm around Renaer's neck without coming fully awake.

Renaer whispered, "Head back out into the hall and turn right. Look for a stone rosebud on the wall."

The four of them moved quickly out of the room and down the passage, soon followed by Vharem, who ran up the stairs with two armloads of parcels, from one of which jutted two long loaves of bread. The hallway past Dagult's office ended at a deep curved recess in the wall, stone roses carved in relief all over the back of it.

Meloon chuckled. "First the sewers, then a secret door privy, and now a garderobe. Lovely smells follow our adventure at every turn."

Renaer smirked, and nodded to the sorceress. "Elra, turn that last stone rosebud on the right-hand side toward us, please?"

Laraelra shifted the books into one arm, and she did as directed. Above the pulse of the battering ram, they heard the grinding of stone as a circular stair descended from the ceiling down into the garderobe. A slim pillar of stone rose from the floor of the garderobe to add support to the center of the stairs as well. A chill breeze came down with the stairs, as did Madrak's voice. "Hurry masters and milady, the Watch is almost inside!"

They mounted the spiral stairs, Renaer having to choose his steps gingerly and make sure Vajra's head did not hit anything as they ascended. When they reached the top, they found themselves greeted by Madrak, all wrapped in a heavy cloak. Once all of them were up the stairs, Madrak shoved a metal bench over the stairwell, and the stones recoiled back into place.

"I'm not seeing a way out of here, Renaer!" Laraelra looked over the rooftop garden, its plants in decay or wrapped in burlap to help them survive the coming winter. The entire roof was a meticulously designed garden with tiled paths and a walkway around the perimeter that might have an arbor of roses arcing overhead in summer. With the winter, the terraces and flower beds and arbors were bare mausoleums of dead vegetation. "Do you mean for us to jump down to the roofs of your neighbors?" Laraelra saw the look of excitement on Meloon's face and frowned at him. Despite the strong sunlight, the slight wind made it bitterly cold.

"Be quiet and follow me, all of you. Madrak, if you please. We'll meet you later, if or when you can join us. If Father or the Watch continues to hunt for me, tell him or them I'm off with some lissome young priestess learning about yet another god and its promises—and no hinting at malefic gods this time, mind you."

Renaer and Madrak each winked and smiled at each other, and then moved across the roof. Meloon and Laraelra hurried to keep up with the short butler.

His white hair whipping in the wind, Madrak stopped in one corner in front of a small statue of a kneeling elf maid, her hands cupped as if drinking water. The halfling whispered, "While I pour water into her hands, the gate remains open. Go quickly, and may Brandobaris grant your feet speed."

Renaer nodded and stepped inside the arbor, cradling the still-unconscious Vajra. As Madrak poured water into the statue's hands, Renaer stepped forward and was gone. Meloon stepped back in surprise, while Laraelra said, "Fascinating. Not even any flash or hint of magic."

"Get moving and follow him!" said Madrak. "This only works once a day and only with one stream of water. Now hurry!"

Vharem smiled and followed Renaer's footsteps exactly. "Thanks, Madrak!" he said as he vanished into thin air.

Laraelra stepped under the arbor and along the same path as Renaer. She also rushed into nothingness. Meloon timidly followed suit and vanished just as Madrak's bucket poured the last of its water into the statue's hands.

Madrak smiled as not one drop of water remained to betray what he'd been doing. He quickly walked back to the servants' exit, hugging himself for warmth. He left his cloak on a peg just inside the three-foot-high hidden exit. When he descended through the passage down to the kitchen, he stopped and peered through a spyhole and found exactly what he expected—a cadre of Watchmen bullying the staff for information.

Time to buy the young heroes some time to do some good, Madrak thought. 'Tis about time someone did.

Inside the door, he had left an empty slop bucket to explain what he'd been doing—throwing kitchen scraps onto the compost on the roof. As he had done exactly that, there was no way for anyone to claim he lied. Now he simply had to stall for time and keep the Watch from asking too many questions about his lord.

CHAPTER 8

More has been lost in Waterdeep's City of the Dead than the innocence of youth. Its shadows hold far worse than a chill. Its stones cover more than bones and ossuaries.

Savengriff, *Swords, Spells, and Splendors*,
Year of the Harp (1355 DR)

10 NIGHTAL, YEAR OF THE AGELESS ONE (1479 DR)

Khondar nearly jumped out of his chair when an unexpected knock on his door disturbed his inadvertent nap. The tome he had been reading before he fell asleep tumbled to the floor. Already, his dream of a wizard in charge of each ward of the city faded to obscurity.

"Who dares disturb me?" he snapped. He picked the tome off the floor as he adjusted his chair. He placed the tome inside his desk and closed the drawer.

"The Blackstaff," came the reply.

"Come in, come in," Khondar said. "I'm honored by the Blackstaff's presence." Behind the closed door, Ten-Rings grimaced at the irony of what he said, given his hatred of the man whose guise his son wore.

The man entered the chamber and closed the door behind him. "Can we talk here?" the Blackstaff asked. "Is it safe?"

"Yes," Khondar said. "One of the few benefits of this poor office location is that a previous tenant set rather durable spells to prevent anyone from hearing anything from without."

"She finally gave up some secrets, Father." The Blackstaff's form shimmered, and the bearded face of Khondar's son smirked at him.

"What are you prattling about, boy?" Khondar said. "She's been out of our grasp since last night—thanks to your and Granek's failures."

Centiv frowned at the reprimand, his shoulders slumping, and he said, "I've already apologized for that. There was nothing I could do, short of being captured myself. I stabbed her to keep her from talking and hid her as best I could in short time."

"They're children and amateurs, Centiv," Khondar said. "You should have just blown them all away." Khondar turned away and stared out his window.

"In those tight corridors? I'd have roasted myself!" Centiv growled. "Not all of us can hide behind so many magical rings to protect us from spells blowing back on us."

Khondar's face blazed with tight-lipped fury, but he kept his temper when he asked, "What was it you came to tell me? How does Vajra spill her secrets now?"

Centiv beamed. "I had a tome and quill magically recording everything said within her cell. I'd hidden it behind an illusion in the cell across from her. After I left Roarke House with those records and books just ahead of the invaders, I used one of my other illusory guises and went to her chambers we keep over on Keltarn Street. I spent much of the night reading the transcript. Vajra had babbled a few things—names, locations, dates, item names, and the like—but we never thought they were anything more than random thoughts or words to stall Granek's next wound. She repeated them at night when Granek and we were gone, as if she were talking to herself. When you look at them all at once, they have a pattern—"

Khondar got up from his chair slowly, glowering, and asked, "You recorded everything?"

"Yes, and when I found—"

"*Everything?* Centiv, you fool! That's now evidence of our direct involvement!"

"I already destroyed the evidence, Father—once I confirmed she spoke the truth."

"What?"

"I found a pattern in a few passages of the transcripts. Each place she mentioned also corresponded to a person's name she blurted out. I've spent the day looking at every place she mentioned and found every person she named. Once my status as the Blackstaff cowed people out of my way, I could search for secret chambers or compartments in their locations. I found a few scraps of parchment hidden in each location. By themselves, the parchment scraps are nothing but trash. But together . . . well, here."

Centiv tossed the dozen fragments up into the air and cast a minor spell on them as they floated. They fell into place as one scrap on Khondar's desk. They spelled a single name: *Sarael*.

Khondar looked up at his son, irritated, and raised an eyebrow in question. Centiv smiled and motioned with his hand to flip the parchment over to reveal Elvish script on it.

Khondar sighed. "You know I don't read Elvish, Centiv. Stop showing off and tell me what you know."

"It says, 'The first heir of his body points the way to a new heir of his spirit. The Tears light the way.' I am certain this refers to Khelben Arunsun, the first Blackstaff. His first son was Sarael Arunsun, whose mausoleum resisted the Spellplague, unlike many others. We simply need to wait for moonrise and visit the tomb of Sarael Trollscourge in the City of the Dead. There, we should find what we seek."

Khondar thought long and silently, his fingers steepled in front of his face, his gold and silver rings all glistening. He nodded finally and looked up at Centiv. "Very good work, Son. I'll send Eiruk Weskur with you in case you run into trouble. He's loyal to a fault and will just assume this is guild business. He'll meet you at the gates of the cemetery at nightfall."

"I don't need his help on this," Centiv said. "I could have done all this without telling you, after all. I might have just brought you the secrets after the fact!"

"Well, you didn't, and this isn't the first time you've had the chance to show initiative and failed me. I'm not going to let your tendency to panic when confronted with the unexpected ruin our plans. Now take Weskur with you and we'll mind-wipe him later if we must. Just get whatever the Blackstaff has hidden in that tomb."

"But I don't—"

"*Enough!*" Khondar slammed his hands down on his desk. "I will *not* be questioned by my own child! We'll meet at Roarke House when you have the secrets."

Centiv wrapped himself in the illusionary guise of Samark "Blackstaff" Dhanzscul. His illusions did not disguise his anger, though, and he slammed the door behind him. Khondar shook his head. He and his third son shared so much, like the magic that drove them from the superstitious backwater of Sundabar more than two decades ago. Unfortunately, they also shared a temper, and Khondar wondered how much longer their scheme would hold up before someone's temper lost it all.

>———W———<

"Of course, I know that," the Blackstaff told the guard. "My predecessor was the one who created that law. Now step aside. I mean to honor that predecessor's son this night, on the anniversary of his greatest victory. Worry not. Only benefit shall come from blind eyes toward us."

He levitated a large bag of coins at the guard, who took it, then nodded at his younger compatriot who unlocked the gate.

"Come along, Weskur," the Blackstaff said, waving his companion forward.

Eiruk Weskur complied, following the older wizard through the gates. He shuddered despite himself, knowing full well that there were many reasons why people were locked out of the City of the Dead at night. He shivered beneath his heavy wool cloak and hood, wishing he'd not recently cut his black hair to a short skullcap. Still, to work directly with the Blackstaff was worth the discomfort. He just wished he knew what they were doing, as he had only the spells he'd already prepared that day and two wands given to him by Guildsenior Khondar Naomal before he was told to meet the Blackstaff here two bells after sundown.

The two of them left Mhalsymber's Way through the Weeping Gate, so named for an unidentified ghost whose sobs could be heard only on the night of the new moon. Eiruk was glad Selûne shone nearly full and bright tonight, if only to keep that ghost at bay. Inside the gate, the moon shone brighter still, as the interior walls were mirror-smooth and reflected the light, even though they remained worked stone blocks on the street-side. Eiruk had not been in the City of the Dead in quite some time, and he was shocked at how ill-tended it seemed to be. The wide paths, cobbles that had become glazed smooth slabs under the Spellplague chaos, were cracked, and weeds jutted out everywhere along the avenues among the mausoleums. The once-carefully manicured lawns lay untended, rife with weeds and badly in need of trimming. More than a few trees were obviously dead, while others grew out of proportion or unnaturally. The shadowtop in their path looked like a wooden fountain, its trunk shattered and spreading out to fall back and reroot in fifteen different points around itself. That tree proved healthy and strong, even if it did grow over a small tomb, which now lay in rubble beneath its boughs.

Worse yet were the mausoleums and tombs. Eiruk knew they used to hold portals built by Ahghairon the Open Lord himself, allowing more burial space in uninhabited dimensions. The dangers of those portals had been put on display when the Gundwynds buried three of their own shortly after the Spellplague first hit Waterdeep. All those who entered the family's tomb and went through its portal were transformed into trolls or giants. All were maddened by the pains of transformation and rampaged through the city. While they were stopped by the Blackstaff and a contingent of the Watchful Order, no one could be restored, which led to the end of the Gundwynd Waterdeep clan in 1388. Ever since, scouts did extensive magical reviews before anyone entered any of the tombs—especially those warped by the Spellplague. At least a dozen tombs either winked out of existence or exploded in the magichaos of that time, while others morphed or shifted, their stone melting like butter at highsun. Only a handful remained utterly unchanged by that time, and the pair of wizards approached one of those now.

An adamantine statue of a warrior stood proudly atop its blue Moonshavian marble base, as it had since its creation more than three centuries ago. Eiruk liked the look and strength of Sarael the Trollscourge, his face clean-shaven, strong-jawed, and smiling triumphantly, his hair flowing in a breeze and frozen in metal. The warrior wore chain mail from shoulders to toe, his shield resting upside-down on its straight top, the point of the three-sided shield resting on his left knee. His arms held two battle-axes crossed high above his head, and as clouds passed over the moon, reducing the light, a slight blue glow shimmered around the axes. Eiruk remembered an old dwarven forge-magic called blueshine that might explain that. What he couldn't explain was why he was following the Blackstaff as they walked two complete circuits around the base of this small memorial. He had been busy looking at the statue, while the older wizard stared at the marble base. The Blackstaff swore when the moon's light faded, as if he were looking for something by moonlight.

"Watch for any changes or signs on the statue or the base when it's in moonlight," said the Blackstaff. "Tell me immediately if you see something."

With that, the old man pulled his hood close around his balding head. Eiruk peered carefully at the tomb as he walked three circuits around the base, passing the distracted wizard multiple times. As the Blackstaff looked low and at the base, Eiruk looked higher at the statue or their immediate surroundings. On his fourth circuit, Eiruk spotted a hidden blue glow, visible only to his mystically sensitive eyes, and said, "Blackstaff, I see something."

"What is it?" The Blackstaff scurried to his side.

Eiruk pointed and said, "Look there. It points to something."

The Blackstaff sighed loudly. "I've no desire to waste energy on a detection spell or analysis. Just show me where it points."

Eiruk and the Blackstaff stood between the tomb and the northern wall of the City of the Dead. Looking through the wide stance of Sarael's statue, he saw thin lines of magic glimmering in response to the moonlight. Two points led from the axes and intersected with a third line from the point of the shield. When the lines intersected, they became a stronger white beam that pointed directly to one spot on the back wall of a tomb within the shadow of the Beacon Tower.

"There are magic beams directed from this statue to the Ralnarth tomb there," Eiruk said as he pointed.

"Why that tomb?" The Blackstaff wondered aloud. "And what do the beams do?"

"The Ralnarths bought all holdings of the Estelmer clan," said Eiruk, "and I think the Estelmers were allies of the first Blackstaff long ago. That might be the connection. As for what they do, I can see they're conjurations overlaid with illusions, but I can't tell you more. If Vajra were here, she could easily discern these spells. If I may ask, where is your apprentice? She can do this task far better than I." Eiruk hoped he kept his face impassive as he asked. He respected the Blackstaff and his power, but he still pined to be close to Vajra, despite her love for the older man.

"You may *not* ask, underling."

Eiruk became uncomfortable beneath Samark's long and angry stare. He returned his attention and concentration to his spell.

"Show me where the beams touch the tomb," the Blackstaff said.

Eiruk stepped up on the marble dais and crouched to maintain his line of sight. As he squatted, he rested his hand on the cold statue. A stabbing headache suddenly formed behind his eyes and a ghostly shimmer of the lights appeared in normal sight.

"Ah! Very good, Weskur!" the Blackstaff exclaimed.

The Blackstaff moved away to the back of the tomb and began chanting, weaving his fingers through a few simple spells directed at the wall. Eiruk realized that while the statue and his hand were cold, his fingernails glowed the same as the beams.

Eiruk could not discern what spells the Blackstaff cast at the beam's final point, but the younger mage's vantage offered him new insights. Eiruk watched the wizard mutter more arcane phrases, snapping his fingers through spell after spell to no apparent effect and then swear at the wall. The young man had worked briefly with the Blackstaff thrice before in the six years he had been with the Watchful Order, and now he could see that whoever stood before him, it was definitely not Samark Dhanzscul. That older man never swore, even in battle, and always used people's given names. Samark also spoke kindly and respectfully to everyone, from the lowliest servant to the guildmasters and Lords themselves. The contempt Eiruk heard in his voice should have warned him sooner. This person, while a decent enough actor to cow most with his illusionary form, was rash and impatient when faced with the unexpected. As Eiruk watched the wizard move, he detected a shimmer around the Blackstaff and another dark-haired form beneath his skin. He squinted, trying to see the man's face, but he couldn't over the distance with only moonlight.

Eiruk felt a tingling beneath his hand and turned his attention back to the statue. The inside of the shield that rested against Sarael's leg shimmered slightly with the same blue glow as the axes. Maintaining his contact with the statue but moving his hand along the cold metal, Eiruk shifted closer to the left leg and tentatively reached toward the shield with his right hand. He expected to touch cold metal, but instead felt warmth. He felt a throb of heat on his palm, and then the surface yielded and his hand sank inside—but not through—the shield. Eiruk could only feel warm air and the edges of the shield. He smiled, fascinated by the curious magic set by a long-dead wizard, one who truly earned the title of the Blackstaff—an honor for which Eiruk fervently wished.

The open hand of peace and a loyal heart gains you alone entry. Eiruk heard the deep voice in his head and struggled to keep his face from revealing his shock. He felt another stab of pain behind his eyes and heard the voice again. *If ye truly be friend, Blackstaff Tower will welcome you. All others will only enter to gain knowledge in accord with their hearts.*

Eiruk felt a searing sensation in his palm. It ended swiftly, and then he felt stone scrape against the top of his knuckles. A large bundle apparated beneath his touch. He closed his hand, hooking his fingers beneath what felt like leather bindings, and pulled a large parcel out of the shield. As he did so, the light emitting from the statue and the light inside the shield both winked out. Eiruk found no visible mark on his palm, though he felt magic pulsing beneath his skin. He would have to study it later—on his way to Blackstaff Tower for more answers. The leather bundle in his hand was sealed with a complex sigil unmistakable to many Waterdhavians—the wizard mark of Khelben Arunsun, lord of Waterdeep and the first Blackstaff.

"What happened?" The false Blackstaff turned around, angry at the interruption of his activity. "What did you do, Weskur?"

When he saw Eiruk held something, he dashed forward and snatched the leather bundle from his grasp.

Eiruk kept calm and said, "When you cast spells at that spot, the statue's shield here became some sort of portal. I reached in and withdrew this."

The false Blackstaff tore at the leather bindings, ignoring Eiruk and the significance of his predecessor's mark on the parcel.

Inside the surprisingly supple and warm leather wrap were two bundles. One, wrapped in lighter kid leather and stamped with an Elvish rune Eiruk didn't recognize, was round with an obvious bulge on one side. The other was an elaborate scroll tube carved from a dragon's leg bone and set with gold-plated runes and many gems. From the weight of the bundle, Eiruk also knew the tube held far more than the usual few parchments.

Eiruk watched the Blackstaff examine the parcel and tube. The young man resisted the urge to expose the imposter before him. Eiruk knew there was no one here to help him, and his foe's power might be far stronger than his subterfuges. For now, the young wizard held his tongue. Perhaps Maerla Windmantle, another guildsenior of the Watchful Order and one with whom he usually studied and worked, would be able to help. If he could find Vajra, they could expose this fraud of a Blackstaff.

The false Blackstaff looked up at Eiruk. "You should smile, for you've done well. You have the Blackstaff's thanks." The false Blackstaff retied the leather straps and tucked the bundle into his belt pouch. "Let us return to the Towers of the Order and show Master Naomal the fruits of our work tonight."

Eiruk could resist no longer. He had to test the lying wizard as the pair of them headed back toward the Weeping Gate. "As you wish, milord. If I may, will you tell your apprentice Vajra that I asked after her welfare? If she is ill, I'd be happy to visit any apothecary."

The Blackstaff shot a look back over his shoulder at the younger man. "Thank you for your offer, Eiruk, but no matter. Vajra suffers naught. She merely winters with her family down among the hills of Tethyr. She returns with the spring." With that, he pulled his hood tight around his head and said nothing more.

Eiruk worried that this imposter had harmed Vajra. While she only returned his love as friendship, Eiruk knew Vajra would not leave the city without saying farewell.

No, Eiruk thought. Maerla needs to learn of this tonight, no matter how late.

"Thank you, Eiruk," Ten-Rings said. "That will be all. *Return to your room and remember nothing of this night but a long, peaceful sleep.*"

The wizard finished his spell, and Eiruk Weskur walked calmly out of his office and down the stairs toward the younger guild members' dormitories. Once he was gone out of sight, Khondar closed the door, turned around, and said, "Not here." He rested his hand on his companion's shoulder and said, *"Oralneiar."*

The two men disappeared from the Tower of the Order with a chuff of imploding air.

They reappeared in a small, cold room lit only by a meager fire. Two tables flanked the hearth, both piled with scrolls and books. The table farthest from the window held a sculpture of two human hands carved from hematite, rings winking on every digit.

"Show me," Khondar said. "Show me, boy!"

Ten-Rings muttered a few arcane words, and two glowballs flared to life above the tables in his work chamber.

"I wasn't sure what we had, but I recognized both Khelben's mark and the Elvish rune." Centiv's face shimmered back into focus as he dropped his Blackstaff illusion. He reached to the rough table beneath the window and handed his father the tome Samark had brought with him out of Khelben the Elder's tomb. The sigil on the cover matched the one on the kid leather bundle.

Ten-Rings muttered, "That book's protections proved beyond our skills."

His hands out of Khondar's sight, Centiv clenched his fists in frustration against the constant jabs. He had spent eleven days more than Khondar studying the tomes, and he knew the words and letters just swam about, as if he tried to read the book through a foot of wind-shimmered water. When he could catch a recognizable letter or sigil, he could only tell it was a word in Dwarvish, the next in Elvish, another in some form of Draconic. Centiv hated that his father rushed to judge what was beyond Centiv's skills when Khondar's own proved lacking.

"I *know*, Father." Centiv said. "But given that sigils on the covers match, perhaps this can help us with the book." Centiv unwrapped the kid leather to reveal a hand-sized lens of clear amber crystal.

Khondar snatched the crystal away from Centiv with a growl and held the crystal over the first page of the tome. Through the lens, the page swam as usual, but after a moment, both could see the letters stop shimmering and settle into place. Better still, the letters reformed into Common, and both men read the title.

Lore and Awareness of the Dark Archmage's Acolytes: On the Assumption of Power as the Blackstaff or the Blackstaff's Heir.

Beneath the title page were five signatures—*Khelben Arunsun, Tsarra Chaadren, Kyriani Agrivar, Krehlan Arunsun,* and *Ashemmon of Rhymanthiin*—and their wizard marks after them.

Laughing loudly, Khondar threw an arm around Centiv's shoulders, a move from which his son initially flinched before smiling at the show of paternal pride.

"You've done it!" Khondar said. "You've found the way we can make the Blackstaff's power our own! Now if we can just make sure that Tethyrian bitch stays out of the way . . ."

"In a way, I did so earlier today . . ." Centiv's flush of pride deepened as he thought about the report his agent Charrar brought to him the previous dawn. While he bristled at the costs in lives and gold, Centiv was grateful he had had to silence only one agent instead of six to cover his tracks. He marveled at the luck Renaer and his friends seemed to have. They had very nearly caught him, all thanks to that skinny witch's muting spell. Before this was over, Centiv knew he had to rip the secret of that spell from her, both to resist it and to exploit it. With that spell, he might even force his father to acknowledge him as an equal . . .

Dagrol, the Watch armar, entered Shank Alley along with an accompanying wizard of the Watchful Order, both of them with their staves at the ready. The five other Watchmen were either in the alley already or at either end, keeping folk from entering and disturbing the scene. Dagrol approached his firstblade and asked, "Who found her, Barlak?"

"He did," the watchman pointed at a young boy taller than Dagrol. Despite the cold, the boy wore no shirt beneath his apron, and his muscles showed Dagrol he was used to hauling around loads of heavy fish. "His name's Karel."

"Talk to him, would you?" Dagrol asked the wizard at his side, who nodded and walked away. "Where's the victim?"

Dagrol's impatience was well-known by his patrol, and the young man nodded up the alley to the left. Dagrol found his best vigilant assessing the scene. Tasmia looked up at him, gray eyes somber and haunted.

The body lay tucked against the rough rear exterior of the Filleted Filliar hearthouse. The woman's body had been shoved roughly behind and beneath large stacks of discarded garbage, fish guts, and other assorted offal. Her body was a mass of welts, scars, and wounds, but Dagrol's eyes fell on two wounds in particular.

A dagger jutted out of her right eye, and a short sword had been driven up beneath her ribs and directly into her heart. The blades were ornately decorated along the hilts.

"You ever seen work like that before?" Dagrol asked Tasmia, who knelt beside the body.

"The killing blows, yeah," Tasmia said. "Standard moves to make sure someone's definitely dead, despite all other wounds. Overly showy blades are all the rage right now among the rich, too. The details on that basket-hilt sword, though, give up our suspect right away."

"Who is it?"

"Well, those arms—the bear's claw atop a diamond, all atop a field with three stripes from dexter to sinister—belong to the Neverembers. Unless you think the Open Lord's killing women in alleys these days, I'd say we need to find young Renaer Neverember.

And we'd better do it quickly." Tasmia pulled a rough woolen blanket over the body, and whispered a quick prayer. "Selûne keep her soul safe from the predators that claimed this body."

"Aye." Dagrol nodded, sighing deeply. "Anybody else recognize her?"

"Just me, Dag," Tasmia said as she stood, brushing mud off her leathers. "She's Vajra Safahr, lover and heir of the Archmage of the City. If we want justice served, we'd better arrest Renaer and any accomplices before the Blackstaff finds them."

"Gods help us if that happens." Dagrol shuddered. "If he's like his mentor Ashemmon at all, we'll need a lot more gravediggers."

CHAPTER 9

No one ever knew what happened to old Varad Brandarth. Many said he went mad. I knew he was mad before the Spellplague, so it couldn't have been that. I suspect he had one or three hidden safeholds of which only he knew.

Elchor Serison, *Sorcery & Trust*,
Year of the Silent Bell (1435 DR)

10 NIGHTAL, YEAR OF THE AGELESS ONE (1479 DR)

Renaer stepped into darkness. His footsteps echoed loudly. "Kamatar," he said, and fires flared to life in the two hearths on opposite sides of the room.

Vajra stirred in his arms and opened her eyes. Renaer flinched as he saw her eyes waver between the red-black maelstrom orbs and normal eyes of different colored irises. She grimaced, creasing her brow, and her eyes briefly focused into almond-shaped eyes of deep mahogany brown.

"Where am I holding me wait aren't you no a friend carry a vampire's victim?" she said.

Vharem appeared behind them, followed by Laraelra and Meloon. All of them stumbled slightly when they apparated.

Vajra, whose attention shifted quickly to look over the new arrivals. "I don't know . . ." Vajra tapped Renaer on his shoulder and pointed down with her eyes.

"Welcome to Varadras, milady Safahr, everyone," Renaer said, setting her on her feet. Renaer noticed the others looking around the room, but the skies beyond the windows were dark, and snow and ice covered much of their openings. Renaer said, "Palnethar," and torches flared to life on each wall and inside a long hallway leading out of it. Cobwebs covered many surfaces and corners, and the chamber warmed now only due to the presence of the hearthfires.

"Neat trick, Renaer," Vharem said. "You never told us you were studying wizardry."

"Varad taught you don't know where how we'll survive when you are mage?" Vajra said, and while she rambled, she approached and touched Renaer, her fingers glowing with magic. "No he casts not words for any safehouse fine for now don't trust it calm down among friends." Renaer heard her voice change inflections and pitch as she spoke. Her eyes shifted as well, flitting between different colors and shades of gray, brown, green, purple, and a dark blue. Still, she stood steadily, looking around the room and smiling.

"You knew Varad?" Renaer asked.

Vajra's only response was an arched eyebrow and a nod of her head toward Vharem.

Renaer remembered how frustrating it was to talk to wizards who liked their secrets. "She's right, if I understood her correctly," her said. "I'm not a wizard, but I've been studying up on this place and my ancestor who built it three generations ago. He set a lot of magic in place, and most remained stable despite the Spellplague. Mostly, Varadras is just a place to get away. My father has no way of finding me here. The manor house is invisible to those outside of it unless you approach within a certain range."

"So where are we?" Meloon asked. He stood at the nearest window, scraping away some ice and rubbing a window clear. "I only see a lot of trees around us. We're not in Waterdeep?"

"We're about a hundred miles due west of Beliard, the town near the Stone Bridge," Renaer said. While he spoke, he led his friends down the hallway, and more torches lit up as they approached, those in the distant entry chamber snuffing themselves accordingly.

Renaer led them past three doors before he stopped, opened a broad pair of double doors, and said, *"Dornethar."*

Inside that chamber, fires flared to life on three hearths and on six torches set high on the walls. The group entered a carpeted study with shelved books lining the walls. Unlike the other chambers festooned with cobwebs, this room was pristine and cold, though warming quickly. A massive desk of dark wood loomed to the right of the main fireplace, its surface disturbed only by a gleaming ball of dark red crystal and a massive tome lying open.

The five of them rushed toward the hearths opposite or flanking the doors to warm themselves. Vajra, who had followed the group with Laraelra guiding her like a child, rushed over to the right, approached the shelves behind the desk, and pushed in a single tome. Without a sound, the shelves swung inward, revealing a secret passage, and Vajra disappeared into the darkness, chuckling.

"Where does that go, Renaer?" Laraelra asked.

They all moved toward the secret door. Laraelra slammed the set of books she carried on the desk as she passed it, heading into the dark room. She muttered a short series of magical syllables, and her fingernails took on a blue glow as she walked.

"I don't know!" Renaer said. "I didn't even know that was there. It's not mentioned in any of the notes or plans." He repeated the words "palnethar" and "dornethar," but no torches sputtered to life inside the passage.

Laraelra finished casting a spell, and a blue glow filled the room. The small windowless chamber lay revealed as a wine cellar, racks of bottles lining the back and side walls and the left-hand long wall left empty to allow passage without disturbing the bottles. Many racks were empty along the right, but the back wall still held nearly its full complement of bottles.

Vajra stood at the center of the wine cellar holding a bottle of wine and blowing off its mantle of dusty webs. She laughed and said, "Varad kept his best never been here how'd she do never mind we must oh bother let's just drink it no share it not for dining keep clear head." She kept muttering and arguing with herself so that she didn't resist when Vharem eased the bottle out of her grasp.

When he looked at the bottle Vharem's eyebrows rose and he whistled a low unbelieving tone. "Renaer, this single bottle's probably worth a tenday's worth of tavern jaunts! The Surrilan vineyards died out in the drought seventeen summers back—and this bottle's more than eighty years old!"

"So that's good wine, then?" Meloon asked, reaching for another bottle.

"Some of the best," Renaer replied. "Vajra, how did you know this was here?"

The dusky woman smiled, her eyes flitting from purple to gray to blue to sea green. "Varad Brandarth was . . . a good student . . . faithful friend. Stingy with his wine . . ." She reached up for another bottle and wiped the dust and webs off on Laraelra's robes before the sorceress could stop her. She smiled and said, "Pikar Salibuck introduced us. Many secrets shared . . . best was this." She waved an arm around to indicate the room. "Gods, we tried . . ."

As Vajra whirled with her arms outstretched, her eyes rolled into the back of her head, and she collapsed. Laraelra grabbed enough of her sleeve to slow her before her head slammed into the stone floor, and Vharem made a mad dive to catch the falling bottle of wine. Laraelra shot him a look as she tried to settle the unconscious wizard onto the ground.

Vharem shrugged and said, "What? You had her, and we can't have her rolling around on shards of glass or soaking in priceless wine."

Meloon lifted Vajra and headed with the others back to the study. Renaer kept looking around at the contours of the room, nodding to himself, and examining the bookshelf-door and its triggering book.

"Care to explain all that?" Meloon asked as he placed Vajra on a long divan in front of the small hearth on the eastern wall.

"Varad Brandarth and Pikar Salibuck were both wizards of some note decades past," Renaer said. "They had a friend and mentor in common across the years—the Blackstaff, or at least one of them anyway. I think Vajra is possessed or has some memories of the previous Blackstaffs."

"Just realized that?" Laraelra said.

Renaer opened his mouth to respond, and then exhaled loudly and forced his hands to relax at his sides. "We're all on edge with everything that's happened, and we've had no sleep or food. Fellows, let's leave the ladies here while we find some food to go with this wine." Renaer set a bottle down on a side table, and wrestled the other two from Vharem's grip.

Laraelra sighed and said, "You're right. We all need some rest. Then with a brighter day, we can approach this with clear heads. Maybe remember things we're forgetting now. Renaer, I—"

"Offer apologies by watching her?" Renaer said, nodding at Vajra. "Thank you. Stay warm while we go forage some more food."

Meloon grabbed a few furs off the pile he'd dumped in a corner, and gave two to Laraelra and draped another over Vajra.

"Pikar was Madrak's father, by the way." Renaer said, over his shoulder. "When I was a child, I heard loads of stories that are in few histories about the hin sorcerer of Blackstaff Tower. I'll have Madrak share some of them later."

Renaer led Meloon and Vharem out of the room and closed the double-doors. The three men all shivered as they left the warm chamber for the chilly corridor. Renaer led them to the end of the hallway, down a flight of stairs, and into a large kitchen area. Renaer stayed silent, so the hearth fires did not flare up, icy downdrafts alone disturbing the cobwebs at the chimney. Meloon looked out the kitchen windows, only to see the swirl of heavily falling snow. They walked through a large pantry and down another short flight of stairs into a root cellar filled with dried herbs and bushels of potatoes and such.

"Awfully big place, Renaer." Meloon whistled. "Who did you say lived here?"

"Varad Brandarth, my grandfather's uncle. He was a wizard and one of Khelben the Blackstaff's last students. This place he kept secret from most of his family. My mother discovered the hidden portals leading to it almost thirty years ago. Varadras was empty for more than forty years after Varad died until Mother found it."

"And old Dagult doesn't know about this?" Vharem said. "Seems a piece of property he'd love to get his hands on."

"Mother always thought of this as her secret place," Renaer said, "and she shared it with me alone. Apparently, she found Varad's hidden journals by accident her nineteenth winter, and she hid here whenever she needed. Even though she held few secrets from Dagult, she never told him everything about her family or its holdings. He has never heard of this place. Nor will he."

The young lord led them through the root cellar, tossing an empty bushel at Vharem and then launching a dozen potatoes and half as many onions at him to collect in it.

"So your mother was a wizard?" Meloon asked.

"No," Renaer said as he examined a ring of dried apples before setting it back on its hook. "Neither one of us could read his spellbooks, but his journals are mundane and readable. They recorded most of the words that activate magic around the manor. Even you could activate them if you knew the words."

The trio now entered one room with three archways off of it, all stone walls and ground whereas the root cellar had a bare dirt floor. Their breath clouded the air around them, as it was only slightly warmer in here than outside in the blizzard. Renaer opened one jar the size of his head and sniffed. "Hmph. If we take this up with us, the honey should thaw out by the fire. Good stuff too. Varad kept bees here, and his honey was among the few trade goods that supplemented his stipend from the family coffers."

"If all this was here, why did I need to bring food along?" Vharem complained as he examined a few large crocks of pickles.

"The only stuff Madrak and I keep here are things that won't spoil easily," Renaer said. "Unless you wanted to eat only dried meat, honey, and pickled vegetables, what we brought with us should help keep us fed for a day or so until we return to the city."

"Why wait a day?" Meloon asked. "I think Vajra needs some help."

"I think it's something to do with the Blackstaff's power, not her health. We'll have to ask her when she revives."

"Let me guess," Vharem said. "The portal that got us here only works once a day?"

"Close enough," Renaer said. "Besides, Meloon and Vajra are the only ones who've actually gotten any sleep. We need to eat, rest, and then we'll plan our return."

Meloon smiled and said, "Hey, that's a good idea." He reached up and grabbed a large cured ham covered in dusty white mold. "Let's eat this too, then."

Renaer paused as he entered the farthest larder and said, "Wait a moment. Something's been here since I was here a few months back."

"Probably just a rat or three." Vharem snorted. "Not even wizardry can keep those things out if there's food to be had."

"Bigger than a rat, and I don't know of vermin that stack things to reach high cupboards," Renaer said, nodding toward a haphazard column of boxes atop a chair in one corner.

Meloon looked close at the disturbed dust on the floor and said, "Big feet, too."

"Thanks." A dry laugh answered them from the shadows.

The trio launched into action. Meloon whirled, his axe in his hands. Vharem whipped out his newest short sword on loan from Neverember Hall. Renaer flicked a dagger into each hand and yelled the word *"Ronethar!"* In response, the very air in the room took on an amber glow, illuminating every corner and leaving no shadows in which to hide.

Lying atop one of the high cupboards and peering down at them was a young halfling, now grinning. The hin's bushy sideburns were a chestnut brown, like the curly hair on his head, and he dressed in black, which had helped him hide from them in the dark. Silver rings glinted in his left nostril and earlobe. He rolled onto his back and giggled, swinging his feet down off the high cupboard on which he lay.

"Well, if the gods aren't chuckling!" the halfling said between bites of a raw potato. "Hiya, Renaer, Vharem! Whatchaguys doing here? Who's the big blond axeman? Anybody got any tinder to start a fire? I'm freezing."

⟜—W—⟝

The double-doors to the study opened, and a halfling stumbled through them, followed by Renaer, who shoved him forward. Vharem and Meloon, each laden with food, followed.

"Everyone, meet Ellial's son and Madrak's grandson, Osco Salibuck."

Osco recovered from his stumble, cartwheeled across the remainder of the room, and landed easily on a footrest by the fire at the center of the southern wall. The hin gleefully rubbed his hands and buttocks, standing to absorb more warmth from the fire and sighing with pleasure. "Haven't been warm for three days, thank Brandobaris for this," he muttered, and then turned back to the group. "You used to be nicer to me, Ren, when we were the same height," He raised his eyebrows when he noticed Laraelra and Vajra stirring on the divans across the room. He slicked his hair back and jerked his thumb toward Renaer. "We grew up together, you know, and I could tell you stories about him. Why, when he was five—"

"We'd rather hear the story about how you got here," Renaer said, narrowing his eyes.

"Oh, enough about me," Osco said. "What are you doing here?"

"Uh-uh," Vharem said. "This little one's got a talent for avoiding questions—usually because he's filched something or stuck you with his tavern debt."

Osco clutched his hands over his heart and fell on his knees.

"Oh, such barbs from one I called fellow and comrade!"

Vharem rolled his eyes.

"Answer me, Osco, or Madrak'll hear where you've been trespassing without invite."

Osco rolled his eyes and sat down hard. "You're no *fun* anymore, Ren. Just because I found out how you get here doesn't mean I'm going to *take* anything. There's no trust anymore."

Vharem cleared his throat, produced three silver forks, and waved them at Osco, who patted a belt pouch and then scowled at the slender human. He crossed his arms and sulked, muttering, "Just needed a place to lie low for a few days. Figured you'd not be here until spring. Sorry for intruding where I'm not wanted."

"Who're you hiding from, Osco?" Renaer said. "And how did you find out about this place and how to get here?"

"You and Gradam are always plotting," Osco said, "and I just made it a point to follow you around, quietlike. I watched you disappear from the garden and you returned the next day, so I figured, wherever it was, it was a safe place. I got Sharal to pour the water for me and ended up here three days ago. Three miserably uncomfortable days, mind you, as there's no fireboxes of wood around here. How'd you guys get this fire going?"

"Magic," Laraelra said. "I know you, little halfling, or at least I've heard of you. Someone matching your description posed as a cellarer and stole a lot of gems a few tendays ago from a client in Trades Ward. My father's still fighting with the Gralleths over that, and the only thing keeping it out of Lords' Court is the indisputable fact that there are no halflings in the Cellarers and Plumbers' Guild."

"You wound me, Lady Harsard," Osco chided, clasping his hands over his heart. "Besides, it could have been anyone shorter than him, as Malaerigo and Lord Chalras can't tell a halfling from a gnome or a dwarf, let alone identify any hin among hin."

"While that might be true," Laraelra said. "I never said which Gralleth was robbed."

Osco grimaced and then shot a wink and grin up at Meloon. "Women with brains. They'll be our downfall in every way, eh?"

Meloon looked down at the halfling and said, "And so the wagons roll, little friend."

"Enough!" Renaer yelled, and everyone started and looked at him. Vajra stirred a moment on her couch before settling back into unconsciousness. "Osco, you're coming back with us tomorrow when we leave. Stay with us, and maybe we can help you with whatever problem had you hiding out here. If you don't want to come back, good luck, but you're not staying here without someone to watch you."

"But it just got more comfortable," Osco whined. He shot a sly glance at the two women and said, "And it just got far better looking than it's been."

Vharem said, "I vote we just chuck him out in the snow. He'll only draw down more trouble on us."

"Oho! Renaer and Vharem are fleeing from trouble?" Osco's face lit up. "Did you get hired to help them out, big axeman, or are you all conspirators, kidnapping the Tethyrian over there?"

"No!" Meloon said.

Laraelra snickered at his shocked look. She snapped her fingers to get Osco's attention and said, "You're very good at deflecting attention off yourself, aren't you, little hin?"

"Yes, he is," Renaer said, "but I know him well enough to know when he's lying. Osco, help us out when we return to the city, or we'll just let Laraelra turn you over to her father and let the taols fall where they may."

"You'd betray a childhood friend, just like that?" Osco said. "Is that why that overgrown hin Faxhal isn't with you now? You left him to his creditors or something?"

Laraelra and Vharem gasped at the halfling, and Renaer felt like he'd been slammed in the stomach again. While others turned away, he met the halfling's gaze, his eyes watering, and Osco realized something truly bad had happened.

"Faxhal's dead, Osco," Renaer whispered.

Osco cleared his throat and said, "Sorry, Ren. Really."

For a few long moments, the only sounds were the crackle of flames in the fire grates. Then Renaer stood, opened a bottle of wine, and took a long drink. He passed it on, and Vharem, Meloon, Elra, and Osco each drank, then held the bottle toward the fire, silently saluting Faxhal. Osco returned the bottle to Renaer, who drained it. "Sleep, friends, and we'll leave come dawn."

Osco, his voice softer, asked, "Ren, why leave at all? This place is stocked well enough to keep us a while. Some of us can hunt for food too. Can't we hide out here until spring?"

"We must help Vajra. She's been tortured for the past month or more."

Osco's curly eyebrows shot up, he shot a glance toward Vajra, and then shrugged. "She looks fine to me. Must not have been too bad. They torture her with feathers?"

"I've had healers cure her body, but they can't repair her mind. She's the Blackstaff's heir, and there's someone back in Waterdeep posing as Samark the Blackstaff. He and Khondar 'Ten-Rings' Naomal, the Watchful Order's most arrogant guild-senior, are up to something, and they need her secrets."

"Why?" Osco asked. "What could she tell them? And why should we get involved in the Blackstaff's mess? It'll just lead to *us* being tortured—the kind *without* feathers!"

Vajra sat bolt upright on the divan, leveled steel blue eyes at the halfling and said, "You know many secrets that lie beneath black stones, Osco Salibuck. Do these deeds for me, and know the Blackstaff rewards his friends well." Her tone was grave and stern, but then she looked quizzically at Osco and asked, "When did your eye get restored?"

When Osco just looked at her strangely, the blue-eyed wizard stopped speaking, and then she collapsed back onto the couch, unconscious.

Osco looked at her, then Renaer, and the others, and said, "Bet she's fun at parties. I've never met her before in my life, so I don't know how she knew my name. And I've *no* idea what else she was blathering on about."

When Vharem shot him a disbelieving look, he pleaded, *"Honestly!"*

"She does that," Renaer said, "but she rarely speaks as clearly. Normally it's like there's a bunch of folk fighting to talk through her. I think if we take her to Blackstaff Tower, it might help her. At least it'd be a safer place for her to hide."

"So how does that make it our problem?"

"Because they knew we're aware that they're up to something, fool," Vharem said as he sliced off a large hunk of cheese from the wheel he'd brought with him. "Besides, if someone else steals her power as the Blackstaff, they could kill Renaer and all of us far too easily. Not to mention anyone else associated with Renaer, like a certain family of hin servants?"

Osco blanched, his connections to the trouble made clear. "Depending on where we can return to in the city, I can probably keep us all hidden from anyone looking for us. Anyone human, at least."

"How can you do that?" Meloon asked.

"Yes, how do you plan to help us avoid being caught?" Renaer said. "We're not even sure who our pursuers are other than Ten-Rings."

"I'll lead you through the Warrens beneath the city. It'll help me avoid others meself."

"Do the Warrens lead anywhere near Blackstaff Tower?" Renaer asked.

Osco's brow furrowed, and he said, "Not that I know of, but I'm sure we can get close."

"Is that easier than using the streets?" Laraelra asked.

"Easier?" Osco said. "Not for you tall ones. Safer? Yes. The Watch and most humans never had much presence in the Warrens beyond a few token gnome and hin Watch. Mostly because the

Lords're too big and too arrogant to think that things among the small folk are worth noting. That's why there's a lot of things going on down there that make me gradam think I'm up to no good."

"Well, you skulk in the shadows pretty well," Renaer said, "and you always seem to be in trouble or fleeing from one moneylender to the next."

"And that hardly makes me worse than most of the young nobles and nigh-nobles of Sea Ward now, does it?"

"He's got a point," Laraelra chimed in, smirking.

CHAPTER 10

Blessed are those enfolded by the Cloakshadow, for their enemies shall see them not, know them not. Things entrusted to the Illusory remain secret, until the time comes to draw back the cloak and reveal what Baravar held dear.

Ompahr Daergech, *Pantheonica, Volume IV,*
Year of the Guardian (1105 DR)

10 Nightal, Year of the Ageless One (1479 DR)

"Master Ompahr," Roywyn yelled, "we need your help!" She hated trying to talk to the nigh-deaf elderly priest. Even her shouts barely penetrated his awareness.

"You can't have my heart, curse you!" The bald, white-bearded gnome half-sat up against a mound of cushions and pillows at the back of his somewhat sumptuous burrow. His quarters filled the back of the subterranean temple to Baravar Cloakshadow, his honored presence as the elder high-priest of the order apparent from the richness of the trappings about his personal burrow. Ompahr Daergech himself was a frail, wizened gnome who almost disappeared amongst the pillows.

Instead of answering, the young priestess took a helmet off a nearby shelf and handed it to him. It was a curious object—a metal skullcap with two ram's horns mounted over the ears. In opposite fashion from some overdone fighter's helm, the points of the horns went toward the ears and the open ends of the hollowed horns faced outward. The old gnome grudgingly took the helm and grumbled as he put it on. "What are you disturbing my meditations for, granddaughter Ellywyn?" His voice dropped as he realized how loudly he had been speaking.

"I'm Roywyn, Grandsire Ompahr—Ellywyn's granddaughter," she explained in a lower voice, now that he could hear better.

"Well, what do you want, whoever you are?" Ompahr's growl was now more playful. Both she and her ancestor knew each other, but continued the game nonetheless for their own amusement.

"There's someone here bearing your seal—your *green* seal," Roywyn said. Her hands communicated even more to Ompahr that would not be overheard in the tunnels. She knew their guest was wrapped in at least three spells—one illusion, one transmutation, and one divination spell—and that he was impatient and not terribly respectful. His hands also glowed brightly of magic, even though they appeared bare. The child continued talking while her hands flew fast to tell her great-great-great-grandfather all this. "He is a halfling who has come to pay his respects and asks a boon of you." Her final hand-signals elicited much giggling out of the aged gnome, as she explained that if he was truly a halfling, she was a hill giant—after all, he turned down their standard offer of something to eat when he crossed their threshold.

"Send the lad in, then," Ompahr said, "and leave us be." Ompahr's silent hand-signals told Roywyn to stay close but hidden, along with two other priests who could overpower their foe—or at least dispel his active magic and any more he planned to use.

When Roywyn returned, she escorted a male hin. He wore a nondescript cloak and leathers, his hood thrown back, and a pair of short wands tucked into his belt. He bowed, and Omphar looked at him with spell-enhanced sight. He saw who the man was beneath his transformations and illusions—a completely bald man with merged eyebrows and a thin salt-and-pepper goatee and mustache. He noted the ten rings on his fingers—only two of which glowed magically—and saw an additional wand strapped to his inner right forearm. Ompahr didn't know who he faced, but he grinned nonetheless. He hadn't had any fun with strangers in quite some time.

"Greetings, honored Ompahr Daergech," the halfling said as he stood up. "I bring you this—"

"Don't waste my time, boy!" Ompahr roared at him, far louder than he needed for his own hearing. "I'm too blasted old! Show me what you've brought, silly fool of a hin! And give me a name, or I'll call you Puckerpaws and make you match the name!"

The hin coughed once, nervously, and said, "Call me Harthen," and held out his left hand, palm up, to show the gnome priest a rolled scroll closed and impressed with a green wax seal. Written in the old Common trade tongue on the outside of the scroll was, "Take this to Ompahr Daergech or his heirs. They will guide you to your rightful legacy."

Ompahr wiggled his ring finger and the scroll levitated off Harthen's palm. "Hold your palms up to me, Harthen," he said.

Ompahr saw nothing, either on Harthen's palms or on the man's real palms beneath his spells. Well, he didn't find these himself or he'd have the mark on one of his hands, Ompahr thought. I wonder how he found an honest person to do so. The priest wiggled his index finger, and the seal popped off the scroll, the ancient parchment unrolling and brittle edges cracking as it did so.

Ompahr saw an empty scroll for a moment, and he whispered a prayer to his god. "Baravar, draw open the curtains of deceit over this and let me see what secrets we hide from ourselves and others."

Words shimmered into view—words in a strong hand, written in Gnomish. *"Your oath is fulfilled, friend. Give the bearer the right hand passkey, if my marks are on him."* In Ompahr's own hand—written so long ago there was no tremble or waver in his lettering, the scroll read, *"Grant the scroll's bearer the keys of the left hand, if he should come ablustering without the marks to show he passed Khelben's test."*

"So be it," Ompahr whispered. "No marks. No mercy."

"What does it say, wise one?" The halfling asked, lowering his unmarked palms.

Ompahr did not answer for a few breaths, and it amused him

slightly to see his guest get increasingly agitated. While Ompahr loved playing games, he suddenly felt tired as his mind washed over memories of friends long fallen and oaths nigh-forgotten. Finally, he snorted. "Well, at least you're as properly impatient as a hin, I'll give you that. Your disguise is lacking, as is your subterfuge, wizard."

"How did you—" the figure exclaimed, then shook his head. "It matters not. Just tell me what the scroll bids, and I'll be back on the streets above where I belong."

"Unless we choose to cancel your magic." Ompahr leaned forward, his hand aglow with his threat. "You'd hardly be able to cast effectively or move easily, once your full form unfolded in my warren."

"Don't threaten me, gnome," the wizard said. "I've bested every challenger I've ever faced in arcane combat or otherwise. Some newcomers digging beneath my streets don't worry me, no matter their age or god."

Ompahr's smile drew tight and thin, his bushy eyebrows rising. "Supercilious shapeshifter. The Warrens have been here longer than ye know. Some existed long before there were human buildings up above us—well, aside from Hilather's Hold and a few temples. We just knew how to hide them better in days past. Once we told the hin about them, though, they invited everybody down here. Our secrets held for centuries among us and the dwarves, but once you tell a halfling a secret, it's a rumor in a breath and a fact by next highsun."

Ompahr's guest drew back, a confused look on his face.

"Did you think the dwarves and humans were the only ones drawn here to this upland?" the old gnome continued. *"Every* race in Faerûn feels the call of this place, one time or t'other, one road or t'other. Not all roads lead to Waterdeep, but precious few lead to more worthy destinations. Magic—not just a good harbor and defensible highland—drew folk here, till they fulfill their purpose on or under the shadow of the mountain. Me, I have a role to play yet. That's why I'm still here after so long—my oath to that scroll and him what wrote it with me."

Confusion danced across his enemy's face, shifting into anger every other moment. Ompahr delighted in toying with the intruder, and he chose to play his hand out in full now and see whether his foe would reach for the prize given or seek out more.

"The scroll talks of keys. Keys to power. I am bound to give them to the bearer of the scroll—save when that bearer brings false face and false name to me. Tell me a name I can believe, and they will be yours."

"Give me the keys, old fool!" His hands fidgeted and two of his rings glowed.

"Yer spells will avail ye little here, boy of ten hidden rings." Ompahr enjoyed the look of shock on the false halfling's face, but continued, making his voice its most serious in decades. "I've not used my sorcery in three times your lifetime, and I can still shrug off your worst with that and the Cloakshadow's blessings."

"I doubt that you understand my full measure, gnome," the man said. "Call me Ten-Rings, then. You'd not be alone in that."

Ompahr chuckled, then broke into a hoarse coughing. The ancient gnome fell back and turned away on his cushions, a wet phlegmy cough ending his seizure. When he regained his wheezing breath, he looked with one eye back at the man. "Ten-Rings," mused Ompahr. "So a senior of the Watchful Order comes scraping for the Blackstaff's power, does he?"

"You know of me, then?" Ten-Rings asked. "Then you know I work toward the city's good, not my own."

"I hear tell of a wizard whose pride and paranoia has him wearing ten rings to hide his magic and show it off at the same time," Ompahr said. "Some of my kin are among your guild, 'tis true, and they speak of your arrogance and magic."

"I am not proud. I simply acknowledge my own abilities. Unlike many others, I do not hide them."

"Why do you seek the keys, then?"

"The city has no Blackstaff nor heir," Ten-Rings said, "and I would put that burden on myself for the sake of the city."

Ompahr snorted and began a great long belly-deep laugh. When he finished, he wiped tears from his eyes and locked them on Ten-Rings. "You might fool others, but orcs make better lies to my face than you just did. You're after power, plain and simple."

"No!" Ten-Rings said. "Our city fares better beneath the rule of wizards like Ahghairon or Khelben, and I willingly shoulder that burden. I only seek to restore the city to its rightful stature again—with the rule of magic as well as law."

"Khelben never ruled outright," the gnome corrected. "And you hardly compare to Ahghairon either, wizard or no."

"I am mighty in magic and wise in the politics of the city," Ten-Rings said, "and I know I can serve the city better than that coin-pincher Dagult."

"That might be, child," Ompahr said, "but that neither makes you Open Lord nor Ahghairon, and I should know. He and I were students in Silverymoon together. I helped him make the first Lords' Helms."

"Challenge me to a duel of wits or spells. I shall prove my worth!"

"I'm too old and tired for such games," Ompahr said, "and a gnome has to be plenty aged to be saying that, to be sure. I have naught to prove, and you need nothing other than that scroll and your bearing it to me."

"Then why bother with this pretext? Why follow an oath to those over a century dead?"

"Across five centuries, I have been many things, but never oath-breaker," Ompahr said. He gestured, and the entire dais on which his pillows and cushions rested rose. In a recess beneath the platform lay a small chest. Ompahr sighed. "Take what I have held for long years, and remember that you took this burden on yourself."

Ten-Rings held his ground, casting a spell or two, and then said,

"No protections on it, no illusions, no traps. I thought gnomes kept things hidden better than this." He leaned forward and grabbed the chest, pulling it close to his torso.

"Hidden better?" Ompahr said, "You're the *first* to come looking for it since I took the oath with Khelben twenty-three decades ago, so I consider that well-concealed and protected. May you deserve all that that coffer brings you."

Ten-Rings clutched the strongbox tight to his torso, nodded to Ompahr, and said, "We shall talk again, old one, when I am the city's archmage and you can tell me more of our Firstlord and the city as it once was."

"No," Ompahr said. "I doubt I shall survive to see the year out, with my oaths now fulfilled. Should you need my wisdom, commission a copy of my journals from my temple—if you have both the coin and the shelf space for seventeen volumes of lore."

The old gnome's final smirk and dismissive wave sent Ten-Rings out of the temple of Baravar Cloakshadow in the Warrens.

Roywyn returned and said, "Grandsire Ompahr, do you feel ill?"

The old gnome cackled until he was overcome by another fit of coughing. When he regained his breath, he smiled and said, "Child, I feel better than I have since Caladorn's investing as the Open Lord. Ready my litter and the acolytes. There'll be fireworks on the mountain tonight we have to see!"

"How do you know?"

"Khelben the Blackstaff was the only human I ever knew with a sense of humor to best a gnome's. I swore to hide two coffers and give one to him who asked for it and bore his hidden mark on his palm. Since Ten-Rings did not, I gave him the second coffer, but I never knew what either held. By the gods, I'd even forgotten about them entirely until I saw that scroll! Good thing I used the green seal on the scroll; that reminded me to give him the proper reward."

"But why risk going uptop? The way you talked, I'm worried you don't expect to live long!"

"Pish-posh, Roywyn," Ompahr said with a broad grin. "You

think I'd tell *him* the truth? I've got a few more years left in me than teeth, by the gods' blessings. Besides, I may not know all that the Blackstaff had planned, but his pranks were only ever exceeded by Baravar himself!"

In his entire life, Centiv doubted if he'd ever seen Khondar as angry as he was upon his return. Khondar slammed the door and roared, "If I *ever* set foot in the Warrens again in my lifetime, it shall be to *raze them!*"

Centiv hovered over the burden his father set down, only half-listening to the rant. The strongbox's outside was nondescript, a brass chest with iron banding on its edges. He could not detect any magic on the small chest itself, having examined it from every angle and picking it up easily with one hand. Some weight shifted inside but made no noise against the metal. Khondar's tirade proceeded unabated.

"The mongrel races that pollute our city weaken and reduce Waterdeep to a stew of problems. Were we to winnow out all but the most useful of them, we would have no problem restoring prominence and greatness to this city!"

"Father, you're overstating," Centiv said, "and you're losing your focus. Just because some old gnome rattled you doesn't mean—"

"Do *not* accuse me of losing focus!" Khondar raged, grabbing a handful of Centiv's robes. "That gnome laughed at me—despite all I plan to do for—"

"Yes, Father," Centiv said in an oft-repeated litany. "He didn't recognize all you do for us, for the city."

Centiv knew Khondar's temper flared whenever he felt old or belittled. Centiv wondered if Khondar sought the Blackstaff's mantle for the secret of long years, or if it was simply his hatred of Samark. Still, he needed to calm Khondar down and get back to the task at hand. He kept his voice neutral and only fed his father what he wanted to hear.

"Father, you can address those insults later. For now, let's see what that gnome gave you. The work is old and well-done, but I'm no smith. All I can tell you is that there are no spells on the chest itself or its locks. It should open easily and safely. Let's do this, please?"

Khondar's face drained of its red rage, and he exhaled loudly, his shoulders dropping. "Very well. Time enough later to deal with disrespectful dirt-grubbers. Let's see what they kept for our city's archmage."

There was an emblem at the front of the chest and Khondar rotated that sunward until it clicked and the chest's lid popped up. He opened the lid, and inside lay a bundle of red kid leather. Khondar unwrapped it to expose a small garnet-pommeled dagger in a silver sheath set with three more garnets and two large heavy iron keys covered in runes with wolf's heads for their handles.

"Yes," he whispered. "The book you found talked about keys to Blackstaff Tower, worn as amulets rather than wielded, for there are no locks on the tower—just locks in the mind."

Centiv bristled, as Khondar had kept him busy with other errands, collecting spell components and preparations for tonight's work. The elder Naomal had locked up the book, keeping what it said secret from him. He trusted his father not to steer them wrong, but he ached to have that knowledge for himself. Then he could prove his worth to his father and to everyone. "Father," he asked, "of what else did the book talk about? Do we need more magic prepared than those scrolls provide?"

"Of course we will, fool!" Khondar snapped without taking his eyes off the key he rotated in his hands, looking at it from all angles in the late afternoon sun. "We must go back to the Towers of the Order and meditate, then memorize our strongest spells. The scrolls and keys will gain us entry to the tower, but we shall have to win the Blackstaff ourselves."

"But I thought the keys—"

"Khelben Arunsun and his successor Tsarra Chaadren were the last to allow a door on Blackstaff Tower. Since their deaths, none but the Blackstaff, his or her heir, or their chosen guests have entered the tower. Part of that is due to its lacking a door. The keys allow us safe passage through the outermost defenses and make us seem to be heirs to the tower. When used in concert with the scrolls, the keys allow us to unlock other secrets that might normally trap intruders."

"Couldn't we use the Duskstaff we already have? We know we can move that with Ncral's Ring. Having a weapon crafted by the Blackstaff might come in handy."

"Very good, Centiv, and well planned. As it will support your disguise as Samark, I was going to suggest that very thing. After all, we can't teleport inside the curtain wall around the tower, and the book suggested we would need a staff to open the gate. I assume that, should we take it into the tower, we can use it to sense for sympathetic enchantments and track those to the Blackstaff's seat of power."

"So all we need do now is wait for the fall of night and then we breach Blackstaff Tower, to claim its power for ourselves?"

"Yes, my son," Khondar said, looking away from the keys for the first time to focus on Centiv. "And with the power of the Blackstaff and this guild behind us, we should be able to force the Lords into working with us to help restore a more proper order in Waterdeep."

CHAPTER 11

That old wizard could escape a noose simply by making the hangman disbelieve his head were attached to his neck proper-like! Varad Brandarth weren't called the Shifter for naught, though he never snaked out of his debts neither—unlike some magic-workers I might mention . . .

Jorkens of Waterdeep, *Journal VII*,
Year of Silent Shadows (1436 DR)

10 NIGHTAL, YEAR OF THE AGELESS ONE (1479 DR)

I don't want to get too close. Marael said she'd heard that Blackstaff Tower drives folk mad who're not supposed to be there."

"I heard it eats the souls of folk who touch it without protection."

"My mother always said Blackstaff Tower stayed strong because of all the ghosts in it."

"Well, you know that if Blackstaff Tower ever falls, so goes the City, right?"

The whispers and rumors flew fast among the Watchmen posted that morning and afternoon around Blackstaff Tower's walls. For the first time in recent memory, the Watch stood guard over one of Waterdeep's oldest landmarks.

"We've been standing out here all day. Why're we here again?"

"You didn't hear? The old man's foreign consort turned up dead!"

"Are we supposed to watch for anyone skulking around the place? Or just guard it?"

"I dunno. I'm not the civilar! I could go for an eel pie right now."

"Stop talking about food. You're making me hungry!"

"So if the Blackstaff's so powerful and this place is powerful, what're we doing here?"

"Jarlon promised the Watchful Order the favor of guarding this place, and he's ordered us here. That's all I know."

"Since when does the Watch work for the wizards of the Watchful Order?"

"Since Ten-Rings and Jarlon learned to scratch each other's back, that's when."

"Stifle it! Here's comes Jarlon. And look who's with him."

"Rorden or no, he looks like a kid begging for a toy from those old men."

"Better not let him hear you say that."

Jarlon, the Watch rorden, walked up the street, and the young Watch officer motioned the guards to let them through the gates. The cordon parted without a word, allowing him, Samark the Blackstaff, and Khondar "Ten-Rings" Naomal to approach. Samark tipped the Duskstaff forward and touched the gates. A ringing sound resonated through the gates, and the ironwork writhed and twisted, the iron rosebushes and staves shifting out of the way to unlock and open the gates. The ringing stopped, and only the slightest of protesting groans accompanied the sound of the gate's hinges.

Once they passed through the open gates and were inside the curtain wall, both men turned to face the Watch. Samark addressed the guard captain. "Thank you, Rorden Jarlon. We appreciate your men's vigilance. Thank you all for keeping watch over my tower from those who attacked my heir during my absence. Now, you may disperse, as your services are surely needed elsewhere."

The watch commander nodded, then shouted, "Stand down, men! Convene back at the Tharelon Street post!"

The two dozen men and women of the Watch did not linger,

though a few muttered as they fell out of formation. Not a one cast another look back at the forbidding stone wall or tower that they would all swear made them feel colder than the chill winds did.

><—W—<

The two wizards stood stock still until the street around the tower's wall was empty. The gates closed and locked, the ironwork reweaving its tangled rose briars across the bars and lock. Only then did the two men turn and walk to the tower.

Khondar forced himself to breathe deeply, keeping his excitement to himself. He'd dreamed of making Blackstaff Tower his for decades, and his dream was at hand—as was the constant reminder of the one who'd stolen his dream. "It still makes me shudder how well you ape that bastard Samark in tone and voice," Ten-Rings said softly.

"Well it's easier than trying to duplicating some of his spells," Centiv whispered. "Now are you sure we have the proper precautions?"

"I have Krehlan's rings, you have the Duskstaff, and we each have a key," Ten-Rings said, reaching into his cloak and removing a large parcel. "We should be safe from immediate defenses. Once we've breached the tower, we simply have to find the true Blackstaff and claim its power for our own. Do we have appropriate cover?"

"For all anyone knows or perceives," Centiv bragged, "you and the Blackstaff have taken to walking a circuit or two around the tower, talking low between ourselves, since I addressed Rorden Jarlon. Should anyone bother to try and listen in, we are currently discussing rumors and gossip among the Watchful Order. That illusion should give us about half a bell's worth of cover and also cloak our physical presence and voices. It ends with the two of us entering the tower anyway, so we won't be seen in two places at once."

"Good planning, Son," Khondar said, clapping a hand on his shoulder. "Here are two spells you must cast on the walls, while

I work on our protections." He handed him a scroll tube with two scrolls, both slightly heavy from the gem-encrusted sigils and heavy metallic inks. In turn, he opened a tube of his own, withdrawing the first of numerous scrolls. The two wizards intoned the phrases from the scrolls, and wisps of smoke rose from the vellum as the sigils disappeared. While cloaked from outside view, the two wizards' forms and the tower wall before them glistened with magic sparks of a variety of colors. Eventually, the sparkles stopped whirling around them and shimmered into translucent fields of blue-green energy. When that happened, Khondar cast his fourth spell, the scroll consumed itself in white smoke, and the stones and mortar glowed with the same energy—as did the two keys that hung on cords around their necks. He nodded, and the two men stepped forward into the walls of Blackstaff Tower.

Khondar stood just inside the wall he'd just passed through and smiled. He'd expected much of the interior of Blackstaff Tower, and this did not disappoint. Instead of a common stone tower with defensive spells flaring to life, this was special. The walls became lost amid a sea of floating stones and random architecture, from flagstones to arches and statues to doors floating free in a dark night lit from behind, as if they now floated among the Tears of Selûne trailing behind the moon. The only stable feature here was a set of stone steps spiraling up into the night, though no mortar or stones lay between each successive step.

Khondar and the illusory Blackstaff each stood upon a patch of solid flagstone floor, but while they entered within a hand-span of each other, they now stood more than a man's height apart, and Khondar actually had to look up and behind himself to spot Centiv. When he did so, he also saw something coming out of what appeared to be a bright red nebula.

"Son, watch out!"

A blast of red energy slammed into Centiv's back, but his aura held firm and the energy ricocheted off to blast some of the stairwell free. A giant hand made of lightning reached around from behind him and wrapped its crackling fingers around him. While a portion of his protections burned up and the pressure was enough to keep Ten-Rings from using his spells, the aura held. Centiv spat out a spell at the hand, making it fizzle out.

"Thank you," Ten-Rings said, and he returned his attention to his bracers, clasping each with the opposite hand. The gems glowed as he thought about his rings that gave him the ability to move objects from afar and the ability to control the elements. He smiled as the rings blinked into view on his hands, replacing Krehlan's shield rings. Khondar hadn't been sure the transfer would happen inside Blackstaff Tower, but the proper rings gleamed on his index fingers. He used their magic to move his stone platform well away from Centiv and toward one of the few patches of wall still floating near them. Once in motion, he withdrew one more scroll from his sleeve and read it.

Centiv tried to disperse any and all illusions around himself, but he still floated aimlessly in a night sky. All his actions managed to do were to set his platform to spinning him upside-down. Centiv noticed Khondar moved farther from him, and asked, "Father, where are you going?"

Centiv's control over the Duskstaff faltered, and the Duskstaff rocketed off the platform away from him. Centiv tried to grab at the staff, but he did not leap off of his only solid perch. The Duskstaff, free of any control, flew straight through a black tear in space and disappeared. His voice quailed as he shouted, "Father, I've lost the Duskstaff!"

Khondar ignored Centiv and continued reading from the scroll and waving one hand in an involved casting.

Centiv tried to dispell the illusions again. "Father! I can't dispel any of this—they're *not* illusions!"

As both mages wove spells of dispelling frantically into the void, rips appeared in the air around them. Out of the rifts flew a wild snarl of translucent blue imps and a shriek of glowing red gargoyles. The creatures descended upon the two wizards' platforms and attacked their protective magic auras—the gargoyles vomiting fire, the imps spitting ice. Just as the attackers reached Khondar, two silver pulses expanded in the air around him and dissipated like smoke rings. Khondar heard the creatures jabbering but could not understand them.

"The shields are holding!" Centiv yelled. He drew a wand from his belt, blasted a gargoyle with orange missiles. "I thought you said the spells would make the tower accept us! These things are speaking Elvish, saying, 'Neither bears the mark. Neither is an heir true!' What went wrong?"

"Don't you have any stronger spells, boy?" Khondar asked, his aura filled with the white smoke of the consumed scroll he had cast. He waved his hands, and white light shimmered around every imp and gargoyle around him. Many froze in place, and with their wings no longer beating, they fell into the void around him or clattered, paralyzed, on the stone platform where he stood. Khondar smiled—until he saw more opponents flowing out of the void.

Centiv snapped his fingers through a quick spell and he and his stone platform appeared in eight different places, hovering at different angles. As the imps and gargoyles spat and clawed their way past the illusory Blackstaffs, two wands flew down the stairs, leaving trails of silver sparkles in their wakes. Weaving paths through the fray, the wands settled into the hands of Ten-Rings.

"Your mirror images will only delay them so long," Khondar said. "You've always relied too much on the misdirection and tricks of your illusions. Time you learned and used real spells, like a real man!"

"Those illusions helped keep you alive and safe and in power at the Watchful Order!" Centiv shouted, as a translucent gargoyle shattered against the blue shield. "They were good enough when you needed them! At least I've never had to rely on items, like you and your rings! And my lies were only spells, not actual treason to guild or city!"

"Everything I've done has been for Waterdeep!" Khondar said, brandishing the wands. "I'll supplant Dagult and return Waterdeep to the proper rule of proper wizards!"

Khondar waved, and the blue shields that wrapped him unfurled and became a wall that shoved all the confining imps off of him and his stone platform. He gestured with his opposite hand, the sapphire on the ring glowing coldly. The corded key around Centiv's neck drew taught and snapped, and the key flew into Khondar's palm.

Khondar looked at Centiv, smiled coldly, and said, "Prove yourself now. Tame Blackstaff Tower, boy! If you can, we'll rule as Open Lord and Blackstaff. If you cannot, you're no son of mine!"

With that, Khondar wrapped the two wands and the key in his cloak and stepped back through the wall of the tower.

Centiv's shout of "No!" fell upon silent stone.

His anger at his father's betrayal vanished as Centiv realized he was alone. The translucent gargoyles and imps all turned to him and smiled. They became more transparent until all had disappeared. The strange void in which Centiv floated began to shrink as the stones assembled and came together as a chamber. There were still holes in many places, and Centiv himself stood as if the eastern wall were the floor, but it appeared to be a standard chamber.

"Father, *no!* Don't leave me!"

"O-ho, someone's fallen into another web of yours, old man."

The voice took Centiv by surprise, its lilting tone arising very near him but without a person attached to it. A light green fog rolled down the stairwell, and Centiv thought he heard a low growling like a wolfpack on the hunt. A tendril of fog slipped ahead and touched the illusory robes Centiv wore as the Blackstaff.

"That form is not yours, boy," said a harsh whisper.

Centiv recognized it as Samark's voice. The illusion he wore of

Samark's form shattered. Centiv stood with his own form and face in the humble blue robes of a Watchful Order mage.

"Congratulations, little illusion-weaver. You and your sire are the first unwelcomes to darken the doorstep of Blackstaff Tower in more than a score of years." Another deeper voice he didn't recognize. It was a man's voice, spoken from the air before him. As he stared, Centiv saw a face coalesce in the green fog—an angry face clean-shaven save for dark sideburns, and long dark hair that swept past shoulders barely manifesting out of the mist. Other beings partly or fully phased out of the fog, their bodies alternating between translucent fog and seemingly solid features. Within a breath, Centiv found himself being watched by multiple fog-forms.

"We've been bored without playthings," said a lissome half-elf with dark hair and a shock of light green at her temples. She whispered into his ear, wrapping her fog-self around his body and teasing his face with a kiss as cold as the night air outside. "No offense, Sammy, but he's prettier without your face on him. Reminds me of one of the Estelmers from times long gone."

"He's not one of your conquests, Kyri. He's a shapestealer, an intruder, and a traitor to Waterdeep. It simply remains to be decided how he shall be punished." The voice, far away from Centiv, drew his attention to an older woman kneeling on the stairs and drawing a bow on him. He wove a shield in the air before him but hardly expected that to do more than delay things.

"I'm not a traitor!" Centiv shouted, and he turned to follow his father's example by fleeing—only to find all but the patch of floor on which he stood to be less than solid. In every direction he tried to move, the stones either tipped and floated off like loose stones as light as feathers or dissipated as illusions. The tautness in Centiv's stomach wrenched another knot tighter. He leaped for what appeared to be the outside wall—only to collide with the same solid spot on which he was now trapped.

"The pack has been hungry since the Night of the Black Hunt

more than two-score years gone," said the male half-elf, his open robes exposing a lightly haired chest of wiry muscle beset with a multitude of sigil tattoos. "Set them loose on him perhaps?"

"Ashemmon speaks true. The pack is hungry." Centiv started as the first face he saw returned at his shoulder, speaking directly into his ears. "And we know what you visited upon our heir, false one."

"I did nothing!" Centiv howled. "It was Father and Granek!"

"Every Blackstaff and heir is tied to this tower," said the darkest, deepest voice. "What you did to Vajra is inexcusable . . . and inhuman." Samark's face, almost white in anger, wisped before Centiv's eyes. "Your lack of moral courage had you stand by while others did her ill. That brands you villain, Centiv Naomal. If I still had a body, I'd share some of her pain with you."

As Samark spoke, the stones on which Centiv stood rolled up and clamped hard around his feet. He screamed as bones in his feet ground together, and he fell backward, his feet still imprisoned.

"Oh wait," Samark said softly. "I *can* share something."

"We are none of us powerless, limited though we are to the tower," said the deepest voice. "We are merely limited until our heir can rise to the fore and face off our second hapless victim."

"Victim?" Centiv asked, panting hard in panic and in pain as the stones continued to press on his ankles and feet. His leather boots began to rip at the stones' edges and blood appeared there. Centiv swallowed. "My father betrayed me and fled!"

"Some of us are familiar with that," the first voice muttered.

The mists wrapped more thickly around the half-prone man. The tattooed half-elf knelt by his face but did not face Centiv. It spoke toward the voice and said, "Krehlan, you let that anger go a half-century ago. You and Khelben made your peace." He then turned back to Centiv and said, "The incantations your sire used allow you to penetrate the walls of the tower. What they also do is set into motion contingencies laid long ago by Arun's Son and Tsarra Autumnfire."

The bow-wielding shade on the stairs said, "You and your father fell into a trap for those who would abuse the Blackstaff's power. The lens only works truly for the one marked by Sarael's tomb. It was neither you, weaver of lies, nor your sire."

"No, Tsarra," Samark's ghost said. "Whose trust did Khondar betray, Centiv? Who found the lens and the scrolls?"

"Weskur? Marked how?" Centiv's attention ricocheted about the room as all the shades began talking rapidly. "Why him? Why not me?"

A disembodied voice glowered all around him. "What I hid in Sarael's tomb could only be retrieved by one who respected others above the self. And he would be marked invisibly with this." Bright green phosphors laced in the air before Centiv's eyes to create the webwork of lines in Khelben's wizard mark.

"So another is marked as heir," Krehlan said. "Why is he not here with you?"

"It's obvious," Ashemmon said. "They betrayed the heir in their greed. They found what they wanted and ignored the signs. They walked the wrong path. As Ten-Rings cast certain spells on himself alone, those spells now compel him to complete his unwitting new course."

"Whatever his previous motivations, he must seek out keys that will pierce the veils around Ahghairon's Tower." The deepest voice manifested a face larger than all the other phantoms. Centiv recognized it from several statues and paintings. He faced the shade of Khelben Arunsun, the first Blackstaff, and he was angry.

"The secrets there are far more dangerous than those here," Kyriani's shade said. "I'm glad we're left a plaything, myself." The dark-haired half-elf materialized atop the prone Centiv, and the stones beneath him pulled at his robes, ripping them and exposing his chest.

"Do you think there's a chance he might actually succeed and harness some of Ahghairon's magics?" Tsarra's shade said.

Samark's shade shook his head. "They have the books I'd

planned to show Vajra to teach her more about those very fields—Melkar's journal and Alsidda's Tome give him more than enough information on how to penetrate the magic around it, if not Ahghairon's Tower itself."

"Tymora always leaves a chance. He may pierce the initial veils, given the power we sensed in him, though how far only chance knows for certain."

"But entering those fields is a capital offense!" Centiv shouted. "He'll be killed!"

"If the Watch is up to its mettle as in times past," Ashemmon's voice mused, "aye."

"Indeed," whispered the shade of Khelben Arunsun.

With that, all the shades dissipated into mist again, though Khelben's dark eyes remained locked and glaring on Centiv for long moments after the rest of his spectral form was gone. His voice made Centiv shudder to the core of his being.

"There still remains the matter of what to do with you, little illusion-caster. No doubt it shall be uncomfortable at best."

CHAPTER 12

The Spellplague-warped Pellamcopse remains tainted after decades. Its mutated guardian and the denizens of the wood protect their home fiercely, but the Blackstaff tells us the Pellamcopse Haunt, in his own way, protects Waterdeep as well.

Arn Gyrfalcon II, *To Walk Lands Afflicted,*
Year of the Wrathful Vizier (1411 DR)

10 NIGHTAL, YEAR OF THE AGELESS ONE (1479 DR)

Well, I don't know about you, but I'm bored," Osco said after having paced around the warm study a number of times.

"If you'd spent last night fighting an archmage and corrupt Watchmen, then fleeing through the sewers before coming here, you'd be tired too, little man," Meloon mumbled as he lay before the fire.

Osco wandered past the large fighter and bent down to whisper in Vharem's ear. "Hey, V, want to explore this place with me? There's some interesting stuff here—and I'm not talking about the wine cellars, though those *were* a good find."

"I don't steal from friends," Vharem said, opening only one eye. "They know where to find you."

"You used to be more fun, V," Osco said. "There were a few locks I wanted you to help me with."

Renaer sleepily rolled over on his couch and faced Osco. "If it's any of the doors in the tower, I've their only keys—and they're all magically locked besides. There's things up there you shouldn't disturb, Osco. Things I know to leave well enough alone."

Osco sulked as he walked to the table and buried his frustrations beneath a flurry of eating, consuming what remained of the large ham and the bread. In between bites, he mumbled, "Just because I wasn't up all night doesn't make lying around all day dull as dwarves."

Vajra, who had remained unconscious most of the day, rose slowly from the divan and said, "The hin speaks true. We must get to Blackstaff Tower. It has chosen a potential heir. I need to become Blackstaff before that path—and my mind—dissolves. I have need of Varad's books and counsel." With that, Vajra vanished.

The only sounds in the room were the crackles of fire and the snorting chuckles of a halfling with his mouth full. The others staggered up from dozing as Osco said, "Guess someone's disturbing things anyway, chief—and I doubt she's gone to the kitchens." With that, he dashed out of the room and cut left down the corridor.

Vharem asked, "Where'd she go?"

Renaer threw off his furs with a growl. "Varad's books are either here or in the tower!"

By the time the whole quartet roused themselves from beneath their furs, Osco's movement had lit up all the torches back down to the entry chamber. Renaer snapped "Stlaern!" as he pushed past a tapestry and through an open doorway mostly blocked by the wall-hanging. Vharem, Meloon, and Laraelra followed him into the stairwell that led up into a high tower. A blizzard howled outside the slim arrow-slit windows. Ice and snow pelted the tower.

They ignored the smaller landings and doors as they raced past two upper levels and found Osco at the third landing, waiting for them in front of a door.

"Well," Osco said. "Saer, 'I've got the *only* key to the tower rooms,' I can hear her rummaging around in there."

Renaer scowled at him and reached into his belt pouch to withdraw a silver key. Osco's eyes widened, as the key was a true work of art. Pure silver with some light runes around the bow end of it, the key's tines were table- and trap-cut emeralds of various sizes.

"Weird key," Osco muttered. "No wonder I couldn't pick the lock."

Renaer unlocked the door and opened it. The five of them entered a chamber that seemed larger than the tower in which it was housed. Renaer noted it was devoid of cobwebs and cold, unlike the lower rooms, and very orderly. Not a single book lay out on any of the three tables, nor were any stuffed haphazardly atop a shelf. The only things on the tables were rows of wooden rods, ivory wands, and other components laid out as if someone were planning to craft something.

In the center of the circular room lay a rune-inscribed circle painted in a variety of colors, twelve different runes in each of three successive circles. At the center of the circles, the floor was painted black. Stars glinted inside that void, and Vajra levitated cross-legged above it with a massive spellbook in her lap. She nodded at the group's entrance.

"How did you get up here, Vajra?" Renaer said. "Varad's tomes said none could enter this chamber without his key."

"I've been here before, youngling," she said, her voice and demeanor far older than she seemed. "The Shifter held few secrets the Blackstaff did not share. Now hush." Silence muffled the room. The only sounds heard now were Vajra's mutterings and the sound of her turning the vellum pages of the spellbook. After a short time, all but Laraelra withdrew from the room to sit on the steps outside the room.

"—really hate wizards, aye." Osco's voice returned as he stepped out of the room. "Was she this much fun to be around earlier too?"

"I liked her more when she needed to be carried," Vharem muttered.

"Could be worse," Meloon said. "If she's getting her head together, that means we might have a fighting chance against Ten-Rings and his fake Blackstaff. I say we keep helping her, and she'll be able to help us."

"I certainly hope so," Renaer said. "If she knows so much about Varadras, she probably knows how to use the portals. I just hope she doesn't use them alone and leave us stranded here another day."

"So where would we end up if we used them?" Osco asked.

Renaer sighed, thinking a moment. "The portal from my garden only leads here—to the receiving hall. There's three command words that take anyone standing on the mosaic back to Neverember Manor, Ordalth House, or a stone circle in the middle of the Pellamcopse north of the city. If the mosaic is used, it can't be used again for at least half a day until its magic restores itself."

"The Pellamcorpse?" Osco blurted. "Why would anyone visit that monster-infested place?"

"It wasn't always as it is now. In Varad's day and before, it was a pleasant little woods good for hunting game within a short walk from the Northgate. The Spellplague corrupted it. I've only read about that link, never used it. Varad's book talks about the arrival point being a place of worship older than the earliest settlements of Waterdeep. I think he tapped into older magic there to make this portal network of his stable."

"Um, are we supposed to know what and where Ordalth House is?" Meloon asked.

"It's a marble four-story grandhouse in Castle Ward, close to Diloontier's & Sons Apothecary."

"You forget," Vharem said, "not all of us study history, the names of buildings, or wander every street and alley in the city."

Renaer smiled and nodded. "Fair enough. We'll go to Ordalth House and Osco can get us into the Warrens from there. Then we'll get as close as we can to Blackstaff Tower without being detected and hope the gods are with us as we dash to the tower. I hope Vajra's presence will get us through its gates."

"Lots of hopes in that plan," Osco said. "Trust in us, not the gods, Ren. We can be counted on more often."

"Tymora'll help us," Meloon said.

"You rely on luck a lot, big guy?" Osco asked.

"I'm still striding," Meloon replied with a wink.

"Well," Vharem interrupted, "I hope that luck's with us, as milady wizard and our friendly sewer-sorceress are done with whatever they were doing in there."

The door thundered and all four heard both women cry out. Meloon shoved the door open and Renaer stepped to the side, his daggers at the ready. Inside the room, a column of green energy roared, Vajra hovering at its center. Lightning crackled off of her, and she spasmed with each pulse leaving her hands or feet. The magic circles above which she hovered absorbed some of the magic, but random bolts arced across the room.

Osco yelled, "Down!" and shoved at Vharem's knees, knocking him out of the path of a blast heading out the door. The halfling looked at Vajra, then yelled to Vharem, "I agree with you—I liked her better unconscious too!"

From behind the open door, Laraelra said, "Just before this started, she dropped that wizard's tome, her eyes went all black, and green lightning crackled all over her. Then she said, 'Chartham, ye stand as traitor,' and slammed me into the door. I can't stop her!"

"Chartham?" Renaer asked.

Vajra's head snapped toward him. Her gray eyes widened and she spoke, her voice deeper than usual, "Slay my heir, would you?" She raised a hand, and Renaer dived behind the table to his right as lightning exploded where he had stood.

"Blackstaff!" Renaer yelled. "You're dead, Krehlan! Let Vajra go!"

The energy in the room dimmed, but Vajra remained focused on Renaer. "Dead? Let who go?" She stared at him, then down at her own outstretched hand, and finally down at her body. "But—oh, we're not in the tower. In an unreadied heir . . ."

With a snap of her fingers, the lightning storm ceased, and Vajra settled down on the ground. Her head kept twitching left and right, and Renaer saw her eyes shimmering in many colors.

Her eyes widened as she saw Meloon helping Laraelra up with one hand, his other holding his axe. As Renaer approached her, she nodded, murmuring something he didn't catch.

"What did you do, Ren?" Vharem asked.

"Chartham Dellenvol killed Krehlan Arunsun, the Blackstaff, over fifty years ago," Renaer explained. "When Vajra said his name, I guessed she might be possessed by Krehlan's spirit. He was the one who was Varad's friend too. All I could do was make him notice he wasn't in the past and hope that'd do something. Guess it did."

"And here I thought reading all those books would never help," Osco said.

Vajra balled her fists and closed her eyes a moment. When she looked up at Renaer, her deep brown eyes stayed focused and alert. "Thank you," she said. "Can we get to Blackstaff Tower soon? The power is . . . unstable. I need to claim it before it claims me . . . or another usurps it . . . and with it, the city. And my life."

"Very well," Renaer said. "Let's go."

Renaer led everyone out of the chamber and down the stairs. As they descended, Renaer said, "We can use the entry hall to teleport directly to another house I have closer to Blackstaff Tower—one the Watch may not know I own. From there . . ."

Osco nodded and said, "We'll improvise."

They entered the receiving chamber, and Renaer said, "Everyone stand on the carpet at the room's center—where we arrived—and hold onto each other. Do we have what we'll need?"

When the others nodded in agreement, Renaer stepped onto the carpet with them. He opened his mouth to speak the command, but Vajra's hand shot out to hit him in the chest. Her eyes were black storms afire with green energy, and she yelled, *"Uarlaenpellam!"*

Renaer shouted, *"No!"* as the six of them vanished—

—and reappeared in ankle-deep snow and a wailing wind. The sky was open overhead, though dark and frigid, and they saw they stood at the center of a stone circle, its ancient arches holding back the thick, dark forest that surrounded it.

"Quality place, Renaer," Vharem said. "Very top coin, this. Roof needs work, though."

"Nice, Ren." Osco snorted. "The one place we don't want to go—"

"I didn't do it—she did!" Renaer grabbed Vajra by the shoulders, hoping for an answer.

She smiled, looking past Renaer at Meloon, and said, "Find something that's been safe here—an ally for today and in times yet to pass. Find your fate." She pointed at the stones to the east, and fired five amber missiles from her fingertips. One lanced through a stone arch, disappearing but leaving a wake of sparks, while the others splashed onto the stones and lit the entire circle with a yellow glow that pulsed upward as a pillar of light. With that, her eyes rolled up into her head again and she fell into Renaer's arms.

"So much for help from the mighty wizard," Vharem said, "or for avoiding notice."

"You know," Osco said, "if all it took was so much fainting, my Aunt Delalar could be considered a wizard."

"What'd she mean?" Meloon asked. He took Vajra from Renaer's arms and hefted her almost effortlessly into his own. "Where's this ally she mentioned?"

"Out there. The quicker we find him, the sooner we can head back to the city." Renaer stomped angrily through the archway and into the forest in the direction of Vajra's missile. The trail was easily followed as the orange sparkles it left behind still hung in the night air.

It was not yet midnight, but the night was icy. The blizzard and its cloud cover at Varadras had not yet drifted south to this area. Selûne and her Tears sent moonlight filtering through bare branches bedraggled by glowing mosses. Lichens and mosses glowed underfoot. The spongy deadfall and undergrowth crunched and crackled as the friends' steps cracked the frost and snow.

"Where are we?" asked Meloon. "I don't recognize the trees or the scent of this place."

"The stars look right for the Sword Coast," Vharem said, "but I can't see much beyond the trees."

"It's odd," Laraelra said. "All the magic around here seems tied up in knots instead of flowing. See?" She pointed ahead and the orange sparkles whirled around like angry gnats and then splashed into a large tree, which quivered in response.

"This place is as far from a normal forest as Undermountain is to a cellar," Osco said. "They say it's a haunted place filled with dead wizards, spell-warped animals, and worse. No one goes through the Pellamcorpse unscathed. The only good thing is that no undead walk here."

"Osco, would you be quiet?" Vharem said

"Would you all be quiet?" Renaer snapped. "Or do you want to attract more attention than Vajra's magic already has?"

"I'd say that's a moot point," Laraelra whispered, pointing down the vine-choked trail toward a clearing, where a shadowed figure blocked their path.

Tall and wide-shouldered, the cloaked figure hunched over on one knee in the center of the clearing. In the moonlight, they could see clouds of its breath curling from beneath its hood. The figure lifted its hooded head, and the moonlight caught a bright patch of white hair on the darkly bearded chin. Little else was visible beneath that hood.

"Khelben?" Renaer whispered. "But he's been dead for more than—"

"Is this the ally we were supposed to find?" Meloon asked. "Doesn't look too friendly."

A snarl cut him off, and the figure leaped straight up, clearing the height of the trees, and his arms threw the cloak wide. Huge black wings threw it off and a massive cat-headed man with raven black wings flew around the clearing. Various white sigils stood out on its torso and arms as if tattooed or bleached into its black body pelt. A long tail lashed behind the figure, its movements swift and angry.

"Oh stlaern," Osco whispered. "The Nameless Haunt!" He looked around for shadows in which to hide, and quickly slipped behind Meloon, who was handing Vajra over to Vharem with one arm while unbuckling his axe.

Laraelra whispered, "I never expected . . . he's beautiful."

Vharem said, "Yeah, like a knife's edge—and far more dangerous!"

While his voice should not have carried across the distance, everyone heard the creature equally well when it spoke. "Intruders," he snarled, "have you come to steal our power?"

The cat-man's hands gestured, and his claws and pinfeathers glowed green. The forest shifted around them, trees sliding backward with groaning, clattering branches. The six heroes found themselves standing in a clearing with the creature diving toward them. He smiled, and his fangs gleamed in the moonlight. The cat-man broke out of his dive and landed in a crouch nearby. "Good," he said. "We've been bored."

"Forgive our trespass," Renaer said. "We come as friends. We mean you no harm."

The Haunt laughed. "You couldn't harm us if you tried, boy. But since you've come as friends, I'll be polite and warn you." His claws wove a spell, and suddenly there were seven identical images of the Nameless Haunt standing in a semicircle, spreading around them. All of them smiled their fanged grins, and said in unison, "Run." With that, the figures leaped toward the group.

Laraelra stood her ground, launching two quicksilver bolts at the images. An illusory Nameless Haunt dissipated under the assault, and the other roared as the silver colored missile slammed into his wide feline snout.

Meloon ran forward, leaped into the air, and swung his axe with a roar. The blades passed cleanly through two more images, popping them like soap bubbles. Meloon landed and rolled along the ground, coming back up in a crouch behind the creature, his axe at the ready.

Vharem carried Vajra back to the trees as quickly as he could, preceded only by Osco running full out. Renaer held up a long sword and backed away, trying to provide cover for them to get their vulnerable friend away from danger.

The claws of the four remaining Nameless Haunts all glowed silver-blue. They raised their arms and wings in unison, and then snapped all sixteen limbs straight out. Shadowy webs shot out of eight pairs of wings and claws to entangle Osco, Meloon, Vharem, and Laraelra.

Meloon whirled with his axe and stumbled out of the dark patch. He encountered no resistance. "Hey! It's nothing!"

Laraelra stepped to one side, her hands cupped together. She finished her spell and unleashed a dazzling display of colored lights over the cat-man and his shadow web. Her magic wiped those images away.

Osco jogged forward, a slight whistling at his side, and whipped his sling upward. The stone bullet easily pierced the head of his feline attacker, and the mirage dissolved.

Renaer stepped forward to help Vharem and Vajra, but yelled, "Hey!" as he found the shadow webs solid, unlike the others. The dark cocoon containing Vharem and Vajra quivered and large batlike wings unfurled from its surface and flapped the cocoon skyward. The sole remaining Haunt flapped its wings and hovered over the clearing, chilling everyone with the cold downdraft of his huge wings. While the dark cocoon flapped off to the east, the Nameless Haunt looped high skyward and then dived toward Laraelra.

Quicksilver bolts flashed from her fingers and streaked straight for his wings, stunning him and turning his glide into a tumble. Laraelra turned and ran, but the Haunt rolled out of his fall and pursued, loping along on his arms and legs like a cat. She reached the trees just ahead of the Haunt, who shoved her into a large tree.

Laraelra vanished.

"No!" Renaer and Meloon yelled, and they broke into a run, brandishing sword and axe.

The Nameless Haunt turned toward the roaring warriors. He gestured, a slight glow of magic on his claws, and a large pit groaned open in their path. Renaer, unable to check his speed, fell in. Meloon leaped, swinging his axe, and landed on the far edge of the pit. He sank his axe into the frozen turf, his weapon holding him up at the edge of the pit. "Climb up me, Ren!" he yelled, but Renaer lay stunned at the bottom of the pit. Meloon shifted around, using his free hand to grab at frozen grass and turf at the edge to pull himself out.

The area went dark around Meloon as the Nameless Haunt glided down to crouch over where Meloon scrambled out of the pit. The cat-man sniffed, growled low, and extended one claw at Meloon's axe. His touch turned the axe's wooden haft to dust, and Meloon yelled as he fell backward into the pit.

Sniffing and growling, the Nameless Haunt looked down into the pit. He called down to the men. "Nameless shall take wizards to talk. You and your friends stay here."

His head twitched to one side, as if he caught a scent, and he lashed his wings back, slamming Osco Salibuck on both chest and back, driving the wind out of him. The Nameless Haunt stepped over to the gasping halfling and picked him up by his cloak and collar, sniffing at him more intently. Osco struggled for breath, made even harder as his cloak pulled taut, pressing the clasp against his windpipe. The cat-man's yellow eyes widened, and he smiled.

Osco winced. "Stop! Don't eat—"

"HappylittlemanPikar! Nameless joyous!" The cat-man pulled the halfling into an embrace and licked his face, then pulled back with a growl. "You are not Pikar, though your scents are similar. Who are you?"

Osco, finally breathing normally, struggled against the creature's greater strength, and said, "Pikar? You've got me confused, saer. I'm Osco Salibuck."

"Osco did not have this." Osco shuddered as the cat-man's claw popped out in front of the halfling's left eye. "He also had a beard and stank of bad pipeweed."

"Sounds like me great-gradam. Hey—you knew him? And Pikar *was* me great-gradam! Say, how old are ye?"

The Nameless Haunt cocked his head, considering Osco's words, and the lightly furred face held a quizzical look. "You are a friend of the Blackstaff?"

"Aye!" Osco nodded, still squirming to break the creature's grip. "At least until you made off with her! Where'd you take her?"

"Home." He carried Osco over to the pit's edge, holding him over the edge as he looked down on the two men. "You are friends with the Blackstaff, too?"

Meloon nodded. He seemed awkward and insecure without his axe.

Renaer rubbed the back of his head and said, "Yes, and if you've—"

The Haunt gestured, and the pit filled up from below, raising the two humans back up to stand even with him. Renaer still held his sword, but he dropped it when the Haunt tossed Osco at him. The cat-man held up his hands and said, "Peace, then. We too are friends of the Blackstaff. We shall go to my home. We carry you, yes?"

"I can walk on my own," Meloon huffed.

The Nameless chuckled, shaking his head. "You cannot reach our home by walking. You need wings."

"Do you vow on the Blackstaff not to harm us? Or those you captured?" Renaer asked.

"Aye. All are safe. We go now."

The Nameless Haunt spread his arms, but Meloon shook his head. "I'm not going with that thing. Not flying."

The cat-man seemed puzzled as he looked to Renaer, Osco, and then back at the cross-armed Meloon.

"Meloon, come," Renaer said. "We know we can't fight him, and he's offered us hospitality. Let's go."

"You go. I'll follow on foot." Meloon picked up Renaer's sword and looked at the cat-man. "Which way do I need to go?"

One claw extended to the northeast. Meloon nodded, then turned and started walking that way. The Nameless Haunt launched a quick spell at his back, which froze Meloon in midstride. He swept his left arm back to hold Renaer back, and said, "He is scared to fly, we think. We go now. Easier. Come."

The cat-man wrapped his left arm around Renaer's shoulders, and Renaer threw his right arm around the Haunt's massive shoulders, above the joints where his wings sprouted from his back. The Haunt shrugged Renaer off the ground and walked to collect the frozen Meloon, wrapping his right arm around Meloon's waist and carrying the paralyzed warrior like he would a large log. He then flapped his wings and took to the air.

Renaer had only ever been this high in the air with a solid tower beneath his feet, and his stomach warred with him as he saw the ground drop away. He gulped and breathed deeply, and the cat-man snorted. "It's easier to not look down. Look up, groundling. Look up."

The Nameless Haunt flew high into the air, and Renaer looked up. The clouds had parted and he could see Selûne brighter and closer than ever before. The Haunt swooped up and over, and Renaer let out a slight gasp of surprise that became a deep laugh as they rushed to the ground. "I never knew flying felt so free! So alive!"

"Hey!" Osco yelled. "What about me?"

The Nameless Haunt snatched Osco by the shoulders with his foot claws. After a moment of wailing and howling, Osco started laughing.

Renaer called down to him, "What's so funny, Osco?"

"You ever have such a view, Ren?"

"Never."

Renaer's worries about the others faded as he focused on the experience of flying. The Nameless Haunt's strange combination of feathers and fur and strong scent mattered little, though Renaer was glad the creature's hard muscles held them aloft rather than fought them. He looked down and around and smiled. Osco was right—to see the world from on high was breathtaking. The moonlit trees were silver and white, and they flew high enough that Renaer could make out the entire southern half of the Pellamcopse. They passed over a small clearing, and Renaer saw a six-legged bear with a white mane leap upon what looked like a deer with two heads. Nearby, a tall collection of conifers stood out above the bare deciduous treetops, though their needles were a blazing red and glowing slightly in the moonlight.

"Amazing," Renaer whispered.

The Nameless Haunt purred. "There's more to see when it's not winter."

As they swooped around the red pines, three tentacles lashed out of the treetops toward them. Renaer saw numerous fanged maws dotting the wide flat limb and he tried to free his sword. The Nameless Haunt growled out a spell, and brilliant light shone down from his eyes. The tentacles snapped out of sight beneath the tree cover. The Nameless said, "The buarala hunger, but they shun light. Much more dangerous beneath the trees."

The quartet flew in silence after that, and Renaer kept his eyes open despite the wind and cold. He loved the sensation of flight and enjoyed the expanded view all around. He could see the Crown of the North far off to his right, and a few fires dotted the night to the south and the east of them and the forest.

"Travelers bringing goods to Waterdeep before winter?" he said.

"Fools should hurry," the Haunt replied. "We scent blizzard coming fast. Two suns or less."

"Speaking of fast, are we there yet?" Osco asked. "It's chilly down here!"

The cat-man looped lower and down to the right. " 'Tis a short flight yet. The forest pulled me far to answer the call."

Renaer asked, "So the Pellamcopse's magic drew you to us? Or was it Vajra's spell?"

"No spell. The Pellamcopse asks us to go to any magical intruder—and helps us do so. Vajra is the one marked by Blackstaff?"

Renaer nodded.

Osco's questions came quickly through his chattering teeth. "Why do you look the way you do? Did a Blackstaff do this to you? Did Khelben curse you to haunt this place?"

The cat-man's growl-like chuckle vibrated against Renaer's side. "Khelben was a friend—and more. The Spellplague made us. We had to become as we are to save our love. We protected Blackstaff so she could guard Waterdeep."

Renaer noticed the cat-man's eyes tearing as he talked, but he cleared his throat with a rumbling growl and then focused on their flight, not saying a word.

For the rest of the flight, the only sounds were the flapping of the creature's wings and Osco's incessant chatter.

". . . big baby—scared of heights. He'll be sorry he missed this view! Hey! Ren, did you see those green owls down there? And those perytons? This forest has some of the nastiest critters alive down there."

>===w===<

They arrived at the Haunt's treetop lair with the stars still bright. The cat-man spread his wings wide, and they came to a soft landing on a balcony formed from three parallel tree limbs. The lair looked like what Renaer had read about elven tree settlements—platforms and rooms shaped out of or into massive trees. The only difference was that Renaer couldn't see any stairs or ways to reach this height without flying. Renaer guessed they were higher than even a five-story building in North Ward.

The Nameless Haunt ushered them into a large chamber, and Renaer gasped at the warmth in what appeared an open-air room. The cat-man set Meloon properly on his feet and relinquished the spell on him.

Meloon said, "Well, which—Hey!" The blond warrior reached back for his weapon, only to find it missing, and he looked around in confusion and anger, scratching his head about how he arrived here.

"We are sorry to enspell you," the Nameless Haunt said to Meloon. "We only wanted to reunite friends more quickly." He motioned to the rear of the chamber, where Vharem, Laraelra, and Vajra sat or lay inside cells within the massive tree trunk, the bars thick thorn-laden branches. The cat-man gestured and the bars all spread wide, allowing them to exit their cells. While Vharem and Laraelra got out quickly, Vajra remained unconscious.

Osco cackled happily and asked, "What happened to you guys?"

"That cocoon dumped me here in this cell along with Vajra," Vharem said. "The place is warm and there was food—but it's still prison!"

"For your own protection." The Nameless flexed his claws, cocked an eyebrow, and asked, "You wish to fight us, boy?"

Vharem fumed, but Renaer intervened. "No, we don't. We just didn't know what you wanted with us, why you attacked us, or why you abducted our friends."

"Wizards more apt to talk than warriors," the Nameless explained. "We only take warrior because he carried her." He pointed at Vajra. "She sick? Nameless know Samark healthy. Did someone kill Blackstaff?"

Renaer nodded.

The cat-man's face glowered, and Renaer suddenly understood the tales of how fearsome Khelben's glare could be, especially now when mixed into leonine features. The cat-man returned to stroking Vajra's hair and face, whispering to her. "She has not been to tower? She needs help to understand her power." He uttered a few quick syllables and his palms glowed as he stroked her head.

Vajra's eyes snapped open, black orbs with storms of green energy. The Haunt shushed her like he would a baby, and continued to stroke her head. Crackles of lightning surged from her eyes, then died down to normal hazel-colored eyes rimmed with tears. "Raegar . . ."

"Tsarra love mistress wife . . . we are glad to see your eyes again." He purred in return.

"It hurts to see you this way, Raegar. What you and Nameless did . . ."

"Had to be done. Now why do you haunt this lass? You belong in tower, as we belong here."

Vajra sat up and looked around. "We're in the Pellamcopse?" When the cat-man nodded, she said, "Vajra wasn't readied. The power transfer happened outside the tower. Someone killed Samark. Why are we here though?"

The woman's eyes clouded to black again, then shifted to cobalt blue eyes. Vajra sat up straighter, her shoulders squared, and raised an eyebrow as she stared around the room. The cat-man bristled slightly, his wing feathers ruffling.

"I brought us here," she said. "Nameless, you've guarded something well for some time, but it needs to return to the city."

"As do you, Khelben. Spirits hurt Vajra."

"I realize the dangers more than you, familiar friend. Let us attend to our task and we'll visit again when we have more time." Vajra's stern voice whispered something only the Haunt could hear, and he nodded.

The cat-man and Vajra both cast the same spell with their left hands, their right hands remaining tightly grasped together. Their magic opened one wall of the room, revealing a small chamber.

"You four men need to see who she'll allow to wield her," Vajra said. "Her time for sleep is over."

"So what befalls here?" Laraelra asked, stepping up and blocking the opening. "Why not me?"

"You shall wield something far greater, girl, should you prove patient enough."

Vharem, Osco, Renaer, and Meloon entered the small chamber, finding it close and small for all of them. At the center of the room was a tree stump, and embedded in it was a beautiful silver axe with a rune-carved double-bladed head, its haft wrapped in blue dragonskin and a star sapphire winked at the pommel's end. The exposed edges of the blades all glowed with a shimmering blue radiance, lighting the chamber.

Renaer stepped forward, whispering, "Azuredge." When he grasped the axe's handle, he pulled hard once, twice, and gave up after the third tug didn't release it. Renaer was crestfallen as he stepped back and let Vharem try. "This axe is legendary. Its wielder is always a great defender of Waterdeep. Ahghairon the first Open Lord himself made this as a tribute to the Warlord Lauroun more than four and a half centuries ago."

"Well, it's useless if none of us can pull the thing free from this stump," Vharem said. "Why do wizards always muck up good weapons by sticking them in things that need a prophecy or destiny or something to get it free?" The slender man grabbed the axe's haft, but rather than pulling, he held it and his eyes wandered and his face lost its color. After a moment, he let go, as if the axe were painful.

"What happened?" Renaer asked.

His long-time friend looked at him, opened his mouth, and then closed it, shaking his head. "Not for me," he whispered. "Told me so."

Meloon, who had been awestruck when he entered, stepped up, but Osco leaped up onto the stump to straddle the axe's handle and pull on it as hard as he could. His efforts were useless, other than to make Vharem chuckle and Renaer and Meloon smile. The halfling opened his eyes after another strained attempt, and shrugged.

"Had to try, didn't I? I get the feeling this thing's meant for the big guy."

"That thing probably weighs as much as you do, Osco." Renaer said. "If you'd drawn it, how could you have used it?"

"Fetch a fair price for the gems, the silver, the dragonskin," Osco ticked off items on his fingers to Renaer's gut-wrenching horror, and then giggled when he saw Renaer's face. He winked at Vharem and said, "I'm not sure. Has he always been *this* easy to tease?" Osco hopped off and clapped Meloon on the calf as he walked out of the room. "Go to it, big man."

Meloon reached over and grabbed the haft of the axe. Blue flames flared around the axe and the warrior. Renaer and the others flinched back, but Meloon stayed transfixed and seemed unharmed by the blue fire.

A bitter wind whistled around Meloon, who found he stood alone on a wooded plateau, seedling trees and shrubs slapping his knees in the wind. He whirled around to the familiar sight of Mount Waterdeep. But all else was strange. No city, no roads crossed the plain where he stood, and the mountain lay bare and untouched by any hand but nature's.

He stood near a crossroads, and he turned toward a rider's approach. Astride a stallion was a woman clad in chain mail, her face framed by the metal garb and a few stray red locks. She stared down at Meloon, her cerulean eyes freezing him in place. She broke eye contact first and stared east, down the lone dirt path. She looked again at Meloon, then directed her eyes west, down toward the deepwater harbor. Meloon could see a log palisade on the mountain spur where Castle Waterdeep would be, and he could see the Spires of Morning, recognizable as the great temple to Amaunator, even though it was still being built.

Meloon asked, "Am I fallen into yesterday? Is this Waterdeep in the past?"

"Will you fight?" the blue-eyed warrior asked.

Meloon nodded. "If the cause is just."

"Or the pay is right?" She cocked an eyebrow at the sellsword's common phrase.

Meloon shook his head. "Take only honest pay from honest folk, or you repay coin with guilt."

The woman smiled, then tossed a double-bladed axe to him. "If the Black Claws descend upon us, how do we protect the city?" She stared to the east, a cloud of dust rising beyond the trees.

Meloon looked east, then west toward the temple and further down the plateau at what he knew as Dock Ward and she knew as the city. He saw the limited trails, the heavier forest to the northwest, and the cliffs to the east.

"The walls protect the docks and the southern city?" Meloon asked. She nodded, and Meloon pointed with the axe at the trees along the trail. "I'd use my axe to fell the trees and block the trail. That forces any attackers into smaller units among the trees or around the whole plateau to attack along the roads to the south. Either way buys you more time for more defenses—or more ways to pick off the enemies. If you have to, set fire to the undergrowth—the smoke will slow them further, and it shouldn't harm the trees much."

The woman smiled and brought her shield up—a serpentine dragon wrapping vertically around a sword resting point down on a green field.

Meloon's eyes went wide, and he said, "Did you copy that from my memory?"

The woman's face became unreadable, as she shook her head. "This is my family's crest. Why?"

Meloon pulled his shirt open to reveal the same emblem—the dragon over the sword—tattooed over his heart and beneath a hairy chest. "It's my family's mark of old. The Wardragons of Loudwater. I was told many Wardragons originally settled Waterdeep, but I'd found none in two years in the city."

The woman dismounted and grasped Meloon by the shoulders. "You found me. You are not only worthy, you are kin. Know me as Lauroun, once-warlord of this place. Now, together, we can both be her defenders." She grasped his hand around the axe and brought them both up, her eyes framed above the blade. The axe burst into blue flames that matched her eyes.

Meloon's eyes focused on what he held in his hand. The runes on the axe head flashed three times, and the entire axe flared with blue flames. Meloon whispered, repeating the voice he heard in his head, "May the weapon be as worthy as its wielder, its wielder as worthy as the weapon . . ."

Meloon blinked and saw the last of the flames wink out as his normal eyesight returned. He came out of the room carrying Azuredge.

Vajra smiled a tight, thin smile, and said, "Good. Wield her well, warrior." She looked back at the cat-man. "When dawn breaks, the magic that created and tied you here should open. We need to redirect it, pulling us home." She reached up with a glowing hand and rested it on his cheek. The Nameless Haunt snarled in pain as she sent magic into his head. She muttered, "I'm sorry for it all," and collapsed into the cat-man's arms.

"We are too, Blackstaff." The Nameless stood and carried her out onto the balcony overlooking the forest. The light of dawn lit the eastern horizon. From their high vantage point in the tallest trees of the forest, everyone could see the distant slopes of Mount Waterdeep and the city huddled around it a few miles to the west.

The Nameless Haunt settled Vajra into Renaer's arms and began weaving a complex spell. He seemed to pull more and more light from the horizon and onto the balcony with them. After a few moments, he turned and said, "Stand here and face the mountain. I'll send you home."

"Thank you for everything," Renaer said. "If there's anything—"

"Not for us," the Haunt said. "Get her to her tower. She needs to touch the true Blackstaff soon. Then all may be better." He looked at them all, then shot a quick look at the eastern horizon and ruffled his wings. "Go now . . . to where we became. Help her and our city. Tell her we love her always. And be her friend, for a Blackstaff's life is lonely too."

The Nameless Haunt's wings spread full, scattering magic all around and over the group, his black feathers edged and glistening with red-gold energy.

Vajra stirred in Renaer's arms and said, "Farewell, love." Tears fell from her hazel eyes and streamed down her cheeks.

The sparkles swirled into a ring of light that settled around and over the six of them. Renaer watched as the air around them grew hazy. The haze shimmered, then a flare of light on its eastern face lit up the entire globe. The silver ring expanded from their feet, rising up around them and above their heads. Renaer closed his eyes and felt his stomach flip, and he had a brief sensation of flight again.

When he opened his eyes, he stood in a small fenced garden, winter bare and frost-rimed. Before him were not the trees of the Pellamcopse but the seaward slopes of Mount Waterdeep. Night still reigned in the skies overhead, but the first rays of dawn lanced beneath the heavy clouds that drifted above from the western sky. What bothered Renaer more was the fact that he stood alongside Osco, but the others had disappeared.

CHAPTER 13

In efforts to avoid the worst of the Second Pestiliars, those who could afford it built upward, scaling the mountain and building upon it, as old protections kept them from burrowing into Mount Waterdeep. Mountainside was borne of panicked nobles and a need for cleaner air.

Kuldhas of Waterdeep, *A Walk in My City*,
Year of Azuth's Woe (1440 DR)

11 NIGHTAL, YEAR OF THE AGELESS ONE (1479 DR)

Renaer did not often come to this area of Mountainside, but he knew the cobblestone road he faced was Mandarthen Lane because of the bright blue doors on every building and the white-stone tiles on the roofs. He also knew most folk, who disliked the abusive Mandarth noble clan and its whaling-derived riches, referred to it as the "Ambergrislide." Below them, Osco and Renaer could see the morning shift change of the Watch on the west wall, as lights bobbed along the length of the walls, new watchmen climbing the tower stairs with torches.

Osco smacked Renaer behind his knees, causing him to fall and land hard on his back. Before he could yell at the hin, the halfling's hairy hand covered his mouth, and Osco's face came close with his index finger at his mouth, signaling quiet. Renaer relaxed, but fought the urge to cough, as a foot patrol of Watchmen wandered past them. They were close enough that Renaer and Osco overheard snatches of conversation.

"—said there's an extra bonus in our pay if we can catch them without the Watchful Order's interference!"

"You ever had to chase him? Renaer Neverember's a greased fish that slips the net every time."

"When it don't matter, maybe. Now, with the murders in Ravencourt, he'll be caught. And he's got friends. They'll be easily enough caught, and then—"

"What? He'll come for them? Anyone who'll do what he did to the Blackstaff's heir isn't worried about retribution and hardly cares what happens to others!"

A third rougher voice growled at the chattering Watchmen. "Less jabber, more seeking, fools!"

"They'd stand out too easily up here," the first voice said. "There's no one awake and on the streets but a few servants heading downslope to fetch mornfeast for their masters."

Renaer could now make out the Watch patrol passing directly in front of their position on the other side of the iron-rail fence. If they looked even an arm span in their direction . . .

In the distance, Renaer heard some commotion, and Osco whispered, "Somethin's disturbed some dogs."

A few breaths later, the shadowed pack of four Watchmen started, as a horn sounded a few streets over.

"Let's see where our fellows need our help!" said one of the Watchmen.

They ran east and up over the slope of the mountain, leaving Osco and Renaer behind them. The two of them exhaled in relief, their warm breath clouding the air around them.

"Sorry, Renaer," Osco said, brushing snow and frost off the human's cloak and vest. "No time for warning. How you humans avoid trouble with such poor eyes and ears is beyond me."

"I suspect avoiding trouble's not on our agenda today," Renaer said. "You heard them and that horn. How much would you wager they've spotted some friends of ours and sounded the alarm?"

Osco beamed a broad smile. "Haven't had a tussle with the Watch in four days myself. Let's see if we can trip them up without them being the wiser, eh? We'll head up Gorarl's Way and over to

Tybrun Ridge, right?" With that, the halfling slipped through the wide rail fence and scampered off into the shadows.

"Osco!" Renaer whispered harshly, but not too loud to draw attention. "I meant we should—grrr!"

Renaer got up and found he could not slip between the rails as the hin did. He found the gate and eased it open with only some noise from its hinges. He headed in the same direction as the halfling and the Watch, and he found it easy to know what direction to travel by seeing the scuffs in the mostly undisturbed frost on the street. He just hoped they'd reunite with their friends before anyone got caught.

——W——

Laraelra slipped and began to fall as the ground under her proved too icy. She felt someone catch her, but she could not see with the rising sun lancing in her eyes. Shielding her face, she realized that Vharem stood behind her, and he kept his feet despite the ice. "Thank you, Vharem," she said.

"Any time I can help damsels in distress." He grinned.

"Any idea where we are?" Laraelra asked as she regained her footing and looked around. The two of them stood in an open court that sat higher on the mountain slope than most of its surrounding one- and two-story buildings. In the shadows of the buildings, untouched by the rising sun, furred creatures stirred and stretched. One or two dogs slipped into the sunlight and approached the two humans, growling and apprehensive.

"Stlaern," Vharem whispered. "Elra, back out of here as calmly as you can, but quickly."

She tried but found her way blocked by another growling dog, a Moonsharran mastiff. "Where are we?"

Vharem did not answer. He reached into his belt pouch and withdrew three large hunks of dried venison, which he now waved to spread the scent. He whispered, "I'm going to toss these. Then we run."

The court exploded with color and light and numerous yelps. Laraelra grinned as Vharem turned to find her casting her spell. She clapped her hands together as if brushing off dust, and said, "Or I can take care of a pack of dogs with a simple spell."

"You didn't get them all—run!" Vharem threw the venison to her right. His aim was true, and the mastiff caught the largest hunk of meat in his jaws instead of lunging at the sorceress. Other dogs now fought over the unclaimed meat as Vharem and Laraelra ran out of the enclosed court and into the small street.

Vharem looked left, saw a number of folks heading east toward them with hands raised to see against the rising sun. Two wore Watch colors. Vharem pulled her to the right and the two ran. No other steps disturbed the morning frost on the streets in this direction. Laraelra realized they were up in Mountainside, racing down the northern slopes of Mount Waterdeep. This road ran parallel and just one block east of Tybrun Ridge, the slope edge of the mountain. She recognized no buildings, as she'd rarely entered Mountainside.

"What was that?" she whispered.

"Wildhound Court," Vharem said as he steered them to the right and onto a wider street that curled back north almost immediately, but ran lower on the slopes. "Whenever dogs get loose up on the mountain, as they do when drunken nobles stagger home in early morn, the dogs get drawn to that court and form a wild pack, no matter how good-tempered they might be normally. Oftimes, folk who wander into it at night are found dead by full morning. It has something to do with some old curse left over from the warlords' time or something. Here!"

Vharem pointed, and he and Laraelra swung left into another court that had an exit opposite them. He rushed them both toward a baker's window just opening for morning business. He flipped a few coppers toward the young apprentice and said, "Fresh bread, and hurry."

The entire time they stood there, Vharem never stopped tapping his foot.

"Do we have time for this?" she asked in a fierce whisper.

"We've got to let those Watchmen go by."

"But why are you nervous now?" Laraelra asked. "You weren't even this twitchy against that fake Blackstaff two nights ago."

"I was sure he didn't know me or carry a grudge," Vharem said. "There's a few Watchmen up here who really don't like me, and I need to get both of us out of here. We need to find the others. Why didn't we arrive together?"

"I don't know," Laraelra said, "but don't worry. We'll find them."

"I'll worry. I've played some pranks on the Watch up here."

The apprentice baker reappeared with two piping hot loaves, which he handed over nervously, apologizing for the slow service. Vharem handed one to Laraelra and moved to keep on walking, when the court exit was blocked by a Watch patrol. One of them pointed, and the rest chuckled. Vharem and Laraelra turned on their heels to leave the way they had come, only to find the Watch armar blocking their way.

The tall man, whose remaining long black hair was tied behind his shaved scalp, rubbed his head and smiled at Vharem without saying a word. He simply pulled his signal horn up to his lips and blew. The high, clear sound echoed in the court.

"Oh parhard," Vharem and Laraelra swore.

Meloon's eyes remained clouded, the haze of silver replaced by a full blue glow. He saw Lauroun's face again, her cerulean eyes, hawklike nose, and strong brow beneath a chain mail headpiece. She smiled at him, and mouthed the words he heard in his head. *Home again. Good.* Meloon tightened his grip on Azuredge, the axe whose voice spoke to him.

A small hand at his belt steadied him before he fell forward, and he shook his head to clear his eyes. Meloon found Vajra smiling up at him. Her brown eyes became purple and she licked her lips while looking at him. The eyes shifted again to sea green, and she said, "Listen to Lauroun. She'll never steer you wrong." Her gaze darted to the magical axe, and she said, "Nameless's portal only works when the first rays of dawn strike the place where he was born. Alas, we alone arrived on target. The others are near, scattered by some whim of magic attached to this mountain. Perhaps the Godstair interferes . . ." Her voice trailed off and Meloon followed her gaze to the peak of Mount Waterdeep. When she turned back to look at him, her eyes were brown again. "We have little time and must get to the tower. They can meet us there."

"No," Meloon said.

"Don't argue with me, warrior. Why not?"

"Because you faint. A *lot*. And I can't fight *and* carry you. So we find the others first." He looked around and found that the cobblestones on which they stood were scorched in the shape of a cat's head. "Did we do this?"

"The Spellplague did a century ago," Vajra said, her hazel eyes shining with tears. "It robbed me of both husband and familiar in one magical blow. The magic marked the city forevermore, even though they have changed the stones seven times in and since my lifetime."

"Vajra?"

"Tsar—Unh," Vajra said. "Fehlar's Bones, this hurts! They keep pushing out of my head!"

"Yet another reason why we need the others," Meloon said, looking out from the intersection in which they stood. The cross-roads led straight along the ridge of the mountain to the south, but zigzagged away from their meeting point down the slopes to the west, east, and north. As he looked down to the city, a brief flash of colors flared up in a court south and east of them, and he pointed. "There!"

Meloon turned to help Vajra along, but she sped off ahead of him, running faster than he thought possible—he had to run full out to catch up. He wished he knew the names of the streets, but they headed down toward the flash, and Meloon's speed showed him why all the roads were switch-backed and zigzagged. If they ran roads straighter in Mountainside, carts or horses would easily get out of control or run too fast down the mountain and shatter legs or goods along the way. During the run, Meloon heard a horn and noticed a number of shutters disturbed by it, as well as some folk either heading toward the sound or away from it.

By the time Meloon caught up to Vajra, she stood outside a court and was casting a spell at the backs of a Watch patrol. The two men and one woman all fell asleep before their bodies slumped to the cold ground. She looked back at him as he arrived and slid to a halt on a patch of ice. She wore a serious mien, and her gray eyes held no humor. "Come. Our comrades await."

Meloon and Vajra entered the court, and Meloon's stomach growled as he caught the scent of fresh bread. He ignored it and beamed as he spotted Elra and Vharem—and the watch armar past them. Just as Meloon focused on the oddly mussed and frizzy hairstyle of the armar, the man's eyes rolled into the back of his head, and he fell forward, unconscious. Behind him, a grinning Osco Salibuck stepped out of the shadows, his sling dangling from his right hand. Moments later, Renaer appeared in the alleyway behind the halfling.

Everyone entered the courtyard, saying nothing but surveying the four downed Watchmen, then the large covered well at the yard's center. The folk who lived and worked in this stories-tall court had opened their windows or doors when the horn sounded, and they yelled out their upper windows and into the streets. "Young Neverember and his friends assault the Watch at Trellamp Court! Murderer on the loose 'tween Sulvan's Way and Three Lords' Crossing!"

"We're innocent!" Renaer shouted. "We've killed no one!"

"Aside from that one-eyed Watchman and his flunky," Vharem whispered to Osco.

An elderly matron of doughy countenance leaned out her window and cackled at Renaer. "If ye're innocent, stay and explain why the Watch lies at yer feet, laddie!"

With more than a few folk yelling into the streets, a warning bell sounded in a nearby temple tor, and the sounds of boots approached.

"Parharding bells." Renaer groaned, and then said, "This way, everyone!"

The six of them sped out of Trellamp Court, racing down Sulvan's Way as if gods themselves dogged their steps.

CHAPTER 14

Pave your path through life with kindness to others and every step forward will reward you with soft landings and little resistance. Pave it with anger or force to others, and your every advance will be hard fought.

Bowgentle, *Meanderings,*
Year of the Bright Star (1231 DR)

11 NIGHTAL, YEAR OF THE AGELESS ONE (1479 DR)

"That way!" Renaer said, kicking a block out from behind a wagon wheel, and Vharem did the same on the other side. "Down Shyrrhr's Steps and northeast on the Garmarl's Dash over to Windless Way!"

The two of them pushed the wagon and sent it careening back down the street to slow any pursuers and distract any observers. They caught up to Laraelra and the others dashing down a short stairwell linking them to an alleyway behind a slate of rowhouses. They looped around a pair of adjoined buildings and a covered well, startling three scullery maids filling buckets there. With Osco in the lead, the group slipped over to the brick-paved Windless Way.

Laraelra stopped dead and rasped, "Osco, stop!" She looked for Meloon, Vajra, Vharem, and Renaer, and spotted another Watch patrol in pursuit behind them. Luckily, the morning sun rose into the Watchmen's eyes, which helped conceal the fugitives. Laraelra could see both Vharem and Renaer keeping their hands in front of their torsos, hiding their directions from the Watch, and pointing her to their right, to the south.

Laraelra held back, letting Osco, Meloon, carrying the swooning Vajra, and finally Vharem and Renaer past her, as she hid behind the side of an apothecary shop. Once everyone was past her, she let the Watch close a little more before she cast her spell, unleashing an explosion of magical colors over them. Of the quartet, three fell unconscious and the armar went blind. She smiled at the effectiveness of her magic and ran to catch the others.

Renaer had led the rest of them down the dark-bricked Windless Way. As Laraelra reached them, they darted onto a black cobblestone alley and into a tiny bricked courtyard. Three doors faced out onto the court, and the southwest-facing upper windows of the three two-story homes were still shaded from the morning sun. Renaer pointed at the door on the far left and said softly, "A friend lives there. He should be able to hide us from the Watch for a nonce."

When Meloon approached the door and raised a fist, Renaer whispered, "Stop!"

The burly man raised an eyebrow in question, and Renaer reached up and used the door knocker—a crude iron sculpture of a bird's head set atop a large plate of iron. The knocker oddly made no sound, but within a moment, a window overlooking the door on the upper floor opened.

"Who's there?" The voice preceded the night-capped head of an older man with a close-cropped gray beard, who fumbled to put spectacles on his long nose.

"Parlek, it's me!" Renaer said. "Let us in, please!"

The older man leaned out, squinted down at Renaer, and gaped at them and at the prone Vajra in Meloon's arms.

"You're wanted for murder, boy," Parlek replied. "Give me one reason to trust you and your friends there."

"I'll give you three—*The Annals of Kyhral*. You'll finally complete the set! The volumes are yours in exchange for safe haven."

The old man's face brightened. "Finally! I knew I'd gain those volumes from you one day, boy!" The old man practically cackled with glee, then caught himself and said, "Er, well, that proves you are who you say, as you're the only one in the city with those volumes. And for you to part with them means you're either desperate or innocent—or both. Come in, all of you."

The man waved, a light bout of sparkles drifting off his hand, and the door below unlocked. As Renaer opened the door, the older man above closed the window.

"We'll be safe here, temporarily," Renaer said, escorting them all into the row house.

They entered a snug antechamber, then walked through a slim passageway to the front of the house and an equally slim stairwell leading upstairs. Down those stairs came a bowlegged old man wrapping his robes more tightly about himself.

Renaer gestured up and said, "Everyone, Parlek Lateriff—sage, sorcerer, and smith of the highest order."

"Stop basting my ego, boy." The old man stopped in midstep, grabbing the railing in surprise. "I wasn't sure . . . but it is! You've got her! That *is* Vajra Safahr, isn't it?"

Renaer nodded. "What exactly are we accused of doing now?"

"The usual, when they want someone caught without having to explain much—murder, dissent against the Lords, and more. Surprisingly, there are specific charges that tell more, if you know how to listen." He motioned them all up the stairs and continued. "The fact that you're protecting someone you're accused of murdering should help your case—or harm it, if they claim you used your connections with many temples to resurrect her so you could kill her again."

Renaer sputtered, "But . . . why—who?"

Vharem smacked him between the shoulders and said, "He's stuck. Lemme help."

"Who's accusing us of all this?" Laraelra said.

"And who might you be, lass?" Parlek asked.

"Laraelra Harsard, daughter of—"

Parlek's eyes widened and he interrupted her, "Malaerigo

Harsard, who claims his daughter has been bewitched into helping a murderer and offers a reward for her rescue. Interesting. Interesting."

Laraelra groaned. "On a brighter day, Father'd not be such a fool."

"Yes, but your own reputation for cool-headedness serves you well. More folk than your loud-mouthed sire believe your involvement is both voluntary and honorable."

Laraelra got a small smile out of that.

"What did you mean when you said the charges tell more?" Vharem asked.

"You disappeared yesterday morning from Neverember Manor. Too many people saw you go in, and none saw you come out. Without someone telling your side of the story, your accusers filled the streets with gossip to support their claims. What'd you do to get on the wrong side of Khondar Naomal, Renaer?"

"How did you know he was behind it?"

"Those slinging the most accusatory statements all had ties to the Watchful Order, and to him specifically. I have some guilded friends who want to know what's going on, since most of them aren't buying the story. The Watch—or at least those few you've shamed in your nightly pranks—believes the rumors and search hard, as do some Order apprentices. Otherwise, most of us use our heads as other than hatracks and wait for the truth to come out at Lords' Court."

"Thank the gods for that," Renaer said.

Parlek led them through a small room toward a doorway in the far wall. "Don't touch anything—especially *you*, Osco Salibuck!"

There were two work tables, on which were fine smiths' tools, vises, and some works in progress—a bracer, a headdress, and an amulet. Above the tables and set on slim support rods were two long planks, on which were gems small and large of various colors. Across from the tables were shelves overflowing with books and scrolls.

Everyone passed through the room quickly. Renaer held onto Osco's cloak, and Vharem held onto the hin's tunic. However, while Renaer and Vharem were broad-shouldered, they were not as large as Meloon. In order to avoid dislodging things from the shelves on his right, Meloon bumped into the table on the left as he passed it, and he knocked its shelf over, spilling its contents on the table and floor.

"Parharding stlaern it!" Parlek swore. "It's going to take forever to sort all that out again! You've ruined my work for the next tenday!"

Meloon blushed and muttered, "Sorry," but whispered back at Renaer, "What's he got all that for?"

"Parlek makes a living by creating replicas of jewelry pieces for nobles," Renaer said. "It allows him to afford better books and time to study on all things ecclesiastical."

While Parlek groaned and shot glares at Meloon, the others gathered up everything that fell off the shelf onto the table.

"You big ox!" Parlek snapped. "I'll never finish that tiara in time!" He pointed at a half-finished headdress of filigreed silver webworks, half its fake gems in place. The parchment on the table illustrated the finished piece, but that was half-covered in loose gems.

Osco hopped up on the stool, produced a lens out of his back belt pouch, squinted to hold it close to his right eye, and began picking small gems up to examine them. "It'll be less than forever and certainly not a tenday, but it'll still take some time. Settle back, gentles, and let me show you glass from class. *Ooo,* nice work there! Almost didn't see the seam."

Laraelra swept all the loose gems together, gestured at the jumbled pile of fake and real gems, and uttered a few syllables.

"Hey!" Osco yelled, as all but the single gem in his hand spun away from him, glowing. The gems glistened and spiraled into eight separate piles—two blue, two red, two clear, and two green gems, one each of fake and real gems. The fake gems easily outnumbered the real gems by ten to one, as there were only two or three real gems of any color.

Parlek gasped, looked at Laraelra, and back at the piles, and both of them smiled.

"It's a minor magic of mine," Laraelra said. "Separates out components and puts like with like."

"I might pay you to teach it to me, lass, but another time," Parlek said. He motioned them forward toward the door behind him. "Let's get out of my workroom and into my parlor. *Please.*" The last word he pleaded, looking directly at Meloon, who gingerly side-stepped his way through with Vajra.

They entered a moderate-sized room flooded with morning light. Two couches and four chairs hugged the walls of the room. Parlek motioned them all to sit, himself taking a seat by the window and the light. They all sat and Renaer said, "Sorry for the disruption of sleep and home, but we need to know everything you've heard."

"Too much," Parlek said. "Tell me what you know and I'll try and fill in the rest."

Meloon chimed in with, "All we know is Khondar and somebody posing as the Blackstaff want us dead because we kept them from killing her. They stuck a knife in her gut!"

"Those two hated each other for decades," Renaer said. "I suspect Khondar killed Samark or had him killed, and then had a trusted lieutenant wear an illusory shape to divert attention or sow confusion."

"We don't know who the illusion-weaver is," Laraelra added, "but they must have enough information to steal the Blackstaff's power. When Vajra's cogent, she talks about getting to Blackstaff Tower before someone takes its power."

Parlek listened to all of them, nodded, and said, "You're right in that you need to get her to the tower—her place of power. I suspect that'll help her just by being there. As for the illusion-wearer, that's probably Khondar's son, Centiv. He's good with illusions, and one of the few that ring-wearer would trust—at least as much as he trusts anyone." He whistled. "You sure pick enemies, Renaer, that's for certain." His gaze happened upon Osco, whose hands shot up into the air to show he didn't have anything in hand despite having passed by a silver serving set on the sideboard.

"The gods' honest laughs," Osco said. "They found all this trouble by themselves!"

"What can you tell us about Ten-Rings?" Renaer asked.

"Once I realized he was the one slandering your name," Parlek said, "I asked friends who know the city's wizards. Naomal only picked up that name about eighteen years ago when Sarathus died and Khondar failed to become Ashemmon's apprentice and heir for the third time. Before that, he'd been a middling wizard with a brief stint in the Watch-wizard corps. In less than a year, he was a power in the guild with his new affectation of a ring on every finger. I heard he searched spellplagued areas in Neverwinter Woods and found some artifacts—including the Jhaarnnan Hands." Parlek smiled, happy to impart his knowledge. "The four sources that discuss them say the items are from Memnon in Calimshan, though all disagree as to their origin. One says they were made by the great djinni lords, one says efreeti, and the third by their wizard servitor-proxies. The fourth insists demons worked to undermine the djinn-rule of the time and made them to do so."

"By the gods, man!" Osco said. "We're hunted! Less story, more information!"

Parlek frowned and said, "Of course, you're right, you're right. The Jhaarnnan Hands are a matched set of gold bracers and sculpted stone hands, which allow Khondar to swap out magical rings he wears with those on the Hands. I assume he wears a ring on each digit to disguise when he changes rings."

"So if we find these hands, we can strip him of power?" Meloon asked.

"Doubtful, but decreasing his power should keep you alive." Parlek shrugged.

"Don't suppose you've got a way to just blink us over to Blackstaff Tower, do you, old man?" Renaer asked, winking at Parlek.

He laughed and said, "Even though magic's more stable in the city, Renaer, there's very few of us who would dare to teleport to Blackstaff Tower—even if we could."

"So we're on our own," Vharem sighed.

"I think you'll find that the only folk who're pursuing you in the streets are the ignorant or those corrupt few who seek to curry favor with those more corrupt above them." Parlek rose and approached another door, which he opened to reveal another set of stairs leading down. "These are the outside stairs leading out onto Firegoad's Gambol. If you're lucky, you can take that down to the Talltumble Stairs, which should get you to Castle Ward. From there, you've a bit of a run to Blackstaff Tower. May the gods whisk you along, friends."

They left Parlek's home and emerged onto a slate-colored brick street that was starting to bustle with activity. When a few folk took note of them because of the unconscious woman in Renaer's arms, he quickly explained, "She's sick. We're looking for the nearest shrine to Tymora."

The fact that she was hooded and heavily wrapped against the cold kept most from recognizing who she was. Some helpful folk pointed out directions, while others shunned them, but they made their way to the top of the Talltumble Stairs as most folk ended their mornfeast and got on to work in the city.

The Talltumble Stairs clambered down the eastern slope of Mount Waterdeep to provide a way for the Watch and others to go up or down into Mountainside. The name came from how folk lost their balance on the shallow steps and oft-tumbled down a bit of the mountain slope. The name remained, even after the Stonecutters' Guild reworked the stairs from one complete straight run to a number of angled stairs with four resting platforms along the way.

The party made its way down the first set of stairs to the Lovers' Landing, so named for its use at night by amorous nobles of Mountainside. The only others on the stairs were merchants carting goods in packs, heading up to the High Market to sell their wares. No one gave the party much notice, focused as they were on simply keeping their balance and their wind while trudging up the steps with their heavy packs.

The party continued to the Dragon's Spout, the informal name for the second landing, at which there was a magically maintained fountain with clear, fresh water. The stone fountain—a carved dragon's head—once topped the Dragontower of Maaril, but that edifice had rocketed skyward during the Spellplague and exploded high over the city. The only piece to have survived was the dragon's head, which was put to use at this fountain.

Osco whispered to Vharem, "Hey, V, is this going too easily or is it just me?"

"No, it's not just you," Vharem said, his hand resting on his sword hilt, as he looked around at all those approaching them.

The group paused to drink at the fountain, and Renaer passed Vajra over to Vharem to stretch out his arms and lean over for a drink. With the group clustered around the fountain, Osco snapped to attention and hopped up onto the fountain's surrounding ledge. "Something's wrong."

"What makes you say that?" Meloon asked.

"It just got really quiet, and those two people on the far side of the fountain haven't stopped talking." He unfurled a whip at his belt and snapped it out into mid-air—and suddenly the air shivered around them.

Within a breath of Osco's whip-snap, nine young wizards wearing the gray robes of the Watchful Order surrounded him and his friends against the fountain.

"How the gods did he know?" A young mage yelled as he came into sight.

His companion lurched over, howling and holding his face. He glared at Osco, the welt on his cheek fresh and bleeding. "You'll pay for that, halfling."

All nine of the gray-robes held wands, aimed at Laraelra and her friends.

CHAPTER 15

Regrets? I haven't wasted my time or energy on them for seventy winters, and I'll not start now. All I do lament are missed opportunities, ignorant fools, absent friends, and good wine spilled.

Kyriani "Blackstaff" Agrivar, *A Life Relentless*,
Year of the Fallen Friends (1399 DR)

11 NIGHTAL, YEAR OF THE AGELESS ONE (1479 DR)

It shocked Eiruk Weskur that these accused murderers traveled so brazenly with an injured person, but he held his wand on the large blond barbarian while Sarkap called out, "Renaer Neverember and company, you are to come with us to answer for your crimes!"

Eiruk knew all of the gray-robes had wands to either paralyze or slow their foes down, but he didn't trust Mauron or Ulik to not have more potent magics at hand. The pair of them were fanatic followers of Guildsenior Naomal, and they followed his every command. While Eiruk respected the wizard, he could not put his finger on why he felt increasingly nervous around him.

Some of the younger apprentices seemed scared even while leveling wands at Renaer and his friends, but the Naomal-loyalists seemed happy to provoke a confrontation, including Sarkap.

"Put down your weapons and throw yourself on our mercy!" Sarkap said.

Eiruk hated working with these bullies, but his tutors tasked him with cloaking them with illusions to take their targets unawares. Eiruk just wanted answers. He'd only heard about the murder of

Vajra that morning and was still numb. She'd been his friend—and now she could never be more than that.

Renaer held up his hands and said, "As you can see, we can't be guilty of someone's murder—"

"Silence!" Ulik yelled. *"Riarlemn!"* His wand fired a blue-gray beam, but Renaer leaped forward and down, avoiding it, and it struck the dragon's head fountain to no effect.

Renaer answered the attack with a dagger, stopping his roll forward but letting the dagger fly as he did so. The ornate hilt of Renaer's dagger stuck out of Ulik's arm, his blood staining the sleeve, and the young man howled as if mortally wounded.

Eiruk watched in horror as his companions unleashed spell-missiles on every member of the party, including the wounded woman. Her hood fell back as she grunted in pain from the missiles her bearer failed to shield her from. Eiruk's jaw dropped. It was Vajra—alive!

His head and heart revolted. Eiruk been ordered to capture her murderers, but here the supposed murderers were protecting her.

"Stop!" Eiruk yelled, but few were listening. They were all trained in the Art, but most had never been in a magical fight. Thus, the apprentices panicked or, like the bullies Mauron and Sarkap, took advantage of the situation to abuse others. Luckily, those brutes focused on those who fought back, not the helpless like Vajra.

Eiruk heard Renaer yell for them to stop, but no cooler heads heard him. Laraelra Harsard unleashed a well-aimed blast of colors that knocked out Mauron and blinded two others, but Raman paralyzed her with a bolt from his wand. Renaer's friend Vharem Kuthcutter, who had set Vajra behind the fountain, slashed an angry wound across Ulik's arm, making him drop his wand. The bully of the third-year dormitories fainted at the sight of more of his own blood. The halfling wielded his whip effectively and managed to trip Gharill, bouncing the wizard's head off the cobbles.

Despite surprise and their better numbers, some younger Watchful Order apprentices panicked, running from the fight when challenged with a blade. The few who remained either missed or aimed only at the biggest target—the blond man named Meloon. However, Eiruk saw the blond man step in front of spells and heard him yell, "Protect Vajra!"

That's when Eiruk made his choice. He focused on the remaining three Watchful Order attackers. He wove his spell carefully, and two of his compatriots fell asleep, slumping to the ground, while the third whirled around to face Eiruk in disbelief.

"Traitor!" Sarkap screamed. "Ten-Rings will kill you!" His attention on Eiruk, Sarkap didn't even see the halfling's whip lash out, wrap around his leg, and pull that leg out from under him. All he saw were the cobblestones rushing up at him to send him to oblivion. Eiruk smiled grimly when he saw two broken teeth fly out of Sarkap's mouth.

Renaer sighed and said, "Thanks, friend," though Vharem, Meloon, and Laraelra all glared at Eiruk with suspicion.

"I did this for Vajra," Eiruk said. "They said you killed her, but I saw—is she all right?"

"She will be, if we can get her to—" Laraelra said

But Vharem interrupted her. "We're *not* murderers. Why not call off your dogs?"

"I tried, but . . ." Eiruk noticed that some of the wizards were stirring, so he said, "Let's go. We'll talk on the way!"

Renaer nodded and picked up Vajra while Meloon unhooked a massive axe from his back, its edges glistening with blue energy. The axe reminded Eiruk of something, but he didn't have time to think yet.

Once the others were past him and down the stairs to the next landing, Eiruk lay a spell down to slow pursuit—he savored the irony of using it to help, not hinder, Renaer and his friends. As he turned to follow the others, Eiruk found Vharem sticking close to him, a naked blade in his hand. "Give me one reason, wizard, and I'll hurt you worse than your men hurt my friends."

"All I care about is *her* safety," Eiruk said, pointing at Vajra. "If that's your goal, we're on the same side."

Yells drew Vharem and Eiruk's attention behind them on the stairs. Two apprentices had reached the steps where Eiruk's spell lay, and both slipped as if grease coated the steps. Both fell off the stairs and rolled a bit down the slope of the mountain. Vharem smirked slightly and lowered the point of his blade, but Eiruk knew it would take more to gain the man's friendship.

The last wizard on that patrol, a fourth-year named Phalan, lit up the morning sky overhead with green fire. The fireball exploded, and emerald sparks showered down onto Eiruk, Vharem, and the others—but no bystanders on the stairs.

"Stlaern," Eiruk swore. "This spell will draw every patrol right to us —Watchful Order and Watch alike!" He and Vharem reached the next landing, halfway down the slope.

The seven of them, their bodies sharing bright green auras, took refuge behind the only cover they had at this landing. Northspur Rock, like other massive boulders on Mount Waterdeep too large to move out of the way, jutted out of the landing constructed around it. Eiruk joined the others behind the massive house-sized rock, shielding them from immediate view. Only then did he realize they were backed into a corner against a sheer cliff of exposed rock with no way out but the stairs.

"*Good* leading, Elra." The halfling's voice dripped with sarcasm. "I *love* being cornered."

The chorus of "Be quiet, Osco!" at least gave Eiruk the halfling's name.

"I am Ei—" he started to introduce himself, but he gasped as Vajra woke to his voice. Instead of the intense brown eyes he loved, she stared at him with lettuce green eyes that reminded him of Samark.

"Eiruk Weskur," Vajra said. "You may accept Ainla's son, friends. He can be trusted, now that his path intercepts ours."

Eiruk's stomach felt like it dropped away. Vajra didn't know his mother's name—but her mentor did. "Samark?" he asked.

Vajra nodded. "All of us . . . we need your help, son."

"Help's what ye need all right," said a gruff voice. The speaker was a squinting, much-scarred man with a patchy scruff of a beard, a rusty chain shirt, and a large number of friends behind him. Only then did Eiruk remember that Northspur Landing was also a mercenaries' gathering place. The leader growled out to his followers, "Boys, I hear there's a price on their heads taller than a tavern. Whatsay we capture these folk before the Watch does it for free? Or before some of them angry wizards yonder steal our bounty?"

Eiruk gulped as they all turned to meet the voice. A score of grizzled sellswords raised weapons.

CHAPTER 16

While I might map all the unseen pockets of magery about the city,
I cannot predict the effects visited upon those who trod upon them.
Northspur Rock alone has blessed or cursed many a guardsman on the
mountain, whether they knew it or no.

Khelben "Blackstaff" Arunsun,
On the Matter of Magecraft and the City,
Year of the Stalking Satyr (1179 DR)

11 NIGHTAL, YEAR OF THE AGELESS ONE (1479 DR)

Sellswords closed in on the party from both sides. Vharem counted at least nine men closing in on them from the far side of the rock, all armed with drawn swords, cudgels, or maces. Laraelra shouted a spell and blasted them with a silent maelstrom of colors; while many of them howled and grabbed at their eyes, only one fell unconscious. Osco jumped up onto the Northspur Rock and scattered caltrops among the men, the sharp metal barbs slowing their advance.

Between Laraelra and Vharem, Eiruk Weskur swept his arms up as he intoned a spell, and a cloud of glittering golden sparkles erupted among the mercenaries closing in on them from the rock's southwest side. All but two of them clutched at their eyes and yelled about going blind. Like Vharem and his companions' green glows, the mercenaries shone in gold light.

Vharem clapped Eiruk on the shoulder and nodded his thanks. "That helps, but we're still trapped. Come, Meloon—Osco's got the right idea. We need the high ground to tackle a lot of them!"

Vharem scrambled up the rougher side of the Northspur and found the halfling whipping sling stones down on the heads of blinded mercenaries and cackling with glee. "I liked the sneaking-about plan better, V!"

"Me, too." Vharem sighed, as he showered the larger crowd near Vajra and Renaer with caltrops of his own.

Meloon clambered up the rough outcropping, his axe dangling from his wrist by a strap. Once Meloon stood next to him atop the rock, Vharem saw the bright blue flames suffusing the axe head.

Atop the Northspur, Vharem saw how dire a situation they were all in. Four of them were hemmed in between the rock and the cliff face by twenty sellswords. From above and below, wizards flew in their direction.

"What do you think we should do?" Vharem said. When he turned and looked up at Meloon, he saw the axe's blue flames filling the man's eyes. Meloon didn't respond other than to swing his axe with both arms, his actions forcing Vharem to fall back onto Osco. Meloon swung the axe in a wide circular arc, twisting his body as he did so, and the blue flames became a pulse of magic that flashed out in all directions. The four wizards flying up from the city and the pair flying down the mountain all dropped out of the sky, trailing light blue flames as they fell.

Lying atop the Northspur, Vharem looked down at his oldest friend and knew he had to help him.

"Vajra!" Vharem yelled, and she stirred, her eyes a blur of shifting color and energy. "Blackstaff, we need you!"

She glowered at him, her eyes focused points of cobalt blue. Her head scanned around and she growled as she got her bearings. "Northspur, good," she said. She began a complicated spell, her voice a low whisper, but her hands never stopped moving. The ground beneath the four of them began to glow.

Renaer whispered, "Everyone get close and ready. I don't know what she's doing, but that glow's staying tight around us.

Vharem, get ready to join us or head out. You know where to meet us."

Osco whipped a sap down at a half-blinded cutthroat who moved toward Vajra, and the man crumpled, falling atop another blinded sellsword. Vharem saw a bull of a man shake his head to clear his vision, and then raise a rusty battleaxe, aiming at Laraelra. Vharem pierced the man's arm with a thrown dagger, forcing him to drop the axe. Laraelra's quicksilver bolts hit him in the chest and head, and he died before he hit the ground. Eiruk Weskur reached past Renaer and cast his spell, entangling the other dozen or more sellswords to the southwest in thick, gray strands of spiderwebbing. The gray tangles blocked off that escape, but it also hindered the sellswords. Curses, swear words, and the futile struggles of the sellswords shook the webs from within.

Meloon drew up to his full height with Azuredge, then he chopped the Northspur rock. The boulder shot blue flames at the eight sellswords on the northeast approach. Those eight flew out of the way like a shipwreck thrown by a wave.

Vajra continued her spell, and Vharem watched the ground beneath them, while still solid enough to stand on, grow transparent. Renaer gulped as he saw a huge pit yawning beneath them, even though it remained solid ground beneath his feet. Vajra's eyes darted up at Vharem, then back at Renaer, without halting her spell.

"Osco, get ready," Vharem said, "and . . ."

Renaer yelled with Vharem "Jump!" as Vajra said, *"Sruahiil!"* and those inside the circle of transparent rock began to slowly sink through it.

Osco stood atop Northspur and said, "You are mad if you thi—hey!"

Vharem grabbed Osco by the belt and yelled, "Elra, catch!" He flung the hin to her in the glowing circle. The halfling nearly collided with Laraelra, closing his eyes at the expected impact, but his plummet became a slow fall in unison with her.

Osco laughed when he opened his eyes, hanging upside-down above the flinching sorceress. He yelled, "Come, V!"

Eiruk sank alongside Renaer, and he grabbed Vajra's face with both hands and kissed her gently. He said, "Stay alive and stay safe, Vajra," then jumped outside of the glowing effect. "I'll remain behind to explain the situation—hopefully, I can at least keep the Watchful Order off your backs. Speed of gods to you, friends."

Vharem noticed that Vajra's face contorted in shock and surprise, but the stone-face returned almost instantly.

Meloon shook his head as the flames snuffed out on Azuredge and in his eyes. "What happened?" he said.

"Later!" Vharem said. "Jump!"

Meloon looked down at the others, all of whom were nodding or gesturing him forward. He leaped off the Northspur and laughed as he entered the spell's effect, sinking slowly just above shrieking Osco.

Vharem braced himself to follow suit, but his last glance around showed him a young wizard with hateful eyes casting a spell from the steps. The wizard's attention focused on Vajra, and Vharem saw lightning crackling in his palms. Too far for a dagger throw, Vharem thought, and no time. Just do it. He'd do the same for you in a heartbeat.

"Renaer, Vajra!" Vharem yelled. "Down!" He leaped directly into the path of a lightning bolt. Vharem spread his arms and legs wide, and his world went white and silent as the lightning overwhelmed his senses. He could not breathe, but he felt his body seize from the energy. He hoped his spread limbs would deflect any extra energy into the Northspur or the mountain rather than his friends.

Vharem could tell he was floating down slowly, and someone grabbed him beneath his arms to pull him close—Meloon, judging from his grip and the size of his hands. His hearing returned, and he heard Meloon shouting, "Vharem? *Vharem?*"

Vharem tried to whisper, "Stop yelling, big man," but he couldn't catch his breath. His sense of smell returned and he could smell acrid smoke surrounding him. Haze still covered his eyes, and it went pitch black. He gasped, jerked his arm, and his body exploded with pain.

As Vharem groaned against the pain, Meloon said, "Vajra just closed the shaft above us, Vharem. You're not blind."

Vharem tried to speak, wheezing for breath. The effort it took to choke out words, and a lightening feeling in his chest told Vharem to hurry. "We made it?" Those words alone forced him to cough, and the tightness in his chest and head faded.

"We're all right," Meloon said. "You saved us all."

Near Vharem's head, blue light flashed, and he could just barely discern the shape of Azuredge casting light all around him. He tried to wheeze a response, but he couldn't breathe, so he just gripped his friend's hand. He smiled, and the light in his eyes grew brighter as the pain disappeared. He shuddered, and then relaxed into death, his hand falling from Meloon's while they drifted down deeper through the mountain.

>——W——<

Renaer could not shake the image out of his head—his oldest friend, yelling at him with resolve in his eye, his body crackling with lightning. He held onto Vajra and sank slowly, silently. He could hear Meloon talking above. Vajra conjured up six pairs of glowing eyes, each surrounded by seven stars, to add to Azuredge's light. Renaer tried to speak, but only coughed, and he could now see Laraelra's tear-slick face, which told him what he dreaded.

"I had to open the shaft to save us all, not just the one," Vajra whispered. "I'm sorry."

Renaer looked away and set his jaw, clenching his fists to fight for control of his emotions. His face quivered only slightly when Osco whispered, "Oh stlaern it. Not V . . ." The halfling punched fist to palm numerous times.

Silence filled the rest of the descent, as the party watched the shaft become a bricked construction, not just a spell-slick hole bored through the mountain. Renaer realized this shaft—or at least some of it—had been built long ago. Vajra—or one of the Blackstaffs in her head—had known about it and used that to escape.

The party settled to the ground, and Meloon and Osco rushed over to help Elra with Vharem's body. Renaer shrugged Vajra out of his arms, since she seemed conscious and lucid. Once her feet stepped onto the stones of the tunnel, Vajra's entire body pulsed with silver light. She grimaced, groaned, then sighed in relief. She opened her eyes again, and almond-shaped mahogany eyes looked into Renaer's. He nodded, then rushed to help the slowly falling Meloon settle Vharem's body lightly on the ground. Renaer fell to his knees and silently prayed while clutching his friend's lifeless hand. *Kelemvor, god of death, if you be kind at all, welcome him to rewards unending for his sacrifice. Welcome and honor him, as I know we must let him pass from this life.*

Vajra hugged each and every person as they surrounded Vharem's prone form. She then knelt down to whisper a prayer over Vharem's body. "We shall always remember and honor your sacrifice, noble rogue." She wove a spell that cocooned Vharem's body in magical blue-gray energy. "That's the best I can do for you now, but we'll pay homage to you soon."

She rose, brushed off her robes, and said, "It's easier for me to maintain control the closer we get to Blackstaff Tower and the things in which our power flows—like these tunnels. No enemies block our path any longer. These tunnels haven't been traveled by other than spiders and rats in many moons. Most folk forgot about these tunnels once the Blackstaff and the Lords stopped being the most congenial of friends. That's what Khelben used them for— secret meetings with the Lords so they could travel unseen and unmolested." She gestured and the floating eye-lights now merged into the stonework, placing their glows into the mortar.

Vajra headed down the dusty and webbed tunnel, its mortar

seams glistening just enough to provide lighting for the path outside of Azuredge's blue light. Renaer remained frozen, his face impassive in the glow of the magical coffin around his lifelong friend. The others paused, and Renaer could feel their indecision and conflict of staying with Renaer or going with her. In silent answer, a grim-faced Renaer picked up the cocoon and wordlessly walked after Vajra. The three others followed in silence.

The group walked a while before Vajra stopped, reached over, and traced her fingers on the mortared wall. Her finger left a brighter trail of white behind it, and she drew an odd rune along the bricks. Without even a protesting groan or scrape, the wall parted. Vajra stepped through the doorway and torches erupted into life on every wall, their flames flaring wide as they burned up the huge clumps of spiderwebs atop and around them. Renaer and the others followed and they entered a small antechamber with a small desk and chair set into the rock wall. To their left, two tunnels yawned before them, inside of which no torches flickered. Across the room lay a small set of steps leading directly into a blank brick wall.

Vajra stood in the room, confused a moment by the three directions. A brief flash of silver in her eyes, then she nodded. She turned back and said, "Come, friends. All you have to do is step on the stairs, say the word *nhurlaen,* and you'll be brought to my study, safely."

"You sure we're safe?" Osco asked.

"Doesn't matter, Osco," Meloon chuckled. "Better to be in the home of a friend than at the blade of an enemy, right? Besides, who wants to stay down here in the dark?"

"Are we?" Renaer asked. "Friends, I mean?" His tone was cold and distant, tinged with regret. The ache he'd fought against now filled his chest. Both of his oldest friends lay dead, and all to help this stranger get to this place. Renaer could keep the anger out of his voice no longer. "Are you friend enough to me to be worth the *costs?* Worth the *friends lost?*"

Vajra sighed, walked over, and placed one hand on Renaer's cheek, the other over her heart. "I've been nigh-incoherent the past few months because the power granted to me was not properly assimilated. Two others paid with their lives—two debts I can never fully repay, save with lifelong amity to surviving comrades. I cannot replace your lost friends. Nothing can, Renaer Neverember. Even if you'd not done all you have, ending my torture and saving my life would have made us lifelong comrades."

"Are you sure Ten-Rings ain't already the Blackstaff?" Osco said. "We been one step behind him all the time."

Vajra looked down at the halfling and said, "Blackstaff he is not, little man. The tower would tell me, as it has told me things during our walk here. It guards itself well, even from those with power enough to breach its outer defenses. However, he may yet be a danger to us and the city, given the power that he stole from here."

"Ten-Rings got in here?" Meloon asked. "Or was it the imposter Blackstaff?"

"Aye, both," Vajra said, "but Blackstaff Tower conquered them, rather than the opposite. We shall discuss and attend to their fates later. But for now, please, come—help me to become the Blackstaff for certain, so we may all find our true paths."

Vajra stepped onto the stone platform. Her eyes flashed with energy. The brick wall ahead of her receded. The stones formed a spiral stair ahead of her, and all could see and hear the magical torches flaring to life further up the stairs. Vajra took three steps up and said the word, *"Nhurlaen,"* and vanished.

After a pause and a shared look among themselves, Renaer set Vharem's coffin on the chamber's desk, rested his hand on it in silent salute, and said, "Good luck, friends." He then followed Vajra and disappeared. Within a few breaths, Laraelra, Osco, and Meloon repeated the procedure, leaving the chamber empty only with the glow of Vharem's coffin and the torchlight.

The torch flames flickered and sputtered, the only sound until a thin, reedy voice called out, "Father? Have you come for me? The ghosts . . . they left me in the dark. Help me. I did it all for you. I did it all for you . . ." The voice fell to sobs as the torches flickered out, restoring the all-encompassing darkness.

CHAPTER 17

Khelben the Elder built that tower like he carried himself—rod-straight like his back, stone as black as his scowl, and bristling with magics unguessed. Only the most foolish would ever attempt to steal into the forbidding tower, let along steal from it.

Drellan Argnarl, *My Walks through the City of Splendors,*
Year of the Lost Lady (1241 DR)

11 NIGHTAL, YEAR OF THE AGELESS ONE (1479 DR)

Osco stepped off the stairwell and gaped. Whatever he'd expected to find inside Blackstaff Tower, it wasn't this. He stood at the top of a staircase opening into a large ten-sided antechamber, corridors leading off in eight different directions, magical green torches flickering every twenty paces or so. The only other feature was a stone statue of a rearing griffon directly opposite the stairwell against a blank wall. At the center of the room stood Vajra, her back to him.

"Vajra?" Osco asked. "Where'd everybody go?"

Vajra turned to him, a lone tear running down her cheek. While she looked in his general direction, Osco knew her eyes didn't focus on him. "I'm sorry, friends, for what we now must endure. I thought it safe, but the tower seeks to prove us worthy to walk its halls." Her form shimmered as she sobbed. "I'm sorry . . . and may Tymora bless you with good luck." As her voice wavered, she faded into a wispy miasma of green mists, leaving Osco alone to contemplate which direction to follow.

"Parharding wizards," Osco swore under his breath. "So . . . we do this by the numbers, as if it's any other place we're casing." Osco started on the first corridor on his left, scanning carefully for any traps or hidden dangers. After he'd gone thirty paces, he discovered doors on alternating sides of the corridor every six paces beyond the first green torch. Scanning down the seemingly endless corridor, he noted seventeen doors before he stopped counting.

Shaking his head, Osco returned to the original antechamber. He chose the next corridor that arced off in a slightly different direction, and repeated the whole process. His eyebrows rose when he found the exact same dimensions and features in that corridor. He looked, but did not spot any of his own footprints, as these corridors were suspiciously devoid of dust. "Hmph. So much for the easy way of tracking."

Curious, Osco took out a small hunk of chalk and marked the first door on his left with an **O** beneath the lock. He retraced his steps back to the antechamber and chose the third corridor. All the details remained the same as the first two, though Osco growled when he approached the first door to find no mark on it. Scratching his head and scanning further down the corridor, he spotted his mark on the third door on the *right*. "So, you want to play games with me, wizard? Send me down the same corridor and shuffle the doors? Fine." Osco rubbed his hands together, then unbuckled his lock picks from the back of his belt, and said, "Let's see what's behind our marked door, then."

The lock appeared clean, unlocked, and without any traps, so Osco opened the door to find himself in a small room, a cot against one wall, a rug at the room's center, and a set of shelves holding a handful of books. Atop the shelves was a statue of a cat made of ivory with sapphires for eyes. Osco's own eyes widened, and he carefully scanned for traps around it before picking it up and slipping it into his backpack. He muttered, "Well, after all, the biglings always take from the hin, so we're due a donation on our parts."

Osco walked around the room, tapping the stones in the corners.

He found no hidden doors there. He flipped up the edge of the carpet to expose the trapdoor he assumed would be there. It was.

Osco opened the trapdoor, only to find his view blocked by a cloud of greenish mist. He poked a dagger through and stirred it around, making the mists swirl but not dissipate. He dipped the dagger lower and lower, and his hand felt no shift in temperature or other danger. He leaned his head in, but mists blocked his sight. He whistled low. From the sound he could tell he was in a larger room than before, but could not tell how big. He whispered a prayer to Brandobaris, the halfling god and Master of Stealth, and dropped a copper, counting the ticks before he heard it stop. When it hit a solid surface, Osco knew it had struck stone and it wasn't more than a typical corridor's height. He rolled himself through the trapdoor, holding onto the edge and dangling uncertainly within the mists. Another whispered prayer of, "Brandobaris, may the risks I undertake in your name lead only to great rewards," and Osco let go. He dropped into the mist, and his stomach lurched when he realized he'd dropped farther than expected. Just as he started to shout in surprise, he landed outside the mists—

Back in the original antechamber.

"Parharding wizards," Osco grumbled, and he stalked into the fourth corridor.

Osco wiped the sweat from his face, then rubbed his hands dry again on his cloak. This lock was tricky, and it was his third attempt at picking it. He'd spent what he thought was at least two bells opening doors, finding hidden doors, and picking the locks on chests. The locks were getting more and more difficult, but Osco liked the challenge almost as much as he liked what he'd filched so far from those locked chests and secret rooms. His pockets, pouches, and bag all bulged with easily fenced goods and gems he'd found along the way. What drove him to distraction was his constant return to that ten-sided room.

Osco had found this room through a series of six locked and hidden doors, though they all shared similar locks, which made them progressively easier to pick. In fact, he actually found that when he looked closely, the lock itself started showing scratches from his own picks before he even started working on the locks.

"Hmph." Osco smiled. "Any advantage given is one step up a hin needs to get eye-to-eye with the biglings, who take advantage of us." With the latest lock picked, Osco pushed the door open into the largest chamber he'd yet found.

Green flames flared from the tops of crystalline pillars almost twice his height, six of them placed around the octagonal room in front of each wall save the one through which he came and the wall opposite that entry. The chamber held two statues, and Osco smiled when he realized this seemed to be a chamber honoring two halflings, rather than the usual human-scaled statuary. The bases were at least as tall as the statues themselves, their plaques identifying the statues. He walked up to the marble statue on the right and gasped. The figure was clad in wizard's robes cut for a slender halfling, and he held a staff also cut to his size, the staff crowned by the carving of a lion's head. He'd seen paintings and drawings of this broadly smiling hin, but never such a lifelike representation, complete down to a dimpled chin still carried by his familial line. Osco's hand rubbed his own dimple as he read the tall base of the statue: *Pikar Salibuck. Friend of Two Blackstaffs. Tamer of the Three Fires of Harland. Vanquisher of Huillethar the Devourer. He Stood Tall in Art and Life.*

"Thank the gods the Blackstaff remembered to honor me great-grandfather," Osco said. "Too bad we only get some backwater chamber buried deep away from everything else. No respect, really."

He turned on his heel and gasped as he saw movement. The marble statue he now faced was far less friendly. A dark scowling grimace seemed to darken the marble from which it was carved. Here was a halfling with long hair bound behind his head and an eye patch over his left eye. He wore older-cut leathers and a cloak and a hin-sized scimitar at his belt. Osco's eyes widened when he realized the statue's details even included the bulges and hints of daggers in both boots and sleeves. Around the statue's feet were bulging stone bags of carved coins, a pile of gems, and, oddly, a penguin. The living Osco read the inscribed plaque as the first line recarved itself anew with two words added to the end of that line. It now read: *Osco Salibuck the Elder. Agent of Khelben. Ampratines' Friend. Infiltrator Extraordinaire. No Fear Hindered Hin.*

Osco groaned at the pun on the plaque, but smiled as he liked the idea that two members of his family—including the man after whom he was named—were remembered by the bigling wizard everyone remembered. As he stared up at the statue's dimple, his hands fell against the bulging pouches on his belt, and he paused. He looked at both statues and how they had been remembered.

"Stlaern it!" Osco yelled, and he began pulling all his treasures out of his bags, pockets, and pouches. He threw them on the ground in front of the one-eyed halfling's statue, which made the honor plate glow green. From out of the plaque stepped an identical phantom image from its statue. The ghost of Osco Salibuck the Elder dusted its arms off and smiled at the very startled Osco, exposing three missing teeth with his grin.

Osco fell back in shock, and then scrabbled backward on all fours like a crab, his breath caught in his throat. He didn't mind ghosts, when he didn't know who they were, but family was another story.

The grizzled and much-scarred face chuckled, "Heh. You done better than I did, lad, the first time I darkened Khelben's door and helped meself to some of his things."

Osco felt more weight in the few pouches in his cloak, and he fished out four small cat's heads carved out of onyx. He tossed them at the ghost, as if to ward him off, and the ghost held his distance. The one-eyed halfling stalked over to the opposite statue and stepped through it, saying, "Wake up, son. Family's come a-visitin'."

The ghost trailed greenish smoke, but it drew out more smoke that soon collected into the visage of Pikar. While Osco still hated the fact that he was trapped in a room with two ghosts, Pikar's smile comforted him a little.

"Great," Osco said as he stood. "I realized that the test is in not stealing from a friend, rather than taking what's owed me. That's not going to have me haunted now, is it? You'll back off, now that I've thrown all that away."

The one-eyed ghost crouched down by the ivory cat statue and raised his eyebrow over his eyepatch. "Ye sure ye want to just toss this away?"

Osco the Younger nodded vigorously, and the elder ghost let out a low whistle. "Worth a fair piece, all this stuff."

"So're friends, and I lost one already today." Osco sighed. "Don't need to lose another. And I sure as sunrise don't want to be a ghost down here the rest of my days."

Pikar's ghost floated closer and put an ephemeral arm around Osco, saying, "We're proud of you, great-grandson. It is tough being friend to the Blackstaff, but the road's an exciting one, and one filled with treasures vastly more valuable than gems."

"Oh joy," Osco muttered. "Lessons from me family what died helping the Blackstaff. That'll motivate me to keep helping Vajra. What'll it get me at best but a statue down here with you ancestors?"

"What makes ye think we're family, boyo?" Osco the Elder's ghost chuckled, and it began to morph, his features and clothes shifting to greenish hues and growing. He grew to twice his original height and the eyepatch dropped away. His long hair unfurled, and his hair grew slightly longer and darker, a widow's peak forming at the top of his forehead. His mustache and sideburns grew together to a full beard with a recognizable lighter patch at the chin. Osco saw the similarities between the Nameless Haunt and this ghost and nodded.

"S'pose I'm to be honored that the oldest Blackstaff chose to test me?" Osco said, placing his fists defiantly on his hips and looking up at the phantom's impassive face.

His only answer was one slightly cocked eyebrow as the wizard-ghost conjured up a pipe shaped like a loredragon, placing it in his mouth and lighting it with a jet of flame from one finger.

"So are you wondering how I knew?" Osco said, nervously pacing about the chamber, kicking now errant-gems into the corners. "Simple. Nobody but nobody puts gems in chests where you can find them. They hide them in plain sight if they've loose gems. Seen some in vases with dried flowers, others in a fish tank. Best place I ever saw were emeralds slipped into tubes set into the legs of a table—those were tricky to find."

Osco realized he had paced around the chamber while he talked, and the ghost did nothing more than puff on his pipe and remain facing one direction. His eyes did trail on Osco when he was in front of him, but he never made any move to turn and watch him when he walked behind.

"Say something, ye parharding spook!" Osco threw a handful of the gems through Khelben's head. Each made a small hole in his features, trailing wisps of green smoke. When the mists coalesced again, the ghost's front had shifted toward him. Osco found it even more unnerving to have the ghost of an archmage smile at him.

"Silence always makes hin nervous, I have found," the ghost said, with a wink, "and they tell more than they should. That seems the same since my time. When did you realize this was merely a testing, not an actual looting of Blackstaff Tower for your benefit, Osco Salibuck?"

"Well," Osco said, "Vajra'd said something about the tower testing me, and it didn't stop me. Not all hin're greedy *and* stupid—count on dwarves for that. I figured the only way to help myself is to not help myself, and when I saw those statues, I figured out that all these temptations were just that—to tempt me away from where I'm supposed to go."

One eyebrow rose over the wreathing cloud of smoke from his pipe. "Oh really? And where is it you are supposed to go, little halfling, filcher and spy?"

"This way," Osco said, walking directly through the green ghost with a wicked grin. He felt the wall a moment before triggering the secret door, and stepping through. Where the door deposited him was unexpected, windy, bitter cold.

And Osco wasn't alone there.

CHAPTER 18

Tonight I test my theories under the darkmoon. I have the keys, I have the will, and I have the knowledge. Tonight, I shall penetrate the innermost sanctuary of Ahghairon himself, and tomorrow, I shall penetrate the old wizard's secrets.

Melkar of Mirabar, *Journal,*
Year of the Shattered Wall (1271 DR)

11 NIGHTAL, YEAR OF THE AGELESS ONE (1479 DR)

The Goreclipse sheds its crimson light over Faerûn one night every 784 winters, and it also sheds light on many a legend. Learn, too, that those things that suffered 'neath Ahghairon's hand unlock many secrets. Should ye gather as many 'neathmountaineers he battled when Selûne and her tears wept blood in his lifetime, ye shall then gain the Tower Impregnable."

The words from his studies haunted him and goaded him on. *I need more keys,* Khondar thought, *and Dagult has them. He doesn't deserve them—no one untouched by the Art deserves them.*

On his best day, Khondar "Ten-Rings" Naomal was one to avoid in the streets, his kindest face a glowering warning to those in his way. Today, even the dogs and cart traffic stayed out of his way as the wizard stalked his way up the Street of Silks to the Palace. Despite the strong highsun glare, the wizard's disposition wove the cold of the early winter more tightly around him, and folk shivered with his passing.

Khondar passed a steaming food cart, its vendor hawking hot buttered payr nuts, the smell of which reminded him of Centiv, who loved the snack. Khondar's step and face tightened as he thought of his last view of his son in Blackstaff Tower, the fearful face, as green mists and blue imps swarmed over him.

I just need those keys, he thought, and I can re-enter Blackstaff Tower as the Open Lord, not an intruder. Then my son can find himself my most favored of children again.

What snapped him out of his reverie were the overheard rumors. "They say the Open Lord's son killed the Blackstaff's heir!"

Khondar's attention snapped back to the nut vendor, who passed on the latest gossip to his customers, a pair of servants wearing the star-headed mace atop the green banner seal of House Korthornt. One of them responded, "Aye, his love of history has got the better of him, what he tries to steal the secrets of Blackstaff Tower itself." The woman elbowed her companion and whispered a response Khondar did not hear. Still, he smiled as his distracting rumors kept the gossips busy and everyone's attention away from him. That would make this easier, and also serve to keep the current Open Lord off his guard—an advantage Khondar would exploit.

Ten-Rings had fled Blackstaff Tower last night, slipping invisibly back to Roarke House to recover his energy. He tried to sleep, but to no avail, so he buried himself in research all night, specifically the books from Samark. The items they took from Samark's corpse glowed with a new light after Khondar's trip through Blackstaff Tower. He now saw a minor enchantment he'd previously ignored as merely a signature of sorts by the items' makers. He realized each of these was a key. Ahghairon and anything he himself enspelled acted as a key to pierce the fields around his tower—and Khondar already had five of the six keys he needed in the amulet, the ring, the dagger, and the two wands he pulled from the grasp of the Blackstaff's Tower.

That realization forced him through the streets on a frosty morning with flurries in the air. All that time he and his son had researched spell fields and protections around Blackstaff Tower had paid off—and now the Ten-Ringed Wizard would pierce veils unbroken for centuries. He would claim far greater prominence as Ahghairon's Successor and the new Open Lord. All he needed was one last key—and he knew that more than one was in Daugult's grasp. First he would take the keys from him, then the Open Lord's throne, and then the city would see the munificent rule of wizards again.

Khondar turned slightly off the main street toward the palace, but he stopped to stare at Ahghairon's Tower. The slim stone pinnacle rose four stories high. It had a conical roof and very few windows—a very plain and most common of wizards' towers. Were it not for its location or its builder's prominence in Waterdeep, few would ever give it a second's pause—until they noticed the slight glow around it and the skeleton that floated within that glow at street level. While most others had never known much about the failed invader, Khondar smiled. One of the books Samark brought out of Khelben the Elder's tomb named that invader— Melkar of Mirabar. Why Samark sought the book was unknown to Khondar, but he learned from it nonetheless. He reread it in the early morning, seeing it in the same new light he now saw the items he claimed from Samark.

Melkar had failed more than two centuries before because he musinderstood the legend. While many still talked of Ahghairon and his deeds to this day, those tale-spinners corrupted things in the telling. Details were lost and secrets obfuscated, either by accident or design. Most Waterdhavians learned "The Ballad of Battle Ward" by repetition and sing-alongs at taverns in any ward, its simple refrain praising Ahghairon's holding the line against Halaster and his pet demons. Most people assume that this long-ago battle involved only two demons and Halaster himself, as few bards bother to learn more than nine verses of the song, three verses per battle. Khondar knew that Melkar believed in that, which is why he only penetrated the first three barriers around Ahghairon's Tower when he attempted his entry. The legend he'd learned suggested the number of keys should match the number of monsters

Ahghairon fought during the Goreclipse, a celestial event where Selûne went fully eclipsed and dark but the Tears of Selûne were stained red.

Khondar's deeper researches and his torture of Vajra taught him that he needed not three—the number of foes assumed by most—but six. That clue came from *Love at Llast,* a rather insipid volume of love poems with the full version of the ballad written in with footnotes detailing what spells Ahghairon used against them. Khondar knew he needed six keys—one for each of the five demons to pierce the barriers, and a sixth key representing Halaster to enter the tower itself. According to the poet Malek Aldhanek, Ahghairon slew the demons on the very spot he built his tower, sealing an otherworldly portal with their blood and sinew.

Khondar felt the two keys he carried with him—the ring and the dagger—thrum with power as he passed Ahghairon's Tower. "Soon," he whispered, "soon, I will claim that as my own. For now, my power is enough to force the Open Lord's attentions—and to claim from him something he's taken for himself." He masked his eagerness and impatience as he mounted the long and deep steps leading up to the palace.

>=w=<

Standing in the central reception hall of the palace, Ten-Rings drifted over to one of Ahghairon's more amusing creations—and one more easily noticed if moved or lost. Resting on a chest-high base, the crystal globe contained a miniature diorama of Waterdeep as it had stood when Ahghairon founded the Lords of Waterdeep. The weather depicted in the globe had accurately predicted the weather as seen at highsun the following day for more than three centuries. Khondar stared into the massive crystal ball, watching the snow swirl around its confines. As he peered closer at Ahghairon's Tower within the globe, a page approached and cleared his throat.

Standing at attention, the sandy-haired lad had the usual

face-rash of early adolescence but the stance and voice of someone trained in diplomacy and courtly manners. "Milord Naomal, I am Milluth. Please forgive my delay. It took us some time to track down the Open Lord, as he oftimes strays from his official schedule, much to our dismay."

"Never mind that, boy," Khondar said. "Just take me to him."

"I can't do that, milord," Milluth replied. "Milord Neverember is in a meeting and cannot be disturbed. If you'd care to make an appointme—"

"No," Khondar said, putting magical compulsions and spells behind his clipped whisper. "You'll find you can, Milluth. Let us go find and interrupt your precious Open Lord."

Ten-Rings was grateful the alcove in which Ahghairon's Globe rested kept any from seeing him cast the spell on the boy, whose glassy-eyed response revealed the spell held him in thrall.

Milluth quickly crossed the chamber, leading Ten-Rings out of the palace proper and to the southeastern tower of the palace—the Parley Tower, where the Lords met with any envoys or ambassadors from lands east of Anauroch. As they crossed the courtyard, Khondar noticed the clouds growing darker overhead and Ahghairon's Tower looming beyond the curtain wall of the palace. He knew it would snow before too long, and he wanted to be inside, preparing his spells and meditating before it did. The pair crossed to the heavy door with its pair of flanking guards. Milluth led them through the door, across the entry chamber, and up three levels. As they climbed, Khondar planned his next move, and with a thought, two rings among his ten blinked with light, and were replaced with a different pair of rings. He looked at his hands and smiled, confident in his protections and magic.

They stopped at the landing and the ornate double doors that topped the stairwell. Flanking the doors were two pairs of guards—two in Lords' livery and two bearing badges with a raven holding a silver piece in its mouth. Khondar recognized the badge and smiled grimly. As Khondar and Milluth approached, all four guards put hands on their weapons but did not draw them. Khondar whispered a spell, unleashed it ahead of the boy, and paralyzed all four guards. He pushed the boy forward and said, "The door, Milluth."

When Milluth hesitated, Ten-Rings concentrated and willed the boy to forego knocking and simply open the doors. Milluth's hand jerkily reached for the key ring at his belt, and he unlocked the doors and opened them in one smooth motion. Khondar cast one spell on himself, in expectation of trouble.

Inside the room, wide windows covered with expensive glass let in much light and allowed guests a good view of Castle Waterdeep, the spur of the mountain, and southern Castle Ward. Dagult sat facing the doors with his back to the windows, both allowing his guests the view and showing he worried little about having his back exposed. Many described Dagult Neverember as a "lion of a man," and Ten-Rings could see how he earned that ascription. His pumpkin-brown hair flew around a furrowed brow, deep-set dark eyes, and an angry mien like a mane. He looked every bit the impressive and forceful ruler, even when taken by surprise. He wore a gold velvet overtunic emblazoned with the Lords' mark, and his black linen shirt and black-bear pelt cape broadened his already-wide shoulders impressively.

Chairs shrieked as people shocked by the intrusion stood or shoved their chairs back from the door. Khondar's reaction was equally swift. From the guards outside and at least two old acquaintances at the table, Ten-Rings knew this was a Sembian trade consortium—Concord Argentraven—meeting with the Open Lord. He rushed to the table at one man, half-risen from his chair, and he punched him hard in the throat. The man fell back into his chair, choking, and Khondar put his left fist to his mouth, uttering a low syllable. Ice erupted into the man's mouth, surged out his nose, and engulfed his entire head.

"What is this?" Dagult yelled. "Guards!" as he snapped a dagger out of his sleeve and into his hand.

Khondar saw all the other delegates in the room had minor weapons in hand. Their attention was on Khondar and his victim, who had suffocated in the ice and now wore a different face than the white-bearded one he wore moments before. The corpse had no beard, but his skin and hair were varying shades of ash gray. It told those assembled much.

"A shade!"

Khondar turned to face the assembly and said, "Forgive my intrusion and attack, milords, but haste was the best course of action here—lest our Open Lord and you be further duped by a cunning shade seeking to undermine our fair city."

Tradelord Amhath Dessultar cleared his throat and said, "How did you know that he wasn't who he appeared to be? I've known Markall Silverspur for more than thirty years, and you dispatched—"

"—a traitorous being who'd impersonated him for more than three years."

"How can you know that?" another Sembian howled, one Khondar had never met.

"Because," Ten-Rings replied, raising his rings, "it's my business as a Guildmaster of the Watchful Order of Magists and Protectors to know."

"Not good enough, wizard," a third Sembian said. "Explain or hang." The woman was the only person without a dagger at hand. She held a small diamond-studded rod in his direction, and her eyes crackled with magical energy thanks to a diadem at her brow.

Khondar glowered at the woman, then said, "I slew Markall Silverspur years ago in Yhaunn when I caught him blackmailing my guild and stealing thousands from our coffers. I had heard of his recent rise in fortunes and rumors had placed him in the city again. Whether grave-risen or replaced by an imposter, the man's insults were enough to garner a second spot of revenge on my part. Just how well did you all know Markall?"

Khondar fought a smug smile as he let that news sink in, the coin-grubbers wondering how much gold or influence they'd lost to hidden subterfuges of the now-dead shade.

"Khondar," Dagult said in a low voice, "I trust what brings you here is of the utmost importance to disturb these negotiations."

"It is, Open Lord Neverember," Khondar replied, sketching a barely respectful bow. "It is only a surprising gift of fate that I was able to prevent the shades from gaining any foothold in trade or other concessions with our fair city. After all, we welcome fair Sembia and its trade, not its insidious back-shadow rulers."

"Watch whom and what you accuse, Naomal," Amhath said. "We know each other and do business, but we are hardly friends."

"True enough," Ten-Rings said. "My business with the Open Lord is crucial for the city's welfare and must be private."

Khondar had been pacing around the table, past the slumped shade corpse, and when he finished talking, he stood at Dagult's right shoulder. He touched him on the shoulder, and the diamond ring on his right hand flared bright. When everyone's sight cleared, both the wizard and the Open Lord were gone.

Madrak ran his feather duster over the collected bric-a-brac on the ledge around the bay window seat in Dagult's office. As he brushed away a tenday's accumulation of soot and dust, he gazed out the window at the light snow falling.

"Auril," he whispered, "be kind to the young master, and use your snows to hide him from his foes, who seem to lurk closer than he knows."

Madrak hopped off the window seat and was picking up dishes and remnants of meals half-consumed off the three tables, the desk, and the floor when four feet suddenly appeared on the carpet in front of him. He stepped back, startled, and looked up into the cold gray eyes of a wizard glaring down at him. Dagult's back was to him, and he seemed to be sitting in a phantom chair. The halfling butler stepped back just in time as the very surprised Dagult let out a roar and fell solidly on his back. The stream of invectives and swear words coming from Dagult as he rose were directed solely at the wizard, who Madrak learned was named Naomal or Khondar and who had questionable parentage concerning lower animals and even lower planes.

Madrak cleared his throat and said, "Er, welcome, milords. Would you care for anything to drink?"

Years of practice kept any hint of amusement or terror off his face as the halfling flicked his glance from Khondar to Dagult. The wizard, however, made his disdain and dismissal of both Madrak and his master quite plain, at least to the butler's eye. Dagult, as usual, blustered and abused those under him privately, despite all his public demeanor painted him an unmatched diplomat and shrewd negotiator.

"By all the gods, when I tell you to stay out of my office when I'm not here, I *mean it!*" Dagult, having risen to his feet, aimed a powerful kick at the old halfling, who ably dodged the attempt and retreated through the hidden door just barely tall enough for him in the office wall.

"Thrice-damnable halflings!" Dagult roared after the retreating butler's door clicked closed. He spun back to Khondar and said, "Always rooting around, sneaking about the house through secret doors I can't fit through."

"Good help is hard to find, indeed," Khondar said, and he found himself remorsefully thinking of Centiv, left to his fate inside Blackstaff Tower. He paced the room to cover his sudden emotional response, and remembered his goal. The key! Unfortunately, getting a word in edgewise around Dagult proved difficult.

"But they're not nearly half as presumptuous as you, Ten-Rings! Our agreement was that no one would ever see us associated together! You've now given any foes a link between us and a suggested past history. Kidnapping me in front of witnesses won't bode well for your trial." Dagult's voice had started loud and barking, but by the time he finished his sentence, it was a cold, hard whisper with an edge of steel to it. "Abduction and threats against the Open Lord is a punishable offense, after all."

"Don't threaten me, little Open Lord." Khondar smiled as Dagult's face paled and his fists clenched at the insult. Ten-Rings continued, keeping him even more off-balance. "You don't have enough power to challenge me, even if that sword at your side truly holds all the magic it allegedly did in the hands of your predecessors. Frankly, I doubt you're able to draw it, and you just wear it to impress."

"That might be, Guildmaster, but what I do know is this—You assaulted me, my aide, my guards, my guests, and slew a member of a trade delegation. Even if they did not see your flashy abduction of me from the Parley Tower, many saw you enter the tower just before the panic began. Tongues are wagging now, even as we speak. No one can turn rumors and gossip into coins like Sembians. Should anything happen to me before I explain myself, all manner of hells will empty upon you and yours. And you have only yourself to blame for that. Beyond all that, there's this matter you seemed to have skillfully dumped into my son's lap. While the boy needs some challenges, I'll not see him swing for your activities, wizard."

"Hmph. Well, be that as it may, we both have our secrets and our sins. You, I'm sure the people would love to learn, have a knack for acquiring things, if only so you can gloat in their having. I sensed it last time I visited here—you keep true magical items of the Lords here, while leaving fakes behind to keep anyone from looking for them." Khondar's theory got its proof by Dagult's face going ashen again. "I'm looking for a key, Dagult. Do you have it?"

"You'll need to be more specific, Naomal." Dagult sneered, trying to regain control of the conversation. "I have hundreds of keys to hundreds of properties, secret places where only the Lords walk, and keys to every tomb within the City of the Dead."

Khondar glared at him. "Where have you hidden Ahghairon's

Key? The one on display in the Ruby Hall at the palace was false—I could sense it! Now show me the real key!"

"If your information is accurate, wizard," Dagult said, "and you can sense fake constructs, you should be able to find it yourself."

Khondar walked around the room, angrily at first, but then secretly delighted that Dagult had given him the excuse to examine the room closely. Like the rest of Neverember Manor, the room was richly appointed with thick carpets and wall hangings in Dagult's favorite red hues. Ten-Rings skipped over all the bric-a-brac in the windows, sensing no magics from them, but his senses sang of magical auras against the back wall. He paced back and forth, seeming to admire a painting hanging there, and he spotted a stone out of place in the corner seam of the wall. He pressed it, and the painting and part of the wall recessed and slid out of the way, revealing a shelf with a number of items on it. Dagult's sigh of defeat was audible across the chamber.

Khondar reached in and picked up a small brass key, the handle of which was Ahghairon's swirling whorl of a wizard mark. It thrummed beneath his touch, and his wizard sight told him this was the genuine article. "What ever did you need Ahghairon's Key for, Dagult?"

"That key identifies and unlocks any door, known or unknown or however barred, when it passes nearby. When my wife died, she left me nothing—gave everything to the boy. I used it to search this entire mansion, finding out every secret door, every compartment, every possible place she might have hidden money, or every place my son might have hidden things from me. I kept it because it amused me to do so and because I'd never know when I might need it again."

"Well, I need it now." Khondar said, dropping the key into his belt pouch.

"That is not yours to hold," Dagult said, his hand on the dagger that rested on his desk. "Return it or find yourself in deeper trouble than even you can imagine."

"No, I don't think so, little man." Khondar laughed. "Should anything happen to me, your son dies." The wizard let that sink in, and while he knew Renaer and Dagult were estranged, he counted on fatherly attachment to stay his hand. Khondar found himself amused by some of the other things in Dagult's hidden cache, from a small metal dragon sculpture that breathed fire when you pressed its footclaw, to a small silver necklace dripping with thumb-sized sapphires, to a singular silver bracer with two palm-sized sapphires set in its guard. He left the recess open and wandered closer to Dagult's desk, where he spotted a gnarled hunk of phandar wood and gasped with what he saw through his wizard sight.

"You have a piece of the Staff of Waterdeep?"

"That? It's just a idle hunk of worrywood I rub when I need to relax."

"Hardly, Dagult, and forget bluffing me. Few can sniff out lies better than I can." What Khondar left unsaid was that the power in this isolated piece of wood tied into greater magic than he dared dream of. While inert on its own, it joined with eleven other fragments to create a fabled artifact tied directly to Waterdeep. Khondar picked up the lump of wood and tucked it into his belt. "I believe the Watchful Order is better prepared to protect this item of Ahghairon's making, rather than leaving it lying about holding down a pile of parchments."

"Put that back, wizard. I don't care if I can't use it. That staff is better kept apart."

"The Staff of Waterdeep saved the city twice!" Khondar whirled and glowered at Dagult.

"And nearly destroyed it! That stays here, or I'll have you and every member of the Watchful Order loyal to you rounded up and imprisoned *at best.*"

Khondar considered Dagult's threat and, seeing no doubt or hesitation in his eyes, bowed deeply. "Enjoy your tenure on the throne, little conniver-merchant. Soon Waterdeep will see Ahghairon's heir rise to take Waterdeep back to the heights it deserves. I shall restore the City of Splendors, and there shall be a reckoning upon those deemed *less than loyal* to me."

With that, Khondar teleported away, the chuff of imploding air being the only sound in Dagult's office until the gnarled piece of ironwood fell loudly back on the desk, knocking over a wine goblet. Dagult watched as the wine soaked into the parchments, causing the ink on the message to bleed and run. The red wine made his hand-scrawled Lords' coat of arms—the torchlike seal of the Lords—blur into a mass of black ink. Dagult shivered, but he could not tear his eyes away from the spreading stains.

CHAPTER 19

*In her long-held guise as Khelben Blackstaff, Tsarra Chaadren held
the Spellplague at bay the first time it struck Waterdeep. Its resurgence
from Undermountain forced her unveiling by shattering her illusory
guise amongst a crowd of nobles outside the palace. This led to the
two long Retributive Years when Khelben's foes descended upon the
city, ne'er expecting the half-elf to bring them to heel like misbehaving
hounds.*

Maliantor of Waterdeep,
My Eyes Open Always: Memories of the Blackstaff,
Year of the Enthroned Puppet (1416 DR)

11 Nightal, Year of the Ageless One (1479 DR)

Meloon stepped off the stairwell and swallowed hard. Whatever
he'd expected to find inside Blackstaff Tower, it wasn't this. He
stood on frost-rimed grass in a tiny clearing, surrounded by a forest
and a starlit sky. Behind him, the stairwell's stone steps descended
under a small hillock. Only one other friend was here with him.
Vajra hovered at the center of the area, standing upside down from
where Meloon stood, the top of her head even with his eyes. The
floating patch of stone on which she stood seemed to be the floor
for her, as her hair and robes all fell toward it.

Vajra turned to him, a lone tear running down her cheek. While
she looked in his general direction, Meloon knew her eyes didn't
focus on him as she said, "I'm sorry, friends, for what we now must
endure. I thought it safe, but the tower seeks to prove us worthy to

walk its halls." Her form shimmered as she sobbed. "I'm sorry—and may Tymora bless you with good luck."

As her voice wavered, she faded into a miasma of green mists, leaving Meloon alone to contemplate what to do. He looked more closely at the trees, the pattern of the woods, and found it slightly familiar. Intrigued, he climbed the nearest tree, securing Azuredge to his back before doing so. He climbed to the top of the tree, confused as it seemed to grow beneath him. When he reached the crown of the tree and looked out onto the forest, he gasped. Dotted in amongst the trees and various clearings were landmarks of Waterdeep—Mother Marra's House, Pamhael's Inn, the Stag and Hawk, Zarlhard's Swordsmithy, the Open Lord's Palace—and others he didn't recognize, like a tower shaped like a dragon, a trio of towers joined at the top by arching walkways that met a solitary tower above them all, a huge mansion he'd seen in ruins down in Dock Ward, and a noble's villa, its curtain wall keeping much of the forest at bay from its six buildings. As there was a slight glow coming from the windows of the villa, Meloon decided to head there, investigating the Stag and Hawk which lay along that direction too.

Meloon clambered down, dropping to the forest floor the last ten feet from the lower branches. He expected a cushioned fall from the usual woodland deadfall, but it felt like he landed on hard stone. Hearing a noise behind him, he leaped and rolled to his left, narrowly avoiding an arrow that now jutted from the ground where he landed.

"Thanks be to the Lady Who Smiles," Meloon whispered as he came up into a crouch, readying Azuredge in his hands. He looked at the arrow and tried to judge the direction from which it came, but the arrow itself dissolved into green sparks as he watched.

Meloon rubbed his chin and decided to continue on his original plan. Whoever was stalking him could follow him, and he'd catch him or her later. For now, he'd head for the light at that villa. Above him, there were only stars in the sky and no moon, so the two brightest lights came from his axe and the villa.

He jogged through the forest, taking a zigzag path to avoid the archer. Frustrated at feeling so exposed, he whispered, "I wish this axe wouldn't be so bright. It's giving me away." With that, the flames on the axehead snuffed out, leaving Meloon wide-eyed and in relative darkness.

Another arrow thunked into the tree ahead of Meloon, and a woman's voice came from it. "She listens to you, despite your callow nature, boy. Do *you* listen to *her?*"

Meloon kept running past that tree, not recognizing the voice. He heard another twang of a bowstring behind him, and the next arrow zipped by his left shoulder, grazing his leather armor. He turned hard to the right, grabbing the vine-covered tree and swung himself around to face his attacker. "Some light would be good now, axe!"

Azuredge flared, its blue fires lighting up the woods around Meloon and revealing the attacker. She stood almost as tall as Laraelra, clad in leathers, and her long hair was pulled tightly back and bound with a silken cord, revealing slightly pointed ears. She held her bow in her left hand, but her right was weaving a spell. What Meloon found most curious about her was the green hue in everything—her skin, hair, clothes, and weaponry.

"Who are you?" he asked. "Why are you attacking me? And where are my friends?"

"You're in no position to demand anything, boy," the woman said. She finished her spell, and all around her in the shadows among the trees, huge eyes reflected Azuredge's blue fires. Eight new eyes, each larger than his fists, stared at him, and he heard a loud growling coming from all sides. One of the creatures stepped into the light, its golden mane and fur glistening. Meloon judged this lion to be at least three times his size. He gulped and tightened his grip on the axe.

Patience, Meloon, a voice said inside his head, its soft tone melding with glimmers of light within the runes on the axe's head and haft. *She is Tsarra. Talk, don't fight. Move toward the light.*

Meloon saw Lauroun's face in his mind's eye, and her eyes matched the shimmer inside the runes of his axe. Meloon stared at the axe for a moment, then his eyes darted at the gigantic lion approaching and baring its fangs.

Tsarra stood back, drawing another arrow into her bow. "Well, warrior? Surrender or a hopeless battle? Which would you prefer?"

"Neither, Tsarra, thank you," Meloon said, and he backed away, ducking behind a large tree to break the charge of the lion. When it hit the tree, Meloon turned and ran toward the villa and the light.

Behind him, he heard arrows striking the trees and the roar of the lions. He felt more than heard their heavy footfalls in the forest around him. He focused on his first goal—the Stag and Hawk tavern mysteriously moved within this grove. When two arrows struck the trees on either side of him, he marveled at his luck that they'd missed him—

Until sprays of webs came from each arrow. Within a step, sticky arm-thick spiderwebs filled the path before him. Meloon tried to turn, but his feet slid out from under him. A spray of dead leaves covered the lower webs as he rolled to the right. He could see his path to the Stag and Hawk cut off.

Behind him, Tsarra uttered a swear word only his grandfather still used. Meloon got up, only to find his path blocked by two of the lions. He turned back to find the other two lions and the webs preventing escape down his previous path. He tightened his grip on the axe and said, "Come on."

He stepped toward the lion in his path, swinging Azuredge, only to see the lion grow more and more transparent. By the time he closed with it, the lion had disappeared. He broke into a run again.

Arrows sprouted thorn bushes, slinging more webs, and even a few gouted fires or noxious gases when they hit. Meloon charged past all of them, calling behind him, "Tsarra, it's obvious you could easily stop me, so why don't you?"

"Haven't had a good hunt in ages," she said, suddenly beside him. "We rarely get to play here."

"Here?" Meloon asked, dodging away from her and out into a clearing on the western side of the noble villa. "So I'm still in Blackstaff Tower? And since when do wizards use bows or hunt?"

He took a quick look behind to see where Tsarra was, but spotted no one behind or beside him. He picked up his pace, arcing around the clearing to the front of the villa. He ran through the open gates, only to skid to a stop on its cobbles. Tsarra leaned against the villa's corner. On one side of her was the servant's entrance tucked to the side, and on the other the main entrance in proud, overdone details of metal banding and highly polished pharnal wood. Light streamed out beneath both doors and the windows high above.

"Wizards don't, but I do," Tsarra said, as she leaned on her bow.

"Did you hunt down my friends too?"

"Hardly," Tsarra said. "There are others tending to your friends."

"Let us help. You're guarding Blackstaff Tower. Let us help Vajra, and we can all help Waterdeep."

"Did she tell you that?" Tsarra nodded toward Azuredge.

"She who? The axe? No. But she has said a few things, like your name. I'm sorry I don't know who you are. I'm not a history student like Renaer."

"I used to be a Blackstaff. You're a sellsword. If we promised you a fortune in gems, would you help the other guardians and me rout the other invaders out of the tower?"

"No."

"Why not?"

"They're my friends. We're here to help the city, not ourselves. I thought that was what Blackstaff Tower was all about too."

"Very good, Meloon Wardragon," Tsarra said. "There's more to you than a great physique and a magical axe. I expected you to fight my harassment long before you ever got here. If Lauroun"—and here the ghost nodded toward Azuredge—"honors you with advice, listen to her. You're both defenders of Waterdeep now, and that's rarely the easiest path on which to walk. Are you certain you choose this?"

Meloon smiled and said, "And so the wagons roll."

"So be it, warrior," Tsarra said. "How do you know which door to choose, then?"

Meloon laughed and winked at her, then strode past her and through the servant's entrance. As he crossed the mist-enshrouded threshold, he heard Tsarra's ghost mutter, "Brawn and some brains when he chooses. Just like you, husband . . ."

Meloon's third step took him through the mists and into a decidedly cooler place.

And again, not where he expected.

CHAPTER 20

I worry for our son, my love. His temper is as yours was, though he has not my mother's gifts to protect him. Krehlan climbs to your example, but 'tis such a fall from so high . . .

Laeral Arunsun, *Lifelong with Regrets*,
Year of the Wrathful Eye (1391 DR)

11 NIGHTAL, YEAR OF THE AGELESS ONE (1479 DR)

Renaer just stood and stared. After all he'd read about Blackstaff Tower, he'd not expected this. No one else was present other than Vajra, and the room itself was tiny with barely room for Vajra and him to stand face-to-face. Its walls were made of some chilling, white energy. Touching them felt like brushing a hand against glacial ice. Pushing his hand farther through, Renaer quickly lost all feeling in his hand. The room's featurelessness frightened Renaer, as he rubbed his hand to restore feeling to it.

"Vajra, what's going on? Where's Vharem? And the others?"

Vajra turned to him, a lone tear running down her cheek. She looked past his left shoulder and said, "I'm sorry, friends, for what we now must endure. I thought it safe, but the tower seeks to prove us worthy to walk its halls." Her form shimmered as she sobbed. "I'm sorry—and may Tymora bless you with good luck." As her voice wavered, she faded into a frail cloud of green mists, leaving Renaer alone.

He turned back to the stairs, only to find them gone. The white walls dissolved into mists that slowly rose and cleared. Renaer gasped, finding himself at an intersection among rows upon rows of bookshelves. In every direction, books rose on ancient wooden shelves up to a ceiling more than three times' Renaer's own height. He let out a low whistle, turned, and walked into another row, only to be faced by the same scene—thousands of books of all conceivable sizes and bindings.

Renaer reached out at random, grasping a red-leather bound folio off the shelf and opening it to its title page. The rich smell of vellum wafted over him as he read in elegant script "An Archmage's Life at Court, by Vangerdahast Aeiulvana." The scribe's notation at the bottom marked this as a personal copy for Khelben Arunsun, penned in the Year of the Crown, 1351 DR. More astonishing were brief scrawls of "Enjoy!" written by Azoun IV, and another hand writing, "Now you owe me your next," followed by an elaborate **V**. Renaer replaced the book with reverence, knowing this tome alone would cost him a month's worth of rents.

Renaer turned and grabbed a more modest brown leather book bound by straps. He gingerly undid them and opened *Wanderings with Quill and Sword* by Mirt the Moneylender, penned in the Year of the Bridle. Renaer's eyes widened as he realized the book had been copied that same day 130 years in the past! He put the book back and wandered down the rows of books, less frequently taking books down for identification as much as absorbing the variety and breadth of the tomes in Blackstaff Tower.

When Renaer turned down his twentieth row, he stopped in his tracks, startled by the appearance of someone in the library. More than ten feet overhead, a man stood on thin air at the high shelves, reading. The man's olive robes and hood hid his features, but Renaer noticed that his green boots showed no wear and tear on their soles.

"Forgive my intrusion, master," Renaer said. "Do you know where I might find Vajra Safahr or my other comrades?"

The figure barely twitched, though the man's left hand began a spell. Renaer watched carefully, but neither moved nor interrupted him. When the spell finished, a brief cloud of sparks surrounded the man's hood. "How did you know?"

"Know what?"

"Not to fear the spell. Most folk would have dodged for cover behind the books when they noticed my working a spell. Are you simple, fearless, or some combination thereof?" The man's tone was haughty and condescending, a combination that set Renaer on edge.

"Even if I can't cast spells," Renaer replied, "I know how to identify which spells mean property or personal damage, and which ones simply mean the caster desires information for which he is too uncouth to ask directly."

The wizard's head snapped toward him, and he pulled his hood back, glaring at Renaer. "The merchant class has grown ruder since my time." The man's hair, skin, and eyes were all varying shades of green, his hair and neatly trimmed full beard a lighter mossy green than the rest of him.

"No ruder than you, ghost." Renaer said. "Now that you're done trying to distract me, why not test me? That's what you're here to do—test me to see if I'm worthy to accompany the Blackstaff inside her tower?"

"She's not the Blackstaff yet, nor are you protected by her hopes and promises," the ghost replied, and he descended to the floor to face Renaer as if he walked down invisible steps. "As for testing, let us commence with something simple. Who am I?"

"Krehlan Arunsun, son of Khelben and Laeral. You were never simple in life, and I doubt you are after death."

The ghost's eyebrows furrowed, but then rose and he chuckled. "Levity in the face of danger. You're a rare one, boy. How did you know me? I was dust before your father's birth."

"I assumed the most likely candidates to haunt Blackstaff Tower were those who bore its burdens," Renaer said, "and as Krehlan's silver hair from birth made him the only Blackstaff with one solitary hue in beard and scalp, it was a simple guess."

"Fairly deduced, Renaer Neverember," Krehlan said, and he smiled at Renaer's surprise. "Now, how do I know your name, if I have been dead and a ghost for two lifetimes or more?"

Renaer stopped and thought, then replied, "I know your previous spell won't reveal my name to you. While you might have been one of the many spirits possessing Vajra over the past few days, only two managed to stay in control for more than a moment or two, so I suspect you never overheard my name. Thus, I'm left to consider that a Blackstaff would know the identity of anyone who walks inside the tower, whether such detection and identification magic can be felt by the target or not."

"Well, which is it?"

"The last. I've read Maliantor's *Eyes Open Always,* which is considered the definitive tome on life in Blackstaff Tower in the fourteenth century. She talked about the Blackstaff knowing the location, identity, general mood, and intent of anyone inside the tower's walls, simply by his or her magical ties to the stones. I doubt that ended with your death, since at least a part of your spirit seems to remain here."

"And how do you know I'm not fully haunting the tower, awaiting resurrection?"

"You once penned a treatise on elven *kiira* based on your study of the *kiira n'vaelhar* worn by Tsarra, Kyriani, and yourself until the Year of Staves Arcane. I've read it, and you describe how *kiira* create a spirit template to hold and personify knowledge within them. They're less the actual person's spirit than a permanent illusion. You obviously did something with the gem and the tower, as your image retains the green of the gem, even though you've not worn it for sixty-four years."

Krehlan nodded, then waved Renaer toward another intersection of shelves. "Very well. You're at least as smart as most of the agents who've trod the halls of the tower in the past century. Why don't you avail yourself of the library? Discover things you'll never again have the chance to read?"

"On any other day, this labyrinth might have kept me enthralled for ages. But not today."

"How can you resist? Surrounding you are books for which any wizard, sage, or halfwit would give both his arms and read using his feet! All you need do is reach out and read them."

Renaer sighed. "I've already lost two arms because of Ten-Rings. Their names were Faxhal and Vharem. They were friends. My right and left arms, according to some. They are dead and gone, and all I can do is make sure they didn't lose their lives in vain."

"So what will you do?"

"Use what I already know. Your parents taught me that." Renaer fought off a smile when he saw the shocked look on the ghost's face.

Krehlan regained his composure and asked, "How did they teach you? You weren't alive in either of their lifetimes, and Father's spirit occupies another of your friends just now."

Renaer waved his hand around, gesturing at the books. "I've read any and all histories I can find about this city and its heroes. Your parents wrote at least seven books between them about the Waterdeep of their long lifetimes, and I own and have read five of them. I've even read Malchor Harpell's *Two Mages' Legacies* and Savengriff's *Swords, Spells, and Splendors*. All of them taught me much about Khelben and how he thought, not to mention a few choice quotes that apply."

Krehlan's left eyebrow rose, and he said, "Indeed?"

"No, that one doesn't apply." Renaer laughed as he walked past Krehlan and faced the nearest bookshelf. "Your father said, 'The door to truth opens with knowledge. The door to knowledge opens when you admit you do not understand.'" Renaer paused as he realized the shelf ahead of him now glowed slightly—or at least around the decoration on the spine of a massive hand-thick tome. He reached forward and said, "I don't know how to escape this room, but I'm willing to learn and accept such learning."

He reached out, grabbed the decoration, turned it, and the entire bookshelf opened outward as if it were a door. Renaer stepped through it, despite the icy cold draft coming from it.

Behind him, Renaer heard Krehlan mutter, "Stlaern. Took me seven years to realize that secret, and he figures it out in less than a day. He'll do just fine."

CHAPTER 21

The golden-haired half-elf Ashemmon carried his mother's grace, his father's guile, and Art both learned and innate. Many said the fifth Blackstaff outshone all but the first in statecraft.

Sarathus Hothemer, *Blackstaves: Their History,*
Year of the Forged Sigil (1459 DR)

11 Nightal, Year of the Ageless One (1479 DR)

Laraelra found herself at the top of a stairway. Behind her, a chamberlain announced in a loud voice, "The Honorable Guild Master Malaerigo Harsard and retinue."

Laraelra was shocked to note her friends were gone, and she was on the right arm of her father, his other arm attached to Yrhyra, his latest companion, a giggly and short but buxom auburn-haired lass several years younger than her. Malaerigo held tightly to Laraelra's arm, leading her into one of her most hated arenas—a noble's feast. She recognized the green-marbled setting as the Ralnarth noble manse off of Vhezoar Street.

Laraelra found herself wearing a summer-weight gown of deep purple with black and red highlights, her boots replaced by heeled shoes of crimson that made her ankles ache in three steps. Her long black hair no longer hung loose and straight down her back, but was up high above her head in an elaborate Mulhorandi headdress. Her dress was immodestly cut and tight, its front dipping far lower than Laraelra liked, as she normally disguised her slender-to-gaunt figure in layers of clothes. Yrhyra in contrast reveled in the attention her nearly exposed and more curvaceous front garnered her.

Malaerigo also had dressed up beyond his usual attire, slicking his normally unkempt brown hair back on his head and shaving, which exposed the line of moles down his right cheek. Laraelra knew this was an illusion, despite all the evidence—including the proper smells and sounds—merely because her father had always been too cheap to own such well-tailored clothing of red silk and black leather.

Laraelra looked around the crowd surrounding them, not resisting the hold her father had for now. She searched for familiar faces—specifically those with whom she had come to Blackstaff Tower. Perhaps they might have answers. While Malaerigo whispered this or that wrong someone in the crowd had done to him, Laraelra spotted Vajra off to one side.

When she made as if to close with Vajra, Malaerigo held her wrist. He continued smiling broadly and nodding at passersby, but his harsh whisper chilled her. "Child, don't shame me in front of these folk. You'll go where *I* direct, not where you will."

Even for an illusory duplicate, Laraelra felt the all-too-familiar anger at her father's intransigence. She considered exposing the illusion for what it was, but decided to manipulate it to uncover its true purpose.

"Father, I merely sought to steer us away from another dreadful encounter with that coin-sucking Amnian harpy, Lady Kastarra Hunabar."

As expected, her father's face paled to an ashen gray as he scanned the crowd and spotted the large olive-skinned woman with blond hair heading their way. Laraelra managed to steer them behind another crowd of folk behind Vajra.

"Vajra?" Laraelra said. "Milady Safahr?"

Vajra turned to her, a lone tear running down her cheek as she looked straight into Laraelra's eyes. "I'm sorry, friends, for what we now must endure. I thought it safe, but the tower seeks to prove us worthy to walk its halls." Her form shimmered as she sobbed. "I'm sorry—and may Tymora bless you with good luck." As her voice wavered, she faded into a puff of green vapor, leaving Laraelra adrift in a sea of politics, people, and pageantry—three things she avoided as much as possible.

"What are you doing talking to the Blackstaff's heir, Daughter?" Malaerigo said. "Like every wizard, she tries to pry secrets out of every honest man's brain. Never trust anyone touched by magic, especially those in power."

Laraelra stopped and stared at her father, wondering how he had forgotten her own abilities.

"Wizards are icky, Mally," Yrhyra cooed at him. "I don't let them use their wands on me now that I got you."

"Hush, Hyra." The guild master's grip on his daughter's arm tightened. "What does that Tethyrian bitch know about you or about our guild? Is that why she was talking to you—trying to muscle in on my control through you? That's *exactly* how our oppressors operate, you know . . . stealing secrets and—" In a heartbeat, Malaerigo's visage and voice shifted from angry diatribe to pleasing sycophancy. When Laraelra responded to his turning her around, she saw to whom his smiles went. "Why, Lord Gralleth, how marvelous to see you! I hope you're happy with the solution we came up with for your property on River Street. Here, my lovely daughter will keep your son from getting bored while we talk business."

Malaerigo nearly shoved Laraelra into the arms of the younger Lord Gralleth. While she was relieved to be away from her father, Laraelra now despaired as the adolescent and far-shorter Rharlek Gralleth boldly placed his cheek against her exposed cleavage, smiling lecherously as he lisped, "A pleathure to meet you, lovely lady. Let uth danth and you may tell me all about yourthelf."

Unlike most other women in the party, Laraelra did not find Rharlek fascinating or attractive, despite his social and financial prominence. She saw him as he was—a squat, poor-complexioned boor with bad teeth, worse manners, two left feet, and a wasted education. Still, she had something to learn here, so she continued to play along.

"Milord Rharlek, I hope nothing is amiss at your mansion on River Street. It's such a marvelous example of modern Tethyrian architecture—definitely something to gentrify Trades Ward, if I may say so."

"You may, my dear," he replied, readjusting his too-tight grip on her hip. It took some work for Laraelra to keep them even barely in step with the dance, not that Rharlek noticed either the beat or the other dancers. "No, there'th nothing wrong, unleth you count thievth coming up through the thewerth."

Laraelra kept her interest from her face. "Surely my father has put the guild to work to prevent any such incursions ever again."

Rharlek nodded. "Yeth, but we're more interethted in where they came from, becauth they theemed to have keyth to many lockth in my houth."

Laraelra gasped, "Oh my goodness!" both to this and to Rharlek's exuberant entry into the next dance atop her right foot. She knew the younger man wanted her to ask what was stolen so he could brag about his family riches, but she took another tactic. "I'm glad no one was hurt by the intruders. Isn't it awful, the lawlessness in the city? You'd think the Blackstaff or someone could do something about that."

With musicians playing an exuberant dance, the pair whirled about the room. Laraelra nodded at a number of other women, all of whom would gladly be in her shoes, no matter how often their feet were trod upon. Her smiles were met with scowls or outright fury, and one woman even stormed across the floor toward them. Laraelra carefully timed her minor magic and prestidigitated the front of the woman's dress beneath her left foot. The youngest Lady Korthornt sprawled forward with a scream, her sliding fall knocking four other dancers down with her.

Rharlek did not even see the woman tumble on the dance floor, but with unexpected deftness, he maneuvered Laraelra into a double-whirl off the floor and through a side door from the hall. With a flick of his wrist, he spun Laraelra onto a divan, and he closed the doors behind them. Before he turned around, his hair lightened to golden blond and lengthened until it nearly reached the floor. His back remained slender but grew taller, and his garish purple velvet outfit became a wide-necked robe of scarlet. The man turned around, and Laraelra saw a variety of sigils and designs tattooed in black and blue across his chest, shoulders and neck, as his torso was exposed down to his lightly haired navel. The man's face was clean-shaven with hawklike features, and while she imagined he could be severe, she found his smile kindly and pleasant.

"You're good, but you overreached there. Do you know where?" he asked.

"Excuse me?"

"What did you do wrong back there? Loved your very deft use of magic on that silly woman. Unless someone specifically watched your hands, no one would think anything other than the clumsiness of an angry, over-wined young woman. Brilliant, really, save for those who watch and truly see."

Laraelra reviewed the last few moments of the encounter and sighed. "I should not have mentioned the Blackstaff. That tells him what I'm more interested in, rather than having him lead me to what he's wishing to tell me."

"Exactly," the man said, as he settled down next to her. "And the rest?"

Laraelra shook her head, stiffened her back, and put her hand out. "I am Laraelra Harsard, and I would know what you are called, master."

"Heavy-handed, lass, but fair," the man said. "And correct in asking what I'm called. We of the Art should never give out names if we do not need to. I have been called Blackstaff in my day. What would you call me?"

Laraelra paused, looking the man over, and said, "You answer also to Ashemmon, don't you? The only unbearded male Blackstaff other than Samark. You look remarkably well, given that you died fifteen years ago."

"Insightful, yet not intrusively so. You shall go far, once you get past your fears."

"Oh? Which fears?"

"Your father's disapproval. The disdain and jealousies of others."

"But I don't—"

Ashemmon held up his hand and said, "Each of you is being tested to see what kind of folk you are, and if you are worthy comrades or agents or merely acquaintances of our dear, damaged Vajra. Your patience and adaptability were found adequate, my dear. However, you failed to confront your father's comments, nor did you face your rivals fairly in there."

"I see rather deeper than that, master. You were known as a political being, Ashemmon, so you know that public arena was not the place for any confrontation with my father. His temper is explosive, regardless of context, and it was more politic for me to swallow my confusion and deal with him when it would not disrupt either his or my plans. As for the jealous women, what I did was the least of what I could have tried—and certainly far better than she treated me at my first noble feast years back."

Ashemmon smiled and nodded. "True, very true. You've my admiration for recognizing when to confront and when to prevaricate. You'll be a splendid help in teaching Vajra to be more politic. I doubt she'll listen much to me. Or Khelben. She's too much like Kyri."

"This was all a test to see if I could help Vajra?" Laraelra asked.

"We know you can do that. We've been watching. We want to know how you might help her in the future. I think you will be a good friend to the Blackstaff."

Laraelra flinched as she realized the colors of her surroundings had been bleaching away, the blond and scarlet on Ashemmon's image slowly shifting to greens.

"I don't know if I'm worthy of such attention," she said. "Besides, my father would explode if he thought I was to work directly with the city's *oppressors,* as he's always called those in and of power."

"He's aware of your talents, is he not?"

"He must be, as I'd inadvertently cast spells on him before I understood what I could do. Most days, I think he chooses to ignore what he knows and operate as if I'm just a tool for him to manipulate for his political games. I don't know if I deserve to—"

"Poor child." Ashemmon's shade became more and more translucent as he spoke, fading almost to invisibility. "Like me, you were so often told your limits—what you could not be—that you fail to see what you *can* be. I see a future unimaginable for you right now—power and privilege with a price, but honor throughout. You and your friends share a noble goal. Do not despair. Do not abandon that dream. We shall not judge. But we shall be watching."

By the time Ashemmon's form became transparent, so too did the Ralnarth manse. Laraelra felt an icy cold draft whipping around her, and she shivered, thinking of her low-necked gown. She hugged herself, and found she was again clad in her heavy wool cloak and her usual beltarma and robes. Her hazy surroundings whipped around with another blast of wind, and where she found herself was as unexpected as her first location inside Blackstaff Tower.

CHAPTER 22

The Art that is true magic cares not a whit for the hands that wield it. It sings in the heart that embraces Art for her own sake, not the sake of power.

> Zahyra Ithal, *Annals of the First Vizera, Volume XXI*,
> Year of the Burning River (-159 DR)

11 NIGHTAL, YEAR OF THE AGELESS ONE (1479 DR)

Unlike her companions, Vajra had been to Blackstaff Tower many times before. She knew to expect the odd architecture, the guardians, and the dissociation when teleporting from one stair to another. She knew she stood in the entry hall of Blackstaff Tower, regardless of how it looked. Free-floating architectural details filled the room, from arches and statues to doors and torches set into walls that were mere patches floating in space. The rest of the air was filled with elements from the royal court at Faerntarn in Tethyr, the lonely hills where Samark died, and her childhood home at Shelshyr House. The most dominant feature here was a set of stone steps spiraling up through the center of it all, and at the foot of them stood Samark.

Vajra's heart leaped, and she tried to dash forward to where he stood, but he shook his head. "You are not whole, darling Vajra, and you are not Blackstaff. Not yet. We must test you, heal you, and then you can move around the tower."

Another ghost wisped into existence before Vajra's eyes—Kyriani Agrivar, a mischievous half-elf spirit of a former Blackstaff. "You and I share two things—we assumed the Blackstaff's power without proper preparation, and we fight wars in our hearts. Until we settle the latter, the former can never be attained." With that, Kyriani simply shuffled sideways, lay down catlike on a divan that floated by perpendicular to Vajra's floor, and drifted off, leaving the young woman alone again.

"We'll allow you one brief moment to address those with whom you arrived," Samark said, "and then all will be called to testing, for Blackstaff Tower is no place for the unwary, the unwilling, or the unwise."

Samark and Kyriani both cast spells, and Vajra saw Osco upside down on a gray stone platform, Meloon standing to her right on a patch of grass, Renaer on her left on a floor near a wooden shelf, and Laraelra alone stood eye to eye with her, though a gap loomed between them. Vajra looked down and saw Vharem's cocoon far below in a dark tomb alongside a number of other sarcophagi.

Vajra looked up again and locked eyes with Laraelra, a lone tear running down her cheek. She spoke to them all, knowing they could hear her if not clearly see her. "I'm sorry, friends, for what we now must endure. I thought it safe, but the tower seeks to prove us worthy to walk its halls." She sobbed. "I'm sorry—and may Tymora bless you with good luck."

Once she finished, her friends faded from view, though the chaotic environment did not. Indeed, it became even more confusing when she saw two more images of herself floating on the platforms with Kyriani and Samark and one closer to her, alone. The closest image was Vajra as a young girl, weaving illusionary fairies in the air. With Kyriani stood a ram-rod stiff figure of Vajra, standing at a bookstand and reading a wizard's tome. Her other image lay with Samark on a hastily conjured bed of cloud, and the sounds of their shared passions drifted to her ears.

"What do I do?" Vajra asked.

But no one answered her. Kyriani simply stared straight at her, while Samark ignored her in favor of the ardorous image of her. This pained her, as she ached for one more moment with Samark.

But this situation held its own message. Vajra fought to remember what she could about Kyriani.

Despite the greenish shades of both Samark and Kyriani, Vajra knew Kyri had purple eyes when she was alive. The half-elf was once one of the *tel'teukiira*—the Moonstars, as humans called them. Kyriani saw the second Blackstaff—Tsarra Chaadren—and her heir die in battle against a coven of vampire-wizards in the Stump Bog. Kyriani honored her friends by taking up the Blackstaff and risking her own sanity to carry its power back to Waterdeep.

What else? As if Kyri could hear her thoughts, the half-elf's eyebrows rose and the ghost idly scratched one of her pointed ears. Vajra furrowed her brow in concentration. Kyri was a half-elf, and there lay a clue.

Kyriani Agrivar had been the daughter of a human wizard and a drow. Vajra remembered weeping the first time she read of Kyri's constant battles to reconcile and merge her warring natures of darkness and light, and how she'd twice been split into separate bodies.

"That's it!" Vajra exclaimed.

"What is it, dear?" Kyriani asked.

The other Vajra on the platform behind her muttered, "Shush. I must study this."

"I've got to reconcile myself—change my self-image," Vajra said. "For so long, I've seen myself as different things, and they're all here." She pointed at the various platforms and images of herself around the room. "I'm a child and a sorcerer, Tamik al Safahr's youngest girl, and the only one born with magic. I'm the Blackstaff's heir, and I must study and learn more and more to be worthy of this honor. I'm a woman desperately in love despite the differences between us."

Kyriani asked, "So why are all those separated?"

"For the same reason you warred within yourself—we get so used to compartmentalizing ourselves and our images of self that we splinter what should be whole." Vajra wept as she saw the image of her long-dead father pick up her child-self and toss her high in the air. "I was fourteen when my father died defending Darromar from assassins. My sorcerer's spells weren't enough to save him, and he and my aunt died for my failures. I had just begun my wizard training with her, and I turned my back on sorcery that day, since it was the wizardry she taught me that helped us save Tethyr's Queen Cyriana and King Errilam."

"Ignoring an essential part of you creates holes in you," Kyriani said.

Vajra nodded, then turned her gaze on Kyriani and the image behind the green shade. "I see myself there as the wizard, the Blackstaff's heir, the capable student. But never a master. I'll never learn enough magic and wizardry to deserve the honor of being the Blackstaff's heir."

"That's a problem, then." Kyriani laughed. "Since you've got to accept being worthy enough to be the heir *and* to be the Blackstaff. Who filled your head with this nonsense?"

"I did," Varja said, casting an embarrassed eye toward the ardor-fueled meeting of Samark and herself. "I came to Waterdeep to learn foreign magic, as is required of any student of Tethyr's Court Vizera. If we challenge the Tethyr Curse and survive for a winter, we may return and enter her apprenticeship, in hopes of serving the Crown directly. I joined the Watchful Order and expected to return to Tethyr three summers ago, but . . ."

"Yes?" Kyri pushed her.

"I never thought love could overpower me," Vajra whispered. "It's a more demanding magic than any Art I'd known. It drove me to his side, and he fled, thinking it improper. Samark was like me."

"How so?"

"We were both so afraid at first. We ignored it, and you know how it is when you don't answer love's call."

"Afraid not, dear." Kyriani giggled. "I never resisted." She winked, and Vajra found herself both blushing and slightly jealous of the woman.

Vajra fell silent, searching her head and heart for the key to reconcile these fragments of herself. Samark's ghost winked out from the divan where he and her other self lay. He reappeared before her, his robes and composure restored. He reached out, and his cold touch ruffled the short hair on the nape of her neck. "Still questioning, my heart?" he asked.

She looked into his green eyes, remembering them as the sea green they were during his life, and she wept.

"I regret what happened to you in our name, love," he said.

Vajra's head snapped up at his words and she gasped. "No, you don't."

Samark and Kyriani suddenly floated free of any platforms, and all of them began to shift around the chamber.

Vajra kept her eyes on Samark and spoke with confidence. "You said it after we finally admitted our love. 'Only regret what is left undone, what is left unsaid. Regretting what has happened that cannot be changed is wasted energy.' Stop questioning and just accept—that was my test." As she spoke, she relaxed. Taking a deep breath and wiping away the tears on her cheeks, Vajra chuckled. "The answer's been so simple and in front of me so long." She concentrated, snapped her fingers, and a Blackstaff shod with silver on both ends appeared in her hands. "Even the heir can summon a simple Blackstaff."

Vajra looked over the room and saw all the sides of herself drifting near and far. She resolved to change that.

"I'm ready now." She closed her eyes, resting her forehead on the staff, and whispered. "I am Vajra, daughter of Tamik al Tamik el Safahr, paladin proud, and Parama yr Manshaka, mother beloved. I accept the gifts with which I was born, the Art in my blood as sorcerer. I am Vajra, apprentice to Mynda and the Princess Zandra, the Court Vizeras of my homeland, and I am worthy of their praise and teachings. I am Vajra, heir and lover of the Blackstaff Samark Dhanzscul, and our love and our magic completed me. I am Vajra, I am worthy, and I am unified."

Vajra opened her eyes to find her other images missing and the entry chamber gone. She now stood in the private library of the Blackstaff, though she focused little on the books surrounding her. She looked upon the true Blackstaff, no longer hidden in its smoked-glass cabinet but floating free before the massive fireplace. The true Blackstaff was a massive entity of rune-inscribed dusk-wood, made black by years of use, melded with veins of silver metal rune-carved. Atop the staff was a large axe head in the shape of a snarling wolf's head, its eyes aglow with green magic.

Drawn on the flagstones beneath the true Blackstaff were six circles, all aglow with runes and magic. Each circle held the silvery wizard mark or sigil of each Blackstaff before her, and each of them hovered above their marks, staring at her. Vajra had met all but the last and eldest in her three years at Blackstaff Tower, but the first Blackstaff usually only manifested by locking doors or appearing as forbidding eyes whenever she sought to explore more of the tower than he thought wise. Today, she faced every spirit of the tower. She quailed inside, but breathed deep and steadied herself. She would face these spirits in chronological order, from the most recent at the outer circle to the oldest Blackstaff at the center.

Khelben spoke, his bass voice thundering. "When the Blackstaff was forged, it was made by the will of my father, myself, and our goddess. Since that time, the assumption of the true Blackstaff has gained its rituals. Step forward, make your claims, and be the Blackstaff, if you so dare."

"By what right do you claim the Blackstaff?" asked Samark, his kindly smile muted for the seriousness of the ritual.

"I claim it by responsibility, for no one stands as the Blackstaff, and Waterdeep needs one to stand for Art, for order, and for good."

With her answer, the shade gestured, and the outermost circle around the staff disappeared, allowing Vajra to step closer to it.

"By what right do you claim the Blackstaff?" asked the shade of Ashemmon.

"I claim it by inheritance, for I am the last heir."

"No, child, you are not. Another has been recruited."

Vajra stopped, the litany in her head disrupted. She stared at Ashemmon's shade in disbelief, then searched her memory. She nodded and smiled. "It's Eiruk, isn't it? Even with Khelben possessing me, we all felt it when he touched us—Khelben's mark is on him."

"Aye, lass, good deduction. He may be your heir, should you choose, though he himself is yet unaware of his potential and his gift."

Vajra hesitated, then said, "He is a good friend, but his feelings run deeper for me than mine do for him. Until I can face that more evenly"—Vajra cast her eyes back at Samark's ghost—"let us leave Eiruk in peace. The Blackstaff needs less passion and more thought at present."

Ashemmon's shade began again. "By what right do you claim the Blackstaff?"

"The Blackstaff before me bound me to this power, this tower, and this time and place."

Again, the ghost gestured and the circle barring her from moving closer disappeared.

"By what right do you claim the Blackstaff?" said the image of Krehlan.

"I claim it by power, having been born of Art with sorcery in my veins."

Another circle gone.

"By what right do you claim the Blackstaff?" said Kyriani's spirit.

"I claim it by knowledge, having learned of magic at the feet of the Grand Wizard of Tethyr's Crown, the Court Vizera and my aunt, Mynda Gyrfalcon-Thann."

Kyri winked at her as she skipped around the circle, the magical barrier dissipating with each playful step.

"By what right do you claim the Blackstaff?" asked the ghost of Tsarra Chaadren.

"I claim it by love, having earned the trust and heart of Samark, the Blackstaff before me."

"By what right do you claim the Blackstaff?" came the stern question from Khelben, the greatest and oldest of the Blackstaffs.

"I claim it by pain, having endured much in its service, having lost friends and lover."

Khelben smiled grimly. "Girl, you have not yet known hurt or loss."

With that forbidding omen, Khelben swept his hand around, and the final barrier between Vajra and the true Blackstaff was gone. Vajra was sure she heard the wolf's head on the staff snarl a warning at her, but her heart pounded in her ears now.

All six of the Blackstaff spirits hovered near, creating a new circle around Vajra and the staff. They joined hands to seal the circle behind her. When they all linked, the floor pulsed with silver and green energy, filling the room with light.

Taking a deep breath, Vajra said, "I, Vajra Safahr, take up this burden willingly, humbly, and with all I was, am, and ever will be."

Her right hand closed about the metal-and-wood amalgam. It felt warm and inviting. The only sensation she felt was a centering, a grounding, as much of her tension slipped down through her body and into the stones beneath her. She shuddered as she expected some explosion of power when she touched it, but she felt nothing new other than a reduced pressure in her head.

She looked at Samark and Khelben, who stood together, surprised. Samark's shade said, "Darling, you've been carrying the full power and knowledge of the Blackstaffs within you for months. It came to you when I died, as it does to the Blackstaff's heir. Alas, since you didn't come to the tower and touch this staff to ground that power, it wreaked havoc with your mind. For that, I'm so sorry. Our spirits remain here in these stones, available for counsel and help, but never to walk the city again."

"You mean I was as powerful as any of you all the time I was

Ten-Rings's captive?" Vajra felt her temper rise, but let it go when Kyriani raised her hands before her.

"No, dear heart. You carried fragments of our spirits, pieces of our knowledge, and only some wisps of power—enough to let us send you aid to keep you alive."

"I don't understand."

Krehlan stepped forward and said, "Woman, when the Grand Mages of Rhymanthiin and I dissipated the *kiira n'vaelhar* that held the spirits of my father, Tsarra, and Kyriani, we bonded its magic to this tower and its sister in the Hidden City. When someone takes on the mantle of the Blackstaff or its heir, a template of their spirit, their intellect, their knowledge, becomes part of the Blackstaff and its place of power. What you had to endure was all that knowledge without sorting or grounding it properly in ritual. While Ashemmon and Samark assumed their power easily inside the tower, you had neither the benefit of a Blackstaff in hand to hold some of the power nor the tower itself to ground it. You held all our spirits and knowledge, but our collective lifetimes and awareness overwhelmed yours."

Tsarra, impatient at Krehlan's long answer, broke in. "We drove you mad because the tower is what should hold twelve centuries of life experiences. That's why Krehlan merged the gem with the tower—so it could be your advisor, rather than have the Blackstaff be a slave to the copied minds of those who came before her."

Khelben cleared his throat, silencing all the others, and placed his hands on Vajra's shoulders. "It is your time now. I see my blood and Gamalon's blood in you, and I know Waterdeep is safe. Go now and be the Blackstaff. Reach out with your feelings, find your friends, and go forth. You all have work to do this day. We shall be here to help if you need us."

With that, he disappeared, and the others did as well, filling the room with greenish mist. The last to dissipate was Samark, who embraced and kissed her before dissolving, leaving Vajra with tearful eyes in the chilling mist.

Vajra cleared her throat, and then did as Khelben bid. She realized her companions stood in chambers below, each of them tested by the spirits of the tower. She knew how to manipulate the tower so that all the doors they opened would lead them to where she was. With concentration, she even could listen in on what they were saying. Vajra knew the secret words that locked and unlocked score upon score of mysteries within this tower. She realized she had no new knowledge of magic or spells, but she knew where to find information and hidden lore to do so. She knew the location and nature of every magical item within the walls of the tower, and some made her shudder with their power or what they held at bay.

Vajra could see another tower—N'Vaerymanth—in her mind's eye, its layout the same as this, but the city over which it looked was far more orderly, far more magical, and she vowed to visit Rhymanthiin, the Hidden City of Hope, when the time came.

All this and more awaited her as the Blackstaff. It was time to let her city know.

CHAPTER 23

The original splendors of Waterdeep were Ahghairon's secrets, which keep us safe today and always, despite the predations of lesser so-called lords."

Agnan Crohal, *Tales Told Tavernside,*
Year of Daystars (1268 DR)

12 Nightal, Year of the Ageless One (1479 DR)

Khondar stood and stretched in the morning sun flooding through his windows. He walked over to the western window. Guards dutifully walked the parapets of the palace, and he could see from this vantage that breakfast had been laid out in his office in the easternmost tower. With a mere thought and a blink of magic on his left index finger, the Khondar became a beam of light and lanced across the distance, reappearing among a gasping group of courtiers, visiting envoys, and various sycophants and servants.

The room proudly displayed the Lords' Arms and the Seal of Waterdeep in massive tapestries on opposite walls. Marble floors and intricate wood-inlay walls gleamed with the polish of human effort, not magic. The palace no longer catered to outlanders or nonhumans, and the city was richer for it and for the rule of mages. Khondar looked out the window to see many tall ships in the gleaming harbor, wizards from many lands coming to this great city and the rebirth of magic.

All around the table, applause scattered and then grew as people cheered his arrival. Above all, he heard Centiv the Blackstaff sing out in pride, "All hail the Open Lord! Long live Khondar, destroyer of the Shadow Thieves, the Dark Brotherhood, and the Cabal Arcane! All hail the Restorer of an orderly and lawful city! All hail the Open Lord!"

The tall doors leading into the chamber slammed open, and Renaer Neverember led a group of dirty, ragged-clothed halflings into the chamber. The female wizards in the crowd fainted at the sight of the lecherous midgets. Renaer loosed a crossbow quarrel at Khondar, who altered the bolt into a magic missile that returned and slammed into Renaer's chest. Centiv cowed the rabble that followed him by making the floor seem to fall open into spiked pits. The rebels fell to the ground, insensate, and Khondar reached down to hoist Renaer up by his now-filthy shirt.

"Why do you resist our rightful rule?" Ten-Rings demanded. "Why do you not let the wizards rule?"

Renaer smiled a cat's grin. "Because the Blackstaff and the Open Lord serve the city, not the other way around."

>——W——<

Khondar Naomal tossed in his sleep, his dreams of power driving him. He rolled over, pulling his furs and covers closer to him. The small fire in the hearth kept the room above the freezing temperatures outside, though the room could hardly be considered warm.

The spell-fields Ten-Rings established around his new home kept out all magical intrusions but those he desired. Wards protected all the doors and windows, and some of Centiv's more ingenious illusions cloaked the entire third floor, where Khondar now slept. Those magical protections muted all noise coming through walls and windows, allowing him rest despite the nearby belltower off the Fanebar or the noise and occasional tumult in the street outside the inns and festhalls in the vicinity.

Normally, he would not have heard the voice on the wind in the Crown of the North that frosty morning. The fact that it launched him out of a sound sleep both irritated and frightened him as soon as the message was delivered. He growled, *"Blast that woman!"*

Khondar threw back the furs with a growl, launching himself out of bed and over to his worktable. With a snap of his fingers, the fire on the hearth blazed up, increasing the heat in the room. He took a quick survey of the table and sighed with relief. All six keys were in place—Aghairon's Amulet, Key, and Ring; the sheathed dagger his research told him was Anthaorl's Fang, a gift to a long-since-dead loyal watchman from Aghairon; and the two wands he'd plucked from the clutches of Blackstaff Tower. He breathed a sigh of relief and reached for a ceramic dome on the corner of his desk.

He lifted the cracked blue cover to expose a crystal ball the size of his fist. "Show me my defenses," he said.

Mists filled the center of the globe and showed swirling images of various rooms and doors, each aglow in shades of pink, ochre, and ash. Khondar exhaled in relief as his survey showed no spells had been disrupted, but he vented his fury. "That bitch bypassed my wards without disrupting them!" He muttered in harsh whispers to himself. "Bah—it matters not! Blackstaff or no, I'll soon have power over her and the entire city!"

Khondar settled on to a cushion next to the hearth, his spellbook on a low stand before it. Time was of the essence, and he needed every spell prepared for the coming battle for Aghairon's Tower—and control of Waterdeep.

CHAPTER 24

With Open Lord Caladorn at her side, Kyriani's proclamation from atop Blackstaff Tower was necessary to acknowledge her legitimacy in the role of the city's archmage. The Blackstaff's proclamation became tradition when the son of Khelben took up the mantle in the Year of Lost Ships and as his long-time friend Ashemmon did in Ches of this year.

Paerl Nhesch,
Architects Arcane: Waterdeep and the Sword Coast North,
Year of the Dog-Eared Journal (1424 DR)

12 NIGHTAL, YEAR OF THE AGELESS ONE (1479 DR)

The Crown of the North awoke at dawn with a woman's voice carried on the snow-laden winds. Her voice echoed through every alley, every privy, every bedchamber, every hearth house, and every nook and cranny within the walls of Waterdeep. Even those places guarded by spells and prayers heard this proclamation. Few folk recognized her voice, but more than a few had heard this oath, or versions quite similar, more than a few times in the past decades—each time a new Blackstaff stood atop the tower to declare the assumption of power.

"Know this, now and hereafter, the Blackstaff has fallen in service to the City. Mourn Samark Dhanzscul and honor his memory. Yet the Blackstaff has been taken up once more. I am Vajra Safahr, and I am the seventh Blackstaff of Waterdeep. Hear my solemn vow—I shall protect the city, its citizens, and its future from all those who would see it harmed. I act as Magic's eye, hand, and heart for the Lords and for the good residents of the city. My predecessor Samark Dhanzscul died due to the predations of power-hungry men. I and my friends shall avenge him, and I shall strive to be worthy of Waterdeep's friendship and respect. Know you that she already has my protection and my loyalty."

As expected, those in the immediate vicinity around Swords Street and upper Castle Ward threw open their shutters to glimpse this event personally. Those farthest off with a high vantage point saw five figures at the top of Blackstaff Tower, four standing in an arc around a solitary figure holding a massive staff almost half-again as tall as she was. The tower gleamed and pulsed with silvery energy in every mortar crack in the tower and its curtain wall. Folk nodded, remembering this happened each time the tower found a new master. Talk flitted about the gathering crowds that the tower had never accepted anyone unworthy of being the Blackstaff—even if she were "but a slip of a girl."

Atop Blackstaff Tower, Vajra turned back to the group assembled around her. "I am very glad to see all of you survived. I know now, moreso than I did before, that you are worthy allies and friends to the Blackstaff. And I'm sorry for all you've suffered and lost in my and Samark's name. Now, I can do more to help us all—and hurt those who so richly deserve it." Vajra stepped forward, and stamped her foot once on the roof.

A flash of light and the five of them stood in a library, surrounded by walls of books save one wall with a massive fireplace. The ceiling rose higher than three men's heights, and book-laden shelves covered every span of the walls, some even floating without floors to support them. Globes of light shimmered brightly and zipped around the books and shelves to put lights over every person's head.

"There's quite a crowd growing outside right now," Vajra said. "More than a few have dozens of questions, not the least of which have to do with my being declared dead and Renaer accused of my murder."

"Can't say I'm surprised," Renaer said, "given how Ten-Rings managed to pin every ill he's done on others. Shouldn't your announcement take the wind out of the Watch's sails? Keep them from bothering to capture us?"

Vajra chuckled and said, "And did your obvious innocence ever stop some less-than-objective officers from chasing you?"

"Fair point."

"I'm all for a little banter to lighten the mood," Osco said, "but don't we have an over-accessorized guildmaster to stop from conquering the city?"

"Listen to you, little halfling," Laraelra said, "talking like a hero. I thought you only got involved in things with profit."

"If that one takes power, there won't be much profit to be had in a city run by magic-users. All that energy goes to their heads, makes 'em crazy." When Laraelra and Vajra shot him hard looks, he stammered, "Yourselves excluded, goes without saying."

"He's right, though," Meloon added, smacking Azuredge's haft into his palm. "Ten-Rings must be stopped."

Vajra reached up and touched him lightly on the arm, her head not even reaching his shoulder. "We will, Meloon. But first we must marshall our energy. To do that, I'll need Elra's help."

"How do you know that nickname?" Laraelra asked.

"I wasn't completely unaware of what was going on around me, and I hope I can call you that and more. I have a favor to ask, and it's not one I ask lightly. I would have *you* be my heir."

Laraelra stared at Vajra, awestruck by the suggestion.

"You can do this, Elra," Vajra said, leaving the true Blackstaff to hover next to Meloon. She placed her dark hands around Laraelra's lighter, trembling hands, and looked deep into her eyes. "I wouldn't ask this if I didn't sense you could handle the responsibility. I need someone I know and trust. Someone with a good head for intrigues." And no romantic inclinations toward me, she added to herself. "We don't have much time. There are very few spellcasters I can trust in this city, and you are one of them. Please help me so we can all help Waterdeep."

"But I'm no wizard," Laraelra whispered. "I'm barely even a sorcerer!"

"Neither Tsarra nor Ashemmon were wizards, and they served nobly," Vajra said, "and I need one touched by magic to be able to carry one of these against Khondar." She snapped her fingers and a smooth Blackstaff shod with silver on both ends shimmered into her grip.

"You can't expect us to face him directly," Meloon said. "He's ten times more powerful than any of us. I'm not afraid of him, but I'm not stupid either!"

"That's another reason why it's important for her to become the Blackstaff's heir. You all know the stakes and the location of our foe. I'll best help you by remaining here in my place of power, sending power and aid through my heir. I cannot do any of this without your help, Elra. Without you, Ten-Rings may get away with it all, and we'll have to fight from the shadows to take back our city."

"Sounds good to me," Osco muttered, and Renaer smacked him lightly on the head.

"Will you shoulder this burden, Elra?"

Laraelra gulped, her palms sweating profusely. Thoughts of her parents raced through her head, urging her not to be seduced by the promises of power. She also hesitated as she recalled Vajra's insta-bility over the past few days. The two women locked eyes. Despite having been nearly comatose for the past three days, Vajra's eyes held no hesitation, no doubts, only confidence and power. Laraelra heard her father's voice in her head, complaining that she was a traitor for allying with those in power, but she knew in her heart that Vajra and the power she promised needed to be held by those who wanted and needed Waterdeep to be a better place, not just a more prosperous one.

"What do I need to do?" Laraelra said.

Vajra waved her left hand, and a rune-inscribed circle appeared on the floor around them. The three men backed away, leaving the women inside the circle alone. "Sit. Calm yourself. When you're ready, all you'll need to do is take my hand in one hand and the staff in the other. I'll do the rest."

Laraelra and Vajra settled cross-legged within the magic circle, the Blackstaff floating horizontally above the floor between them. One intoned syllable from Vajra and the runes flashed green. A translucent emerald dome enclosed them. Laraelra heard only her own nervous heartbeat.

Vajra spoke in low tones, facing down at the staff and the circle, and her voice was a chorus again of male and female voices. Laraelra would later swear she saw eyes and partial faces within the dome's energy as she listened. She didn't understand what Vajra said, but she knew she spoke Elvish. When Vajra faced her again, her eyes shimmered and shifted, the colors swimming from blue to purple to gray, brown, hazel, and green. The Blackstaff held out her right hand and placed her left hand atop the floating staff. Laraelra exhaled, shook her shoulders, and let go of her fears.

With a silent prayer to Tymora, Laraelra gripped Vajra's right hand with her left and closed her right hand over the Blackstaff. She winced, but she merely felt a buzz in her head and a warmth in her palm, as if the staff were a living thing. Vajra's palm was just as sweaty as her own, but her tiny hand held power—as did her eyes. Laraelra felt rather than saw three pulses of magic pass from Vajra's eyes into her own. After the third pulse, Laraelra found she gripped the Blackstaff alone, and she felt its power simmering just inside the duskwood staff's surface.

Vajra cast a final spell, dissipating the energy dome over them, and said, "For as long as you and I concur, you are an heir to the power of the Blackstaff. That won't provide you with any more power at the present time, other than the ability to safely carry and wield a Blackstaff. In days to come, we'll talk more of you learning from me and from the tower."

Laraelra gulped, realizing this meant more time with the ghosts inhabiting the most formidable fortress on the Sword Coast. She started to ask, then coughed nervously, swallowed, and tried again. "How can we stand against Ten-Rings? He's powerful enough to destroy all of us with one spell."

"Once you get to Roarke House, simply say the word *gehrallen,* and my power will be added to the battle," Vajra said. Laraelra smiled, realizing she understood what was to come without having to utter it aloud. She nodded and shifted the Blackstaff to her left hand, resting one end on the ground. "So what next?" she asked.

Vajra seemed distracted for a moment, as if she were listening to something no one else could hear. When her attention snapped back to the group assembled around her, she said, "Forgive me. That's going to take some getting used to. I can hear and see what folk are doing anywhere inside or within a step or two from the walls around the tower. Watch commander Delnar Kleeandur just demanded the surrender of all of you. He wants you to come to the palace for questioning and a possible trial. At least he has the sense to be courteous."

"I'll go," Renaer said.

"What?" Meloon said. "They'll hang you!"

"Doubtful," he said. "The main charge is for the murder of Vajra, who's very much alive. I want to clear all our names. Also, if I'm keeping the Watch busy, they can't get in the way of what the rest of you have to do. I'm less use in a fight than the rest of you, but I can talk our way out of the false charges Ten-Rings dumped on us."

"A sound plan," Vajra said. "Say the word *traeloth* when you step onto the stairs, and they will deposit you at the entry chamber. When you exit the tower, the gates will wrap around you, but not let anyone else enter. Advise anyone trying to do otherwise to desist, as the Blackstaff is not receiving any more visitors today." Vajra hugged Renaer and kissed him lightly on the cheek. "Thank you again, friend, for all your help. We'll discuss things at length later at your home—matters of days past and the future."

Renaer sketched a salute at the rest of the group and headed for the stairs.

Vajra gestured, and a trio of rings appeared in mid-air in front of Meloon, Osco, and Laraelra. "Those should help you all survive the coming battle with Khondar. Consider the rings my thanks. Now, here's the rest of the plan . . ."

CHAPTER 25

. . . and every citizen shall have his say, be it in open Court or in private with the Open Lord.

Ahghairon, *Lords' Writ, Volume II,*
the Year of the Haunted Haven (1039 DR)

12 NIGHTAL, YEAR OF THE AGELESS ONE (1479 DR)

Renaer's steps and those of his Watch escorts echoed from the marble of the floor to the peak of the dome that loomed over the Lords' Court. He held his head high, neither flinching his eyes away from those who met his nor looking at any beyond those in his path. After the trial at Blackstaff Tower, this held little fear for him.

He stood at the center of a semicircular table's arc, his father straight ahead of him and in full regalia as the city's Open Lord. To see his father reminded Renaer that father and son shared much in looks and manners. Long brown manes tumbled past both their sets of muscular shoulders, though Dagult's hair tended more toward pumpkin while Renaer's locks were almost a chestnut brown. Both men preferred to remain clean-shaven, though Renaer's stubbly chin bespoke his past few days of hard pursuit and toil. They both wore clothes of good solid workmanship and tailoring, but while Renaer's clothes were subtle and simply better-made than many of those around him, Dagult stood out, a blazon of color and sartorial excess in his black velvet cloak, ermine-lined vest, red Shou-silk shirt, and the Aglarondan hip boots of deep crimson leather. Dagult's face wore an expression of deep disgust and impatience.

To each side of Dagult sat three gray-robed and gray-helmed Lords. As usual, they appeared identical in form and stature, regardless of whomever wore the helm and robes. No details of gender, girth, or infirmities could be discerned through the robes, as the Open Lord Ahghairon had designed them long ago.

Behind the Lords loomed a giant bulldog of a man, Lord's Champion Vorgan Drulth, looking uncomfortable in his formal uniform as the Open Lord's personal bodyguard. Renaer noted he wore metal sleeves over each of his index fingers, both sharp as claws, and other weapons bulged conspicuously from his boots, sleeves, and belt.

Dagult opened the proceedings by unfurling a scroll and reading it to the court. From the corner of his eye Renaer noticed a quill untouched by any hand, scribbling away the transcript onto a thick tome at a stand in a side alcove.

"Let this Lords' Court be convened on the matter of the death of Samark Dhanzscul, the Blackstaff; the murder of Vajra Safahr, heir of the Blackstaff; and the deaths of Ramok of Red Larch, Jarlan of Waterdeep, and Baentham of Luskan," Dagult said. "Given that the accused is my own son, I have an obvious conflict of interest here. I therefore recuse myself from this proceeding's judgement, but stay in accord with the traditions of the Lords' Court."

Dagult stepped back, handing the scroll off to a masked Lord who had entered the chamber behind him. The same dark robes and helm enshrouded this Lord as they did the other six. The seventh masked Lord stepped into Dagult's place, sat down, and intoned in a hollow, toneless voice, "The accused stands before us. How does he plead to his Lords?"

"Innocent of all charges, milords," Renaer said. Gasps erupted among his guards, the packed gallery of observers, and also from a few of the Lords themselves. Renaer continued, "I beg my Lords' indulgence, but could you identify the last three names you noted?"

The masked Lord on Renaer's far left stood and pointed at him.

"They swing from the shadowtop in Ravencourt, as the tree refuses to give up its dead. We have more than two handfuls of witnesses claiming you led them there to their deaths, and either you or your pet wizard cast the spell that slew them."

"Hardly, but thank you for identifying them. I knew not their names."

This elicited a fresh set of gasps from the gallery and even one shouted, "Hang him too, then!" before the presiding Lord pounded a gavel on the table.

Renaer continued, keeping the proceedings in his favor. "In fact, I am not guilty of any deaths laid before me this morn. Four fell by others' hands and one is not dead, as you all may have heard with her pronouncement at dawn."

"That can be faked," the accusing Lord said, sitting again. "And if not by your hand, all others died at your orders."

"No," the fifth Lord said. "I was on the streets this morning. I saw Vajra atop Blackstaff Tower. Only a Blackstaff true could hold the staff with the wolf's head, make the tower glow silver, and send that pronouncement throughout the city." The Lord's helm turned in Renaer's direction, and asked, "I would know, young Neverember, if Vajra be not dead, who lies in the Castle's crypts with your weapons in her heart and eye?"

"You will probably need the Watchful Order to dispel some illusions on her body," Renaer said. "As for who it is, I suspect it might be an agent who failed my foes—a woman who called herself Charrar. I lost two daggers and a short sword over the past few days due to haste and peril. It would have been an easy matter for my foes to gather and use them."

"And those strangers were party to their deaths?" A new Lord chimed in, pounding a fist on the table in emphasis.

Renaer paused, thinking his way through his personal library. "If my Lords would have their staff consult Quallon of the Six Fingers' book *Ghosts and Spectres Vengeful*—or their own court transcripts from multiple incidents between 1268 and 1300—they will find ample evidence that Magister Pallak Nharrelk's ghost judged and sentenced those men, not I. His presence beneath and in the Magistree killed those men, for they were unpunished for previous crimes."

"What prevarication is this? Centuries-old scrolls cannot help your cause!"

"They will," Renaer said. "Ravencourt's three-centuries-old shadowtop is all that remains of the House Nharrelk noble villa. Buried beneath that tree is a magister of the city who was slain by the corrupt Guildmasters who overthrew the Lords for a brief time two hundred years ago."

The presiding Lord flinched at that and paused, but said, "This court shall recess to test the accuracy of the defendant's statements. Until we reconvene, you are a prisoner and shall—"

As the other Lord was speaking, a court aide had approached another of the Lords and whispered to the side of the helm. That Lord nodded once, twice, and then held up a hand to interrupt both the aide and the presiding judge. "My aide Urlath supports what the accused has stated. The Hanging Tree of Ravencourt, while inactive for more than a century, has been deemed a rightful arm of the Lords' Justice and thus none can be held accountable for deaths caused by it save the victims themselves."

"What of sworn testimony from a guildmaster that you are responsible for torturing young women in hidden cellars beneath a property of yours?" said another Lord. Renaer found it irritating that all the Lords spoke in the same hollow, nondescript voice.

Renaer had to fight off both the lurch of fear in his stomach and a smile, admiring the deftness at which Ten-Rings covered his own tracks. He paced a moment, collecting his thoughts, and then said, "What we do on our own properties to consenting peoples is our own affair, a code to which each of you Lords, if unmasked, would attest. What we do to those unwilling is actionable, I agree. I'd like to face my accuser in open court and send the same charges at him, for he seeks to place his crimes on me. I proclaim Khondar

Naomal of the Watchful Order, the mage oft-called "Ten-Rings," a traitor to the city and one of two persons guilty of the crimes of which I am accused and more. I would accuse another, but he remained cloaked behind illusions. His co-conspirator walked the streets as Samark "Blackstaff" Dhanzscul for at least this last tenday, if not longer."

Tumult erupted both on the floor of the Lords' Court and up above in the gallery of witnesses. As the presiding Lord tried to gavel the crowd into order, Renaer yelled, "I demand a private audience! It is my right as a citizen of Waterdeep to plead my case to the Open Lord before any trial or sentencing is final." With his first statement, Renaer himself quelled the crowd to a watchful silence.

"The Open Lord recused himself from these proceedings," the presiding Lord said.

Another of the Lords spoke up. "Regardless, it is the boy's right as a citizen."

Five other Lords nodded in agreement and looked to Dagult. The one closest to Dagult said, "As it is our right to hold the Open Lord accountable for judgments he proclaims in our collective name."

The Open Lord readjusted his ermine-lined vest and his heavy amulet of office on his chest, and said, "Very well. Guards, provide us our escort. I shall lead the way."

━━W━━

Lord's Champion Vorgan and three guards led Renaer through the back of the Lords' Court chamber, down a slim hall northward, and through a series of stairs and turns until he wasn't sure of his orientation. By the time they reached a set of double-doors, Renaer knew he'd not seen this place before, despite much time spent in the palace over the years. Dagult, ever in the lead, opened the doors, let his son inside, and then closed the doors again, saying to Vorgan, "Remain here, in case of need."

Renaer looked around this private office, sumptuous in its appointing. "The Chamber Emerald. I've heard of it but never seen it." Renaer went around, touching the silk wall hangings of a green dragon in flight flanked by an outward facing pair of black-pelted pegasi with green feathers and manes. "Can't quite remember—this was built with money from a noble family from Impiltur, right? They lost their fortune a few decades later, leaving this as their only surviving legacy. Didn't they lose all their family and fortunes with the Spellplague?"

"Enough scholar's games, Renaer," Dagult said. "You have your private audience. Don't waste my time and yours reciting what you know of House Khearen."

"You know these charges are false, Father," Renaer said. "You know I can prove my innocence beyond what I've already said out there in open court. I'm just here to save face—yours, in fact."

Dagult, drinking from a goblet, spit out wine in surprise and coughed. "What are you blithering on about?"

"You're in this too, Father. I just didn't want to expose you before your fellow Lords."

Dagult spun toward Renaer, his face purple with fury, but before he could unleash his temper, Renaer simply said, "Roarke House."

Dagult deflated and took another breath before he said, "I don't know what you're talking about, boy."

"You're the only one who had access to the deeds and keys to all our holdings, Father," Renaer said. "You gave or sold Ten-Rings that house in return for something. What were you promised for his doing the dirty work?"

"Careful, boy," Dagult said. "You can still be punished by my hand, officially or simply parentally."

"Don't even think to try it," Renaer said, "or I'll simply start asking questions out there as to how Ten-Rings the Traitor got hold of a house owned by the Open Lord. That alone shall lead even dim-thinkers to other questions. And worse answers." He knew his father was shaken by these accusations, even if it didn't show on his face. The fact that he paced without looking at anyone or anything in particular told Renaer volumes.

Dagult took a few breaths before he said, "Don't threaten idly or without proof, Renaer. It's unbecoming. Besides, you're dealing with wizards here, boy." He paced away from Renaer. "They obviously got to your precious hin, charmed him into selling them Roarke House, and then wiped his mind of the memory later. We see at least one case a month like that in court."

Renaer slammed his hand against the desk. *"Don't lie to me!"*

The doors to the chamber burst open. Vorgan and the armed Watchmen entered. Dagult shook his head and waved them back. They closed the doors behind themselves after they looked around, seeing only the two men in the room.

"You have a share of my temper," Dagult said, "as much as you have your mother's wits."

"Father, her wits are what undid you. Them and your choice of agents." Renaer tossed a small pouch at Dagult, who opened it to find a blood-spattered eyepatch. He turned his back on Renaer to stare out the window of his office, only allowing his son to see him crush the pouch and patch. "Granek worked for you on more than one occasion before and after he was drummed out of the Watch. No longer. As for your cover earlier, one of the reasons I trust Sambral to collect my rents and manage my affairs is simple—he seems to be nearly immune to any mind-affecting magics. I am sure you know how many hedge-and-penny wizards and sorcerers try to weasel out of their rent by bending the brains of the collectors."

Dagult froze, his back to Renaer, and then sighed. Without turning to him, he said, "What is it you want of me?"

"I want all charges dropped and a public apology issued for me and my friends. I also want an end to this harassment by certain members of the Watch," Renaer said. "We both know they're more needed elsewhere than they are chasing me and my friends every night."

"Fair enough," Dagult said. "Provided you actually favor me with your presence when I ask for it. For the past two years, the only times I've seen you are when the Watch arrests you and drags you to me."

"I'll not appear simply at your summons," Renaer said. "A meal shared and scheduled once a tenday here at the palace, and I'll bring the wine."

"You do have your mother's penchant for good wines." Dagult chuckled. "Aye. Done."

"I also want independence," Renaer said. "You're the Open Lord, so live here at the palace. Conduct your affairs from here. Leave me Neverember Manor. I'm planning to restore its original name of Brandarthall in Mother's honor. I can oversee the Neverember business, if you wish, or you can find someone else to manage your holdings—openly or in secret. I only wish to manage what Mother left me—her wealth and her family's holdings, which far outstrip what you cobbled together with her money and family's connections. You can even pretend that I'm simply a wastrel son living off his father's money, if you choose to continue that tale. We'll both know who's the larger land holder in Waterdeep—and we'll both know each other's measure. I'll keep your secrets, if you keep out of my affairs."

After a long pause, Dagult said, "Done," but he remained unmoving before the large window.

"Am I free to go, then?" Renaer asked.

"One thing more—do you know where Khondar Naomal is now? Or his illusion-slinging lackey of a son?" Dagult turned to face him. "They, at least, are traitors, and the city shall demand blood."

"I don't know what happened to Centiv," Renaer said, "but my friends were going to face Ten-Rings before he tried to broach the shields around Ahghairon's Tower."

"What?" Dagult's surprise was genuine. "Guards!"

The three Watchmen burst in.

"Summon all forces and surround Ahghairon's Tower!" Dagult screamed. *"Now!* Get a runner to the Watchful Order and get us their most powerful to stop one of their own guildmasters from high treason!"

"Why the panic, Father?" Renaer asked. "It's not like Khondar'll be able to penetrate all the shields. He's under a compulsion to do this, and Vajra believes it to be a suicide run. Thus, the city will get its blood after all."

"I helped raise you, so I know *you're* no fool," Dagult said. "Few know how to penetrate those shields, but those who tried unleashed all manner of magic. Ahghairon's magic helps protect this city and keeps spells more stable here than elsewhere. Should something disrupt that, the only magic left here might be mundane commerce."

Renaer finished his father's thought. "And there's too much coin to be taken from wizards and their ilk to let that happen."

Dagult spun around and spread his arms as if to say, "Of course!" His smile faded when he said, "Another thing we do know is that any intruder who penetrates those fields far enough, a Walking Statue—yes, a monolithic guardian of the City—teleports in from gods-know-where to attack the intruder."

Renaer started to ask where the problem was, but stopped and gasped. "That statue hasn't been summoned. Ever. It could very easily—"

Dagult and Renaer uttered the same conclusion together. "—bring a patch of the spellplague back with it!"

Renaer ran for the door, heading for the same destination as the Watchmen.

>——W——<

Dagult walked quickly back to the Lords' Court, its gallery now emptied as folk chased the commotion outside. "Where is Renaer?" asked the presiding Lord.

"He is free to go, by my hand and by Code Legal," Dagult said.

"We shall have our answers on those other matters soon enough. Come, our best view of a traitor's end may be from the East Tower."

"What happened in there?" another Lord asked.

"My son has become a man, and worse yet, a hero. Something this city has not seen in some time."

CHAPTER 26

The only thing the Watch may count on among lawbreaking-wizards
is this—corner them where they live, and they are loathe to loose spell-
work that damages overmuch.

Ahghairon, *Works and Woes (Volume IV),*
Year of Azure Frost (1057 DR)

12 NIGHTAL, YEAR OF THE AGELESS ONE (1479 DR)

Meloon, Osco, and Laraelra apparated onto the stoop of the Halaerim Club on Kulzar's Alley. They breathed a sigh of relief. No shadows at their feet showed them the invisibility Vajra wrapped around them stayed in effect.

"Eugh," Osco whispered. "Hate that. Always leaves me guts in an uproar."

"We must be as quick as we can," Meloon said. "Catch the bastard before he's ready for us or any opposition—or before this spell fades."

Laraelra held the Blackstaff out in both of her hands, paused a breath, and then said, *"Gehrallen!"* She sighed in relief as the Blackstaff suddenly grew much heavier. The duskwood staff was replaced by a larger staff of twisted black metal topped with a clear crystal. The duskstaff's crystal glowed slightly, and Laraelra heard Vajra, though none of the others could.

Ah, good, she said. *Elra, you'll be able to hear me, and I can cast spells through this staff as long as you hold it. This ought to even the odds against this wizard.*

Laraelra smiled and said, "I'm ready. Let's go."

Meloon and Osco moved ahead, and Laraelra stepped forward to cross Kulzar's Alley. For the third time in as many days they stood at the threshold of Roarke House.

"Ready?" Meloon asked, hefting Azuredge, the blue runes shining brighter than the golden sunshine rising behind them.

"No," Laraelra said, her voice intermingled with Vajra's. "Let us."

She leveled the duskstaff at the door, and a blue-black beam erupted from the globe. Laraelra saw four separate flashes of energy as the beam punched through and dispelled Ten-Rings' defenses. A massive hand of energy formed from the beam, and a blue-black fist punched down the door to Roarke House. A brief shimmer around them all, and their shadows fell across the threshold.

"I suppose this means we can enter," Laraelra said, turning to Meloon and Osco. She smiled. "After you."

She heard a voice in her head from Vajra. *Don't be overconfident, Elra. I can only cast spells and counter those I'm expecting. Ten-Rings is predictable when it comes to his outer defenses, but his spells in combat may be less so.*

The trio moved cautiously into the star-and-moon covered entrance hall, Meloon in the lead. He stepped toward the cellar door, and Laraelra hissed at him, shaking her head. She whispered, "Even if he flees that way, Harug and his friends have some surprises behind every way out down there. What we need to find is probably upstairs." She pointed up the stairs that spiraled up the outer wall and overhead.

"I'll scout ahead and disable any traps or locks I find along the way," Osco whispered. "Just don't expect to see me easily, thanks to this ring." With that, Osco hopped up the stairs silently, slipping into a shadow and vanishing from sight.

Meloon dashed up the stairs after him, Laraelra following. Energy flared out of the crystal, enveloping Meloon and then Laraelra in protective spells, though Laraelra still felt nervous heading into unknown territory. They reached the first landing and paused at the first ajar door. This floor had a number of doors off this hallway while the stairs continued up, winding along the wall. Laraelra barely noticed the ball of flame bouncing down the stairs ahead of them when Meloon grabbed her and forced her through the door. He shoved her inside and kept his shoulder to the door as explosive gouts of flame scorched the wall alongside the partly open door.

"Thanks, Meloon," Laraelra gasped. "How did you—"

"Just lucky, I guess," Meloon said, and he dashed out the door and up the stairs toward the next level.

Laraelra followed, looking up the winding stairwell that led to the third and fourth floors of Roarke House. Dominating the stairwell atrium and facing east on the front wall of the house was a massive stained-glass mosaic filled with crescent moons and stars. She spotted a figure on the stairs ahead of and above Meloon— Khondar Naomal in olive green robes and a bear-pelt cloak, as if he intended to go out in the cold quickly. Elra cast a spell at him, and the purple dart caught him in the throat. His hands stopped glowing and his current spell dissipated, allowing Meloon the chance to catch up to Ten-Rings. He swung the axe and shattered some kind of magical shield around his target, but the mute wizard held his right fist toward Meloon, and a ring on his thumb pulsed with gray magic. As if he'd been shoved hard, Meloon fell backward, rolling down the stairs until Laraelra broke his fall.

On her knees, Laraelra leveled the duskstaff at Ten-Rings, and Vajra's illusory image settled over hers as the Blackstaff cast a spell Elra had never seen. A flurry of tiny feylike beings flew out of the staff's crystal, and they zipped around Khondar, each trailing snowflakes, glowing embers, a high-pitched buzz, and a light green mist. The faeries harassed his remaining shields and unleashed fire, ice, sound, and poison gas upon him. The faeries managed to pierce some of his defenses. He roared in anger. Meloon shook his head clear and got to his feet.

Khondar looked down at his foes and chuckled. "They sent you two to stop me? Is the new slip of a Blackstaff too tired to face me?

Or too afraid?" He squinted and saw the duskstaff in Laraelra's hands. "Ah, so she works through you, scrawny creature. Well, we can't have that. *You cannot hold the staff.*"

Horrified, Laraelra was unable to stop her grip from opening, despite Vajra's voice in her head screaming, *No!* While in a slight daze, Laraelra willed her freed hands into casting a spell, and a cone of blinding colors flashed out of them and up the stairs to envelop the wizard.

"An apprentice's spell, easily thwarted," Ten-Rings said, behind his magical shield.

"Kept you distracted, though," Meloon said as he swung the massive blue-edged axe and let it go. The axe flew straight at the wizard, easily slipping through his spell defenses. Khondar's left arm went up and he lowered it, the wide sleeve torn and darkly wet with blood.

Ten-Rings howled in anger and pain, but his attention was now on the axe, which landed on the stairs beside him. "Ha! You've given me another key, foolish barbarian. The First Lord Ahghairon made Azuredge himself. You've sealed my victory!"

But when Khondar reached for the axe, the blue sapphire set in the pommel flared with light. The axe twisted in Ten-Rings' grasp, as if it tried to get away from the wizard's touch.

"She won't work with anyone but a wielder she's chosen," Meloon said, drawing his little-used short sword from his belt. "A wielder worthy to defend Waterdeep."

"I'm *far* worthier than you, boy!" Khondar yelled, as he stepped backward up the stairs and away from Meloon and Laraelra. "You'll not keep me from my destiny!"

"They kept you from noticing me, Dumb-Rings," Osco said, his voice coming from behind the wizard.

Khondar twisted to see who spoke, and the halfling became visible as he drove his two daggers into Khondar's back, eliciting another raw howl from the wizard. More than twice his foe's size, Khondar's backhanded slap was more than enough to send Osco tumbling down the stairs and colliding with his friends.

Khondar panted, in pain and blooded by the attacks, but he still limped up the stairs by leaning on the railing. His free hand moved furiously, preparing a spell. "I've no time for this or for you. My destiny awaits, but I neither want you three to escape my wrath, nor do I want to damage my house overmuch."

Ten-Rings cast his spell as Laraelra lunged for the duskstaff on the stairs below her, but she could not wrap her hands around it and only shoved it along.

All three of them yelled as the world flipped, and they fell upward.

>———w———<

Meloon grunted as he slammed into the underside of the stairs above him, but Osco and Laraelra, who were closer to the railing, fell up toes over brows all the way to the top of Roarke House. They lay stunned and groaning against the skylight four stories above the hard marble floor below. Ten-Rings stood at the railing, his feet hooked to its underside, while his robes and cloak fell upward. Strangely, the duskstaff made no noise at all when it fell upward to cling to the jagged perch under the stairs near Meloon.

"I'll not waste another spell on you lot," Khondar said, but he held onto the railing with white knuckles. He gritted his teeth as the red gem on his left forefinger ring glowed with regenerative magic, and his wounds closed.

"Khondar, catch!" Meloon yelled from above him.

The wizard's attention snapped upward, and he saw the warrior using his short sword to flip something at him against the pull of the reversed gravity. The duskstaff flipped end over end, and reflex brought up Khondar's arm and hand to catch it or fend it off. The staff settled against his palm with a crackle, and Khondar's eyes went wide as he remembered what happened when unworthies touched a Blackstaff.

The explosion blew Khondar up the stairs and through the

stained glass window, launching him out across Gunarla's Dash and onto the roof of Kendall's Gallery. From his odd vantage point, Meloon could see the wizard laying stunned. Meloon and his friends remained pinned helplessly by his spell. I've got to try to get them before the spell ends, Meloon thought, or they'll fall. Maybe I can reach Elra's staff . . .

Meloon strained against the spell's pressure, sat up, and lashed his belt at the twisted remnants of the stair's railing. It caught, and Meloon yanked hard to pull himself down before the belt came loose again. He stood on the stairs, hooking his feet on the railing as Khondar had done. He looked up and saw his friends stunned atop the house. He called to them without response.

Meloon worked his way up along the railing, bridging the gap in the railing carefully toward the open window. By the time Meloon reached the breach to look out, Ten-Rings stood atop the far roof, glaring at him through the shattered window. Meloon could see two flashes of blue and green light on Khondar's fingers. The axe spun in his grasp, but the wizard held Azuredge over his head with some effort. He yelled, "Revenge can wait, but victory cannot. *Rekarlen!*" and was gone.

Meloon howled, "No!" but was heard only by passersby in the alley outside, drawn out by curiosity and the noise of the battle in the early morn. He felt his stomach flip again, and his feet landed back on the stairs. He watched the slightly stirring Osco and Laraelra began their long fall to the floor below.

CHAPTER 27

Step back, secure your goods and children, then sell tickets or place bets. Your choice.

Savengriff on what common folk could do about spell battles,
City of Mages, Year of the Starving (1381 DR)

12 NIGHTAL, YEAR OF THE AGELESS ONE (1479 DR)

Khondar "Ten-Rings" Naomal reappeared at the apex of the conical roof of Ahghairon's Tower. He halted a moment, assured that one of his rings would keep him aloft. His regenerative ring had healed his wounds, but he growled in discomfort from the aches in his back and arm, exacerbated by the axe that spun in his hand and fought to be released from his grip. He held it immobile with both hands and whispered, "Calm yourself Azuredge. Help me uncover the secrets of your maker. That's all that matters now—the tower and its secrets."

Khondar scanned the dingy rooftops and thick cooksmoke, the sprawl of Fields Ward and Mountainside, and the filth of the harbor and its morass of wood that was the Mistshore. He surveyed all and smiled grimly. "Soon, those secrets will make all this mine, and it will shine under wizards' rule. I shall restore its glory, and they shall call me the Inheritor of Ahghairon!" He looked down at the twitching axe and said, "And we shall find you a far better wielder with whom you can defend the Wizard-City of the North. For now, open the door."

The winds whipped light snow around him as Khondar swung the axe down on the magical field and the crest of the tower's roof.

The impact sounded like a thunderclap, and blue fires suffused the fields all around the tower. Khondar flinched, then realized the effect simply merged Azuredge's magic with the fields, harming him not. He laughed and slowly sank through the first magical field up to his waist. "Thank you, idiot and axe both, for your unwitting help!"

Khondar threw his cloak back behind his shoulders. From beneath the bracer on his right forearm he pulled one of the wands he'd stolen from Blackstaff Tower. He dropped the white ash wand point first onto the surface of the fields, and it lit up the second field with gold energy and emitted another thunderclap before it sank into the magic. The wand remained half-embedded inside the translucent field, the magic fading to a light yellow color. Khondar sank through the fields, the biting wind only reaching his head, shoulders, and heart outside the fields. He smiled, feeling only elation at his impending control of the city.

His grin faded when he saw opposition headed for him. "The fools would try to stop me. It is now time to show them Ten-Rings was ever their better."

>———W———<

"Hang on!" Eltalon Vaundrar's voice rose from its usual mutter to warn his companions as the graying wizard steered his flying carpet through some crosswinds. They dipped close to the near-empty market, its open spaces given over to sellswords or cart races as winter set in and wares for sale were no more 'till spring. Maerla Windmantle and Eiruk Weskur clung to the edges of the flying carpet, their faces serious as heartstop. Eltalon said, "The Blackstaff didn't warn you or us in time, boy!"

"Look at Ahghairon's Tower!" Eiruk Weskur pointed, and the three of them saw the plume of blue fire that surrounded one of the most sacred magical sites of the city. "He's not just robbing me of memories or honor—he's out to steal Waterdeep's greatest secrets!"

"Of that, I'm hardly surprised," Eltalon said. "Maerla, once we're in range, hit him with a cacaphonic burst while I try a feeble-mind on the bastard. Eiruk, hit him with whatever you have. We may only get one or two passes to stop him."

Eiruk gritted his teeth and hugged himself as they flew into the wind and the biting flurry. He kept his attention on the tower as the three of them slalomed around chimneys and taller buildings. Once within range, Eiruk cast the most powerful spell he had with the longest reach, and a ball of fire streaked out of his palm toward Ten-Rings. The fireball engulfed the top of Ahghairon's Tower.

Khondar's smile faded, even though the flames washed around him harmlessly. An apprentice-level spell, he thought, one easily ignored. Ten-Rings willed his blue-stone ring away in favor of another, which he activated the moment it arrived. Additional defenses fell into place around him.

With his other hand, Khondar cast a spell behind the south-ward side of the tower. A massive hand formed from magical force appeared and hovered out of the approaching guildmasters' sights. Ten-Rings held his concentration to maintain the magical hand. He felt but ignored the buffeting and blasting maelstrom of noise around him—Maerla's spell, no doubt. One of his rings protected him from what he knew would be Eltalon's standard mental attack. He saw them now—Eltalon, Maerla, and Eiruk—on the flying carpet speeding toward him—and their doom.

Khondar willed the magical hand alongside the tower and outward. The magical construct grabbed for the flying carpet as it flew past the tower's roof, and the hand succeeded at crumpling it in its grasp. Two figures jumped free of it and floated to the ground slowly, the wintry wind pushing them apart and farther away from the tower. Eltalon, unfortunately, found his right ankle pinned in the massive hand's grip. Despite the awkward position at which he floated above the tower, Eltalon unleashed a cone of grayish waves of energy at Khondar, but to no avail.

"Eltalon, you fool," Khondar said. "Wasted energy, that spell. My own spells easily thwart that exhausting magic—and soon, I'll claim more magic *and* the Open Lord's Throne. I'm doing this for the betterment of the city and its wizards. You'll see! And then we'll discuss if you're still worthy of serving as a guildmaster in *my* city."

The hand carried Eltalon away to the far side of the tower and lowered him out of Khondar's sight. Khondar heard the brief yell when the hand dissipated, dropping Eltalon unceremoniously into the crowd gathered below.

Khondar cast a spell barrier above him, not to close off any egress of his but to prevent being attacked from behind.

"Tymora, let me be in time. Let them have survived that." Meloon dashed down the stairs to the front entrance hall of Roarke House. When Khondar's spell ended, Meloon had landed safely on the stairs and Osco had managed to twist and grab at the railings and lintels as he fell, slowing his descent. The halfling hung overhead, yelling "Ow! My arms!"

Just as Meloon ran past, Osco's grip slipped. However, with no useful magic at hand, Laraelra fell the entire height of the house from its skylight all the way to the hard marble floor below. She lay still in a pool of blood.

Meloon reached her side and yanked the ring Vajra had given him off his finger, putting it on Laraelra's hand. Vajra promised it would heal him once a day from great wounds. Its red gem glowed, and she began breathing more regularly. Meloon looked over at Osco, who sat up groaning a pace or two away, "Let's not do that again. Ever."

Laraelra opened her eyes and smiled up at Meloon, touching his arm. "Ten-Rings?" she asked.

"Gone," Meloon said, "and he took Azuredge with him. At least that Blackstaff of yours gave him a good blast out of here."

Laraelra sat bolt upright and snapped, *"Gehrallen!"* The dusk-staff appeared in her hands, and she sighed happily as her hands closed around it.

The crystal atop the staff glowed, and Vajra's voice said, *Thank the gods. You must move fast! Ten-Rings has breached Ahghairon's Tower.*

"Don't worry, folks." Osco chuckled. "I think I might know how to slow him down."

Renaer ran out of the palace in time to see two of three wizards of the Watchful Order fall as slow as feathers to the ground. The winds outside the palace whipped a light snow, but this discomfort didn't stop crowds from gathering in a thick circle around Ahghairon's Tower—at a respectful distance. None wanted to be *too* close to the semi-visible blue fire shields that still held a skeleton floating in their midst, the warning for the past three centuries that Ahghairon's Tower was sacrosanct and not to be disturbed.

Renaer ran over to a friendly face and helped Eiruk Weskur avoid landing on his head, the winds having spun the feather-light spellcaster upside-down. Eiruk settled back onto his feet and nodded at Renaer. "Thanks. I take it you've cleared your name, then?"

"Aye," he replied. "It's now fairly obvious who's causing all the mayhem, isn't it?"

"Vajra sent a message to us at the Towers of the Order, exposing Ten-Rings's and Centiv's treason. We were supposed to capture him before he tried this, but we were too late. I don't understand why he's so brazen to do this in broad daylight, do you?"

"I think Blackstaff Tower has much to do with that," Renaer replied. "The ghosts of the tower set some spell on him, compelling him to try and breach Ahghairon's Tower. Even if they hadn't, he might have done this anyway before Vajra rallied all her energy as the new Blackstaff against him."

"Where are the rest of the guild wizards?" Eiruk wondered aloud, looking to the east toward the Towers of the Order. "They swore they'd follow either by air or foot."

"Could be some are more loyal to Ten-Rings and hope that by delaying, they'll be in position to garner favor from him in his new position." Renaer smacked his fist in his palm. "Waterdhavians are nothing if not practical, adapting to every changing situation, Eiruk. You know that."

Maerla Windmantle came up behind the two young men, sidling in between them briefly for warmth. "Well, there'll be many a former member of the guild by nightfall, once we determine who stood with Ten-Rings in his treason. Eiruk, stay here, while we try and bring him down from there yet again." With a few words, Maerla launched herself skyward, arcing toward the top of the tower.

>———W———<

Khondar smiled as he felt the magic of this place and its protections wash over him. He thought the fields would have had dangerous magic trapped between them, but he encountered nothing so far. As he looked up, he saw the matronly Maerla launching spells at his barriers to no avail. They would not hold for long, but Ten-Rings knew that he only needed to pierce another field or two before he was out of reach.

The sapphire amulet on Khondar's chest flashed as he drew its necklace over his head. Ten-Rings laid the amulet and necklace to rest on the magical barrier, and another crack of thunder echoed across Castle Ward. Khondar did not hear much of the outcry from below as he sank deeper into Ahghairon's magical defenses.

Khondar was so enraptured by the magic all around him that he failed to notice the sparkles that rose around him until they became a swarm so thick they could not be ignored. He looked up and saw a more solid form taking shape—a long-sleeping defense had awakened, changing the tower beneath him as its stones shifted and slid into place. Khondar blanched in fear, but he laughed when he realized this defense held no danger for him either.

"The tower accepts me! It takes me as its rightful heir, not an invader!" No one but Khondar heard his howls—at least no one outside the tower and its fields.

>———w———<

Osco pushed open the door, and Meloon helped Laraelra walk into the room. She leaned on both the duskstaff and Meloon, having nearly died in her four-story fall. She smiled at him and Osco, and whispered, "Thanks. Let's find his secrets and get them out of here before someone else has the same idea."

"Gods, I thought wizards were supposed to be smart," Osco said. "Ten-Rings had this great bedroom big enough for seven hin, and he slept on a cot in his secret workroom behind it. See?"

Osco stood on his toes and reached a hand up into the left side of the chimney to trigger a switch. A door popped open in the stone-worked mantle, revealing a smaller chamber beyond with a cot, two worktables, and a small bookshelf heavily laden with books.

Laraelra resisted the temptation to sit down and begin reading, but instead hobbled over to the farthest worktable. She pulled away a small green cloth, and found a pair of hands carved from russet sheen. On each of the fingers and both thumbs gleamed a ring. Laraelra started to cast a spell to examine the magics or determine which rings were magical, when Vajra's voice came out of the staff. *Don't bother, Elra. The Jhaarnnan Hands are obviously magical, as are most of Khondar's rings. Gather those and the books, and I'll bring you home.*

"We'd better find a way to seal this place up," Osco said, "or looters'll pick it clean. After all, there's two big holes in the front of the place—and I haven't had the chance to root around much."

Vajra's voice rang out from the staff. *Good thought, Osco. Thank you.* A spell flashed out of the duskstaff and they could no longer hear the howling wind coming up through the atrium from the smashed stained-glass window.

Meloon and Osco shrugged and looked at Laraelra, who held up the sculpted hands and said, "Wards of some kind. Meloon, could you take these? Osco, grab that small chest down there." She gathered the books off the desk, and said, "We're ready, Vajra."

The staff said, *You boys better hold on to Elra now.*

The air glistened and shifted, growing darker amid a vortex of snow and magic. Within that vortex grew solid stone, and the tower itself groaned and scraped loudly as a massive shape formed four stories above the street. Folk below gasped and pointed as the conical roof of Ahghairon's Tower collapsed and shifted, the tower widening at its top to reform as crenellations and a more solid base for the statue that now loomed overhead. The summoning spell abated, and the air above Waterdeep filled with the screeching roar of a massive stone griffon. The Walking Statue that had long waited in reserve to protect this tower spread its stone wings wide with a clatter of carved slate feathers and reared on its powerful hindquarters, its talons digging into the new stone crenellations that formed its perch.

The Walking Statue froze in place, its rearing form and spread wings now making Ahghairon's Tower taller than the minarets in the palace and the tallest structure in Castle Ward by far, save the towers of the castle set high on the mountain.

Standing in the shadow of the tower, Eiruk Weskur looked up at the statue and knew it was almost three times a normal griffon's size. His studies and experiences with magical beasts told him something else: while it might be a magical statue, it acted like a real griffon. Eiruk knew that its preening display was more a show of its power and virility, rather than any attack. In fact, its paralysis and lack of any attack posture gave him hope.

"It's not attacking," Eiruk whispered, smiling.

Beside him, Renaer saw the same clues and said with him, "Because he can't get in."

Maerla Windmantle flew over the two men, pulling her gaze away from Ahghairon's latest wonder to land next to her most-prized apprentice. "Eiruk, what do you two know?"

"The statue's not in any offensive or defensive posture, mistress," Eiruk whispered. "Khondar must not be any danger to the tower or its fields!"

"That might be the reason, but don't assume more than you can prove. Ten-Rings might simply have already been accepted by the tower, and he's controlling the statue. Let us see how this plays out. Keep your wand at ready. If spells start to fray or go wild because this thing brought magichaos with it, we'll need all the help we can get to contain a rebirth of spellplague—especially since Ten-Rings has disrupted one of the city's places of power."

⊱—W—⊰

"And here you are." Vajra's voice shifted in the wind, even though she stood directly in front of them, her hands on the dusk-staff as well as Elra's. Osco, Meloon, and Laraelra shivered in the cold wind atop Blackstaff Tower again.

"Can't you bring us anywhere warm?" Osco complained.

"Not until we've stopped Ten-Rings. Meloon, put the Jhaarnnan Hands down here, please."

"I don't suppose you'd let us try any of those rings out?" Osco asked.

Vajra's voice alone carried enough snap to cure Osco of that notion. "Be content with the gift you have, Osco Salibuck."

"That ring with the blue gem—what does it do?" Meloon asked.

"It looks like a spell-storing ring or one that triggers a pre-set teleport," Vajra said. "Why?" She barely looked at Meloon as she prepared the Jhaarnnan Hands with some spells.

"I want my axe back," Meloon said as he snatched the ring off the sculpted hand, placed it on his own, and said, *"Rekarlen!"*

The warrior vanished as the shriek of a stone griffon rang out across Waterdeep.

Khondar looked closely at his hand, admiring the rings he had collected over the years but focusing on his newest acquisiton. The sapphire ring of Ahghairon gleamed bright, as if carved and set only yesterday instead of four centuries ago. He felt the power of the ring thrum on his finger, and it resonated strongly when he crouched and pressed his hand flat against the next barrier. Again, thunder pealed within the barriers and all throughout the city, but Khondar had stopped laughing. His destiny was at hand, and he was but one barrier away from the tower's surface.

Few had been this close to Ahghairon's Tower since the fabled wizard's nine apprentices sealed it after his death. Only those few possessed by the ghostly Aghairon's Cloak ever broached the barriers or the tower, and none of them retained any memory of what wonders the tower held.

Khondar held his breath and stopped to savor the moment as his form slid through yet another barrier. He whispered, "Ahghairon, hear me. I am Khondar 'Ten-Rings' Naomal, master of the Watchful Order of Magists and Protectors. In tribute to you, I would bring glory and power back to your city. I humbly approach your tower and take up your mantle with all the respect and honor I have. Allow me to serve your city as its Open Lord as you did."

Ending his prayer, Khondar touched the final barrier.

Meloon blinked into existence standing knees deep among blue flames. He lost his balance but soon realized the flames were neither hot nor harming him. Meloon steadied himself atop the flat tower. He saw Ten-Rings within the magical fields directly beneath him. The wizard knelt upon other fields inside, resting a blue ring against a field that pulsed with the same energy, and he apparently hadn't seen Meloon's arrival.

The warrior turned and spotted his axe. He stepped close and grabbed the haft of Azuredge, which now lodged between the toe talons of a massive stone griffon. Meloon tugged at it, and a shriek sounded louder in his ears than the grinding stone of the talons as the statue reacted in pain.

Meloon readied himself to pull Azuredge loose from the magical field, bracing his feet on either side of the embedded axe. In his head, he heard the axe's voice—

Patience, warrior. Vengeance sweetens with patience.

Vajra, Laraelra, and Osco stared out over Castle Ward from atop Blackstaff Tower, amazed at the massive form of the stone griffon. Their argument continued despite their combined wonder.

"Ten-Rings had Azuredge?" Vajra snapped. "Why didn't someone tell me that earlier?"

"You didn't ask," Osco said. "So what's your plan? Can you blast Dumb-Rings by blasting those hands?"

"Something like that." Vajra sent her silent instructions to Laraelra, who nodded, then approached the halfling from behind.

"What do you need me to do?" Osco asked, then stepped back in surprise as Laraelra drew her dagger and dragged a long cut down the length of her index finger. She dripped blood onto the Jhaarnnan Hands and said, "He who has caused me pain, find him through this magic. Find his scent and bring him to ground."

"Just do the same and repeat what I'm saying, little man," Vajra said, "and think of Ten-Rings while you do."

Before Vajra even began her litany, Osco slashed his forearm and repeated with her, "He who has caused me pain, find him through this magic. Find his scent and bring him to ground."

Vajra nodded her thanks, and the duskstaff whirled across the roof and into her hands. With a thought, she exchanged it with the true Blackstaff, and an eerie glow surrounded the metal wolf's head at the staff's end. In her mind's eye, Vajra could see the hidden library of the Blackstaff clearly, even though she remained outside the tower. Four phantom shapes, none distinct enough to be named, hovered around an image of a translucent wolf. The chorus of voices didn't identify which of the former Blackstaffs worked with her, but they told her, *We can lend you some aid for this, which bulwarks our works of old. Be swift though, for this expenditure weakens us all for a time.*

Vajra smiled, and sent back a silent response, *Better to thwart this enemy now. If he is not stopped, we'll be weakened for far longer.*

The Blackstaff loomed almost a full yard taller than the young woman, but her magic and her will stood taller still. Vajra raised and then drove the true Blackstaff hard onto the stone atop Blackstaff Tower, the impact sounding like a giant's hammer blow. She focused and whispered *"Yaqrlueiehar qapeoirl suakr."*

The eyes on the staff's wolf-head glowed green, while Osco and Elra's wounds and eyes glowed white. The energy leeched out of all eight points, and a pair of ephemeral wolves made of white and green energy stalked around the Jhaarnnan Hands, drinking in the scent and magic of their prey. They leaped off the tower and loped their way across the skies above Waterdeep, heading toward Ahghairon's Tower. Unearthly howls filled the air and frosted the clouds across which they raced.

Vajra finished her spell and said, "May this be enough to stop the traitor—and serve to discourage those who would follow his example."

"Actually, I think ol' Dumb-Rings will be discouraged enough when he realizes he doesn't have these." Osco grinned wide as he produced a rune-covered key and a garnet-covered dagger out of his belt pouch. "The fool didn't notice they were gone during the tussle at Roarke House. Guess my fingers must be magical too, eh?"

Vajra and Laraelra stared in shock at the halfling, then giggled, working their way up to exhausted laughter among all three.

>——W——<

Khondar pulled the sheathed dagger off his belt and pressed it against the final energy barrier, but he felt more resistance than usual. He pressed it point first, then flat against the field again, and only sparks arced up his hand and forearm in response.

Khondar pulled the dagger from its sheath and screamed in anger. The blade was simple steel, and Khondar realized the gem in the pommel was an opaque red jasper, rounded and smoothly cabochon cut rather than the rose-cut garnet it was earlier. The blade held the carved words in trade Common, proclaiming the blade "Osco's Luck."

Khondar Naomal found a dry, hollow laugh escaping his lips despite himself. He reached into his belt pouch to withdraw his final item. "Perhaps Ahghairon's Key could force the final barriers open anyway," he muttered, and then realized the key he held was an ornate one to be sure, made of silver with three emeralds for its tines. It was no simple iron key like thousands of others throughout the city, but it was also not the key he needed. Some power hummed within it, but it was not a magic that would help him now. With that realization, the last glimmers of hope flickered out in Khondar.

He looked up through the fields, knowing he could still escape while the previous keys stood in place, and he paled in disbelief.

"You should be dead, boy!" he yelled.

The blond barbarian stood atop the final field, his hands around the blue axe. "I'm still striding, Ten-Rings," he said. "How do the wagons roll for you now?"

Meloon smiled, eyes locked on Khondar's, and brought his left hand up toward his face. Khondar could see the ring on his hand—for it matched the mundane one on his own left hand. His stomach tightened into knots as he cast a spell to fly out of the fields—

—and then he heard the unearthly howls as if they were on his heels.

>———w———<

Meloon's focus on Khondar broke when the first howls drifted his way. He swallowed hard when he saw the magical wolves racing toward him. He wasn't afraid of the wolves, but now that he looked out over the city, he realized just how high he stood above the streets—and his stomach lurched in fear.

He clutched Azuredge's haft as strongly as he could and looked to the west, on the chance some kinder fate wait in that direction. He stared into clouds black as night and a howling wind driving snow and ice their way. Despite it being near highsun, torches and lights blazed on the castle and palace ramparts.

Meloon looked back in time to see the wolves bring their own clouds and cold trailing them as they loped around Ahghairon's Tower. The warrior's fear faded as he realized the wolves paid him no mind, focusing all their dark green stares at Ten-Rings, who had begun to rise out of the fields.

Have faith, kin mine. Face fear and take the leap.

The voice both calmed and shocked him. Meloon looked down at Ten-Rings and knew he had to act fast to stop him. Khondar paused to pluck small items out of the magical fields and saw the wand floating in the energy field near his left foot.

Meloon reached down and grasped the wand with his left hand, keeping his right on the axe. Khondar let loose a roar of anger contrasted with the pale look of fear on his face. Meloon froze, holding both items in his grasp, and Azuredge twisted so her handle pointed out. *Hold and take your leap of faith, my kinsman.*

Meloon swallowed hard, whispered, "Lady of Smiles, I need your guidance," and stepped backward off the fields and the tower.

With the wand in his left hand and the axe handle in his right, Meloon spread his arms above him, wand and axe dragging against the magical fields. They slowed his plummet only slightly. Meloon wondered if the look of horror on his face matched that first look on

Khondar's face when he slid past, pulling away the two outermost keys for Khondar's escape. Any other thoughts soon left Meloon's head as the ground rushed up far more quickly than he liked.

Faith is tested in leaps, not steps, Meloon. Azuredge's voice was calm as ever.

To his surprise, Meloon's racing heart slowed and he calmed as well. "So I've heard," he said, and he looked down as he heard the crowd below scream and yell at his descent. Oddly, the first person he noticed as he approached was Renaer, who pointed at him. Meloon yelled, "For Waterdeep!" and expected to slam into the cobbles of the palace courtyard a breath later. Instead, he slowed to a stop as his weight disappeared and he floated the last few lengths down the tower. He blinked, and then looked down to see the ground a mere fingers-breadth away. He laughed and stepped down, turning to see Eiruk Weskur standing behind him, his hands in casting readiness.

"Meloon, watch out!" Eiruk yelled.

Meloon turned to see Khondar's furious face right before him. He lurched backward, pulling the wand and Azuredge with him. The magical fields snapped with thunderous booms. The recoil knocked Ten-Rings off his feet, but more importantly, the fires around the tower snuffed out.

"The wolves are trailing magic and building another spell field around the tower," Eiruk said, his eyes wide with wonderment. "They're sealing themselves in with Khondar."

The translucent white-green field completely encased the tower and all its subsequent magical fields, coalescing from top to bottom like a snowdrift built in reverse. It closed completely around and beneath the talons of the stone griffon atop the tower. The field shimmered and faded to near-invisibility. The populace watched as the wolves flew sunward around the tower, seeking the traitor Ten-Rings.

Khondar heard the howls, and he heard the claws scrabbling against all the other magical fields. The two wolves clawed their way past the first two barriers through the tears the barbarian's plummeting escape had created. But rather than close with him directly, the wolves each dodged into the spaces between the barriers, harassing and howling at Khondar with only air and energy between them.

Khondar tried to fly straight out, using the tears in the outer barriers to escape, but the fields slowed him, as if he flew through thickening syrup. The tears sealed before he could leave. He lunged toward the fallen Meloon Wardragon, only to see Renaer Neverember and Eiruk Weskur drag the barbarian back to safety. Ten-Rings slammed face-first into the second barrier. He tried to concentrate, but the increased howling distracted him.

Ten-Rings concentrated on his bracers and tried to will his spell-storing ring to him, but no transfer happened.

That Blackstaff bitch found a way to disrupt the Jhaarnnan Hands? Impossible!

He imagined more tortures he would visit on her. Now that Meloon had taken Azuredge away, the wolves closed on him.

Khondar flew up from the base of the tower, using one of his rings to call up an earth elemental from the courtyard stones at the base of the tower. One of the wolves simply grew in size and savaged it to rubble in less than a breath. The second wolf swooped up and ate Ahghairon's Amulet. That barrier slammed shut again with a thunderclap, and Khondar realized to his horror that the barriers that penned him in meant nothing to the wolves. They dived through the tower itself if their paths took them that way. The first wolf flew above and gobbled up the wand floating in the third barrier. When the wand snapped in two in its jaws, the sound echoed, as if it were a century-old phandar falling in a storm.

The howling wolves flew three passes while Khondar flew one circuit up and around the tower, and one last thunderclap told him one of them had removed Ahghairon's Ring from the fields.

Ten-Rings slipped up to the top of the tower and unleashed a chain of lightning bolts, engulfing both creatures, but the energy served only to make the wolves seem even more solid. One wolf bit and slashed at Khondar as it flew past, dislodging the bracer he wore on his left wrist and swallowing it whole. The wizard did not initially feel his wounds, but soon screamed in pain as he realized it had stripped flesh from his arm along with the bracer. He pulled his wounded arm in close and readied a spell with his undamaged hand.

"I'm Ahghairon's heir! You things should be hunting down *my* enemies!"

Khondar "Ten-Rings" Naomal unleashed a dazzling flurry of colored orbs from his right palm, the iridescent blasts from the orbs temporarily scattering the image of one wolf. The second wolf slipped around the tower and came up from below the wizard. It clamped its jaws down on his extended right hand and chewed. The wizard screamed and pulled his arm back. All he retrieved from the wolf's jaws was half his bloodied sleeve and his muscle-clad bones. No bracer, no skin, and no rings. Khondar's last coherent thought as he descended into madness was—I'll need that skin more than they will . . . for spell components.

The cloud of white and green energy drifted around the tower, slowly becoming a spectral wolf again by its third circuit. It chased Ten-Rings four full orbits around the tower before it snapped its jaws closed over his left hand, stripping it of flesh and rings. Khondar blasted the wolf's head off, as many green missiles crackled off his skeletal right hand, but again, the green-white cloud drifted away slowly, lupine features growing back together slowly. The other wolf attacked from behind, snatched Ten-Rings up in his jaws, and worried him left and right, tearing his cloak off his shoulders and rending his tunic to tatters before letting him fly. Khondar fled.

Items clattered onto the cold, snow-covered stones at Vajra, Laraelra, and Osco's feet. The bracer she'd seen Khondar wear, along with a handful of rings, appeared, covered in blood.

"They started with the left hand and arm, I see," Vajra said, dispassionately.

"You mean . . . those wolves . . . ?" Laraelra asked, swallowing hard and gagging as more bloody bits arrived to stain the rapidly falling snow. Laraelra staggered over to the tower's edge and retched. She wiped a hand across her mouth, then pulled at the trap door atop the tower. It opened easily, and she said, "I can't watch this. I'm sorry."

Osco kept his stomach from rebelling, but he too retched when steaming remnants of Ten-Rings's gore-soaked tunic and breeches landed with wet splats atop the pile around the Jhaarnnan Hands. He followed Laraelra into the tower, casting a sad eye back toward Vajra. "You coming?" he asked.

The Blackstaff shook her head without turning.

The Black Hunt delivers what it brings to ground, Vajra recalled reading, but she never realized that the wolves and the Black Hunt magic would be involved when she set her spells into motion. The bloody rain of rent garments continued, followed by the clang of the second bracer and the tinkling of five metallic rings. Vajra steeled herself and swallowed, whispering, "The Blackstaff is as hard as stone."

She thanked Auril silently for the heavy snow that now swirled around, as it helped blanket and deaden the strong smell of spilled blood.

Inside her head, Khelben's voice said softly, *Birth and death always come with blood. Waterdeep has seen a traitor's death and a Blackstaff's birth—and perhaps more still.*

Some mothers dragged their fascinated and bloodthirsty children away, while other Waterdhavians pushed forward or joined the crowd to watch the gory display. People cheered as the wolves clamped onto opposing limbs and pulled. The only things hindering people's views of the carnage were the constantly changing flight of the chase and the onset of winter's first blizzard.

Renaer, Eiruk, and Meloon smiled grimly when Khondar's eyes locked on each of theirs in succession as he passed by while flying from his tormentors. The wizard's brief pause allowed a wolf to catch him again and rend the last rings from his left hand—along with the rest of its flesh. The young Lord Neverember, Meloon Wardragon, and Eiruk Weskur were among the few folk who remained in place, watching this spectacle wordlessly. They were also among the very few who did not begin taking wagers as to which body part would be next to be damaged. They simply waited to see that justice was done. By the time the wolves charged in opposite directions to tear the body of Khondar "Ten-Rings" Naomal in twain, glow-globes shed light down on the snow gathered deep across their shoulders.

EPILOGUE

For Waterdeep to remain the City of Splendors, it needs heroes and folk of valor to carry her banners higher than commerce or politics. Splendor is not a right but a privilege, and one that must be earned by courage, not bought by coin nor conjured by magic.

Aleena Paladinstar, *Of Fathers, Faiths, and Fortunes,*
Year of the Hidden Harp (1403 DR)

20 NIGHTAL, YEAR OF THE AGELESS ONE (1479 DR)

The light of Selûne and her Tears reflected off a fresh snowfall as the private carriage dashed past Ahghairon's Tower.

"Ugh," Lady Nharaen Wands said. "I can't stand that new horror the wizards unleashed." She looked away, pulling her mink-lined hood closer to shield her eyes, but Lord Torlyn Wands could not tear his eyes away.

The now-skeletal remains of Khondar "Ten-Rings" Naomal continue to fly within the spell barriers around the tower, his skull ever turning to spot his pursuers. Also within the barriers lurked two spectral wolves, ever giving chase. Torlyn smiled grimly as the wolves flew in opposite directions around the tower, only to have Khondar's skeleton explode as the wolves tore him in two different directions at once. Lord Wands knew that the skeleton would reform and the chase would be on again—forever a warning to those who sought to abuse Waterdeep's past and its magic.

A good sign for our times, Torlyn thought. *The past watches and warns us always, and we can't ignore it. Still, we have to keep* moving forward—and perhaps we'll be deserving of the gifts of the past in the hopes of a brighter future.

A short time later, the carriage halted at Roarke House, and Torlyn said, "This is my stop, sister. You go on and enjoy the Gralleth ball. If our business gets concluded early enough, Renaer and I will be along."

"Can't I come with you, Brother?" Nhaeran asked. "With Hurnal being found dead, are you sure it's safe for either of us tonight?"

"We're both safe. Our cousin died because of his own dealings with Khondar Naomal. Even if the old wizard hadn't killed him to get at the Blackstaff, Lord Thongolir and his men might have done so rather than just reporting their finding his body." Torlyn smiled, and his reassuring touch on her arm calmed his younger sister. "So go to this feast with a light heart, but don't expect me before highmoon."

"I shall have to set up a number of ladies with whom you can dance when you arrive, Brother," Nhaeran teased.

Torlyn shut the carriage door and shook his head as he approached the door and knocked.

Madrak, Renaer's halfling butler opened the door and waved him in, smiling. "A pleasure to see you again, Lord Wands. This way, please."

Renaer watched from above as Torlyn, the last of his eight guests, arrived. He smiled and finished adjusting his new tunic and jacket before he headed downstairs to the dining hall. According to Madrak, the early arrivals had quickly guessed who had summoned them here to Roarke House, given the presence of the halfling servants and cook staff from Neverember Hall. Still, as requested, all the hin begged off providing any more details when asked by simply replying, "The master will tell you when he's ready."

Renaer entered the room, and Madrak and the three other

halfling servants withdrew, closing the doors behind them. Renaer strode to the head of the table and raised a goblet, toasting all.

"Friends, good health, good deeds, and good fortune to us, those we hold dear, and our city!" He looked on each of them and was glad all were now healthy and healed from their recent adventures.

After the nine of them drained their goblets and filled them again, Renaer strode to the sideboard and pulled a long chest out of the lowest drawer. "I asked you all here tonight—at the sight of our foe's failings—to thank you all for your help in these past tendays and to beg one more indulgence on my part." He placed the large box at his end of the table, opening it and withdrawing its contents one by one.

He passed each of them a small box, which opened to reveal a gold signet ring marked with a crescent moon and a star. "Look inside them as well," Renaer said. Inside the band, beneath the signet, a smooth garnet glinted in the light.

Osco snorted. "What's all this?"

"I want you all to join me in restoring the city to what it should be—the City of Splendors. We need to be heroes like those who used to fill this city. We need to bring hope and honor and trust back to the streets."

"And we need rings for this?" Eiruk Weskur asked. "One would think after Khondar's fall, you'd not want anything to do with rings for a while."

"Not particularly, no," Renaer said, "but I wanted a badge or symbol of some kind for us. When I had those rings made, I was thinking I might try and restore the Moonstars, who were former Harpers and personal agents of the Blackstaff."

With that, every other head in the room turned to Vajra, whose silver-shod Blackstaff rested upright of its own volition next to her chair. She finished what she was eating and wiped her mouth.

"You're not personal agents of *mine*," Vajra said. "That was more than a century ago. I'm happy enough to call you friends and staunch allies. Nor am I a leader of folk—at least, not yet. Know that while Renaer and I talked about this, I am not the driving force behind the idea—Renaer is—though you're all welcome to use the name of the *Tel'Teukiira*. I know those who came before you would be honored. I will happily work with you, but my responsibilities force me to remain apart from your group for now."

"I remember most of them Moonstars dying at the Stump Bog fighting some group of vampires or something," said Harug Shield-sunder. "Year of the Fallen Friends or something."

Parlek Lateriff said, "That's right. Many did. But not all. The most significant change from that battle was the death of Tsarra, the second Blackstaff. The *Tel'Teukiira* are a dubious group to follow, Renaer, with a less-than-charmed legacy left behind."

"Why not be the Red Sashes?" Osco piped up. "Isn't that where you were going with the hidden red gem, Ren?"

The only response he got from Renaer was a sly smile as he lifted his goblet to his lips.

Torlyn Wands snorted and said, "Depending on whom you ask, the Sashes were either the agents of a rogue Lord, a lawless band of brigands who thwarted the Watch from ever changing Dock Ward, and even some who claimed they were demons hiding in the city and slaying those who dared try and send them back to their home planes."

"Well, I don't want to be linked to that!" Meloon said, slamming his mug down. "What's all this about linking us to some old group long-dead? Not all of us have our heads stuck as much in the past as you do, Renaer."

"I'm hardly stuck in the past," Renaer said, placing his goblet back down quietly as he got up. "It's more about honoring the past efforts of those who kept Waterdeep a good . . . nay, a great place. But above all, it's not the name we call ourselves as much as that we acknowledge the past while forging a new way for the future. Change is all around us, and it's inevitable. I just want us to make the city change for the better, whether we use old names or new."

"Count the Wands as allies in secret," Torlyn said. "I for one love the idea of aiming for a better city—one filled with heroes and magic like my ancestors built, rather than the one the Spellplague did, full of mistrust and fear. Old Maskar would have loved this."

"I'll do it," Laraelra said, "provided we can honor Vharem and Faxhal with posthumous membership in this group of ours."

"Already done, but thank you for bringing them up, Elra." Renaer paced around the long table, touching her shoulder as he passed. He raised his goblet and said, "To Vharem Kuthcutter and Faxhal Xoram, to lives of friendship and honor, and to fighting for what is right and true. May the gods smile on all who thrive or fall while pursuing such lives."

Everyone drained their goblets and mugs and Renaer began again.

"Vharem and Faxhal are both interred in a tomb Harug and I converted from one of the storerooms in that hall of doors beneath us. Their sarcophagi each bear the crescent moon and star. That's why I want to use Roarke House as a base for this group. I don't want this place to only be half-remembered as a house of a traitor. I want it to hint at but not confirm that our group is indeed here."

"But if you want us to be heroes and inspire folk, why operate in secret?" Osco asked. "Other than to keep your cards close to the vest?"

Again, Renaer's only answer was a sly grin.

"Mirt's Mysteries," Vajra giggled. "Well done, Renaer. We approve."

Harug also grinned beneath an ale-foam-soaked moustache.

Meloon looked at Vajra and Renaer, and said, "Huh? What's she talking about?"

Parlek smiled as he said, "It's an old idea of the Lords, attributed to Mirt the Moneylender, from whom all the modern usurers take their name. 'If you want people to talk about things in Waterdeep, suggest that folk keep it a secret. It'll be on everyone's lips without your ever having to utter a word.' "

Eiruk and Meloon started talking over each other, soon joined by Elra and Osco and Harug. Only Parlek, Vajra, Torlyn, and Renaer kept their council as everyone fought over what to call themselves and why. They argued long into the night, never deciding on their group's name, nor attending any solstice ball, but cementing friendships that would last years. Renaer had no doubt that these comrades would help him foster new changes. He looked forward to seeing increased valor and bravery on the mean streets of Waterdeep for the first time in a long time.

GLOSSARY

Armar—Second officer's rank in the Watch (equal to a sergeant)

Aumanator—God of the sun, dawn, light

Aumarr—Fourth officer's rank in the Guard (equal to a captain)

Castle Ward—the heart of the city, home to governmental buildings (the Palace, Castle Waterdeep)

City of the Dead—walled cemetery for the city against its eastern cliffs

Civilar—Generic term for officers above armar-rank and below senior commanders

Crown of the North—Waterdeep's common title/honorific (since the Spellplague)

Daern—Dwarven term for "familiar"

Delvarin's Daubles—Dwarven term for "digger's treasure" (ala "finders-keepers")

Dock Ward—the southernmost and oldest ward on land, filled with warehouses and danger

Downshadow—the undercity that was once the uppermost levels of Undermountain (the city's dungeon)

Field Ward—the ward between North Trollwall and the new city walls, home to many demihumans

Guard—the bodyguard and external army/guard for the City and Palace, supplementary to the Watch

Hin—racial name that halflings call themselves

Mistshore—the former naval harbor filled with wrecks and debris, now a dangerous floating slum

Mountainside—north/northeast faces of Mount Waterdeep, homes for those of rising fortune & the rich

North Ward—the northwestern ward filled with nobles, Waterdeep's "old money" neighborhood

Orsar—Fifth officer's rank in the Watch, envoy to guilds, noble houses, etc.

Rorden—Fourth officer's rank in the Watch, in charge of a Watchpost, barracks, or five to six patrols

Sea Ward—the northeastern ward for nobles and social climbers, the "new money" neighborhood

Shieldlar—Third officer's rank in the Guard (equal to a lieutenant)

South Ward—the southeastern ward of the city, home to caravan drovers, carters, and many adventurers

Taol—the common trade-coin of Waterdeep

Trades Ward—the eastern ward abutting the City of the Dead and home to scribes, business folk, and guilds

Valabrar—Fifth officer's rank in the Guard (equal to a major)

Undercliff—newest ward at the base of the eastern cliffs and includes subterranean links up to the city

Warrens—subterranean territories beneath Dock and Castle Ward, home to smaller demihumans

Watch—the police force for Waterdeep

Zzar—Waterdhavian wine that tastes strongly of almonds

FORGOTTEN REALMS®

A Reader's Guide to

R.A. Salvatore's
The Legend of Drizzt™

THE LEGEND
When TSR published *The Crystal Shard* in 1988, a drow ranger
first drew his enchanted scimitars, and a legend was born.

THE LEGACY
Twenty years and twenty books later, readers have
brought his story to the world.

DRIZZT
Celebrate twenty years of the greatest fantasy hero
of a generation.

This fully illustrated, full color, encyclopedic book celebrates the
whole world of The Legend of Drizzt, from the dark elf's steadfast
companions, to his most dangerous enemies, from the gods and
monsters of a world rich in magic, to the exotic lands he's visited.

Mixing classic renditions of characters, locales, and monsters
from the last twenty years with cutting edge new art by award-
winning illustrators including Todd Lockwood, this is a must-
have book every Drizzt fan.

FORGOTTEN REALMS®

They were built to display might.
They were built to hold secrets.
They will still stand while their builders fall.

THE CITADELS

NEVERSFALL
ED GENTRY
It was supposed to be Estagund's stronghold in monster-ridden Veldorn, an unassailable citadel to protect the southern lands . . . until the regiment holding Neversfall disappeared, leaving no hint of what took them.

OBSIDIAN RIDGE
JESS LEBOW
Looming like a storm cloud, the Obsidian Ridge appears silently and without warning over the kingdom of Erlkazar, prepared to destroy everything in its reach, unless its master gets what he wants.

THE SHIELD OF WEEPING GHOSTS
JAMES P. DAVIS
Frozen Shandaular fell to invaders over two thousand years ago, its ruins protected by the ghosts and undead that haunt the ancient citadel. But to anyone who can evade the weeping dead, the northwest tower holds a deadly secret.

SENTINELSPIRE
MARK SEHESTEDT
The ancient fortress of Sentinelspire draws strength from the portals that feed its fires and pools, as well as the assassins that call it home. Both promise great power to those dangerous enough to seize them.

Stand-alone novels that can be read in any order!

TRACY HICKMAN

PRESENTS

THE ANVIL OF TIME

With the power of the Anvil of Time, the Journeyman can travel
the river of time as simply as walking upstream, visiting the
ancient past of Krynn with ease.

VOLUME ONE
THE SELLSWORD
Cam Banks

Vanderjack, a mercenary with a price on his head, agrees out of
desperation to retrieve a priceless treasure for a displaced noble. The
treasure is deep within enemy territory, and he must survive an army of
old foes, a chorus of unhappy ghosts, and the questionable assistance of
a mad gnome to find it.

April 2008

VOLUME TWO
THE SURVIVORS
Dan Willis

A goodhearted dwarf is warned of an apocalyptic flood by the god
Reorx, and he and his motley followers must decide whether the
warning is real—and then survive the disaster that sweeps
through their part of Krynn.

November 2008

EBERRON

Sword & sorcery adventure from the creator
of the EBERRON® world!

KEITH BAKER

Thorn of Breland

A new war has already begun—a cold war, fought in the shadows
by agents of every nation—and Thorn does all she can as a
member of the King's Citadel. But her last mission has left
her with gaps in her memory, and she'll have to work out what
happened as she goes—after all, Breland won't protect itself.

Book 1
The Queen of Stone
November 2008

The Dreaming Dark

A band of weary war veterans have come to Sharn, hoping to
find a way to live in a world that is struggling to settle into an
uneasy peace. But over the years, they have made enemies in
high places—and even places far from Eberron.

Book 1
The City of Towers

Book 2
The Shattered Land

Book 3
The Gates of Night

In the shadow of the Last War, the heroes aren't all shining knights.

PARKER DeWOLF

The Lanternlight Files

Ulther Whitsun is a fixer. When you've got a problem, if you can't find someone to take care of it, he's your man—as long as you can pay the price. If you can't, or you won't . . . gods have mercy on your soul.

Book 1
The Left Hand of Death

Ulther finds himself in possession of a strange relic. His enemies want it, he wants its owner, and the City Watch wants him locked away for good. When a job turns this dangerous, winning or losing are no longer an option. It may be all one man can do just to stay alive.

Book 2
When Night Falls

Ulther teams up with a young and ambitious chronicler to stop a revolution. But treachery may kill him, and salvation comes from unexpected places.

July 2008

Book 3
Death Comes Easy

Gangs in lower Sharn are at each other's throats. And they don't care who gets killed in the battle. But now Ulther had been hired to put an end to the violence. And he doesn't care who he steps on to do his job.

December 2008